Gaslight Grimoire

Fantastic Tales of Sherlock Holmes

Edited by J. R. Campbell
and Charles Prepolec

EDGE SCIENCE FICTION AND FANTASY PUBLISHING
AN IMPRINT OF HADES PUBLICATIONS, INC.
CALGARY

Edge Science Fiction and Fantasy Publishing
An Imprint of Hades Publications Inc.
P.O. Box 1714, Calgary, Alberta, T2P 2L7, Canada

Interior design by Brian Hades
Interior illustrations by Phil Cornell
Cover Illustration by Timothy Lantz
ISBN: 978-1-8964063-17-3

EDGE Science Fiction and Fantasy Publishing and Hades Publications, Inc.
acknowledges the ongoing support of the Canada Council for the Arts and the
Alberta Foundation for the Arts for our publishing programme.

Library and Archives Canada Cataloguing in Publication

Gaslight grimoire : fantastic tales of Sherlock Holmes / edited by
J.R. Campbell and Charles Prepolec.

ISBN: 978-1-8964063-17-3

1. Holmes, Sherlock (Fictitious character)--Fiction. 2. Detective and
mystery stories, Canadian (English). 3. Detective and mystery
stories, American. I. Prepolec, Charles, 1966- II. Campbell, J. R.,
1963-

PS648.D4G38 2008   C813'.087208351   C2008-904666-8

FIRST EDITION
(p-20080909)
Printed in Canada
www.edgewebsite.com

Contents

Ghosts May Apply
David Stuart Davies

Arthur Conan Doyle was an accomplished practitioner of the supernatural tale and created some classic narratives in the genre. 'The Ring of Thoth', for example, was very influential within the realm of mummy stories. The idea of an ancient Egyptian achieving immortality and the setting of a museum after closing time became the essential ingredients of the 1932 movie, *The Mummy*, starring a very desiccated Boris Karloff. Other Doylean horror gems include 'The Brazilian Cat', 'The Terror of Blue John Gap', 'The Leather Funnel' and 'The Nightmare Room', to name a few — stories which are particularly chilling and memorable.

It must therefore have been a little frustrating for Doyle not to be able to involve his detective hero Sherlock Holmes in this mysterious and frightening world. What exciting scenes, puzzling scenarios and scary moments he could have created if he had allowed himself this guilty pleasure. But he had established Sherlock Holmes as a purely rational detective investigating real crimes with logical solutions. He knew that he would be weakening Holmes' appeal and powers if he involved him with ghosts and other creatures from beyond the grave where logicality had no foothold. As Holmes memorably observed in 'The Sussex Vampire', 'This Agency stands flat-footed upon the ground and there it must remain. This world is big enough for us. No ghosts need apply.'

Nevertheless, Doyle did tease his readers with suggestions of supernatural interventions in two of Holmes' cases. In the aforementioned 'The Sussex Vampire' it was implied that a bloodsucking fiend was at work in the Ferguson household; and in *The Hound of the Baskervilles*, for some time the reader is unsure whether the phantom beast of the title really does exist. Even at the climax of the novel, when the hound finally makes its appearance — 'Fire burst from its open mouth, its eyes glowed with a smouldering glare, its muzzle and hackles and dewlap were outlined in flickering flame' — we are still not absolutely certain that the thing is of flesh and blood and not a spectre from the pit. It is only when the creature howls with pain after Holmes has shot it several times that we are assured that the beast is mortal.

Despite these deceptive forays into the realms of the unknown Doyle actually stopped short of presenting the Great Detective with a real supernatural mystery. Other writers, perhaps seeing a niche gap in the market, took advantage of Doyle's reticence and around the end of the nineteenth century there was a rack of ghost detectives materializing in print. 1898 saw the first appearance of Flaxman Low in *Pearson's Magazine*. Low was a sleuth cast clearly in the Holmes mould: clever, well read, possessing strong deductive powers with the ability to discern clues where others failed to do so. The marked difference between Low and his Baker Street counterpart was that he specialized in solving problems of a supernatural nature. Low was the joint creation of Kate Prichard and her son Hesketh who published the tales under the pen name of E. and H. Heron. Hesketh was a friend and admirer of Conan Doyle and the Holmes influence on the stories is marked, especially in the two final cases where Low encounters the Moriarty-like figure of Kalmarkane. This collection brings Low and Holmes together as an intriguing double act in 'The Things That Shall Come Upon Them'.

Other spook sleuths followed in Low's wake. Most notably there was Algernon Blackwood's John Silence, who first appeared in 1908, and Carnacki the Ghost Finder penned by William Hope Hodgson. Carnacki, who made his debut in 1910, is of particular interest because not all his cases turned out to be supernatural ones. On occasion human agencies were at the root of the various upheavals. Usually there is a chamber or a specific location that needs to be examined and carrying his trusty electric pentacle, Carnacki approaches the scene in very much the same way that Holmes does in many of his cases, with a close observation of the area searching for clues. You can observe how these two sleuths fare together in 'The Grantchester Grimoire', one of the tales in this volume.

As the twentieth century rolled on other psychic detectives followed in the footsteps of Low, Silence and Carnacki. There was Alice and Claude Askew's Aylmer Vance, Dion Fortune's Dr. Taverner, A. M. Burrage's Francis Chard and Seabury Quinn's Jules de Grandin to name but a few. None really achieved the notoriety of Silence and Carnacki and certainly none approached the success of earth-bound Sherlock Holmes. Maybe the reason for their failure to catch the imagination of the mainstream reader is that these fellows not only believed in, but embraced the idea of the supernatural. They did not need convincing that there was a goblin in the cupboard, a vampire in the cellar or an ogre up the chimney. There was no surprise for them when they faced their demons... literally. The appeal then of these stories falls into two camps: the unusual nature of the haunting or supernatural event and the strange methods used by the psychic sleuth to alleviate the problem. These methods of course for the main part are invented by the author and have no roots in reality. This fanciful approach tends to rob the stories of suspense.

What is appealing about the prospect of Sherlock Holmes facing and battling the dark forces is that he is not a believer. The supernatural world is a fairy tale to him. No ghosts need apply because to his mind there are no such things.

When I wrote my first Holmes novel I took the brave or foolhardy step of pitting Holmes against Count Dracula, the king of all vampires. I don't do things by half measures. However, the novel began with Holmes holding exactly the same opinions as he did in 'The Sussex Vampire', decrying the idea that such fantastic nocturnal creatures exist:

'It should be clear, even to the most elementary of scientific brains, that the explanation of such beliefs lies not in the supernatural, but in the acceptance of weird folk-tales as factual occurrences. For the simple mind, the line between reality and fantasy is blurred, but the educated brain should reject any such nonsense without hesitation.'

And, indeed, Holmes continues to reject any such nonsense until he encounters one of these blood-sucking fiends himself and then is schooled by Van Helsing in vampire lore. I believe that Holmes' gradual and reluctant acceptance of the supernatural world and his understanding that certain rationalities can still apply to it is one of the interesting aspects of this exercise in Sherlockian fiction. The fact that Holmes approaches any problem which may have supernatural connotations with scepticism and doubt adds extra interest and tension to the narrative, which is missing from those tales featuring ghost detectives. It is a subtle difference but it adds a richer and more engrossing element to the story.

Sherlock Holmes has always been a supremely gothic character with a strange costume, emerging himself like a ghost from the eerie fog and investigating bizarre crimes which take place in various ancient houses. The scenario of 'The Speckled Band' with bells ringing in the night, an unstable step father and a snake slithering down the bell rope are all elements that could have been plucked from one of Edgar Allan Poe's nightmare tales. Consider also the conclusion of 'The Creeping Man' (a good ghost story title if there ever was one) where we have a respectable academic turned into a libidinous monkey, swinging through the trees. Is this any less believable than one of Carnacki's poltergeists?

The point I am making is that in reality it is not too giant a step to take Holmes and Watson into the twilight world of the supernatural — Doyle brought them close to it on several occasions. As long as Holmes can still function as a detective, surprising Watson and others with his deductions, the introduction of a werewolf or an avenging spirit adds an extra frisson to the Baker Street scenario.

Doyle had to defend himself when critics observed that the stories in his final collection, *The Casebook of Sherlock Holmes*, lacked the freshness and ingenuity of the earlier tales. He explained that in repeating the basic formula of the stories there was bound to be a sense of *deja vu* about them, a certain tiredness which was inevitable. If that was the case with Doyle, think how much more apposite it is to all the pastiches which have followed in the wake of the great man's work. In an attempt to replicate Doyle's style and approach, so many pastiches end up being pale imitations with that awful sense of repetition. 'Great heavens,' Watson will cry, 'How did you know I've just been to the tailors/been playing billiards/had a romantic liaison with Irene Adler/just shot your brother Mycroft.' Holmes will smirk and say, 'Elementary, Watson, you're wearing a new waistcoat/there is billiard chalk on the index finger of your left hand/there is lipstick on your earlobe, the hue of which is peculiar to Miss Adler/I saw a bullet with Mycroft's name on your dressing room table this morning.' We've read that kind of stuff a hundred times before. The formula needs perking up. And maybe giving Holmes a taste of the supernatural is just the fillip needed. Of course it has been tried before. In recent years there's been a volume of the Lovecraftian extravaganzas, *Shadows over Baker Street* (2003), Caleb Carrs's ghostly stab at Holmes in *The Italian Secretary* (2005) and a collection called *Ghosts in Baker Street* (2006). However in general these stories were penned by writers who, for want of a better expression, were having a go at a Holmes tale unlike the authors featured in this volume who are very well-versed in the world of Sherlock Holmes and Doctor Watson and so can effectively blend the world of Baker Street with the world of the unknown. I can guarantee you a good time here. Expect a few shivers along the way.

How will Holmes cope with things that go bump in the night? Well you'll have to read the stories to find out, but let me leave you with this thought. What better detective is there to delve into the unpredictable and frightening world of the supernatural than the one whose motto has always been: 'When you have eliminated the impossible, whatever remains however improbable must be the truth.'

Introduction

An Introductory Rumination on
Stories for Which the World Is Not Yet Prepared

Charles V. Prepolec

Never underestimate the impact of the fantastic on an impressionable child, be it in print, film or television. You never quite know where it may lead, or when it might bite you on the ass. In my case, it eventually led to the creation of *Gaslight Grimoire: Fantastic Tales of Sherlock Holmes*, so feel free to hold the likes of Alfred Hitchcock, Homer (the Greek chap, not Simpson), Alexander Korda, Stan "The Man" Lee, Lester Dent, Ray Harryhausen, Creature Feature presentations on Saturday afternoon television, Otto Penzler, Hammer Films and, of course, Arthur Conan Doyle accountable for the book you now hold in your hands. Although, to be perfectly fair, H. G. Wells, Jules Verne, R. L. Stevenson, Bram Stoker, and Greek myth in general should probably shoulder some of the blame too, but for now we'll stick to the shortlist. You see, as an only child, I spent a lot of time exploring fantasy worlds wherever I could find them — and quite frankly, I found them everywhere!

Hitchcock's *Three Investigators* (okay, Hitch himself is off the hook since he didn't write a one of them) were probably my first exposure to slightly scary mysteries. Well, at least some of the covers were sort of scary. One that had a glowing disembodied head on it had to be safely put away before the lights went out in my bedroom each night. My thanks to those fine folks at Scholastic Books (the same fine folks who, if memory serves, were inexplicably responsible for making me aware of Sawney Bean while I was still under ten years of age) for messing with my young mind! Right about the same time, through a chunky paperback book found in my school library, Greek myth popped into my life with *Jason and the Argonauts*, which in turn led to a far too early reading of Homer's *Odyssey*. Jason, Hercules, and the clever Odysseus became early heroes. My sense of heroic fantasy, heroes and their heroic deeds, was forming, although a strange fear of cannibals was lurking in there somewhere too. Thank you again Scholastic. At about the same time I also had my first brush with Sherlock Holmes. I found myself reading *The Hound of the Baskervilles*, but at the time I didn't find it terribly engaging and didn't finish it. Anyhow, that Greek myth interest was further fuelled when Ray Harryhausen's *Jason and the Argonauts* turned up on television. Harryhausen's stop-motion animation gave magical life to creatures that had previously only existed in my imagination. In short order I was begging to be taken to see his Sinbad films (for the record, Kali has always been my favorite Harryhausen creation), which indirectly took me back to Alexander Korda's *The Thief of Bagdad*. Now that was the mother load for skewing this kid's idea of fantasy. It was the most magical thing I had ever seen, and it had the best villain ever in Conrad Veidt's Jaffar! He made Tom Baker's Prince Koura seem like a boy scout by comparison. What kid wouldn't want to be Sabu?

So with a major itch for heroic fantasy, I did what most geeky kids would do, start reading comic books and developing the first stages of 'collector's mania'. *The Mighty Thor*, *Iron Man*, *Dr. Strange*, *Tomb of Dracula*, the *Uncanny X-men*, and on and on went the list of Marvel comics. Stan Lee had a lot to answer for when he had the idea to infuse the tired superhero books of the 1950s with the soap opera antics of romance comics. Can you say addiction? I knew you could. It was all the perfect fodder to fuel my fascination with heroic fantasy figures. It also led me to discover the world of pulp heroes in a roundabout way. At the time, the mid-1970s, Marvel was producing a line of black and white magazine sized comics and amongst them was *Doc Savage: The Man of Bronze*. Incidentally, there was also a two-part adaptation of *The Hound of the Baskervilles* in *Marvel Preview*, which was my second brush with Sherlock Holmes. The pictures helped, but I still wasn't terribly impressed. Through that Doc Savage magazine I discovered the near perfect heroic fantasy character. Doc Savage combined the best of everything I'd encountered up to that time. He was built like a hero from Greek myth, with bronzed skin and freaky gold eyes, blessed with a brilliant mind, surrounded by a band of lesser heroes, each with their own scientific specialty and had adventures that almost always had a huge fantasy element. Suddenly used bookstores entered my life as part of the quest to accumulate as many of the Doc Savage paperback reprints that I could get my hands on. It became an all-consuming passion. I must have been driving my poor parents nuts with my obsession, but they thought reading was good for me (can't imagine what they would have made of the Bond books or John Norman's Gor series I was also reading at the time) and so indulged me in my interests. I can vividly recall successfully convincing them to drive me some 300 kilometers north just so that I could scour the virgin territory of Edmonton's used bookshops. I eventually managed to accumulate about 102 of the paperback reprints, before moving on to another obsession, but not before reading Phil Farmer's curious Doc Savage bio *Doc Savage: His Apocalyptic Life* and being introduced to the inbred wonders of his Wold-Newton family tree. Suddenly there was a thread, however tenuous; tying together all these fantastic fictional heroes, and look, there on a low branch is that Sherlock Holmes guy again. I also discovered The Avenger, The Spider and, of course, The Shadow! Like Doc Savage, I first encountered The Shadow in comic books, although the fact they were published by DC bothered me no end! Still, Denny O'Neil's stories and more importantly Mike Kaluta's unsurpassed artwork did the trick. "Who knows what evil lurks in the hearts of men?" became my catchphrase. Rarely got an answer to that one, but what did I know about 'evil' or 'the hearts of men'? I was a twelve year old kid and The Shadow

was cool. So cool that when I spotted him in a book called
The Private Lives of Spies, Crime Fighters, and Other Good Guys
by Otto Penzler, and discovered there were films with The
Shadow, I simply had to have it! While The Shadow chapter
was pretty thin, I was introduced to a whole new genre
that captured my imagination, however fleetingly. The
detective in print and film had entered my life ... and there
was that Sherlock Holmes guy again. I can recall being quite
taken with a photo of John Barrymore as Holmes holding
a gun on the grotesquely featured Gustav Von Seyffertitz
as Moriarty, but little else.

Unfortunately my detective interest was immediately
sidetracked by another book, Alan Frank's *The Movie Trea-
sury: Monsters and Vampires* with a garish cover image of
Christopher Lee being staked. Suddenly I wanted to see
monster movies, and lots of them. Happily every Saturday afternoon there was a *Creature Feature* program on
television to feed that particular craving. More importantly
it had the added benefit of sending me back to the literature.
I ended up reading *Dracula, The Strange Case of Dr. Jekyll
and Mr. Hyde, The Hunchback of Notre Dame, The Picture of
Dorian Gray, The House on the Borderland, Carnacki the Ghost
Finder, The War of the Worlds, The Invisible Man* and who
knows how many horror anthologies edited by the late
Peter Haining. My interest in fantasy had shifted away from
the bright and shiny, clean cut heroes of childhood and
drifted down the dark gaslit alleys of the macabre. Comic
books grew less important and gave way to somewhat more
esoteric reading materials. Yup, you guessed it; puberty
had begun to work its own peculiar magic! Sexual repression seemed to be the order of the day as my fantasy worlds
began to take on a distinctly Victorian tinge. It seemed to
me that the era was simply one big heavily populated playground for monsters, madmen and murderers, and thanks
to Hammer Films on television, apparently they all looked
an awful lot like either Christopher Lee or Peter Cushing.

While my reading interests went all over the map at that
point, bloody 80's horror, trashy true crime thrillers,
Herbert's *Dune* series, Tolkein's *The Lord of the Rings*, Anne
McCaffrey's Pern, and God knows what else, the concept

of an almost homogenous Victorian nightmare world remained firmly lodged at the back of my mind. My teen years came to an end and on a fateful day in 1986 I found myself in a comic shop. Browsing the racks I was drawn to the brightly painted image of Sherlock Holmes standing in a graveyard. It was the cover of the first issue of Renegade Press' *Cases of Sherlock Holmes*. The text was Conan Doyle's "The Beryl Coronet", but it was accompanied by the wonderfully atmospheric black and white artwork of Dan Day. Was that Peter Cushing's face staring out at me? Yes, it was, although in the next panel it was Basil Rathbone's, and in the one after that John Barrymore. Hmm, that Victorian playground concept was flashing back into my mind so I picked it up, went home and read it. Here was that Sherlock Holmes guy that I kept running across, but largely ignored, throughout my childhood. Sherlock Holmes, turned out to be calm, cool, insightful, larger than life fantastic hero and best of all, he lived in my Victorian fantasyland. By the next day I was in a used bookstore looking for a copy of *The Adventures of Sherlock Holmes*. I found myself reading the words *"To Sherlock Holmes she was always the woman"*, and considering I was floundering after a bad break-up with my girlfriend, I was utterly and completely hooked. By the weekend I had Peter Haining's *The Sherlock Holmes Scrapbook* and discovered there was a whole world of Sherlock Holmes related material out there, including something called a pastiche. Back to the used bookshops I went. Fred Saberhagen's *The Holmes-Dracula File* fell into my hands, Loren D. Estleman's *Dr. Jekyll and Mr. Holmes* followed suit, then Manly Wade Wellman's *Sherlock Holmes's War of the Worlds*, and oh look, Phil Farmer's Wold-Newtonry was back in my life with *The Adventure of the Peerless Peer*. Apparently I wasn't the only one who thought the Victorian era was a literary fantasyland, but best of all, my new hero, a classic one that seemed to embody the best qualities of all my childhood interests, served as a guide through this nightmare world. To be sure, some of it was truly dire in terms of quality writing, but it was the most fun I'd had in a lifetime of reading, and fun is the key to entertainment.

Flash forward some 20-odd years and here I am, still having fun in my Victorian fantasyland and exploring the ever-expanding world of *Sherlock Holmes*. From the distance an early 21st century vantage point provides, the idealized Victorian and Edwardian world Sherlock Holmes inhabits is to the modern reader, in its own way, as strongly realized and alien a fantasy setting as Tolkien's Middle Earth or Baum's Oz and just as much fun! *Gaslight Grimoire: Fantastic Tales of Sherlock Holmes* will, I hope, communicate some of that sense of fun that I've been enjoying all these years.

Throughout this rambling rumination I've made mention of a number of Conan Doyle's contemporaries and successors who worked the rich vein of fantasy fiction. In the stories ahead you will perhaps find echoes from some of their works or their characters. The connection may be very subtle or it may come through loud and clear as it does in Barbara Hambly's "The Lost Boy", a bittersweet tale of Sherlock Holmes and J. M. Barrie's Peter Pan. Considering Conan Doyle's one-time collaboration and longtime friendship with Barrie, it is a perfect starting point for our collection. Christopher Sequeira's "His Last Arrow" is a cautionary tale, possibly inspired by Sir Richard Francis Burton's translation of *The Book Of The Thousand Nights And A Night*, which drives home the adage that you should be careful what you wish for as Watson appears to have brought home more than a war-wound from his time in Afghanistan. Barbara Roden's "The Things That Shall Come Upon Them" contains our first pairing of Holmes with a classic 'psychic detective', in this case Hesketh-Prichard's groundbreaking Flaxman Low. Holmes and Low both find themselves investigating, from decidedly different perspectives, strange occurrences in a house that is sure to be familiar to readers of M. R. James' "The Casting of the Runes". The Flaxman Low stories are a perfect example of Conan Doyle's direct influence on a contemporary, as the Low stories began appearing in *Pearson's Magazine* in 1898, less than a year after Hesketh-Prichard met Conan Doyle at a writer's dinner. Another, earlier, writer's dinner was also a meeting point for Arthur Conan Doyle and Oscar Wilde, who's *The Picture Of Dorian Gray*, seems to have an echo in M. J. Elliott's "The Finishing Stroke", a grisly tale of art gone wrong. Martin Powell brings in Conan Doyle's other great creation Professor George Edward Challenger in a *Boy's Own*/pulp styled two-fisted adventure tale that could only be called "Sherlock Holmes in the Lost World". In Rick Kennett and A. F. (Chico) Kidd's "The Grantchester Grimoire", Holmes meets his second 'psychic detective'. In this case it is arguably the best known, and certainly best loved, example of the breed, William Hope Hodgson's Carnacki the Ghost Finder. Kennett and Kidd have previously collaborated on a highly recommended collection of Carnacki pastiche available under the title *No. 472 Cheyne Walk* (Ash-Tree Press 2002). In "The Strange Affair of the Steamship Friesland", a direct follow-up to "The Five Orange Pips", journalist Peter Calamai presents Holmes with a unique method of correcting an early failure after consulting a certain familiar doctor with an address in South Norwood. Lewis Carroll's Alice may have disappeared into another world, but any comparison with J. R. Campbell's "The Entwined" stops right there, as the girl in this story dreams of nothing that could be described as a Wonderland. An aging Watson finds himself faced with the horrific power of strong remembrances when Chris Roberson delves into the untold tale of "Merridew of Abominable Memory". When a private investigator on the mean streets of 1940s Los Angeles finds himself faced with a corpse that won't stay down he turns to the greatest detective still living for help, bringing together influences as widely removed as Bram Stoker and Dashiell Hammett in Bob Madison's humorous and hardboiled story "Red Sunset". Our final entry takes a decidedly different turn in that Sherlock Holmes is nowhere to be found; instead Kim Newman has Professor Moriarty, along with Colonel Moran, waging a highly personal and often hilarious *War Of The Worlds* in "The Red Planet League".

At the beginning of this long-winded and wandering introduction I wondered what the impact of fantastic fiction on an impressionable child, might be? Well, now you know, in my case it eventually led to the creation of the book you hold in your hands. A little horror, a little pulp-style thriller, a little comic book adventure, a little ghostly spook story, a little bit mystery and hopefully a whole lot of fun. Not your traditional selection of Sherlock Holmes stories by any means, but what is the fun of that? After all, as Watson noted in The Speckled Band "...*he refused to associate himself with any investigation which did not tend towards the unusual and even the fantastic...*" so why should we?

Enjoy!

Charles Prepolec, 2008

The Lost Boy
by Barbara Hambly

When the Darling children disappeared without a trace from their nursery one night, their father took the case at once to Mr. Sherlock Holmes.

Mrs. Darling came to me.

"You know how George is," she said, when the first spate of anguish, of terror, of speculations both probable and grotesque had been talked out over tea. I had been in the Darling night nursery innumerable times, listening to the tales Meg Darling — Meg Speedwell she had been, when first I knew her at Mrs. Clegg's dreary boarding school in the north of England — would tell small Wendy, smaller John, and baby Michael of pirates, mermaids, red Indians and the fairies that dwell in Kensington Gardens.

I knew the distance from that high window to the street below, and that the drainpipe was at the back, not the front, of that narrow brick mansionette in its row of identical dwellings. I knew how big a dog Nana was, and the sturdy Newfoundland's ferocity where the children were concerned.

"George says—" Meg began, and then stopped. For a time she sat turning her saucer round and round, forty-five degrees at a time, a habit she'd had when we were girls, and she was thinking about how best to say something that the adults had told us we shouldn't say or even think.

And I knew then that what — or who — she was thinking about, was Peter Pan.

"Do you remember Peter Pan?" she asked, after a long, long time, in the small voice one usually only hears late at night, when the other girls in the bleak cold dormitory have gone to sleep.

I nodded. I didn't say, *How could I forget*? I think Peter Pan was the reason that I didn't kill myself when I was seven or eight — and it's a mistake adults make, to think that children who are sufficiently unhappy don't want to try to end their own lives. Mostly we just don't know how. That I'd lived through Mrs. Clegg's ideas of how to operate a girls' school was entirely because I learned to dream, and in those dreams I'd met Peter Pan.

It was what we called him, Meg and I, because Meg dreamed about him, too. We both knew he had another name, a real name, and that other children had called him other things over the years. We both knew — the way you do in dreams — that he was more than he appeared to be, and more than he himself realized he was much of the time. We were both certain that it was possible for him to cross through the film that separates the Neverlands from the damp chilly world of girls' schools, and account-books that don't add up, and bleak London streets, and knowing one is going to die.

Meg had told me once back then — and I believed her — that she had seen him do so.

Now she said — and I believed her — "I saw him in the night-nursery, a week ago." She watched my face as she said it, knowing of course that John — my John, after whom her own seven-year-old son was named — was a doctor, and fearing that my immediate conclusion would be that she was mad.

When I said nothing, she went on softly, "It was only for a moment. I dreamed he had rent the film, that separates the Neverlands from us—" That was what we'd called them, Meg and I: those endless skerries of islands, where children go when they dream. "I dreamed the children peeked through, and saw. I woke, and he was there still, looking just as he always did." She shook her head, at the shared memory of that shock-headed child clothed in skeleton leaves, smiling his ageless brilliant smile.

"Did the children see him?" I asked, and she hesitated, calling the scene back to her mind.

"I think so," she said slowly. "I screamed, and he flew away through the window, like a swallow flies—"

How well I remembered — though I had not until she said it — the motion of his flight, a darting swoop, the tiny lights of whatever fairies he had with him just then flicking in his wake.

She whispered, "He left his shadow behind."

John came home early that evening, though he had stopped at Baker Street to visit with Mr. Holmes. I was ill a great deal that year, and though John kept closer to home than he had before, he also saw a good deal more of Holmes. He would stop at Baker Street for a half an hour on his way back from his rounds. Though I would take a Bible oath that he never so much as mentioned to Holmes his fears for me, nor did Holmes offer so much as a shred of a reassurance that he would have disdained as illogical, still, John would come home comforted, and full of the details of whatever case occupied his friend's keen mind.

Thus that evening I heard all about George Darling's visit to Holmes. "Old George kept his head remarkably," John said, as he stirred cocoa for us both in a little pan on the bedroom hearth, while I lay among my pillows sorting through his medical notebook. It was my duty always to keep track of his patients, and tot up the bills which half the time John then left uncollected. "Holmes could not have done better. George knew the height of the window-sill from the pavement, the names of the cab-men at the corner of the road; before he came to Holmes, he went through the whole of the rear yard examining the ground there, and found no marks of a ladder, nor smudges on the window-sill, nor signs on the drain-pipe that it had been climbed. Of course Holmes returned to the house with him in any case, but he found nothing, either."

I nodded, and the part of me that had years since ceased to believe in that small, shining boy with the wonderful smile wept with sickened shock, that the three children John and I loved as if they were our own might

at that moment be dead. Or if not dead, in the hands of
the human horrors that he and I both knew too well populated the adult world.

John wrapped his hand around mine as he handed me
my cocoa. "They'll be all right, Mary," he said, looking
into my eyes. "Holmes will find them. They'll come to
no harm."

I whispered, "I know."

The medicine I was taking then was bitter and strong.
Though it gave me the sleep I needed, it also sent dreams,
more vivid than I had known in adult life. In dreams that
night I walked in Kensington Gardens, leaving the paths
that John and I followed on our summer afternoon strolls
and seeking the tree-hidden stillness along the far end
of the Lake, where the fireflies' reflection played above
water like black onyx. This was where the fairies lived,
Meg had whispered to me when we were children. This
was where Meg herself had disappeared one evening
when Mrs. Clegg had brought the lot of us down to
London for I forget what occasion — it wasn't a treat for
us, that was all I knew — and had not reappeared for
almost two days. Mrs. Clegg had hushed it up, of course,
and pretended that it hadn't been more than a few hours.
But though we were quite small — five or six — I remembered it clearly.

It had been two days.

And Meg had told me, that she had been in the
Neverlands, with Peter Pan, for what seemed to her then
to have been many weeks. She was never quite the same
after that. Happier, as if she carried in her heart the assurance that things would all come right in the end.

I knew, too, from conversations with Martha Hudson,
that Mr. Holmes' logic and studies extended far beyond
what people like John — bless his kindly, literal heart!
— regard as the Real World.

Thus I wasn't at all surprised to see Mr. Holmes in
Kensington Gardens, walking quietly in the cool blackness
barred with moonlight, not only listening but touching
the tree-bark, the grass-blades, the dew upon the leaves
as he passed. I couldn't imagine how he knew about

Kensington — Mrs. Clegg had certainly never reported that long-ago disappearance of her charge to the police — but he moved like a man who knew the place well, and knew what he sought. When a fairy darted in a sparkling skim of pale-blue light across the lake-surface he only stopped, as it swooped up before him, hung in the darkness a yard in front of him for the space of a second or two, then whipped away.

Whether Mr. Holmes carried something in his pockets that signaled the fairies of his benign intent — and I think he must have — I did not know. But they flickered from the woods, followed him thicker and thicker, as he walked unerringly toward the belvedere that only exists in the park sometimes, usually after the sun goes down: the rest of the time you cannot find it, no matter how systematic your search. But Holmes went straight towards it, coming out of the circle of willows to see it standing in its little meadow, with the fairies hovering around it like dragonflies above standing water in the darkness.

And as he came into the open, about thirty feet from the ghostly circle of marble pillars, he met Peter Pan.

Or, rather, Peter seized Holmes by the sleeve and dragged him back into the willows: "Hist! Beware!" His dagger wrought of meteor-iron, its handle carved of dragon's bone, caught the moonlight in his other hand.

Holmes dropped at once to one knee at the child's side, so that their eyes were nearly level; followed his gaze toward the open meadow, the belvedere. "What is it?"

"It's the Gallipoot," whispered the child. "The Thing Cold and Empty. It haunts the zone of shadow between your world and the Neverlands. It waits for the veil to open, so that it can slip through and hunt."

"What does it hunt?" asked Holmes.

"Souls on this side," Peter replied. "Dreams on the other. It slices them up and swallows them, and all the little pieces of them wave shrieking about it like bloody flags in agony, forever." His eyes burned somberly. It was hard to tell from where I stood, half-hidden among the willows, whether Peter was pretending or not, because he *did* pretend... only the things that he pretended often came to pass. "I've sought to drive it back through the belvedere into the zone of shadow, but it's eluded me, and I dare not call upon my henchmen, for it would make short work of them."

Holmes took a flute from his pocket — an ivory one he'd acquired in Tibet — and said, "Will it come to the music of souls?"

Peter nodded.

"I will stand before the opening into the zone of shadow," said Holmes, "and play. When it lunges at me, I will leap out of the way, and you must drive it through with your weapon."

The child nodded again, trying not to look impressed — I couldn't remember whether Peter could play the flute himself or not. Holmes and Peter walked toward the belvedere together, and I noticed that all the fairies had disappeared. The air of the summer night grew cold, and strange, directionless movements seemed to stir the darkness, with a smell of sulfur and mould. Far, far off, as if at the end of an endless corridor, I could hear shrieking, as of the bleeding fragments of a thousand souls.

I did not know whether at that moment I qualified as a soul or a dream. All I knew was that this was real, this was happening in Kensington Gardens, even as I lay deep in sleep at John's side not many streets away. If it caught my soul, I would never wake up.

I had thought Holmes would play one of those strange airs that he learned in Tibet, or the weird gypsy music that he sometimes coaxed from his violin. But he played the air from Vivaldi's Concerto in D Major for Lute, and the Gallipoot drew closer — I could smell it, hear the trapped souls screaming, feel its nearness in the bone-hurting cold. When it broke from the trees I tried to cry out in my sleep, tried to scream so that John would wake me, but I couldn't. It was well I didn't, for I realized a moment later that if I screamed it would become aware of me, come for me...

It rolled, oozed, surged toward the belvedere, and the exquisite melancholy song of the flute didn't waver, though the screaming of the trapped and devoured souls rosc like the wail of storm-wind. Through its darkness the marble pillars glimmered, then vanished, and I felt in my bones the wrenching of the fabric of the world as it struck.

A shriek like a thunderclap pierced my skull like lightning, and in the blackness that swallowed the moonlight, I saw the flash of Peter's knife—

Then Holmes was stepping down the shallow platform of the belvedere, the world normal again and as it should be, tucking his bone flute into his pocket with one hand.

In the other hand, he held Peter's knife.

"Give that back!" Peter came leaping out of the belvedere, grabbed for Holmes' arm.

Holmes sidestepped him like a dancer. "When the Darling children return to their home, you shall have your knife back."

"Who are the Darling children?" Peter doesn't always remember things.

"Wendy, and John, and Michael," said Holmes. "The children who went away with you to the Islands last night." I don't know how he learned this — perhaps he'd only guessed it, until he actually encountered Peter — but then, as I said, Holmes studied extensively the writings concerned with other realities than those of the material earth. Someone, at some time, must have written about the Neverlands — or the Islands, as they were apparently also called, and they had other names as well. Certainly Meg was not the only child who had inexplicably disappeared, without any traceable sign of human agency, in Kensington Gardens or elsewhere.

Peter said, "They're my friends. Wendy is to be my mother, and take care of me, and look after my Lost Boys in a secret house below the ground."

Holmes nodded gravely. "You are renowned for looking after your friends," he said, as one recalling a legend — or a set of instructions, as to what one must say to a dragon or a fairy — "in the face of any and all danger to yourself."

Peter smote his chest proudly. "I am." Peter never could resist renown.

"Then promise me this," said Holmes. "When the Darling children return home — as return they will, one day — promise me that you will see to it, that they will do so on the day after they departed. That way," he added, "you will have your knife back in only two days."

The fairies were gone, and the moon sinking, as Holmes walked back toward the paths of the more populated parts of the Gardens. In the shadows of the willow circle he stopped, as if at a sound, and turning his head his eyes met mine. He had encountered the fairies, and Peter — not to mention the fearsome Gallipoot — without a blink, but now his eyes widened, first startled, then filled with shocked grief. "Mrs. Watson?" he asked softly.

I know that we do not look the same to others, when we encounter them in dreams.

I put my finger to my lips, and slipped away.

Holmes and Peter met a number of times that summer, usually in Kensington Gardens, where Holmes would go walking when all of London slept. Peter did get his knife back within two days, for as Holmes understood from those strange — and sometimes very ancient — accounts of mysteriously-appearing children over the centuries, time spent in that other world is notoriously elastic, and bears no relation to the seasons by which we live.

As my illness ran its course I would dream of them, when sleeping under the influence of my medicines. Holmes taught Peter boxing and single-stick on the fringes of the lake by moonlight, and the intricacies of baritsu throws, in exchange for whatever Peter could tell him of the worlds that lie beyond our own. Peter, for his part, was fond of displaying his knowledge. Though his accounts varied wildly from interview to interview, still I think Holmes gleaned sufficient information to unlock certain clues in those cases that he never told John about. I know that it was from Peter that he learned the secret behind the events at Rowson Priory, and the riddle that saved his life and John's, years later, during the affair of the Covyng Stones.

But about such matters as Red Indians and pirates, Peter found Holmes shockingly obtuse. And Holmes had enough of Peter in himself, to take umbrage when a boy who didn't quite come up to his elbow scoffed at his researches into the habits of the Cherokee and Sioux. "They're not Sioux, they're Indians," Peter almost shouted at him. "And they'll scalp any white man who comes in their midst!" I think they finally parted over Holmes' contention that the giant ants that lived on one island of the Neverlands archipelagoes could not exist because it was scientifically impossible for them to breathe. "You're wrong," cried Peter. "You're wrong, I've seen them — I've slain one with my knife!"

He stamped his foot, and the impact launched him glittering into the air. He was gone before Holmes could speak.

I think Peter would have cheerfully made up the quarrel, had he remembered to go back to the Gardens, but he didn't. Peter *does* forget things, and people, too, alas. Nearly a year went by, in which Holmes would patiently walk the byways of Kensington Gardens, looking for the paths that had once led him to the belvedere beyond the willow circle — paths that were no longer there and never had been. Holmes continued elsewhere his education in the lore of the Beyond Realms through other connections in London: through a strange young antiquarian who had a house on the Embankment, and the white-haired proprietor of a junk-yard at the end of Fetter Lane.

It was Peter who came to me, for help in finding Holmes again.

I was delighted to see him again. My illness weighed heavily on me just then, made worse by the fact that I knew John was nearly frantic, between the costs of caring for me, and fear that I wouldn't pull out of it, and the sheer insanely mundane burden of running a house. I had dreamed more and more of the Neverlands, hearing in the distance the pounding of the surf on their shores, and the singing of the mermaids among the rocks, but this was the first time Peter appeared in one of the dreams.

It wasn't in the Neverlands, either, but in my own bed-room — John had taken to sleeping on the couch in his study, for fear of disturbing me — and when Peter swooped in through the window I could see he was almost incandescent with rage.

"Mary, where's Holmes?" he demanded, as if it hadn't been decades since we'd parted. He grabbed my hand, and as he pulled me to my feet I was as we all are in dreams, perfectly healthy and much younger than in real life. "You have to show me where he lives. I need him."

He was as he had always been. I was as well, the long blonde hair that had been cut off with my illness (that's how sick I was) now lying intact again in pigtails on the shoulders of my white nightgown, and my nails chewed off short. (I'd quit biting them the minute I left Mrs. Clegg's).

Of course I said *yes* immediately, and being Peter, he completely forgot about putting fairy-dust on me to fly until we were standing on the window-sill, and then Ten Stars had to remind him: Ten Stars was the fairy he flew with by that time, and much less jealous by nature than her predecessor. Tinker Bell would never have bothered to keep a human — dreaming or not — from crashing to the pavement. To do her justice I don't think Tink ever really understood why it wasn't funny.

We flew over London, something I had always wanted to do. And it was as glorious as I had always known it would be.

It was not so very late: Big Ben was striking eleven in the distance as we stepped through the window at 221B Baker Street. We entered through the bedroom that had been John's, now crammed almost floor-to-ceiling with Mr. Holmes' books and souvenirs. I could hear the strains of Mr. Holmes' violin from the parlor, smell strong shag tobacco with an intensity I hadn't experienced since I was a child. By the sudden chill on my bare ankles I knew that Peter and I had stepped from dream into reality, and panic filled me at this thought. Peter, still keeping a grip on my hand, barged through the parlor door saying "Holmes!"

but I hung back in the shadows, suddenly shy of meeting, in my changed dream-state, a man I knew as an adult in the cold adult world.

Holmes had already started up from his chair and the violin was out of his hands — I think he had a pistol tucked behind the chair-cushion — but he saw it was Peter and his eyebrows went up with astonished delight. The next second his glance went to me, still half-hid in the dark bedroom doorway, and his expression changed, but before he could speak, Peter jabbed a finger at him and snapped,

"You have to help me, Holmes. I am being accused of kidnapping — *kidnapping!* — and you must help me clear my name!"

The boy's name was Robert Lewensham and his father was the Earl of Wylcourt. Peter didn't know these things, of course; Holmes looked them up while I poured us all out tea. Peter's account was only that Bobbie had come with him to the Neverlands twice — "He's a tremendous sport and the Black Knight of Ravensmire lives in terror of his blade," — after first meeting him in the bleak fells of Yorkshire, where one of Ten Stars's relatives had gotten lost and Peter went to find her.

"This last time, he didn't get back home," Peter said. "It isn't my fault. Bobbie knew the way. Only now his father's hired men — wizards, some of them quite wicked — to find him, and the King of Dreams is saying, that this kind of thing can not be tolerated, and that if need be he will shut the Gates of Horn and Ivory that lie between this world and the Neverlands, so that no one may cross. He's always saying things like that," Peter added sulkily. It was the first time I'd ever heard him mention the King of Dreams. "And it isn't fair."

"It isn't," I added, a little timidly. "What about all those children who've never gone to the Neverlands, Mr. Holmes? What becomes of them?"

Holmes glanced across at me, the line between his brows telegraphing his uncertainty. In the shadows he had thought he'd recognized me, but sitting on his sofa before the fire — where so many times I'd sat in my adult life, all dressed up in proper gray delaine with a corset, bustle and husband — I could see he didn't know why he'd thought so, or who he'd imagined I might be.

"What indeed?" Holmes remarked dryly, and turned back to Peter, who was devouring biscuits left over — like the contents of the teapot — from Holmes' own tea earlier that evening. "Might your friend have been seized by something that haunts the space between the worlds, like the Gallipoot? There are other things as well—"

Peter waved impatiently with a biscuit. "*We* can get away from them," he boasted — by *we*, I assume he meant, himself and his Lost Boys. "The Gallipoot only eats people like pirates and Red Indians and black knights."

"Does it, indeed?" Holmes had crossed the room to the most recent of his scrapbooks, and the newspapers piled on top of it, sorting through the headlines of the past week with swift sureness, as if he knew exactly what he sought, which indeed he did. "I thought this sounded familiar," he remarked in a moment, and extricated the *York Evening Star* from three-quarters of the way down the stack. "Robert Lewensham, Viscount Mure — h'rm — heir to the Earl of Wylcourt — born 1885 — police are seeking gypsies — believed to have vanished on the Yorkshire fells three miles from the village of Kethmure — bird-watching — blue jacket, blue cap — A shocking paucity of detail." He plucked out another newspaper, handed it to me, got another for himself.

I'd worked with John enough to know what Holmes sought, and located the follow-on article without trouble. "They add little," I ventured, after scanning the columns. "They do say, Bobbie disappeared on the ninth—" I looked at the date of the paper in my hands, then turned, shocked, to Holmes. "Is the paper you have the day before this one?"

Holmes nodded, regarding me again with that questing speculation in his eyes. "So the papers — and presumably, the police — didn't learn of it until the twelfth. Either the boy's guardians are singularly neglectful, or they had some reason to believe him safely elsewhere for two days. This last time, did Bobbie say he'd been visiting anywhere?"

"Bobbie never visits anywhere," replied Peter promptly. "He goes to school in the city, and when he's at his home he's alone." For the first time since I'd known him, Peter's voice had a note of real distress in it, of concern, not that he, Peter, was being accused of kidnapping children from the real world, but that his friend was somewhere in trouble. And that his friend lived the sort of life that he, Peter, had all his existence fled.

When he's at home he's alone. There was a dismal world of Mrs. Cleggery in those six words.

"Most interesting." Holmes pulled another scrap-book from the overflowing shelves. "Do the fairies often get lost on the fells?"

Peter nodded. "Mostly they find their way back at dawn. Ten Stars's cousin Cloverberry's just a little fairy, though, barely more than a bud, and you know how fairies are. Ow—!" he added, because Ten Stars, who was sitting on Holmes' desk blotter, indignantly threw a collar-button at him. "I met him when I was looking for Cloverberry."

"And is this place near a ring of stones?" From between the pages of the scrap-book Holmes extracted one of his vast collection of Ordnance Survey maps, and spread it on the desk. Craning to look over his shoulder, I saw Wylcourt Hall marked, and the village of Kethmure.

"In the middle of one," affirmed Peter. He couldn't keep out of his voice the awed surprise of one who sees magic done. A small circle within two miles of Wylcourt Hall was labeled, *Stone Circle — Fairies' Dance.*

"And the boy's father has hired wizards to find him. Well, well." From the bottom drawer of his desk — the locked one where he keeps certain poisons and lists of names — Holmes brought out a thick, much-dog-eared notebook with a scribbled paper label on it, SPIRITUAL-ISTS—THEOSOPHISTS. Prior to his journey to Tibet, Mr. Holmes had compiled a catalog of known frauds and fake adepts in matters occult, the way he compiled catalogs of every other sort of criminal and confidence trickster he heard of: details cross-referenced in his mind.

Yet he had returned from those years of travel with a
different outlook than he had taken out of England with
him. And he had never, even when I first met him, been
a close-minded man. I knew — not from John, to whom
he never mentioned it, but from Martha Hudson — that
Holmes had continued his catalog with the names given
him by his various contacts in that portion of knowledge
that lies along the boundary between the world we know
and the multitude of worlds that we do not, and it was in
this rear section of the book that he now searched.

"Tell me, Peter," he said after a time, with his long
forefinger resting on a column of names, "is there an ill
wizard in the Neverlands, who commands a group of black
knights? Faceless knights," he added, seeing Peter's hesitant frown. Black Knights are as common as black birds,
in the Neverlands, and come in all sizes and varieties.
"Knights who do not bleed, when stabbed by a foe."

Peter's eyes widened again. Then he quickly readjusted
his features, as if he realized how much like a very little
boy he looked, a little boy the first time a birthday-party
magician produces a penny from behind his ear. Casually,
he replied, "That would be Nightcrow. He has a dreadful
fortress at the farthest end of the Neverlands. He seldom
ventures forth, but sometimes one sees him—"

Peter's voice sank. It was the first time I'd seen him
troubled: not frightened, because Peter doesn't frighten
easily, but deeply uneasy. "His island lies within the realm
of nightmares. Even the pirates won't go near it, and they'll
sail just about anywhere."

"So I thought," said Holmes. Looking over his shoulder,
I saw — as well as I could make out his strong but nearly
illegible handwriting — the entry on the notebook page:
Krähnacht, Jakob — 37 Barsham Lane, Deptford — followed
by a long series of notations in Holmes' personal short-
hand, which as far as I know only Martha can make out.

Hesitantly, I asked, "Why would this Mr. Krähnacht
wish to kidnap Bobbie, even if he did know where he
would come out of the Neverlands? Surely there are
children in London—"

"Obviously," said Holmes as he drew a half-sheet of paper to him and picked up a pencil, "he was paid to do so. By whom, can be deduced fairly easily once we have the boy himself back safe. Can you bring Peter to this place," he asked, turning round to me the sketch-map he'd made, "in three hours? It's down-river a good ways, but I can be there by then in a cab."

Mischievously, I said, "Why don't you fly with us, Mr. Holmes? I'm sure Peter and Ten Stars could fix you up."

Peter's eyes flamed with delight at the thought of Mr. Holmes, Inverness flapping like some vast cinder-hued bird, soaring through the night sky in a trail of fairy-dust. But Holmes shook his head and said primly, "I shall take a cab. Like most adults, I do not travel — at least in this instance — without baggage. I shall see you in Deptford at three."

He laid emphasis on these words and met my eye with a look that said, *Can you make sure he gets there?*

I gave a tiny shrug and a grimacing nod: *I'll do my best.* It came to me that he knew Peter as well as I did.

Barsham Lane lay on the far side of Deptford, far enough back from the river to be half in the countryside still. Number 37 was part of no ribbon-development, but rather lay apart, in its own grounds and about three-quarters of a mile from the last of the suburban villas. It took Peter and me exactly three hours and ten minutes to get there, and we swooped down out of the sky just as Mr. Holmes' cab was disappearing into the thickness of the river mist, leaving him standing by Number 37's iron gate.

As we came down through the fog I asked Peter softly, "Did you know Mr. Holmes before?"

"Of course I did, silly." Peter dove in a circle around me, to pull my pigtail. "He helped me slay the dreadful Gallipoot, that haunted Kensington Gardens. You were there."

I hadn't thought Peter had seen me. "I mean before that."

"Look," said Peter, pointing, "there he is. D'you think he's brought some more of those biscuits in that carpet-bag?" For Holmes did indeed have a large carpetbag at his feet. He wasn't looking at his watch, but into the fog above him, as if he knew we would take just as long to arrive as he did.

"Tell him to save me one," added Peter, and flashed away over the wall in the direction of the house, Ten Stars like a glittering comet-tail behind him. The mud of the drive was very cold and nasty between my toes, and the gravel hurt my feet. I waved to Mr. Holmes but came down on the other side of the gate, lifting the bar there that was heavy to my child's strength.

Holmes whispered, "Good girl, Mary," as he slipped through, and shut the gate behind us. He stood for a moment looking down at me — he stood many inches taller than even my adult, real-world self — and though the fog made it too dark to see more than his outline against the dim reflection from his dark-lantern, when he spoke again I could hear the concern in his voice. "Can you find your way back to your home without Peter?" he asked quietly. "You know that you are not dreaming now—"

"I know." I reached out, took his hand — cold, the way they always were, even through his gloves — and pinched his wrist with my fingernails, hard. His hand jerked back and I grinned up at him, then sobered again, when I saw that in my swift smile he almost recognized me. "But I'm not really real, either — or perhaps I'm more real than I've been in many years. And I know the danger is real. If something happens to me..."

I hesitated, not knowing what would become of me — where my self, my true self, whatever that true self was, would go.

"Peter," I went on hesitantly, "doesn't understand. He's never really lived in this world, not since he was a tiny baby..."

I glanced back toward the house, invisible in the absolute blackness, save for the swift-moving foxfire glow that was Peter Pan, scouting every window, chimney, and door for signs of occupancy.

Then I went on, "But we can't let the King of Dreams... It isn't just about finding Bobbie Lewensham, you know, though of course he must be rescued. But if indeed some mage in this world has found the way through to the world of dreams — or even through to the borderlands that lie between them — he must be stopped. Even for the good mages of this world to go tampering on its borders is ... dangerous. Too many of us need the Neverlands, to let the King of Dreams close its gates."

Holmes whispered, "Yes." I thought he would say something else, but after an intake of breath, he was after all silent.

Peter came whipping back in a shower of brightness that lit up the fog around him like diamonds. "Cravens! The house is deserted!"

"Excellent." Holmes picked up his carpetbag. "Krähnacht is presumably still back in Yorkshire, in whatever place he breached through to the Nightmare Castle when he ambushed our young Viscount upon his emergence from the Neverlands. Whatever that entrance is — almost certainly close by the stone-circle — the Fairies' Dance — where you first met Bobbie Lewensham, Peter — it will be heavily guarded. But Krähnacht has been in and out of the Neverlands before."

"The Wizard Nightcrow!" I cried excitedly. And when Peter looked blank, I said, "Krähnacht is German for..."

"I knew that," said Peter loftily. "I'd just forgot."

Holmes gave me the lantern to carry (of course Peter sees like a cat in the dark), and, when we drew near the house, the carpetbag as well. "It's very heavy," he warned, uncoiling from it a good twenty-five feet of insulated wire, at the end of which was rigged what I recognized as a crude electromagnetic coil. "But whoever doesn't carry it has to get near them, and I'd rather that were me."

"Get near who?" I asked, hoisting the unwieldy burden and staggering under its weight.

"The Black Knights," Holmes said, "of course."

Ten Stars — who was tremendously helpful and obliging (unlike some other fairies I could name) — lit on the corner of the bag like a butterfly, and smeared it with fairy-dust, which made carrying it much easier, although it did develop a tendency to want to travel in its own direction and had to be pulled fairly firmly. Still, that was better than carrying fifteen or twenty pounds of electrical batteries all by myself.

Jakob Krähnacht had his laboratories on the ground floor, strange rooms filled with crystals and mirrors, and a workshop with a small forge. There was a conservatory creeping with foul-smelling plants, and all the carpets and wallpaper stank of smoke and worse things. Much worse things. Ten Stars refused to go in, when Holmes picked the lock on the side door, but Peter walked just ahead of Holmes in the darkness, calling out softly, "Bobbie? Bobbie, it's Peter..."

The darkness thickened, and thickened, until the rays of the lamp couldn't pierce it, as if a hand of invisibility were slowly closing around the light-source, crushing the glow back in. Peter's voice ahead of us suddenly sounded a vast distance away, dimming down a long corridor. "Bobbie? We're here to save you—"

Holmes stopped. What little light remained showed me a wall ahead of us, dark and seemingly soot-stained. Holmes put out his hand to touch it, yet I could hear Peter on the far side of it, his voice fading, "Bobbie—"

I said, "We can go through. We only think it's there." I'd encountered such walls in the Neverlands. Evil Wizards use them all the time. "Close your eyes—"

I set the carpetbag down — and it settled with a metallic rattle to the floor — and closing my eyes, walked forward, hands outstretched.

After perhaps a dozen steps, I could hear the sound of the breakers, far off on Neverland's shores.

I turned around, and Holmes was gone.

I was in the blackness of a dungeon, cold rock under my feet. By the taste of the air, the smell of horror and damp, I knew I was in the Nightmare Realm somewhere, and I knew there was evil close-by. Peter darted up beside me, his face grim in the tiny glow shed by Ten Stars — goodness knows where she'd come from — and his knife in his hand. "Did they get him?" he whispered. "The Black Knights. They're everywhere..."

I shook my head, grieving and very frightened, at least in part because I suspected that Peter did not hold the power here in these realms that he had in the kindlier skerries of dreams. "He can't come through," I whispered. "He doesn't remember the way. Mr. Holmes!" I called, as loudly as I dared. "Mr. Holmes, just close your eyes! Walk forward!"

We stood for what felt like an eternity — what *could* have been eternity, I was well aware, for this realm was neither in the real world nor the Neverlands themselves, like a pocket of darkness in the curtain that separates them. An old pocket, filled with the smell of things that belong in no child's dreams.

"Holmes!" Peter cried, a little louder, and somewhere in the dark behind us, I heard the soft, deadly whisper of metal on metal, the distant clicking of machinery, like a dozen vile clocks.

I kept my voice steady with an effort. "Mr. Holmes," I said. "Mr. Holmes, if you can hear me... What was the first song you learned to play?"

I listened hard in the darkness, in my mind and my heart, but heard nothing from him.

Peter whispered, "It was this one." He took from his pocket (the only pocket he had, hanging from the belt where he carried his knife) his pipes, and played: it was an Irish tune that I'd heard Mr. Holmes weave into fantasias of melody on his violin. Yet it was very simple, the kind of thing a boy might whistle, when he's been locked in his room for seeing too clearly, and for making deductions about his elders from what he sees.

Behind us the clicking grew louder, and by the glow of Ten Stars' fairy-light I could see them, at the far end of the corridor. Four Black Knights, towering and identical. Faceless, as Holmes had said, only through their helmets' visors I could see the cold glitter of something moving steadily, mechanically. Peter's eyes widened, but he kept playing, playing as he and I slowly backed from them, until we reached the wall at the end of the corridor, trapped by that pocket of blackness. The lead knight raised its hand, and I could see that instead of a hand it had glittering steel blades coming straight out of its wrist, blades that whacked back and forth like saw-toothed scissors.

In panic, in despair, my adult self somewhere in dreaming cried, *John*—!

Then Holmes was beside us, stepping out of what looked like a pocket of still-deeper blackness by the wall. Ten Stars flickered, dove about him as he dropped the heavy carpetbag, dug from it a second electromagnetic rod. "We'll only have current for a moment," he warned as he handed it to Peter. "Mary, when I yell *Now*—"

"—throw the switch," I finished, because there was a switch among the neat maze of wires and batteries visible in the bag. "Is it a magnet?" I called after them, as they went striding, gray-clothed man and green-clothed boy, trailing wires down the corridor toward those faceless dark shapes, those whirling blades. The corridor was narrow, the Black Knights crowded one another, jostling, two behind two as they lifted their deadly slashing hands.

Holmes said, "Absolutely," and lunged like d'Artagnan, thrusting the rod into the center of the metal attacker's breastplate at the same instant that Peter thrust his. "*Now!*"

There was a blazing shower of white sparks, a flash of lightning when whatever was still trying to power the clockwork mechanism of the attacking knights imploded as metal fused to metal. The second pair of knights, running into the first pair, magnetized from them and also froze in a shower of blue sparks.

Peter's eyes shone blue and wild, brighter than the lightning with delight. "Super!" he breathed.

The Black Knights completely blocked the corridor, so Peter put his shoulder to the nearest one, sending all four crashing. "That tears it," said Holmes, kneeling to wrap up his electrical rods and batteries. "We must find Bobbie and flee, for Nightcrow will come, and he won't make the mistake again, of using the technology of the real world in this realm."

Peter whispered confidently, "This way."

We found the boy Bobbie Lewensham in a stone cell, its barred door standing open to the dank blackness of the corridor. His head was pillowed on his rolled-up blue coat and his little blue cap; he was profoundly asleep. Holmes tried to wake him, and then Peter, to no avail. I stood looking down at that thin, peaky-looking little face — he was very young, no older than John Darling. *What is it that you were fleeing, Bobbie, that opened your heart so fully to the realm of dreams?* 'Bobbie never visits anywhere,' Peter had said. 'When he's at home, he's alone...'

Alone with at least one person who knew or guessed about the Neverlands, and knew where to hire a kidnapper who would hide him in the other world forever.

"He's been drugged." Holmes scooped the boy up in his arms as if he were a kitten. "Drugged or a spell. Peter, listen. Can you keep him in the Neverlands with you for another two days? It will take me that long to find the man who hired Krähnacht — Nightcrow — and make sure he's not in a position to make a second attempt on the boy."

"He'll be safe with me." Peter inclined his head like a young king. He always liked to turn orders or suggestions around so that they were actually his idea.

And behind us, the barred door clanged.

We all whirled. And there he stood in the corridor, the nightmare wizard Nightcrow: a chubby gray-bearded man in the sort of tweeds you see hikers wear in the countryside — he had, of course, been in Yorkshire. And behind his spectacles, the coldest blue eyes I had ever seen.

"A mortal man," he said thoughtfully, regarding Holmes with those awful eyes. "A dream-child—" He looked at me, as if I were a butterfly in a net who'd make an interesting addition to some tray in a library. "And..." He looked at Peter. "And what have we here?"

"We have here your doom, Nightcrow!" trumpeted Peter, striding to the bars. "I am Peter Pan, and I have come here armed with spells for your destruction! Holmes, play your magic flute!"

"Holmes?" Nightcrow's salt-and-pepper eyebrows ascended; he wasn't in the least disconcerted. "So old Wylcourt's hired occultists have given up trying to find the Gate I opened, and he's hired Mr. Sherlock Holmes, eh? Now, that *is* a piece of news."

Holmes laid Bobbie back on the stone bench where we'd found him and said coldly, "I have nothing to say to you, Herr Krähnacht, except that I advise you to flee as fast as you can. For you are indeed doomed." Then, when Nightcrow only folded his arms with the air of a man expecting to see an interesting show in complete safety, Holmes sat down on the edge of the bench, turned his back on Nightcrow, took his flute from his pocket, and began to play the air from Vivaldi's Concerto in D Major. Peter flung up his arms, uttered a long wailing "Oooo-oo-ooo-ah-ah-ah-ooo-ooo-ooo," and began to chant a string of nonsense syllables, coils of fairy-light (courtesy of Ten Stars, hiding prudently behind his back) ribboning from his outstretched fingers.

I realized what was going on, and began to hop around Peter in the best imitation I could contrive of my friend Delphine Tremlow's Ancient Grecian Dances that she teaches shop-girls.

"Fascinating," Nightcrow murmured, not disconcerted in the least. "You can't do a thing to me, you know. We are neither in reality nor the dream world, and this enclave has its own laws. I look forward, Holmes, to observing you here over the next several years. As for Peter Pan — *the* Peter Pan — Well! I have a number of experiments I am eager to try—"

"Silence, fiend." Peter paused in his chanting. "I am weaving your Doom."

"I await it," smiled Nightcrow sarcastically, "with bated breath. I've heard about you, of course — Did you come because young Viscount Mure was calling for you? He did, you know. For years now I've sought the secrets that lie within the realm of Dreaming, and now they're within my grasp. My dear young lady, I hope your parents..."

At that point, summoned by Holmes' piping, the terrible Gallipoot emerged from the darkness behind Nightcrow in a rush of sulfur stench and the wailing of a thousand chewed-up fragments of souls, and devoured him down to the last morsel. When the Thing Cold and Empty rolled, surged, oozed away down the corridor and vanished once again, all that was left of Nightcrow was his spectacles, his watch, and the key to the cell, lying on the stone floor a few inches outside the bars, in a puddle of Gallipoot slime.

"You did tell him to run away," said Peter, in a satisfied voice. He knelt to retrieve the key. "Grown-ups never listen, do they?"

"Never," lamented Holmes.

There is a crossroads on the borders of the ocean of sleep, a tiny islet of rock and sand in the vast archipelagoes of the Neverlands that stretch into eternity, and from there I could see, far away across the darkness, my bedside lamp burning low, and John asleep in a chair beside my bed.

If I turned my head I could see the other way, toward the Neverlands, world after world of forests and rainbows, of mermaid lagoons and pirate ships, of castellated islands and magic horses and caves full of enchanted books. Peter and Bobbie stood hand in hand where the gray arm of the crossroad led in that direction: "I'll have him back at the stone circle in two days," said Peter. I guessed that if Peter forgot, the King of Dreams would remind him.

"It was Mr. Gower, you know," said Bobbie to Holmes. "Mr. Gower's our business manager — Father's, I mean. I never liked him — he was always asking questions about the fairies, and the Neverlands. When I came back through at the stone circle last time, he was there, he and Nightcrow..."

"He shall be dealt with," promised Holmes, with grim quiet. "He will be gone, by the time you return."

"If we see the King of Dreams," said Bobbie, "I'll tell him you've taken care of the problem."

"You're sure you won't come with us?" asked Peter, looking up at Holmes. "Your tree's still there, and Old Chief Walking Wolf would love to see you again."

Holmes smiled, and shook his head. "I have to go deal with Mr. Gower," he said. "To make sure that the Neverlands will still be open, the next time Bobbie — or your friends Wendy and John and Michael — wish to come through. But do indeed give my regards to the Chief, and to Melegriance the White Wizard, and to the Evil Queen of the Night Island, and all the others. And thank you." He held out his hand, and Peter shook it, very man-to-man.

Peter said, "Any time," though Holmes and I both knew how quickly he would forget.

After Peter and Bobbie had gone, I asked softly, "Were you one of Peter's Lost Boys?"

Holmes gave me a sidelong look. "Certainly not. How would I have come to be Lost in the Neverlands?"

"How does anyone?" I asked. "Will you be able to get rid of this Mr. Gower when you get back? He's obviously studied occult matters, the same as you have, to guess about Bobbie and the stone-circle and the fairies and the Neverlands, and to know to hire Mr. Krähnacht. If he's their business manager, must he not have been speculating with the Earl's money, while the old Earl's been sick? That's why he wanted to hide Bobbie in another world — so no one would find a body. It would be years before he'd have to be accountable for money he'd lost."

Holmes smiled down at me. "I see you've grasped my methods, Mary. Since the matter is one of financial peculation, it should be easy enough to bring home to him, and to put him out of the way. Even had I not spoken to Bobbie, the culprit would have been simple to find. Quite elementary, my dear..."

The word stopped on his lips, and his face changed, in the starry twilight of that crossroads, as he recognized me at last. First enlightened, then filled with a rush of comprehension, as he understood at last why I had come to be so free within the Neverlands, followed by pity and grief. And it seemed to me that I no longer looked up so far at him, though as I've said he was always far taller than I. But it seemed to me that I was as he saw me, not my child self, nor even the woman I'd been when first we'd met, but a gaunt and shorn-haired invalid in the final stages of consumption.

"My dear." He put out his hand, and where once it had felt cold against the healthy heat of my child-hand in dreaming, now his was the warm one.

"Don't worry," I said gently. "I'll be returning to John, at least for a short while."

In his face I saw his knowledge, of how short that time would be.

"Take care of him," I said, simple and matter-of-fact.

"Of course."

"It's been good to have an adventure with you," I said. "I always wanted to. They never let girls."

Holmes opened his mouth to reply — almost certainly with some sentence beginning, *The female of the species...* then thought about the words, and closed it again. At length he said, "That has been my loss."

We were silent, on that crossroads island, the dark bridge that led back toward my own room — and to Baker Street, for him — disappearing into the star-sprinkled gloom before our feet. In the other direction I could still see the Neverlands, sparkling in sunlight and joy.

Holmes asked, "Will you be all right?"

"Oh, yes. Peter will look after me, and go with me the first part of the way. It is the one thing he always does."

He nodded, knowing this to be true. "Until we meet again, then, Mary."

And we went our separate ways.

His Last Arrow

by Christopher Sequeira

The following is transcribed exactly as it appears on many handwritten sheets of paper. The original document itself was the sole contents of a plain brown envelope that had at one time been sealed with wax, which was found amongst a large selection of items in a house in Crowborough, East Sussex, in England. The envelope and many items of value were believed to have been stolen property, accumulated by a gang of burglars who were apprehended after successfully robbing several houses in the vicinity. Some of the goods the thieves had taken appeared to have come from the home of the late Sir Arthur Conan Doyle, however, when the brown envelope was proffered to the late author's family, and it was noted that the seal was broken, a legal representative of the Doyle family examined the documents and announced the papers had never at any time been in the possession of the family, and then took the unusual step of expressing the view in writing that any attempts to claim otherwise would meet with legal action.

⊹✛ ✛ ✛⊹

In 1894 I had returned to Baker Street following the failure of my marriage. I had concealed the full ignominy of my situation by revising the beginning of a story that was just about to see print in The Strand magazine so that the tale began with a contemporary reference to the ending of the union as a 'bereavement'. This was artistic sophistry, of course, for the woman I had married was still on this earth, she had simply decided she could tolerate no more of my involvement in the activities of my friend, Sherlock

Holmes. What my other friends and acquaintances, as well as my readers had no appreciation of, however, was how well I knew this deception would take on a life of its own, and surely enough, it did. Within months old friends like Thurston, Murray and Stamford were speaking of my former wife as if she had passed from this world.

My return to Baker Street and resettling of some of my personal effects seemed to interrupt Holmes not at all. He seemed to be cocooned in a realm of chemical formulae and calculations, and would sit for hours painstakingly measuring droplets of fluids and solutions that he mixed and boiled on his Bunsen burner. When he did speak of his current work he claimed he was seeking an alternative chemical explanation for a spattering of dye stains he had found on a murderer's dye-apron, because that killer's height and infirmity of the left elbow precluded his wielding a left-handed blow that killed his much taller attacker. Due to the fact I was in sombre spirits I made a poor attempt at humor and suggested the killer might have stood on a ladder and turned his back to his victim, stabbing that poor person with his right hand, but in a backwards thrust. Holmes glared at me curiously and instead of expressing disgust or amusement he became quite absorbed in the notion. He proclaimed "Watson, you have increased your deductive capacity greatly since our last shared occupancy — that was positively luminous!" and he spoke not another word for the remainder of the week as he completed his investigations.

So I had much to ponder in those first days back in the old digs, and much to ponder without the company of another's conversation. I surveyed our old quarters, noticing that Holmes had changed little about its character and appearance. Cigars lay sequestered in the coal scuttle, tobacco was to be found in the toe of a Persian slipper Holmes kept near the gasogene, and a bust of Napoleon near a window often served as a hat rack. I wandered to the mantelpiece cluttered with the essential items that marked Holmes' day — tobacco dottles, correspondence answered and unanswered, souvenirs of his most recent case — and here I stopped.

The mantle-corner was the place he always left a souvenir of his last effort; be it a coin, a letter; anything that allowed him to reflect on the relative successes and failures of his last inquiry; and the object always remained there until replaced by the next dirt sample, bent hairpin or scribbled cryptogram that merited his scrutiny.

The latest item was a curious flattened stone, almost perfectly triangular but with rounded corners. On the uppermost side there was carved into the surface a writing of some kind, vaguely like Sanskrit or the Arabic language, whilst on the reverse I was surprised to discover a sort of pictograph; an image carved into it. The writing meant nothing to me, but the image was another matter, infuriatingly, it seemed familiar yet impossible to place into context. The image was clearly a face of some kind, but a monstrous one, of a leering, demoniacal caricature, an ugly fetish, bulging-eyed and sporting a jaw full of menacing teeth, clearly meant to frighten the simple-minded and superstitious. Although it seemed unlike that of the native art of any cultures of the Middle East I had encountered — though I was far from an expert I had spent many years abroad — I felt the nagging sense I'd come across such a totem before.

I knew Holmes would ignore me if I asked him about a recent case whilst he was engaged on a new one, so I decided to wait until he had finished his chemistry work. I could not put the issue, and my possible memory lapse, from my mind easily, but I consoled myself by recalling that during the frantic events of my time of service in the East, including the brush with death that my one-time orderly Murray had saved me from in Afghanistan, there were many experiences that were lost or blurred in the turmoil of gunfire, heat and blood; or the delirium of terrible fevers.

Some degree of relief to the mystery of the stone came in another form the following morning. I had breakfasted alone — Holmes had left a note that he was on one of his mysterious excursions — but as I finished my toast I heard the door downstairs open and close and then the familiar tread of Inspector Gregson on the stairs. Moments after a sharp double-rap at the door and a yelled "Halloa", the man himself entered the room.

The long-faced Scotland Yard man looked older than just the year or so since I had last seen him, and I discerned something unhealthy about his physique; he seemed wasted and drawn, his eyes slightly yellowed, although his greeting was hearty enough.

"Doctor, Good Lord, man, I wasn't aware you had returned here, I am so sorry about your wife, sir."

I muttered a reply, and waved him to a chair, and brought forth some cigars and cigarettes. He smiled and pointed at the silver coffee pot.

"Thank you, Doctor; I wouldn't say no, if I might also partake of a cup of Mrs. Hudson's coffee, she always brews it just right."

"She does indeed, Inspector, so help yourself. Mrs. Hudson has doubtless told you that Holmes is out, but I take it since you opted to come upstairs anyway that I may act as the sounding board of old? Now, what criminal enigma brings you here today?" I said.

Gregson sipped his coffee and exhaled a plume of Egyptian tobacco smoke. He gave me a grin.

"Murder of the most unusual stripe, sir, very much in Mr. Holmes' line. There's an antiques appraiser, name of Spencer Pethebridge, lives in Bloomsbury, but maintains an office in the Commercial Road. He's considered extremely knowledgeable, especially about Oriental artifacts, and has exposed more than a few forgeries, I'm told. And only an hour ago he was found dead, in his office, probably murdered."

I leaned forward, my attention fully engaged.

"Inspector, you should not tease me after I've only just returned to this house of riddle-solving. Probably murdered, you say? How can a murder be only probable to a Scotland Yard man?"

Gregson saluted me with his cigarette. "Bravo, Doctor, I was seeing if you were in the frame of mind for the business again. I do say 'probably', because although there was all the appearance of a suicide, the method of death was so out of the ordinary that murder has to be countenanced."

"Unusual?" I said, feeling a strange sense of dread rise in my chest, rather than the excitement of curiosity that I had felt in the days of old. I was surprised at this reaction, and concealed it from Gregson. I wondered if I was not myself because of the circumstances that had brought me back to Baker Street, the sense of failure, or regression.

I wondered if I was merely growing too old too soon.

"Oh, yes, unusual it was. Mr. Pethebridge shot himself, straight through the heart. With an old arrow, fired by a crossbow."

I was about to ask a question — exactly what I cannot now recall at all — when the door to the room was flung open, and a weird individual stood on the threshold, staring at us both.

He was a tall man in his late fifties or early sixties, with sun-baked, heavily creased, skin. He had a military bearing, but wore a strange hodge-podge of clothing, partly European, in terms of his boots and his trousers, but his long shirt and robe-like cloak was cotton and loose-fitting, and his head was adorned with the many windings of a turban. A few loops of beads were draped about his neck, some holding shining stones and metallic links of a sort not seen in Europe, and in his hand he clasped a very tall stick; more a staff than a cane. Although obviously of the Asian continent in origin, he reminded one more than anything else of that wonderful citizen of the Crown who lived life as much in the world of the Orientals as he did England, the late Sir Richard Burton. He flung a yellow-nailed hand out at Gregson, and spoke in a high, clear, but accented voice, assuredly Middle Eastern.

"The man Holmes, are you he?" he said; then turned to me. "Or are you?"

I stood and approached the fellow, extending my hand, cautiously, although this took enormous effort, for I found I was fearful of the fellow and his blazing brown eyes.

"Mr. Holmes is, I'm afraid, not here," I said, "However if you would state your business I might be able to assist you, Mister...?"

The visitor stamped a foot impatiently, almost in temper. "I cannot delay! I cannot delay!" he said. "I must return to my own city soon. I have no time!"

"I am Holmes' closest associate," I ventured, "if you would just explain what you want, it may help."

The man jumped forward, so fast that I had absolutely no time to anticipate him, and found my forearms gripped with a coiled strength that could have been painful had he exerted much more pressure. Gregson moved to his feet to assist me somehow, but it was not necessary, I was not, apparently in any danger.

"The Doctor! I was told you no longer dwelt here, that you had..." The stranger paused and a look passed over him. He stared at me, searching my face for I knew not what. "I mean that you no longer lived here, with the man, the detective, Holmes," he finally said. "Please, when will Holmes return here? I have a message that he must receive, I took an oath to bring it to him."

I tried to explain to the visitor that Holmes' movements were not easily predictable when he was on a case but the man seemed to lose all interest. Gregson was becoming impatient with the fellow, too.

"I think that's about all Dr. Watson really needs tell you, sir, unless you are prepared to give a name, or something a bit more substantial. And as a member of her Majesty's Scotland Yard detectives division I would suggest you heed him."

Our guest looked at Gregson, and then shook his head, but there was no hostility, only sadness.

"My name is Faroukhan. I will try to find Mr. Holmes elsewhere. If you see him, please tell him I will return no later than four o'clock this afternoon if I have not found him by then. I stay with friends, but only until seven o'clock tonight, then I must return home."

"Do you wish to leave me the address of where you stay, sir?" I asked.

The stranger shook his head, and without another word he turned and left.

Gregson, bless his soul, could sense the strain this odd intrusion had on me, so newly returned to the world of Holmes and his parade of strange clients.

"Don't worry, Doctor, you'll get used to things again, I dare say. Here, why don't you come to the Commercial Road with me, we'll leave a message with Mrs. Hudson and perhaps Mr. Holmes will end up joining us there if we're lucky."

I agreed that this sounded an excellent plan. We left and took a cab.

Once in Commercial Road we stopped outside a small house-front where two constables were guarding the door in a largely futile effort to dissuade a group of curious on-lookers from loitering. Gregson nodded at the men and escorted me inside.

It was a terrible sight. There was a large desk and chair in the middle of the room whilst the walls were covered by a multitude of shelves featuring reference books of many shapes and sizes and glass cabinets containing a small museum's worth of oddities and artifacts. Ancient weapons, old bronze vessels, aged and cracked tools lay in various cabinets within the shelving. All of this paraphernalia only served to heighten the ugliness of the scene of the dead man at the desk.

He was a dark-haired man of between thirty and forty, clean-shaven, and he sat back in the chair, a look of pain frozen on his white face. A crossbow was clutched in his fingers, and indeed an arrow was embedded in his chest — just the angle and appearance of the corpse made me feel certain that the weapon had pierced his heart and killed him almost instantly. But what cast an eerie aspect upon the whole scene was the item that lay on the desk, largely under the dead man's hands and the crossbow. It was a photographic plate, the type that appears in textbooks illustrating a particular item, and a ragged edge made it quite clear that it had been torn from the pages of a book.

Naturally enough my first thought in this room of many books was that the original volume the page belonged to might be somewhere at hand, recently pulled from a shelf, but no tomes seemed to have left their home on the bookcases.

What the photographic plate depicted was a dying man, in eastern clothing lying on a mat on a dirt floor in some sort of tent, surrounded by grieving women and children. The man however had one arm outstretched and his eyes looked in that direction, even though, judging from the emaciated state of the man, the act of rising even that small amount seemed to be an effort. The curious aspect of the plate was that where the man looked to, where his hand was stretched to — there was nothing, no other hand grasped his withered palm to comfort him, and despite the look in his eyes, he met no other face with his gaze. The caption read simply *"The Shaman asks for Mercy on his Deathbed"*.

Gregson explained that the neighbors had neither heard nor seen anything out of the ordinary this morning. Pethebridge had arrived at his office, very early, at eight o'clock, as was his custom. He would normally read and drink tea for an hour before opening his doors to his appointments. A curator of one of the collections at the British Museum hoped Pethebridge might have some available time that day to inspect a new shipment of Egyptian articles they had received, so a commissionaire had been sent here at half past eight to deliver a message. The messenger entered and had found the body just as we saw it here, and alerted the police.

I examined the actual arrow that was in the dead man's chest. It was of a strange construction, it seemed to be made of old bronze — ancient bronze — rather than wood, which gave me great doubts about its flight capabilities over any sort of distance. The arrow was one of five that appeared to be part of a set that belonged in an old leather quiver of some kind, almost petrified by age, which stood on the desk near the corpse. Of the four remaining arrows in the quiver all were bent or had broken heads, none other appeared, through dint of age, to be in a state where it could be loaded into the crossbow. Of the crossbow itself I noted that it seemed to have a different vintage and origin than the arrows and quiver, for it seemed more like an ancient English device, of the type that can be found in many a native crafts and hunting exhibition; I dared think it was more than fifty years old. So, to kill himself, it seemed Pethebridge had opted to combine a mismatched cross-bow and bolt.

Gregson expanded on what he thought was a feature of interest. "Now, according to the fellow who owns the haberdashery opposite, not a person entered this premises between seven thirty and eight thirty, other than Mr. Pethebridge. Therefore we need to consider an entry from another part of the building as a possibility, such as a window or back door, but, I've been unable to locate any that aren't securely bolted on the inside, so a death by suicide certainly seems supported, but really, Doctor, I find it very difficult to conceive of a man killing himself in such an awkward way."

"Of course, there is an alternative, gentlemen," came a clear voice. We looked up and saw Holmes standing in the doorway.

Gregson shook Holmes' hand warmly. "Glad to see you, sir. You have a theory, already?"

"Not one theory as yet, Gregson, for I have in fact con-ceived of eight workable hypotheses based on the facts as I know them from your men outside and my first glance about this room. However, I am optimistic that I can elimi-nate several with a proper examination of this scene," said Holmes.

Holmes examined the quiver, he pulled a lens from his inside coat pocket to look at its entire surface, and then he carefully studied the remainder of the arrows. He then looked carefully at the dead man, paying particular atten-tion to the scalp of the deceased, especially at the back of the head. He sniffed at the remains of a cup of tea found on a side-table, and then performed a number of calcula-tions in a notebook drawn from his pocket. He clucked and looked around the room. From out of another pocket he drew a long-stemmed pipe and idly tapped it against his leg. Having replaced the pipe, he stood near the centre of the room and slowly turned around in a perfect circle; I could see he was surveying the room again, but particularly the shelving, until at one moment he paused — staring, his eyes darting back and forth over the rows of books — I followed his gaze intently hoping to see a volume recently displaced or some other item out of the ordinary, but all seemed in perfect order and no different to any other shelf.

But it was clear Holmes saw something I did not, and he was quite aware that both Gregson and I were scrutinizing him. He darted forward to the book case and, professorially, held up a hand.

"Note, if you will, that although this room is relatively free from dust — indicating it is regularly cleaned — that on this shelf, and this shelf alone, there is a great streak of dust — five furrowed streaks of dust, in fact. What does this suggest?"

I looked to where Holmes pointed. "Why, that could be a dusty hand-mark." I exclaimed. I felt a weird queasiness as I said it for I had earlier examined the shelf myself and seen nothing of the print in the dust.

"Indeed," said Holmes, "as if someone were firmly grasping the edge of the shelf while they exerted some effort to pull free one of the books tightly placed there, correct?"

"Yes, that is feasible," I said, and noticed Gregson nodding in accord.

"My, how we can see without properly observing!" Holmes then said triumphantly. He grasped the shelf where the dust-mark was and pulled whilst holding in a knot of wood. There was a clicking sound followed by a creak and Holmes suddenly pulled an entire section of book case from the wall to reveal a hidden doorway and some sort of descending stair case!

Words were limited to exclamations of amazement as we swiftly followed Holmes down, below the building, and through what appeared to be some sort of sewer tunnelling that finally terminated after coming up through an empty cellar doorway behind a public house around the corner.

Holmes immediately saw an empty cab-stand across the street and sprinted over to an adjacent newspaper seller's box, where he engaged the lad in a quick exchange and contributed lavishly to the boy's takings for the day.

"We are in luck, the boy saw our man and he knows the cabbie who picked him up quite well; they often chat when things are slow. His name is Charles Netley. His number is 522."

Gregson beamed. "Right-o. I'll arrange for Mr. Netley to be interviewed and we'll soon have the address to which this fellow was delivered. Would you like to come along for that part of the investigation, Mr. Holmes, Doctor?"

Holmes rubbed his hands together briskly, and agreed that we would.

Holmes and I were dining at Simpson's some hours later when an officer from Scotland Yard interrupted us to advise that Inspector Gregson had news of the case. We immediately abandoned our meal and after paying our surprised hosts we headed off in a Scotland Yard-arranged carriage. It was not long before we reached a quiet street in Camden and alighted to find our friend the Inspector surreptitiously watching a particular house.

"Gentleman, a week ago that house was let to a fellow who arrived with a large selection of items bound for the British Museum. The Museum had paid a small fortune for these acquisitions and was planning a major exhibit about them.

Holmes surprised me again by adding to Gregson's information. "Yes, Inspector, and an anonymous letter was received by the head of Collections that the bulk of the material was not authentic, that what had been examined in Cairo was carefully substituted en route to England, and the real artifacts were in fact being shown to French Museum officials next week — this was part of a systematic stratagem to sell worthless copies that the Museums would be far too embarrassed to publicly admit they had been cheated, or so I've been advised by my Baker Street Irregulars."

I was astonished. I had been with Holmes all day and his ability to progress a case whilst scratching a violin or smoking a pipe was as marked as ever. I had seen him go to the door once and take a note from a street urchin, but had not inquired what it meant at the time.

Gregson nodded. "The culprit is in that house, I am sure you are right, but let us be clear, gentlemen, this is a ruthless, ambitious man. The fact he knew the location of Pethebridge's secret exit-way suggests that he knew of its existence beforehand, and that tells me that Pethebridge was likely his accomplice."

Holmes clapped the inspector on the shoulder. "Yes, Pethebridge was to authenticate the fakes, not expose them, but some dispute between the two men destroyed their plan."

We quietly approached the house. Lights were on, but no sound could be heard. Gregson and his officer went first, and knocked on the door.

Amazingly it swung open at their touch. They paused, listening, but no sound came, so with the two official men at the front the four of us entered the house.

The place was almost bereft of furnishings, save for the living room where a chair and table gave the room some sense of habitation, and a roaring fire filled the grate. On the mantelpiece, over the fire, there rested an unbroken arrow just like the one that had killed Pethebridge, and above the arrow, on the wall, hung a framed photo of a collection of soldiers and native tribesman loosely gathered around together. I studied it carefully and found myself rudely surprised. I turned to Holmes. I felt ill, I felt as if I did not know what I was talking about, but the words tumbled from my lips as if forced.

"This man in the centre, the one in local garb — Holmes, he's the man who came looking for you this morning! Faroukhan! He is much older now, but that is him, I'm certain."

Holmes seemed stunned. "Watson, I dare say you are right, and this bodes poorly for us. I fear that what you say means he meant me ill, that he knew I would be consulted in a case like this. Can a man this well prepared be caught off guard by such an obvious approach as we have just made? Perhaps we had better—"

There was a blood-curdling cry and I turned.

Faroukhan stood in the room with a scimitar raised before him.

He lunged at Holmes with the weapon but the detective dived for the floor. The blade followed, but was stopped by the table, and sent wood splintering in all directions. The sword-wielder turned to me, and I felt my life was to end there. He shook his head, actually looking at me with sadness, when without warning, Gregson's pistol sounded three times, and bullets tore through Faroukhan's neck and chest. He seemed struck with disbelief but still he clutched the sword. Again, he turned towards me, this time he did move forward, but only to collapse against me, his fingers grasping for my coat.

Faroukhan's lips parted one last time, but only to spill frothy blood while his eyes pleaded with me. He died then, his hands so tightly locked on my shirt-front that I had to pry them free. In one was an object that I could feel before I even looked at it. I was struck with a desire to conceal it, to examine later, when the horror of this moment was behind me. I discreetly pocketed the item.

"An ugly, demented affair, old fellow. The anxiety of which I should have been able to spare you, had I been less concerned with my own sense of drama," Holmes said. "Forgive me, old friend, I am not yet used to having you at my side again."

I did not know what to say, but there was much going through my mind. I was silent until we arrived back in Baker Street, where I then excused myself to have an early night.

Before I went to bed I looked at the triangular piece of stone that I had earlier secreted in my pocket; it was identical to the one I had found on our own mantel.

That night I slept fitfully. After struggling for several hours I arose, and in the darkness I dressed and went quietly out into the night. At first I just walked the city's thoroughfares aimlessly, but eventually found myself standing before the empty house in Kensington that I had lived in with my wife. Although I owned it I scarce knew what to do with it and had not put it up for sale or lease. I realized, as I stood there in the dark, that I was expecting her to return at any time and allow us to step back into the home we once shared so contentedly, and I knew then, that it could never happen.

I found a cab and sent it hurrying through the night to the house where Faroukhan had dwelt. Giving the cabbie a small financial incentive I bade him wait whilst I circled the property. Finding a window at the back of the house I smashed it, unlatched the frame, raised it and climbed inside.

Having turned up the gaslight I stood in the room looking at the picture on the wall. After a few moments, or perhaps an eternity, I found the front door, went out to the cab and after giving the driver some instructions, sent him back into the city.

It was cold, so I relit the fire and waited...

Holmes arrived an hour later — I heard the cab approach and met him at the front door, letting him in, I stood watching as the cab driver drove off. Holmes looked sympathetically at me.

"Watson, I never get your limits. But one thing is doubtless, old friend, I am acutely aware of how compassionate a fellow you are. You worry about the family of this man, Faroukhan, do you not?"

I nodded. I showed him the large framed photograph which I had taken down from the wall during my vigil.

Faroukhan was many years younger, as he laughed and joked with the soldiers, but he was not the only one. I pointed to an officer in the picture, one I had not observed before, no matter how impossible, there was no mistaking the man in the back of the shot if you looked closely enough. It was myself in uniform, one of the optimistic souls in a dirty war in a strange land, where friends were few.

Holmes nodded. "He had been friendly to you and the rest of the Fifth Northumberland Fusiliers, had he not? You considered him a man whose reports from enemy lines had saved you all from a horrible death — the man who had got word the enemy was coming and enabled you all to break camp and escape before an attack came, is that not so?"

"Yes," I said. "He was a man who believed that he had shared an honor with us, one that would last beyond the day we ever saw each other again, and it was largely due to me. When I had arrived in his village I had treated his niece and saved her from an agonizing fever, succeeding more by luck than any of the limited medical supplies I had to hand. He swore an oath promising a bond to me from that day onwards."

"Yes," said Holmes. "So how did this obligation come to be twisted into such evil intent? What misfortune befell this poor, superstitious fellow that turned him against you so?"

"I suppose that is the explanation — of course." I said. I sighed, exhaustedly, and bent over a little, steadying myself on the nearby armchair. "I think I have punished myself enough, Holmes, would you help me hang the photo back up again?"

Holmes clapped me on the back softly and then turned to heft the picture. "Rest easy, old friend, it shall take me but a moment."

With both his hands full and the picture partially obscuring his view of me, Holmes could not see me pull, from inside my coat, the last of the bronze arrows, where I had hidden it by tearing a hole in the lining. Using both hands, and all the strength I could muster, I plunged the arrow into my friend's chest.

Instantly he dropped the picture and screamed. One of his hands flailed out at me, catching me on the face. My nose was smashed and I actually heard the cartilage break a moment before blood began to gout from it. I instinctively jumped as far back from Holmes as possible in my state, and watched him slowly sink to his knees, blood spurting from his chest, his arms jerking like some strange puppet.

He slumped to the floor, then onto his side and was screeching as he struggled, weakly, to pluck the arrow from his chest. The ichor that flowed from the wound and down his shirt-front, was no longer red, but was changing even as I watched, turning as black as his eyes. Finally, only one hand tugged uselessly at the arrow imbedded in his body. The other began to scratch the floorboards, effortlessly digging deep furrows in the hard, smooth surface. It was clear there was terrific strength in that form, but thankfully it could do nothing against the enchantment of the arrow.

Then, Holmes began to spasm and twitch; the heels of his shoes beating an awful tattoo on the floor. He began to weep but only briefly, soon he was silent, simply twisting and jerking like a landed fish breathing its last.

He looked at me. I shuddered, for the hatred I saw in those coal-black eyes was incalculable; it was the fierce burning hatred of one natural enemy for another.

Then, Holmes finally died. His body began to change, to warp and take on a different hue, his hands knotting and twisting as if suddenly desiccated by years of age. What he became was a creature that only resembled a man in base configuration, but this was no man, of any kind. Blue-skinned, blue as a corpse, its skin was more a lumped and pitted hide. The limbs were much, much longer than Holmes' had been and now stuck out in an ungainly fashion from the sleeves and trousers of the clothes it had adopted. The hands were six-fingered, without nails and like the roots of plants, long and gnarled; the feet seemed equally distended, lying slack within Holmes' boots.

The thing's face was just as abnormal. A large, narrow head with a gigantic jawbone and a cranium that extended backwards, the creature looked like some nightmare version of a primitive man, heavy brow-ridge and bulging eyes combined with an over-sized mouth, full of protruding, tusk-like, teeth... the face on the triangular stone.

I collapsed on to a chair and waited in that room for hours, too horror-struck, too filled with shame and loathing, to do anything. Finally, the sun's rays began to creep into the chamber, and I took to my feet. The natural light, the friend of we who can only pretend to have made this planet our kingdom, gave me courage, and the spell that had afflicted me for so many years was completely lifted from my weary shoulders.

I remembered all. I recalled how I had lain in a ditch in Afghanistan, my body afire with the wounds I had sustained, begging, screaming for Death to come, and crying out to the gods of that strange land to grant me mercy. Death had not come, but instead this djinn appeared, this awful, parasitic creature of antiquity. When it had leant over me and whispered to me in a language I ought not to have understood, I had no will to deny it. It reached into my mind and plucked out my most naïve and childish desires, fuelled by the discontent I had at being a failed medical practitioner, and had asked me whether I would like to have not only my life saved, but my fondest wishes fulfilled, to forever be known as man of courage and heroism, who would be renowned through my homeland as a vanquisher of evil, I said yes! In that moment I would have agreed to far worse. The demon smiled a ghastly smile, pressed an odd triangular piece of carved stone into my upturned palm, and then disappeared as suddenly as he had come.

And so it was that I found myself miraculously rescued by Murray and, with my health broken, returned to England. Once there, young Stamford, in some weird trance, had come to my flea-ridden hovel and taken me to Bart's hospital where I had descended, as if in a dream, to the morgue, where Holmes appeared like some spectre amongst the cadavers — an event I later glamorized when I wrote of it. I was to change many a weird event in the next several years as the foul thing performed its work. I suspect the creature had actually created its body, its form, from the cadaver of some poor lost soul lying in Bart's, some nameless, hapless victim of disease or accident.

So began the years in Baker Street, where my mind and body were put into a strange servitude. The creature would prowl the streets of London, and sometimes, the country-side much farther afield, wreaking terrible murder and misfortune, and then concocting the most perfect, yet utterly fantastic scenarios that would explain the outrages, even affecting the minds of the very victims and witnesses; condemning many a man and woman to imprisonment or even the gallows. At times the creature was content to actually solve genuine crimes, its ability to partially glimpse men's thoughts made that a simple matter, but it had a perverse sense of drama, and so created strange means of homicide and assault that defied reality but fuelled the fantasy. The speckled-band — that never-before heard of swamp adder that killed the Stoner girl; the impossible serum that transformed Professor Presbury into a creeping man; the impossibly agile, dart-throwing dwarf assassin at Pondicherry Lodge; the chemically irreproducible Devil's Foot narcotic that slew a room of people instantly; all these were some of the terrible instruments of death that the djinn had conjured into being by sheer force of will, as plot elements in its cavalcade of murder and depravity. All done just so that Holmes and myself could triumphantly appear on stage to explicate and bring down the final curtain with a solution only we could furnish.

A solution I would then write of... for the adulation of millions.

My wife knew, of course. I don't know how long it took for her to see through the veil of Holmes' inhumanity, but she knew he was not what he seemed, but she was careful, she never challenged him directly; I am sure such action would have been fatal. No, Mary simply asked me to make a choice, as I had made a choice on that bleak battlefield years before, shivering with pain and ague. I wanted her to stay, but I could not admit why she was really leaving, so ultimately I let her go, because I was weak, I still wanted this life of fame, this life of international acclaim, as a stalwart of justice, and crusader against the wicked.

Somehow, across the years, across the miles, my old friend Faroukhan had sensed that my moment of truth was coming, and knowing I would fail, had come to repay the old debt, the debt that began with my helping his niece, and was compounded when I left his country carrying an evil native force with me, unbeknownst to him at the time.

He had come to help me fight valiantly, with honor, as I had not done, as I had only pretended to do all these years since leaving Afghanistan. How he knew of my plight I know not, but he must have consulted a shaman of some kind and obtained the arrows that would rid the world of the djinn.

I was, I am, an utter fraud, no matter the sort of influence I was under all these years, no matter how confused my mental state when in proximity to the wretched creature. I know that now. I have my service revolver at my side. I have managed to rouse the fire in this room. I have dragged the djinn's body into the fireplace and liberally doused much of the furniture in this place with oil. I will wait until I have satisfied myself that the thing's body is adequately consumed and then ignite the room; that will take some hours, but the time has given me an opportunity to write this narrative.

After all else, I think I loved the writing more than anything, more than the money, the acclaim. How small and how sad were my desires.

I shall finish this missive and place it outside, in an envelope addressed to my old friend, Conan Doyle; he may do with it as he pleases. Then I shall return here, touch the flames to the furniture and put my service revolver to my head and do what I should have done in Afghanistan many, many years, and many, many lives ago. Hopefully I will become like Holmes, a thing of fantasy, nothing more than a creature of the imagination.

The Things That Shall Come Upon Them

by Barbara Roden

"Do you recall, Watson," said my friend Sherlock Holmes, "how I described my profession when we first took lodgings together, and you expressed curiosity as to how your fellow lodger was related to certain comments which you had read in a magazine?"

"I certainly do!" I laughed. "As I recall, you referred to yourself as the world's only consulting detective; a remark prompted by my less than effusive statements regarding the article in question. In mitigation I can only say that I did not realize, when I made those statements, that I was addressing the article's author; nor did I have the benefit of having seen your methods in action."

Holmes smiled, and bowed his head in acknowledgment of my words. "Your comments had at least the charm of honesty, Watson."

"But what prompts this recollection, Holmes?" I asked. My friend was not, as a rule, given to thoughts of the past, and I suspected that some event had given rise to his question. In answer he made a sweeping gesture which encompassed the many newspapers littering the floor of our Baker Street rooms.

"As you know, Watson, I make it a habit to familiarize myself with the contents of the many newspapers with which our metropolis is blessed; it is astonishing how even the smallest event may prove to have a bearing on some matter with which I come into professional contact. And yet it seems that every time I open a newspaper I find myself reading of yet another person who has followed where I have led."

"Imitation is, as they say, the sincerest form of flattery."

"In which case I am flattered indeed, Watson, for my imitators are numerous. When our association began there were, as I recall, no other consulting detectives, or at least none who called themselves such; yet even the most cursory glance at the papers now shows that I have, however unwittingly, been what our North American friends might call a trailblazer. Here" — and his long white arm stretched out to extricate a paper from out of the mass which surrounded him — "is an account of how Max Carrados helped Inspector Beedel of the Yard solve what the newspapers are, rather sensationally, calling 'The Holloway Flat Tragedy'; and here is a letter praising the assistance given by Dyer's Detective Agency in Lynch Court, Fleet Street. These are by no means isolated instances; and it is not only the newspapers which record the exploits of these detectives. The newsagent boasts an array of magazines in which one can read of their adventures; a turn of events for which you must assume some responsibility."

"How so?" I exclaimed.

"Your records of my doings have, I am afraid, given the public an appetite for tales of this sort, so much so that every detective worthy of the name must, it seems, have his Boswell — or Watson — to record his adventures. The doings of Mr. Martin Hewitt appear with almost monotonous regularity, and I can scarcely glance at a magazine without being informed that I will find therein breathless accounts of the cases of Paul Beck or Eugene Valmont or a certain Miss Myrl, who appears to be trying to advance the cause of women's suffrage through somewhat novel means. I understand there is a gentleman who sits in an A. B. C. teashop and solves crimes without benefit of sight, or the need of abandoning his afternoon's refreshment, while Mr. Flaxman Low purports to help those whose cases appear to be beyond the understanding of mere mortals; truly the refuge of the desperate, although from what I gather the man is not quite the charlatan he might seem." Holmes chuckled, and threw down his paper. "If this continues apace, I may find myself contemplating retirement, or at least a change of profession."

"But surely," I replied, "your reputation is such that you need have no fear of such a fate just yet! Why, every post sees applications for your assistance, and Inspector Hopkins is as assiduous a visitor as always. I do not think that Sherlock Holmes will be retiring from public view at any point in the immediate future."

"No; I may fairly claim that the demands upon my time are as frequent as they have ever been, although I confess that many of the cases which are brought to my attention could be as easily solved by a constable still wet behind the ears as by a trained professional. Yet there still remain those cases which promise something of the *outré* and which the official force would be hard-pressed to solve." Holmes rose from his chair, crossed to the table, and extracted a sheet of paper from amongst the breakfast dishes. He glanced at it for a moment, then passed it to me. "Be so good as to read this, and tell me what you make of it."

I looked at the letter, and attempted to emulate my friend's methods. "It is written on heavy paper," I began, "simply yet elegantly embossed, from which I would deduce a certain level of wealth allied with good taste. It is in a woman's hand, firm and clear, which would seem to denote that its writer is a person of determination as well as intelligence."

"And pray how do you deduce the intelligence, without having read the letter?" asked my friend.

"Why, from the fact that she has had the good sense to consult Sherlock Holmes, and not one of the pretenders to his crown."

"A touch, Watson!" laughed Holmes. "A distinct touch! But now read the lady's letter, and see what opinion you form of her and her case."

I turned my attention to the paper, and read:

Lufford Abbey
Warwickshire
Dear Mr. Holmes,

Having read of your methods and cases,
I am turning to you in hopes that you will
be able to bring an end to a series of distur-
bances which have occurred over the past
two months, and which have left our local
constabulary at a complete loss. What be-
gan as a series of minor annoyances has
gradually become something more sinister;
but as these events have not, as yet, resulted
in a crime being committed, I am told that
there is little the police can do.

My husband is in complete agreement
with me that steps must be taken; yet I will
be candid and state that he does not agree
that this is a matter for Mr. Sherlock
Holmes. I hasten to add that his admiration
for you is as great as mine; where we differ
is in our ideas as to the nature of the events.
I firmly believe that a human agency is at
work, whereas my husband is of the opin-
ion that we must seek for an answer that lies
beyond our five senses.

I fear that any account which I could lay
before you in a letter would fail to give a
true indication of what we are suffering.
However, suffering we are, and I hope that
you will be able to see your way to meeting
with us, so that we may lay the facts before
you. I have included a note of the most con-
venient trains, and a telegram indicating
your arrival time will ensure that you are
met at the station.

I thank you in advance for your consid-
eration of this matter; merely writing this
letter has taken some of the weight from my

mind, and I am in hopes that your arrival and
investigation will put an end to the worries
with which we are beset.
   Yours sincerely,
   Mrs. John Fitzgerald

"Well, Watson? And what do you make of it?"

I placed the letter on the table. "The letter confirms my opinion of the lady's character and intelligence. She does not set down a jumble of facts, fancies, and theories, but rather writes in a business-like manner which yet does not conceal her anxiety. The fact that she and her husband have thought it necessary to involve the police indicates that the matter is serious, for Mrs. Fitzgerald does not, from this letter, strike me as a woman who is given to imagining things; unlike her husband, I might add."

"Yes, her husband, who believes that the solution to their problem lies beyond the evidence of our five senses." Holmes shook his head. "I have never yet met with a case which is not capable of a rational solution, however irrational it may appear at the outset, and I have no doubt that this mystery will prove the same as the others."

"You have decided to take the case, then?"

"Yes. As the lady was so thoughtful as to include a list of train times, I took the liberty of sending a telegram indicating that we would travel up on the 12:23 train. I take it that your patients can do without you for a day or so?"

"I can certainly make arrangements, Holmes, if you would like me to accompany you."

"Of course I would, Watson! A trip to the Warwickshire countryside will prove a welcome respite from a damp London spring; and I will need my chronicler with me, to record my efforts, if I am to keep pace with my colleagues." My friend was smiling as he said this; then his face became thoughtful. "Lufford Abbey," he said slowly. "That name sounds familiar; but I cannot immediately call the circumstances to mind. Ah well, we have some time before our train departs, and I shall try to lay my hands on the details."

⁜ ⁜ ⁜

My long association with Sherlock Holmes, coming as it did on the heels of my military career, had made me adept at packing quickly and at short notice. It was an easy matter to arrange for my patients to be seen by one of my associates, and well before the appointed time I was back in Baker Street and Holmes and I were on our way to Euston Station, where we found the platform unusually crowded. We were fortunate enough to secure a first-class compartment to ourselves, but our privacy was short-lived, for just as the barrier was closing a man hurried along the platform and, after a moment's hesitation, entered our compartment. He was middle-aged, tall, and strongly built, having about him the look of a man who has been an athlete in his youth and maintained his training in the years since. He gave us both a polite nod, then settled himself into the opposite corner of the compartment and pulled a small notebook from his pocket, in which he began to make what appeared to be notes, frequently referring to a sheaf of papers which he had placed on the seat beside him.

Holmes had shot the newcomer a penetrating glance, but upon seeing that our companion was obviously not one to intrude his company on others relaxed, and was silent for a few minutes, gazing out the window as the train gathered speed and we began to leave London and its environs behind. I knew better than to intrude upon his thoughts, and eventually he settled back into his seat, put his fingers together in the familiar manner, and began to speak.

"I was not mistaken, Watson, when I said that the name of our destination was familiar to me. As you know, I am in the habit of retaining items from the newspapers which might conceivably be of interest, or have a bearing on a future case, and this habit has borne fruit on this occasion. An article in *The Times* from July of last year reported the death, in unusual circumstances, of an English traveller at Abbeville, who was struck on the head and killed instantly by a stone which fell from the tower of a church there, under which the unfortunate gentleman happened to be standing. His name was Mr. Julian Karswell, and his residence was given as Lufford Abbey in Warwickshire. It would not..."

But my friend's words were cut short by an exclamation from the third occupant of our compartment. He had laid aside his notebook and papers, and was looking from my companion to myself with a quick, inquisitive glance which avoided mere vulgar curiosity, and instead spoke of something deeper. He seemed to realize that an explanation was needed, and addressed himself to both of us in tones that were low and pleasant.

"Excuse me, gentlemen, but I could not help overhearing you speak of a Mr. Karswell and his residence, Lufford Abbey. Both names are known to me, which accounts for my surprise, particularly when I hear them from the lips of Mr. Sherlock Holmes. And you, sir"— he nodded his head towards me — "must be Dr. Watson." He noted my look of surprise, and added with a gentle smile, "I heard your friend address you by name, and it was not difficult to identify you from your likenesses in *The Strand Magazine.*"

"You have the advantage of us, sir," said Holmes politely, "as well as the makings of a detective."

"My name is Flaxman Low," said our companion, "and I am, in my small way, a detective, although I do not expect that you will have heard of me."

"On the contrary," answered my friend dryly, "I was speaking of you only this morning."

"Not, I fear, with any favor, to judge by your tone," replied Low. "No, Mr. Holmes, I do not take offence," he continued, forestalling my companion. "A great many people share your view, and I am accustomed to that fact. You and I are, I suspect, more alike than you think in our approach and methods. The difference lies in the fact that where I am Hamlet, you, if I may take the liberty of saying so, prefer the part of Horatio."

For a moment I feared, from the expression on my friend's face, that he would not take kindly to this remark; but after a moment his features relaxed into a smile, and he laughed.

"Perhaps that is no bad thing, Mr. Low," he remarked, "for at the end of the play Horatio is one of the few characters still in the land of the living, while the Prince of Denmark is, we presume, learning at first hand whether or not his views on the spiritual world were correct."

Flaxman Low laughed in his turn. "Well said, Mr. Holmes." Then his face turned grave. "You mentioned Lufford Abbey. May I enquire as to your interest in that house and its late owner?"

Holmes shrugged. "As to its late owner I admit of no knowledge, save for the fact of his death last year. The house, however, is our destination, hence my interest in any particulars relating to it." He gazed at Low thoughtfully. "I am not mistaken, I think, in stating that Lufford Abbey is your destination also, and that you have been summoned thence by Mr. John Fitzgerald, to look into a matter which has been troubling him."

"You are quite correct, Mr. Holmes," acknowledged Low. "Mr. Fitzgerald wrote and asked if I would be available to look into a series of events which is proving troubling to his household, and appears to be beyond the capabilities of the local police force."

"And we have received a similar letter from Mrs. Fitzgerald," said Holmes. "It appears, Mr. Low, that we shall have a practical means of comparing our methods; it will be interesting to see what results we achieve."

"Indeed." Low paused, and looked from one of us to the other. "You say that you know nothing of Julian Karswell, save for the few facts surrounding his death. Perhaps, if you will allow me, I can give further elucidation as to the character of the late owner of Lufford Abbey."

"By all means," said Holmes. "At present I am working in the dark, and any information which you can provide would be of the greatest interest."

"I am not surprised that you know little of Julian Karswell," said Low, settling back into his seat and clasping his hands behind his head, "for while I, and a few others who knew of him, felt that he had the makings of a distinguished criminal, he never committed any crimes which broke the laws of man as they currently stand."

Holmes raised his eyebrows. "Are you saying that he committed crimes which broke other laws?"

"Yes, Mr. Holmes. Karswell was interested in the occult, or the black arts — call it what you will — and he had the means to devote himself to his studies, for he was reputed to be a man of great wealth, although how he acquired this wealth was a question for much speculation. He used to joke about the many treasures of his house, although no one that I know of was ever permitted to see them. He wrote a book upon the subject of witchcraft, which was treated with contempt by most of those who bothered to read it; until, that is, it appeared that Mr. Karswell took a somewhat more practical approach to the occult than had been suspected."

"Practical?" I interjected. "In what way?"

Our companion paused before replying. When he did, his tone was grave. "Certain people who had occasion to cross Mr. Karswell suffered fates which were... curious, to say the least. A man named John Harrington, who wrote a scathing review of Karswell's book *The History of Witchcraft*, died under circumstances which were never satisfactorily explained, and another man, Edward Dunning, made what I consider to be a very narrow escape."

It was my turn to utter an exclamation, and both Holmes and Low turned to look at me. "Edward Dunning, who belongs to the _____ — Association?" I asked.

"Yes," replied Low in some curiosity, while Holmes gazed at me quizzically. "Why, do you know him?"

"As a matter of fact I do," I replied. "He came to me on the recommendation of a neighbor — oh, eighteen months or so ago — and we struck up a friendship of sorts; enough that when he was seriously incommoded by illness in his household I invited him to dinner."

"When was this?" asked Low, with an eagerness which somewhat surprised me.

"Why" — I paused to think — "this was in the spring of last year; April, as I recall. His two servants were struck

down by a sudden illness — food poisoning, I suspect —
and the poor man seemed somewhat lost, so I invited him
to dinner at my club. He seemed more pleased than the
invitation itself would warrant, and was reluctant to leave;
almost as if he did not want to return to his house. Indeed,
he was in a rather agitated state; distracted, as if he were
continually turning some problem over in his mind."

"You are very close to the truth, Doctor," said Low
gravely. "The agitation which Edward Dunning displayed
was occasioned by Karswell, and certain steps which that
person was even then taking; steps which almost led to
Dunning's death."

"Death!" exclaimed my friend. "Surely that brought
Karswell within reach of the law?"

"Yes and no," replied Low after a pause. "You see,
gentlemen," he continued, "Karswell was a very clever man
in some ways, and was familiar with practices which would
allow him to exact revenge against someone while ensuring
that he himself remained safe from prosecution; there were
rumors that he was preparing another book on the subject, although nothing came of it. Unfortunately for him,
he ran up against two people — Edward Dunning being
one of them — who were prepared to use his own methods,
and thus escape harm by throwing Karswell's own agents
against him."

"Are you saying that you believe this Karswell used
supernatural means to accomplish his ends?" asked Holmes
in astonishment.

"That is precisely what I am saying, Mr. Holmes,"
replied Low gravely. "I agree with the words of St. Augus-
tine: *Credo ut intelligam*."[1] Holmes shook his head.

"I am afraid I must side with Petrarch: *Vos vestros servate,
meos mihi linquite mores*.[2] It has been my experience that no
case, no matter how bizarre or otherworldly it may seem
when it commences, cannot be explained by entirely natural
means. Surely your own experiences, Mr. Low, will have

---

[1] I believe in order that I may understand.
[2] You cling to your own ways and leave mine to me.

shown you that man is capable enough of evil, without ascribing its presence to the supernatural."

"As to your last point, Mr. Holmes, we are in complete agreement. Where we differ, it seems, is in our willingness to accept that not everything we see or hear or experience can be rationalized. I enter every case I undertake with a perfectly clear mind, and no one is more pleased than I when it can be proved that something which appears to be supernatural has a completely logical explanation that would stand up in a court of law. And yet it is my belief that we are standing on the frontier of an unknown world, the rules of which we do not comprehend and can only vaguely grasp, in flashes, as our unready senses catch broken glimpses of things which obey laws we cannot understand. One day, perhaps, this other world will be understood, and mapped as fully as any known country on earth; until then we can only advance slowly, storing away pieces of the puzzle in hopes that they can be fitted together in the fullness of time."

It was an extraordinary speech to hear in the prosaic surroundings of a first-class carriage rattling through the placid English countryside; but Flaxman Low's earnest face and steady voice carried a conviction that it was impossible to ridicule. I could tell that my friend was impressed despite himself, and when he replied it was in a tone more restrained and conciliatory than would have been the case only a few minutes earlier.

"Well, Mr. Low, we must agree to disagree on certain points; but I look forward to the experience of working with you on this case. Perhaps, if you would be so good, you might tell us more of Mr. Karswell."

"But what can he have to do with this?" I interjected. "He died almost a year ago, and surely can have nothing to do with the matter in hand."

"Possibly not," said my friend, "but the fact remains that a man who appears to have died in questionable circumstances, and who himself may have been involved in the death of at least one person, has left behind him a house which is now, in turn, the scene of mysterious occurrences.

This may prove to be mere coincidence, but it is not something an investigator can ignore. The more facts with which we are armed, the more likely that we shall bring Mr. and Mrs. Fitzgerald's case to a speedy — and satisfactory — conclusion."

I will not try the patience of my readers by detailing the events which Flaxman Low laid before us; Dr. James of King's College has since provided his own account of the case, which is readily available. Suffice it to say that Mr. Julian Karswell appeared to have been a deeply unpleasant person, quick to anger, sensitive to criticism both real and imagined, and with the fire of vengeance burning within him, so much so that any who crossed his path appeared to have very real cause to fear for their safety. He was, according to Low, responsible for the death of John Harrington, and very nearly killed Edward Dunning, although Holmes refused to believe that he used supernatural means to accomplish his ends; nor did he believe that Karswell's sudden death at Abbeville was anything other than the accident the French investigators deemed it to be. "For if a man will go walking about in a site where extensive repairs are being carried out, we cannot be surprised to hear that some mischance has befallen him," he said, while Flaxman Low shook his head but said nothing.

Our companion had scarcely finished narrating his story when our train began to slow, and our stop was announced. We were among only a handful of passengers who alighted, and before the train had pulled away we were approached by a coachman, who nodded his head respectfully at us.

"Mr. Holmes, Dr. Watson, and Mr. Low, is it?" he enquired. "You are all expected, gentlemen; I'll see to your baggage if you will kindly follow me."

We left the station and found a carriage awaiting us, a fine team of horses standing harnessed in front of it. Holmes ran his keen eyes over them.

"I see that we have not far to go to Lufford Abbey," he remarked, and the coachman glanced at him.

"No, sir, little more'n a mile or so. You've been here before, then?"

"No," interjected Low, before my friend could reply, "but the horses are fresh and glossy, which would indicate that they have not travelled far to get here."

Holmes' lips twitched in a slight smile. "You evidently see and observe, Mr. Low. Excellent traits in a detective."

"I have learned from a master," replied Low, giving a small bow. "Indeed, I may say that it was reading the early accounts of your cases, as penned by Dr. Watson, which first gave me the thought of applying your methods to the investigation of that frontier which we were discussing during our journey here. Indeed, one day it might come to pass that you are acknowledged as being as great a forerunner in that field as you are in the science of more ordinary detection."

Our bags had been loaded in the carriage, and we climbed in. The coachman called out to the horses and we were on our way, rumbling through the main street of a pretty village crowded with half-timbered buildings which spoke of a more peaceful way of life than existed in the bustling metropolis which we had left. The tranquillity around us contrasted so sharply with the story Flaxman Low had told us in the train, and the dark deeds hinted at in Mrs. Fitzgerald's letter, that I could not help shivering. Low, who was sitting opposite me, caught my eye and nodded.

"Yes, Doctor," he said, as if in answer to my thoughts, "it is difficult to believe that such things can exist when the evidence of our senses shows us such pleasant scenes. I hope, in all honesty, that our clients' case may prove to have an entirely logical and rational solution; but given what I know of the late owner of Lufford Abbey, I confess I fear the worst."

It seemed that we had scarcely left the village behind us when the carriage turned through a set of massive iron gates, and we found ourselves driving through beautifully maintained grounds. Bright clumps of yellow daffodils were dotted about a wide sweep of grassland, which led in turn to a thick plantation of trees on both sides of the drive. Ahead of us lay Lufford Abbey itself, an imposing building of mellow stone which seemed to glow in the warm afternoon sunlight. I did not have time to contemplate the house, however, for as soon as the carriage drew up the front door opened, and our host and hostess came out to greet us.

They were an interesting study in contrasts, Mr. and Mrs. Fitzgerald. He was tall and slender, with dark eyes set in a pale face, and an unruly shock of black hair, a lock of which he was perpetually brushing back from his forehead. His wife, while almost as tall as her husband, was more sturdily built, and her blue eyes looked out from a face which I guessed was, under normal circumstances, ruddy-complexioned and clear, as of one who spends a good deal of time in the open air. Now, however, it wore a look of anxiety, an expression shared by Mr. Fitzgerald, who stepped forward with short, nervous steps, wringing his hands together in an attitude of embarrassment.

"Mr. Low?" he enquired, looking from one of us to another, and our companion nodded his head.

"I am Flaxman Low, and these gentlemen are Mr. Holmes and Dr. Watson. We understand from your coachman that we are all expected.".

"Yes, yes, of course... oh dear, this is really most awkward. I do not know how I came to make such a terrible mistake. The dates — of course, I put the wrong one in my letter to you, Mr. Low, and it was only when I spoke with my wife after that I realized what had happened. We did not intend... that is to say, we meant... such a dreadful mix-up..."

His words trailed off, and he wore a look of contrition that was almost comical. His wife stepped forward firmly and placed a hand on his arm.

"My husband is correct in saying that this is an awkward situation, gentlemen; but such events happen in the best-regulated of households, and I believe that when you hear our story you will excuse us. Matters have been somewhat" — she paused, as if in search of the correct word — "fraught here in recent days, and we were both so anxious of a solution that we proceeded independently of each other, with the result that you now see. We will, of course, understand perfectly should one of you decide that he would rather not stay."

"Explanations are unnecessary," replied Holmes, and Low nodded. "My friend and I were not previously acquainted with Mr. Low, but a fortuitous chance has ensured that we had an opportunity to discuss the matter — so far as we know it — on the way here, and I think I may safely say that we see no difficulty in combining our efforts."

"Mr. Holmes is quite correct," added Low. "While we may differ in certain of our beliefs, we are united in our determination to put an end to the difficulties which you face."

"Thank you, gentlemen," said our host, relief sweeping across his face. For a moment the look of anxiety left him, and I was able to see traces of the good humor which I suspected his countenance usually wore. "I cannot tell you how relieved we both are to hear this. Of course, we really must explain why it is that..."

"Yes, we must," interrupted Mrs. Fitzgerald, firmly but kindly. "However I do not think, John, that the front drive is the place for explanations."

"Of course; you are quite right, my dear." He turned and smiled at us. "Forgive me once more; my manners have quite escaped me. The maid will show you to your rooms, and then we will lay all the facts before you, in hopes that you will see light where we see only darkness."

Less than half-an-hour elapsed before we were assembled in a pleasantly furnished sitting-room with our host and hostess, and provided with refreshments. Both Mr. and Mrs. Fitzgerald seemed to take pleasure in the everyday ritual of pouring tea and passing cakes, and for a moment their cares and anxieties seemed to fade in the flow of casual conversation around them.

"Yes," said Mr. Fitzgerald, in answer to a question of Low's, "there was an abbey here, although nothing of it now remains apart from a few relics housed in the parish church. Most of it was destroyed in 1539, and what little was left — mainly stables and the Abbot's lodging, from what I gather — has long since vanished. Some outlying domestic buildings were the last to go; according to village gossip there was an old man who, early in the eighteenth century, could still point out the sites of some of the buildings, but this knowledge appears to have died with him. I cannot think of another similar monastic house which has disappeared so completely from the ken of man."

"You are a student of such things, then?" enquired Holmes.

"In a very modest way. Being a gentleman of leisure, I have the time and opportunity to indulge myself in that way; and have a natural inclination towards such subjects, tinged with melancholy as they are. Parts of this house were built very shortly after the abbey was dissolved, and I suspect that many of the stones from the original monastic building found their way into the construction of it, hence the house's name. Inigo Jones added to it in the seventeenth century, so we find ourselves in possession of a very interesting piece of our country's history."

"And in possession of something else, it appears," said Low. "Your letters, however, provided little by way of information on that point."

Mr. Fitzgerald's face clouded, and there was a sharp clatter as his wife placed her teacup somewhat unsteadily in its saucer. "Yes," our host replied after a moment's pause, as if summoning up strength. "The truth is, gentlemen, that I — we — found it very difficult to convey the facts of the case in a letter."

"What my husband means, I think," said Mrs. Fitzgerald, "is that the recent... events here sound, on paper, so inconsequential that they would appear laughable to someone who has not experienced them."

"I assure you, Mrs. Fitzgerald," said Low earnestly, "that none of us are inclined to laugh. I know something of the man who lived here before you, and informed Mr. Holmes and Dr. Watson of the facts surrounding him, and the manner of his death. It is not a laughing matter."

Husband and wife glanced at each other. "We are agreed," said Mrs. Fitzgerald, "that Julian Karswell — or rather something to do with him — is in some way responsible for the events which are taking place; but we do not agree as to how or why this should be. My own feeling is that there is a logical explanation behind everything, whereas my husband feels that—" Here she stopped, as if uncertain how to proceed, or unwilling to give voice to what her husband thought. Mr. Fitzgerald took up the thread.

"Elizabeth is trying to say that I feel Mr. Karswell, although dead, is still influencing the events in his former house." He gave a somewhat hollow laugh. "My father was Irish and my mother Welsh, gentlemen, so I have inherited more than my fair share of willingness to believe in what others disdain."

"Perhaps," said Holmes, with a touch of asperity, "we might hear of these events, so that we may have some idea of why, precisely, we have been invited."

"Of course, Mr. Holmes," said Mrs. Fitzgerald. "Shall I begin?"

"Please do, my dear," replied her husband. "We are in no disagreement as to the facts, and you will tell the story so much better than I."

Low and Holmes both leaned back in their chairs; Low with his hands clasped behind his head, Holmes with his fingers steepled in front of him and his eyes half-closed. I settled back into my own chair as Mrs. Fitzgerald began her tale.

"As you gentlemen know, we have not lived here very long. My family comes from Warwickshire, and I longed to return here, and when we heard that Lufford Abbey was available — well, we fairly jumped at the opportunity. It did not take us long to realize that there was considerable ill-feeling in the village towards the previous owner, about whom we knew little more than that he had died, suddenly, while on holiday in France, and that in the absence of next of kin his house and effects were being sold. We attended the sale of his possessions, as did many of the people from the immediate neighborhood; largely, I suspect, in order to see the house for themselves, as the late owner had guarded his privacy to a quite extraordinary extent, and had not been known for his hospitality towards his neighbors. There was also, I believe, some talk of great treasures in the house, although nothing that was sold struck us as being deserving of that name.

"When Mr. Karswell's things had been disposed of we were, quite naturally, anxious to take up residence, but events conspired to make this impossible. The house, while in good repair for the most part, needed a certain amount of work done to it, particularly the rooms in which it was apparent that Mr. Karswell chiefly lived. He appeared to have kept a dog, or dogs, and they had scratched quite badly at the paneling in one of the rooms, so much so that it needed to be replaced. Some of the furnishings, too, proved difficult to dispose of; more than one person who had purchased items had a change of mind after the event, and declined to remove them, so in the end we kept one or two of the larger pieces and disposed of the rest as best we could."

"And the workmen, my dear; do not forget them."

Mrs. Fitzgerald shuddered. "How could I forget? We had no end of difficulty with the workmen we had employed to carry out the repairs. What should have been a very straightforward piece of work, according to the man who was in charge, became fraught with difficulty. Some of the men took to turning up late, or not at all, and there were delays with some of the materials, and scarcely a day went by without some accident or other. Oh, they were very minor things, we were assured, but troubling nonetheless, and at one point it seemed the work would never be completed. At last we resorted to offering a larger sum than initially negotiated, and eventually all was finished and we were able to take up residence."

"One moment," said Low, at the same time that Holmes interjected with "A question, if I may." The two detectives looked at each other; then Low smiled and waved his hand towards my friend. "Please, Mr. Holmes."

"Thank you." Holmes turned to the Fitzgeralds. "The workmen who were employed: were they local men, or from further afield?"

"There were a handful of local men, Mr. Holmes," replied Mrs. Fitzgerald, "but the man in charge had to obtain most of the workforce from further away, some as far as Coventry. As I mentioned, there was some considerable ill-feeling towards the late owner of Lufford Abbey."

"Considerable indeed, if it extended even after his death," remarked Holmes. "Were you both here while this work was being carried out?"

"No; it would have been far too inconvenient. We had regular reports from the man in charge, and my husband would come by on occasion to check on the progress — or rather the lack of it."

"Thank you," said Holmes. "Mr. Low?"

"I was going to ask about the dogs," said Low, "the ones which you felt were responsible for the damage. Do you know for a fact that Karswell kept dogs?"

"No," replied Mr. Fitzgerald slowly. "Indeed, it did strike me as odd, as from what we knew of him he seemed unlikely to be a man who kept pets."

"This damage they caused; was it general, or confined to one particular place?"

"Again, it is very odd, Mr. Low. One would not expect dogs to be particular as to where they caused damage, yet it all seemed to be located in the one room, on the first floor. It is a very fine room, with views out over the park, and we understood that Karswell used it as his study."

"What sort of damage was caused?"

"Well, as my wife said, it appeared that the animals had clawed around the base of the wooden paneling in the room. Quite deep gouges they were, too, which is why the wood needed to be replaced."

"Do any of the marks remain?"

Mrs. Fitzgerald drew in her breath sharply, and Mr. Fitzgerald's already pale face seemed to go a shade whiter. It was a moment before he answered.

"When we took up residence my answer would have been no, Mr. Low; none of the marks remained. However, since then they... they have returned."

"Returned?" said Holmes sharply. "What do you mean?"

"I will come to that in a moment, Mr. Holmes," said Mrs. Fitzgerald. She paused, as if to gather her thoughts, then continued with her tale.

"As I say, we took up residence; that was in early March. At first all was well; we were busy settling in, and there were a hundred-and-one things to do and be seen to, and anything odd we put down to the fact that we were in a very old house that was still strange to us.

"Gradually, however, we became aware that things were happening which were not at all usual. It began with a sound, very faint, in the room above us..." She broke off with a shudder, and Mr. Fitzgerald looked at her with concern.

"Margaret, would you like me to continue?"

"Yes please," she said in a quiet voice, and her husband took up the tale.

"At first we both thought that it was one of the maids, cleaning; it was only later that we realized the sounds were heard at times when there should not have been anyone in the room. You will forgive us, gentlemen, for being somewhat slow to remark on this fact, but at first it seemed such a trifling matter that we gave it little thought.

"The next thing that occurred was a cold draught, which always seemed to play about the room. Now one must, I fear, expect draughts in a house as old as this, but we did not notice such a thing anywhere else; indeed, the house was, as my wife said, very sound, which made it all the more odd that it should be confined to this one room. We examined the windows and walls and around the door, and could find nothing to account for it. It began to be quite uncomfortable to be in the room, which I used, as Mr. Karswell had, as a study. I had hoped that as the spring approached the draughts would stop; but if anything they seemed to get worse.

"The sounds had continued all this time; not constant, by any means, but frequent enough to become unnerving. We told ourselves that it was some trick, perhaps related to the draughts; but one evening we heard the sounds more distinctly than before. They seemed changed, too; if we had heard them like that from the first we would not have mistaken them for the footsteps of a person. It was a dull, heavy, dragging sound, rather as if a large dog was moving with difficulty about the floor. I would go to investigate, but I never saw anything, although I found that I did not care to be alone in that room.

"Then, one day, one of the maids came to us, almost in tears, poor thing, because she said that she had been in the room to fill the coal scuttle and had heard what she thought was a growl, as of a large dog. She said that she had a careful look around the room, thinking that perhaps some stray animal had got in, but could see nothing untoward, and was continuing with her work when she felt distinctly something large and soft brush heavily against her, not once but twice, as if a dog had walked past her quite close and then turned back.

"Of course we went to look — it was all we could do to persuade Ellen to go back in, even though we were with her — but found nothing. We reassured the girl as best we could, and my wife took her down to the kitchen so that she could have a cup of tea, and I took one last look round; and it was then that I saw the marks on the wall."

"These are the claw marks to which your wife has alluded?" asked Holmes.

"Yes. As we explained, the paneling in that room was ripped out and completely replaced, and I remember thinking to myself what a fine job the men had done. So you can imagine my surprise and consternation when I saw marks on the woodwork. At first I thought that perhaps they had been caused by something being bumped against the wall accidentally, but when I examined them

I saw that they were quite deep, and identical in every way with the marks which had been there before. I must admit, Mr. Holmes, that I was startled, to say the least, and I was glad that my wife had left the room, particularly in light of what happened next. For as I stood there, trying to make sense of it, I heard a soft, shuffling noise, such as a dog or other large animal might make, getting up and shaking itself. And then, before I could move, I felt something brush against me; something heavy, and soft."

"Did you see anything?"

"No, I did not; nor, I will say, did I stay to look about more closely. I was on the other side of the door, and had closed it, before I could think clearly once more. When I did, I locked the door, and later told the servants that we would not be using that room for a time, and that they need not bother with it unless we told them otherwise."

"The servants," said Holmes thoughtfully. "Have they been with you for some time, or did they work for Mr. Karswell?"

"None of Mr. Karswell's servants stayed on, Mr. Holmes," said Mrs. Fitzgerald; "they were dismissed immediately upon his death. From what I heard of them I would not have wished to employ any of them. A queer, secretive lot, apparently, who were disliked almost as much as their master. No, the servants here have all been with us for some time, and I trust them implicitly."

"Has anything else untoward happened?" asked Holmes. "Have either of you noticed any signs of your things having been tampered with, or has anything gone missing that you cannot account for?"

"No, Mr. Holmes," said Mrs. Fitzgerald. "The — disturbances — seem confined to that one room."

"I think, then, that we should take a look at this rather singular-sounding room," said Holmes, rising. "Will you show us the way?"

We followed the Fitzgeralds out of the room and made our way up the stairs. The spring day was drawing to a close, and the lamps were lit throughout the house. Was it my imagination, or did the hall seem a trifle darker outside the door before which our host and hostess halted? Such a thought had, I felt, occurred to Flaxman Low, for I noticed that he glanced sharply up and down the hall and then up at the light closest to us, which seemed dimmer than its fellows. Before I could remark on this, however, Mr. Fitzgerald had produced a key from his pocket, unlocked the heavy door in front of us, and pushed it open.

A sudden cold draught played around my ankles with a force which startled me, as if a tangible presence had pushed at me from within the room. I could see from the looks on the faces of my companions that they had felt what I did, and I confess that I hesitated for a moment before entering the room.

It was a large room, and I imagined that it would have been pleasant in the daylight, with its wide windows looking out over the expanse of lawn, and the paneling on the walls creating a warm, rich glow. However, in the evening dusk, with lamps the only source of illumination, and the strange tale we had been told still ringing in my ears, it presented an aspect almost of malignancy. I had a sudden feeling that we were intruding in a place which contained dark secrets, and if one of my companions had suggested we leave I would have followed willingly. However, both Holmes and Low advanced to the centre of the room and stood looking about with penetrating glances, taking in every detail. Holmes turned to Mr. Fitzgerald.

"Where are these marks of which you spoke?"

"Over here, Mr. Holmes." We followed him to one side of the room, where he knelt and pointed to a section of wall beside the fireplace, which was surmounted by a carved mantelpiece embellished with leaves and branches. We could all see plainly the deep scores running along the wood; they did, in truth, look like the claw marks of a large dog, although I would not have liked to meet the beast that made them. As Mr. Fitzgerald went to stand up, he glanced to one side of him, and uttered a soft exclamation.

"There are more!"

"Are you sure of that?" Low's voice contained a note of urgency which was not lost on Mr. Fitzgerald.

"I am positive! The last time I looked they extended no further than this panel" — he pointed — "but now you can see for yourselves that they continue further along the wall, up to the fireplace itself. I don't understand it! The room has been locked for the last week, and no one has entered it, of that I am sure. What could be doing this?"

"I have an idea, as I am sure Mr. Holmes does," said Flaxman Low quietly; "although whether or not these ideas will agree remains to be seen." He straightened up from where he had been crouching by the wall, running his hand along the marks, and looked around the room. His gaze seemed to be held by a large, ornately carved desk which stood close by. "You said that you purchased one or two pieces from the estate of Mr. Karswell. May I ask if that desk was one of those pieces?"

Mrs. Fitzgerald gazed at Low in astonishment. "Yes, it is; but how did you know?"

"Tsk, tsk," said Holmes, approaching the desk, "it is quite obvious that while the other pieces in the room were chosen by someone with an eye for symmetry and comfort, this desk was not; it does not match anything else in the room. Furthermore, it is one of two desks in the room; the other is quite obviously used extensively, to judge by the papers, pens, ink, books, and other items on its surface, whereas this one is singularly clear of any such items. Not, therefore, a piece of furniture which is in regular use, which rather suggests an afterthought of some sort, here on sufferance only."

"You are quite right," said Mr. Fitzgerald. "That was one of the items we bought from Karswell's estate, as the original purchaser unaccountably decided against buying it. At the time it seemed a reasonable enough purchase, but for some reason..." His voice trailed off.

"You found yourself unwilling to use it, and uncomfortable when you did," supplied Low.

"Precisely," said Mr. Fitzgerald gratefully. "It is, as you can see, a handsome piece, and I had some thought of making it my own desk; but for reasons that I cannot articulate I always felt uncomfortable when working at it, and it was not long before I abandoned it altogether in favor of the other desk."

Flaxman Low walked over to the carved desk and ran his hand over it. "Karswell's desk," he murmured to himself. "That is certainly intriguing."

"Yes," said Holmes crisply. "For there are few things which can tell us more about a man than his desk. Tell me, did you find anything in it?"

"That is a curious thing, Mr. Holmes. When we purchased it the desk was, as we thought, quite empty, and I made sure that nothing had been left in it; there could have been something valuable which his executors should know about. I found nothing; but a few days later, I happened to be opening one of the drawers, to place something within it, and it stuck. I pulled and pushed, and gradually worked it free, and found a small piece of paper at the back of it, which had obviously fallen out and become wedged in behind."

"Do you still have this paper?" asked Holmes eagerly, and Mr. Fitzgerald nodded towards his desk.

"I put it with my own papers; although I confess I do not know why, as it seemed without value." He moved to the other desk, where he rummaged around in one of the drawers. The rest of us stood close together, as if by common consent, and waited for him to return. When he did he was holding a small piece of yellowed paper, which he handed to my friend, who held it out so that we could all read it. There, in a neat hand, we saw the following:

> Nonne haec condita sunt apud me et signata in thesauris meis.
> Mea est ultio et ego retribuam in tempore ut labatur pes eorum iuxta est dies perditionis et adesse festinant tempora.

"What on earth does it mean?" I asked in some puzzlement.

"Well, I wondered that myself, Dr. Watson. My own Latin is not, I am afraid, as good as it once was, but after a little thought I realized it was from the Vulgate — Deuteronomy 32, verses 34 and 35 — and translates as 'Is not this laid up in store with me, and sealed up among my treasures? To me belongeth vengeance and recompense; their foot shall slide in due time: for the day of their calamity is at hand, and the things that shall come upon them make haste.'"

Both men gave a start, and I could see that they were thinking furiously. "Treasures," said Holmes thoughtfully, while Low murmured "Vengeance and recompense." Both turned at the same moment and gazed at the section of wall where the claw marks were most visible. My friend glanced at Flaxman Low.

"I believe our thoughts are moving along the same lines, Mr. Low," he said quietly.

"Yes," replied the other, "although I suspect that our conclusions are slightly different." He turned to the Fitzgeralds, who were gazing from one man to the other with a bewildered air, and addressed our host. "Will you kindly bring an axe and a crowbar? This may prove a difficult job."

"Why, yes, of course," replied Mr. Fitzgerald. "But what is it that you are going to do?"

"I — that is to say we, for I believe Mr. Low and I have come to the same conclusion — believe that there is a concealed space hidden behind that section of wall. That is an outer wall, I take it?"

"Yes; yes, it is," said Mrs. Fitzgerald. "Do you mean... do you think that..."

"It is too early yet to say what I think," replied my friend grimly. "But I believe that the solution to this mystery lies behind that wall, and the sooner we investigate the sooner we will put an end to the events which have puzzled you both."

Mr. Fitzgerald departed to find the required implements; but in the end they proved unnecessary. While he was gone both Holmes and Low searched the fireplace, running their hands along the carvings, and within a few moments of our host's return Holmes gave a small cry of satisfaction. "Here we have it, I think," he said triumphantly, and we all heard a click which, slight as it was, seemed to echo throughout the room, so still were we all. Our gaze turned to the section of wall which we had previously examined, and I do not know which of us was the most startled to see a section of the panelling move slightly, as if it were being pushed from behind by an unseen force. Indeed, this very thought must have occurred to each of us, for we all remained motionless for some moments. It was Low, followed closely by my friend, who finally stepped towards the disturbed section of wall, and together the two men grasped the edge of the piece of panelling which, we could now see, had moved. I stepped forward with a lamp, as did Mr. Fitzgerald, while his wife stood behind us, peering anxiously over our shoulders.

The two men pulled at the wood panel, and for a moment it did not move, as if it were being held from the other side. Then, with a sound very like a sigh, the panel pulled away from the wall, leaving a rectangle of inky darkness behind it.

We all stepped back as a blast of icy air came from out the space thus revealed. After a moment we moved closer, and I held the light up in order that we could see inside.

I do not know what I expected to see, but it was not the sight which was presented to my eyes. A small table, like an altar, had been erected inside the space, which was barely wide enough to accommodate a man, and hanging above it was an inverted cross made of some dark wood, which Low dashed to the ground with an exclamation of disgust. A set of what looked like vestments was draped over one edge of the table, on the top of which was a book bound in cracked and faded black leather, and several vials of dark liquid, while the topmost of the two drawers contained pens, ink, and several thin strips of parchment. When the bottom drawer was opened Low gave an exclamation which mingled surprise with satisfaction, and withdrew a series of notebooks tied together with string, which he slit with a penknife. He glanced through the books and looked up at us.

"It is as I thought," he said quietly, and Holmes nodded.

"Yes," said my friend, "we have found what I expected to find," and he gestured to his left. Twisting our heads and looking down the narrow aperture, we saw that a set of rough stone steps was carved into the floor of the chamber, and apparently carried down between the inner and outer walls. "I have no doubt," continued my friend, "that when those stairs are examined they will prove to communicate with a hidden door on the outer wall of the house, or perhaps a tunnel which leads to some secluded spot."

We were all silent, gazing down into the black depths which seemed to swallow the light afforded by our lamps. As we stood clustered together, there came again that blast of icy air, and a faint sound, as of padding footsteps. Low immediately moved back from the opening, and motioned for us to do the same.

"I think," he said gravely, "that we would do well to close this now, and seal the room until morning. Then we can take the necessary steps to prevent any further disturbances."

By common, unspoken consent we refrained from discussing the matter that was uppermost on our minds all through supper, when servants were in and out of the dining-room. After supper Mrs. Fitzgerald retired to the sitting-room and we gentlemen were not long in following her, as we knew that she was as anxious as her husband and I to hear what the two detectives had to say. When coffee and brandy had been poured and Holmes and Low had lit their pipes, we sat back and waited for them to begin. Low motioned for my friend to go first, and Holmes addressed himself to us.

"My reading of the case began with the character of the late, and apparently unlamented, former owner of Lufford Abbey, Mr. Julian Karswell. Shorn of melodrama, what I knew of him amounted to this: that he was a man of some wealth who had a good many enemies, who chose to live in seclusion, and who died in circumstances which, though certainly out of the ordinary, could not be considered overly mysterious. Shortly after arriving I learned that his house, Lufford Abbey, was built during a time when, for various reasons, it was thought expedient by some families to have a secret room or chamber built, in order to conceal a person or persons from over-zealous eyes.

"That Karswell knew of this chamber is obvious, judging by the effects we found there; and I suspect that at least one of his servants would also have known of the existence of the room, in order to prevent a mishap should the master of the house find himself locked in and unable to emerge. In my experience, even the most secretive and close-mouthed of servants will, under the correct circumstances, divulge information of a sensitive nature, perhaps to secure esteem or reward, and I would not be surprised to find that Karswell's secret chamber was not, perhaps, the secret he thought it was amongst some of the villagers. Hence we have a man of secretive nature and some wealth, who dies suddenly, and whose household is scattered to the four winds almost immediately. That there was considerable ill-feeling towards him locally has been established, and I think it probable that some of the locals amongst the workmen who came here discovered the hidden chamber during the course of their repairs, and then found it expedient to delay work on the house, so that they might have time to examine it for more secrets.

"As to the noises of footsteps you heard, and the cold wind: all this can be explained by some person or persons — as the footsteps sounded like those of two distinct people — using the stairs and the secret chamber as a means of entering and leaving the house in order to search for something of value that they felt might be hidden; for you spoke of treasure, Mr. Low, as did you, Mrs. Fitzgerald, and these views are borne out by the passage which we found in Karswell's desk, which specifically mentions treasure. It was stated, however, that no treasures had been amongst Mr. Karswell's effects. This would suggest that his treasures were well hidden, and that someone knew — or suspected — as much, and decided to continue the search. I wager that there are more hiding spaces in this house than the one we found tonight, and that a careful search will reveal Mr. Karswell's treasure; while blocking up both entrances to the hidden chamber will eliminate the noises, and sounds, which have troubled you so much."

"But what of the feeling of something rubbing against me, Mr. Holmes?" enquired Mr. Fitzgerald. "Ellen the maid felt it too, yet neither of us saw anything."

"I suspect that the maid was imagining things, Mr. Fitzgerald; she was overwrought, as your wife stated. When you went up to the room you remembered her words, and something as simple as a draught of air became a phantom shape."

"What of the claw marks, and that odd note we found in the desk?" asked Mrs. Fitzgerald. She had brightened considerably over the past hour, as if a terrible burden had been lifted from her; but her husband, I noted, still wore a worried and drawn expression.

"Those are very easily explained. The note was, I think, meant as a taunt for any who presumed to look for Karswell's treasure, by mentioning it particularly; and I daresay that if one were to take a chisel to the panelling, one would make very similar marks to those we saw. When a person is looking for what he thinks is hidden treasure, he is not apt to be overly concerned about leaving traces of his handiwork on the walls, particularly if they are being ascribed to supernatural means which allow him to search without fear of being discovered."

Holmes sat back in his chair, and Mrs. Fitzgerald clapped her hands together softly. "Thank you, Mr.

Holmes," she said quietly; "you have taken a great weight
from my mind. I felt sure that there was a perfectly natural
and logical explanation for these strange events, and I
have no doubt but that you have hit upon the correct
solution. I am sure that if we take your advice and seal
up the chamber properly, there will be no further disturbances at Lufford Abbey."

"By all means seal up the chamber," said Flaxman Low,
who had listened attentively to my friend's explanation,
"but not before you destroy all the items found within
it — as well as the desk, and any other items which belonged to Karswell — by burning them, and with as little
delay as possible."

"Why do you say that, Mr. Low?" asked Mr. Fitzgerald.
He, too, had listened attentively to Holmes' speech, but
did not seem as convinced as did his wife.

"Because I believe that Julian Karswell was an evil man,
and that anything associated with him carries that stamp
of evil, and will continue to do so until it is destroyed
by the purifying element of fire. Only that will put an end
to your troubles." He glanced towards my friend. "Both
Mr. Holmes and I agree that the cause of the disturbances
in this house is Karswell; but I am prepared to grant him
a much larger part than is my colleague here.

"Karswell made it his life's work to not only study and
document the black arts, but to dabble in them himself.
He believed, as many others have before him, that he was
capable of controlling that which he unleashed; and as
so many others have found, too late, he was greatly mistaken.

"We know him to have been a man both subtle and
malicious, and one who desired to protect and keep secret
what belonged to him. He had written a book on witchcraft, and was rumored to have written — if not completed
— a second volume. For a man such as Karswell, would
this manuscript not have been a treasure beyond price?
The years of work poured into it, and the price that was
doubtless extracted from him for the knowledge he received, would have made him value this above all else,

and I believe that he would have ensured that it was... well guarded during his absence in July of last year. That this absence was to prove permanent did not, of course, occur to him; and once set in place, the guardian appointed by Karswell would continue to do its duty, neither knowing nor caring of the death of its master."

"You speak of a guardian, Mr. Low," said our host in a low voice. "What precisely do you mean?"

Flaxman Low shrugged. "Guardians can take many shapes and forms," he replied, "depending on the skill and audacity of those who call them up. That Karswell was an adept in the field of magic is not, I think, in dispute; we have the death of one man, and the near-death of another, to attest to this. I believe that Karswell summoned a guardian that was in a shape known to him; possibly something not unlike a large dog. It was this guardian which was responsible for the claw marks on the walls, and the soft, padding sound which you heard, and the cold draught which you felt: manifestations of this sort are frequently accompanied by a chill in the atmosphere, sometimes quite severe. I also think it unlikely that the workmen discovered the chamber; there were no signs of anything within it being disturbed, and I am sure that its discovery could not have been kept a secret. The door was, as we saw, quite cleverly built, and I believe the workmen did not realize it was there."

"But why did this guardian not venture outside that one room?" asked Mr. Fitzgerald. Like his wife a few minutes earlier, he now looked considerably more relieved than he had been since we arrived; the prospect of putting an end to his troubles by following Low's advice had obviously taken a weight from his shoulders.

"Without knowing the specifics of what Karswell did to conjure it up in the first place, I cannot say. I do know, however, that very powerful constraints must be laid on these creatures, lest they turn on those who create them. It could well be that Karswell's guardian was restricted to that place, near its master's treasure." He paused, and gazed thoughtfully at his hosts. "From the manner in which the sounds it made changed, I should say that it was growing stronger as time passed, and that it is as well that we arrived when we did, before it grew even more powerful."

"And what did you make of the note, Mr. Low?" asked our host. Low smiled gently.

"I, too, took it as a taunt, although I interpreted it somewhat differently to Mr. Holmes. He seized on the word 'treasure', whereas I was struck by the use of the word 'vengeance', and the reference to 'the things that shall come upon them'."

There was silence then, as we all pondered what we had just heard. Looking upon the faces of Mr. and Mrs. Fitzgerald, I could see that their troubles were, if not quite at an end, at least fading rapidly. Mr. Fitzgerald, it was clear, was prepared to believe Flaxman Low's interpretation of events, while his wife believed that Holmes had hit upon the correct solution. I caught the latter's eye as I thought this, and he must have read my thoughts, for he laughed and said, "Well, we have two solutions, and three listeners. I know that two of you have already made up your minds, so it remains for Dr. Watson to cast the deciding vote. Which shall it be, friend Watson? Tell us your verdict."

I glanced from the one detective to the other: both so alike in their methods, so sure of their case, yet so different in their explanations. I took a deep breath.

"I am glad of my Scottish heritage at this moment," I said, "for it allows me to answer, quite properly, 'Not Proven'." And further than that I would not be drawn.

There remains little to tell of this strange case. The following morning, as soon as it was light, a proper investigation of the secret chamber was made. Nothing more was found beyond what we had already seen; and the stone steps did, as surmised, lead down through the thickness of the outer wall to a tunnel which stretched away from the house and emerged in a small outbuilding some distance away. The tunnel was in surprisingly good repair, leading Holmes to believe that his theory of treasure-seekers was correct. Low said nothing, but I noted that he spent some time scrutinising the floor of the tunnel, which was,

I saw, free from any marks that would seem to indicate the recent passage of any corporeal trespasser. The entrances to both chamber and tunnel were sealed shut so as to make both impassable; but not before everything had been removed from the chamber, and everything of Karswell's taken from the study, and burned.

I have not heard that the Fitzgeralds have been troubled since that time; nor did I ever hear of any treasures being found in the house.

One other item, perhaps, bears mentioning. Low had been invited to travel back to London with us, and we found ourselves with some time to spare in the village before our train was due to arrive. We walked, by common accord, over to the small parish church where, we recalled, some of the items salvaged from the original Abbey of Lufford had been stored, and spent a pleasant half-hour therein, admiring the church and its relics. Holmes, indicating that it was time to leave for the station, went outside, and I looked around for Flaxman Low, whom I found staring intently into a glass case which contained some of the remains of the old Abbey. As I paused by his side he turned and smiled at me.

"Ah, Dr. Watson," he said; "or should it be 'Gentleman of the Jury'? Do you still find for 'Not Proven', or have you had any second thoughts?"

I shook my head. "I do not know," I said honestly. "I have worked with Holmes for many years, and am rather inclined to his viewpoint that there is nothing that cannot be explained logically and rationally. And yet..." I paused. "I am not, I think, more imaginative than my fellow man, nor a person inclined to foolish fancies; yet I confess to you that as we stood outside the door of that room, I would have given a good deal not to go in there; and all the while we were inside it, I felt that there was... something in the room with us, something malignant, evil." I shook my head. "I do not know," I repeated, "but I am prepared to weigh the evidence and be convinced."

Low reached out and shook my hand. "Thank you," he said quietly. Then his eyes returned to the case which he had been studying, and he pointed at an item within it. "I was reading this before you came over," he said. "It is one of the relics from the Abbey of Lufford, a tile that dates back to the fifteenth century. The original is in Middle English, and rather difficult to make out, but a translation is on the card beside it. I wonder if Karswell ever saw it; in the unlikely event that he did, he certainly paid no heed to the warning."

I gazed at the card, and read the following words from Lufford Abbey:

Think, man, thy life may not ever endure;
what thou dost thyself, of that thou art sure;
but what thou keepest for thy executor's care,
and whether it avail thee, is but adventure.

The Finishing Stroke
by M. J. Elliott

Some may call it a tragedy, others a fantasy. My friend Sherlock Holmes will not have it that those terrible events surrounding the Tuttman Gallery are capable of anything other than a rational, albeit unorthodox, explanation. While he admits that the violent death of Anwar Molinet is beyond our ability to explain at present, he is insistent that future scientific developments will one day show how such a thing might be possible. I confess, I do not share his confidence — should I call it hubris? — and to this day, he chides me for ever daring to suggest a supernatural solution to the mystery.

"Can it be, Watson," he says, "that you, a trained man of science, have fallen in with the spiritualists, soothsayers and other such frauds and self-delusionists?"

I make no reply, and never shall. But I set down here the full, unbiased account of our most mysterious adventure, and leave it to the reader to decide.

Sherlock Holmes did not, as a rule, encourage visitors at 221B, but he frequently made an exception for Inspector Lestrade. I confess, I have never understood his fondness for the company of the rodent-faced policeman over other officers for whose intelligence he expressed a higher regard, but I have rarely seen my friend happier than when sharing a bottle of the Beaune with his old adversary. It was common on such occasions for Lestrade to voice his concerns regarding any recent problematic investigations. I expected today would be no different, but this afternoon the police official appeared agitated, glancing at the clock on the mantelpiece from time to time.

"Are we keeping you from your duties, Inspector?" asked Holmes, with more than a touch of mockery.

"Er, no, Mr. Holmes. Not just at this moment. I was just thinking... it should be happening soon. Cawthorne's post-mortem, I mean."

It took very little effort on my friend's part to persuade him to elucidate.

"Anwar Molinet was the fellow's name," Lestrade explained. "Murdered in broad daylight, in the middle of a busy restaurant."

"Oh?"

He consulted his notebook. "*Les Freres Heureux*, it's called. Ever heard of it?"

"Your pronunciation could stand some improvement, Lestrade," I remarked. "But, yes, I believe we've dined there once or twice. An excellent cellar."

"Although the manager's cigars are quite as poisonous as I have ever experienced," Holmes added. "It's the curse of the modern age, I fear. I find it hard to believe that a detective of your undoubted abilities would experience even the mildest of difficulties running the culprit to ground. You seem to have an over-abundance of witnesses, and more than adequate supplies of the energy required for such a task."

Lestrade twitched visibly. "You might think so, Mr. Holmes, but... well, it's a peculiar thing... impossible, even."

"I make it a habit to eliminate the impossible before proceeding in an enquiry. Come, come! Surely this is a matter for which the old hound remains the best."

"I should have thought so, too. But you tell me what it means when a man is brutally murdered in front of some twenty-odd people and yet not one of them claims to have seen a thing... Almost as though the killer were *un*visible."

"Brutally?" I wondered aloud.

"You're a medical man, Dr. Watson, and a soldier to boot but I doubt if even you have ever..." Lestrade's voice failed and I imagined for a moment that he was actually stifling a sob. "You'll never see anything like it this side of hell, I swear it."

Holmes rose to his feet and stuffed his pipe into the pocket of his dressing gown. I saw at once that his mood had altered from extreme languor to devouring energy.

"If we are content to sit here chatting about it, I too swear that we will never see it. You said that the post-mortem is due to begin at any moment. If we make a start now, we should be in time to interview the surgeon. Watson, Professor Cawthorne is a member of your club, yes? Then we should have no difficulty in breaching the inner sanctum of one of London's most respected police surgeons. No, no, Lestrade, you need not accompany us. I see from your haggard features that you have already had far too much of the unsavory side of this investigation. By all means, finish your drink, and show yourself out when you are ready."

I was struck, upon entering the mortuary, how long I had been away from the world of practical medicine. The smell of carbolic and decaying flesh could never be described as palatable, but our ability to become accustomed to even the most unattractive circumstance will invariably out. On this occasion, however, it took some effort on my part not to gag as the odor assailed my nostrils.

Cawthorne was soaping his hands as we entered, and gave no more than a brief backward glance. It was not his way, however, to be ungracious, even in the most morbid situation.

"Why, John, what a pleasant surprise. Though I shouldn't really be surprised at all, I suppose. And Mr. Holmes." The two men exchanged no more than a nod of assent, for feelings were somewhat cool between them, ever since Holmes had called Cawthorne's competence into question during our investigation into the shooting of a vagrant on the grounds of Colonel James Moriarty's Chelmsford home. "You're here about the late Mr. Molinet, I imagine?"

With his stick, Holmes indicated a corpse beneath a bloody shroud. "This is he?" he asked.

"It is. I've more or less finished with him, but you're welcome to take a look. I confess, there are still a good many questions concerning the nature of his death I'd like answering. You have George's permission to be here, of course?"

It took a moment before I realized that Cawthorne was referring to the Inspector, with whom, it seemed, he was on first-name terms. To Sherlock Holmes and myself, however, he was simply 'Lestrade'.

I explained, in the most diplomatic terms, that our mutual acquaintance had chosen to remain behind at Baker Street, rather than view the body once more.

"You won't judge him harshly, I hope. This is a shocking matter, even for an old war-horse like George. Indeed, your joint experience in examining dead bodies notwithstanding, you should perhaps prepare yourselves for something you may not have seen before."

He tugged back the sheet, and we found ourselves looking at what had once been a man but had now been transformed into a nightmare. I made no remark; no gasp of astonishment escaped my lips. I seemed, in fact, utterly incapable of speech at that moment.

"Well, well," Holmes breathed, "you do not exaggerate, Professor."

"Whoever did this to Mr. Molinet aided my examination considerably. As you can see, I had no need to make a single incision."

In the moments that followed, I heard only the whistling of my own breath, as we three gazed in silence at the hideously mutilated corpse, his innards visible through the gaping hole in the stomach. I had witnessed something similar when examining the body of the unfortunate Catherine Eddowes, but on that occasion, identification of the weapon had been a simple matter.

"These tears are deep but also ragged," Holmes observed, without apparent emotion. "This was not done with a blade of any sort. Claws, perhaps... or teeth. Have you ever seen the results of an attack by a wolf, Professor?"

"Very few wolves in London, Mr. Holmes," Cawthorne replied.

"Not the four-legged variety, in any case."

"In any event, there is an even greater mystery to be overcome, as you can see, since it would appear that this beast — whatever it may have been — clawed its way *out*, not in."

I heard someone say "There is devilry afoot," and it was a moment before I realized that the words were mine, the first I had uttered since the hideous corpse had been uncovered.

"I have, in the past, voiced the opinion that life is infinitely stranger than anything which the mind of man could invent," Holmes murmured, "but this is perhaps *too* strange even for life as we comprehend it." But I knew that he could not do anything other than proceed with his investigation, for he refused to associate himself with any matter which did not tend towards the unusual and even the fantastic. And I, who share his love of all that is bizarre and outside the conventions and humdrum routine of everyday life, could do nothing but follow in his wake.

For Holmes' sake I attempted, so far as seemed appropriate, to make light of the matter. "Well, Holmes, we have a rare little mystery on our hands," I commented, as we rattled along in the four-wheeler we had flagged down outside the mortuary.

"Your propensity for understatement never ceases to amaze me, Doctor. We seem to have been presented with someone's waking nightmare masquerading as a case. Molinet is slashed to pieces in a public place, apparently by a ferocious animal and in a manner that beggars belief... and yet no-one seems to have seen anything."

"Witnesses to a particularly vicious crime are often unreliable," I noted. "I'm certain I don't need to remind you of the conflicting accounts we heard following the Pennington Flash Murder. Shock can play peculiar tricks on the mind."

"In one or two cases, I might agree, Watson, but surely shock cannot have affected every single diner and member of staff in one of London's most fashionable restaurants."

"Perhaps we are approaching the matter from the wrong end," I suggested. "It may well be that knowing why Molinet was murdered will give us some indication of how it was done."

"Excellent, Watson! Really, you are coming along! How can I take you for granted when your clarity of mind comes to my rescue?"

Holmes had never said as much before, and I must admit that his words gave me keen pleasure, for I have often been piqued by his apparent indifference to my assistance.

Upon our return to Baker Street, we were advised by Mrs. Hudson that Lestrade had only recently departed, and in a state of some merriment. Our long-suffering landlady was less than cheered, however, to learn that Holmes and I would not be staying for dinner, nor could we say when we were likely to return. Holmes searched through his ever-reliable index until he found the address of the late Anwar Molinet.

My earlier intuition, alas, proved of little use when we were confronted with a locked door. There were no servants at Molinet's Belgrave Square address, no-one to answer our persistent knocking.

"Our first broken thread, Watson," Holmes noted, and though there was no malice in his tone, I could not help but redden with shame at the thought of a wasted journey taken at my suggestion.

"You'll find no-one at home, I'm afraid," a strident female voice called to us. We looked about, and saw that the voice belonged to the occupant of the house next door. Though not born to the purple, she gave an excellent imitation, save for the fact that she had chosen to lean out of her window in order to address two perfect strangers.

"Anwar's nephew gave the servants notice as soon as he heard. The place has been locked up ever since. You're Sherlock Holmes and Dr. Watson, aren't you? You're not unlike your pictures, if I might say so."

I raised my hat. "Madam, you were a friend of Mr. Molinet?"

"An acquaintance would be the better term," she simpered. "Neighbor, really. The last time I saw him was at the auction. Oh, I'm terribly sorry, I haven't introduced myself. What on Earth would my husband have said? Mrs. Serracoult is my name. Actually, would you care to come inside? Susan was about to prepare tea."

I accepted cheerfully. Holmes, whose mistrust of the fair sex seemed to increase in direct proportion to their ebullience, murmured: "Watson, I leave this interview entirely in your hands."

In an experience of women which extends over many nations and across several continents, I have met none so flighty as Mrs. Serracoult. She rushed about her sitting-room as though in a constant panic, half-remembering some errand before forgetting it once again.

Holmes emitted several loud groans at this very feminine behavior, but our host was far too preoccupied with at least half a dozen things simultaneously, and I am relieved to say she never noticed.

"Mrs. Serracoult," I said eventually, having sat through several tedious anecdotes regarding her late husband's social connections, "you mentioned that the last time you saw Mr. Molinet was at an auction?"

"At the Tuttman Gallery, that's right, Doctor. Which reminds me, I've been suffering from an unpleasant burning sensation recently, right here."

"I'd be happy to examine you, dear lady, but I regret I left my stethoscope at home." I turned my hat in my hand as I spoke, hoping to conceal the bulge made by the instrument. "Now, this auction..?"

"At the Tuttman Gallery, yes. Do you know the Tuttman Gallery?" I shook my head. "They're very particular about their customers — perhaps I could put in a good word for you both, next time I'm there. Anyway, there was rather a fierce bidding war over a Redfern."

Holmes, who had the crudest notions regarding art, raised a quizzical eyebrow. "Redfern is a painter?" he asked.

"One of London's most exciting new talents, Mr. Holmes." Without warning, she shot from her chair, rattling the tea things as she raced to a handsome landscape upon the wall. I knew that my companion could have no appreciation of its excellence, or of the artist's choice of subject, for the appreciation of nature found no place among his many gifts. "Rather marvellous, isn't it?" our host enthused. "And hideously expensive, of course. But that fact seems to make the very owning of it even more exciting. And I do so long for excitement. Curious, isn't it, Doctor, how one can be very, very bored and very, very busy at the same time?"

Despite never having experienced this condition, I expressed my sympathy. I was in the middle of lamenting the state of a society in which such a complaint could be allowed to arise, when Mrs. Serracoult let out what I can only describe as a strangled shriek, and collapsed back into her chair. I did not even have the chance to enquire as to the cause of her distress, before she regained her composure and desire to speak.

"Goodness! It just occurred to me, Dr. Watson — the last time I saw Oliver Monckton was also at the Tuttman."

I had no notion of who Oliver Monckton might be, or whether he had any bearing upon our current investigation, but I persisted nevertheless.

"Did you outbid Mr. Monckton also?"

"Heavens, no! I hadn't even heard of Redfern then."

"So Monckton bought a Redfern also?" Holmes asked. Mrs. Serracoult nodded, but before she had time to expand upon the fact, Holmes rose to his feet. "Well, thank-you for the tea, Madam," — I noted that his cup was untouched — "but our duties require our presence elsewhere."

"The elusive Professor Moriarty, no doubt."

He gave a thin-lipped smile. "No doubt. Come along, Watson."

Our rooms were ankle-deep in newspapers, reference books and crime periodicals. From time to time, Holmes added to the general scene of chaos with another carelessly discarded document. I have made mention of this frustrating anomaly in my friend's character elsewhere, but under the circumstances, I had little cause for complaint; I had no keener pleasure than in following him on his professional investigations, and in admiring the rapid deductions with which he unraveled the conundrums submitted to him.

"What exactly are you looking for?" I asked in frustration as a crumpled-up copy of something called *Police News of the Past* flew by my face.

"This!" He announced, triumphantly, presenting me with a copy of the *Journal de Geneve*.

"Some of us have only the one language, Holmes."

"Please excuse me, old fellow. This article relates to the sudden death of Englishman Oliver Monckton while holidaying in Switzerland. I recall that the details were few, but I was struck by the journalist's claims that certain unsavory details were suppressed by the coroner."

The word 'unsavory', which I recalled Holmes had used earlier, certainly suggested to my mind a connection between Monckton and Anwar Molinet, although I wondered whether any description could do justice to the horror I had witnessed in the mortuary.

"And Mrs. Serracoult said that both men had purchased Redferns at the Tuttman Gallery, wherever that may be."

"It is in Knightsbridge, I believe — formerly the Gaylord Auction Rooms. The question is, if a connection exists, does it relate to the paintings, the artist, or the gallery? We are in unfamiliar territory, Watson; my own art collection consists solely of portraits of the last century's most notorious criminals."

"And my army pension would hardly stretch to spending afternoons at the Tuttman Gallery in the company of Mrs. Serracoult," I added, ruefully.

"Then you must be thankful for small mercies, Doctor."

"Holmes... I have been thinking."

"This is turning out to be a day of remarkable occurrences."

"Really, you're the most insufferable fellow alive."

"Quite possibly. Please, go on; I should be grateful to hear your theory."

I marshalled my thoughts with the aid of a stiff whisky. "Remember the affair of the Christmas Goose, or the busts of Napoleon? Might there not be something hidden away, perhaps within the frame itself?"

"A provocative notion, Doctor. And though it does no harm to theorize, we are at sea without—"

He got no further along his train of thought, however, for at that moment we were interrupted by a knocking on the door. I imagined it might be Mrs. Hudson, and wondered what her reaction to the present state of the room might be, when the door swung open to reveal the familiar figure of Inspector Lestrade, his features more haggard than before, if such a thing can be imagined.

"Our good fortune, Doctor!" Holmes cried. "Inspector Lestrade, here to help us through the morass of officialdom. And with a gift of a somewhat unconventional nature, I see."

"Hardly that, Mr. Holmes." I saw that he held in his right hand what had once been a ladies' shoe. From its charred appearance, I supposed he must have extracted it from a bonfire.

"Where did you come by this singular souvenir, Lestrade?"

The police agent waited a moment before responding. "This shoe, Mr. Holmes... is all that remains of Mrs. Bernice Serracoult."

My friend has so often astonished me in the course of our adventures that I am ashamed to admit a sense of fascination at witnessing his complete astonishment. A flush of color sprang to his pale cheeks as he listened in silence to the Inspector's account of Mrs. Serracoult's demise. Approximately half an hour after our departure, the maid, one Susan Foxley, had been alerted by the screams of her employer.

"She described being conscious of a peculiar odor for several minutes — an odor we now know to have been burning flesh. When she reached the sitting room, Mrs. Serracoult was fully ablaze."

Holmes had been on the point of reaching for his pipe, but evidently thought better of it. "How much of the house was destroyed in the fire?" he asked.

"None, Mr. Holmes."

"None?"

"Mrs. Serracoult was burned to a crisp, but the chair she sat upon was not even singed."

"Impossible," I protested. "Such things might occur in Dickens novels, but never in real life."

"And yet it happened," Holmes noted, "suggesting that it is simply a badly-observed phenomenon. I have said many times that life is infinitely stranger than anything the mind of man could invent, but we must stick to reason, or we are lost."

"Unlike Mr. Holmes here, I don't believe in coincidences," interrupted the haggard policemen. "I can't explain it, but when the neighbor of a man who died a horrible death suddenly bursts into flames... I don't know, gentlemen — it beats anything I've ever seen, and Lord knows, I'm no chicken."

Holmes hurried Lestrade from our rooms, and a few moments later, we were in a cab, on our way to the Tuttman Gallery.

I attempted to draw Holmes into conversation about our present investigation. When he would not be drawn, I sought to engage his power to throw his brain out of action and switch his thoughts to lighter things by changing the topic to Cremona violins, warships of the future and the obliquity of the ecliptic.

"It... hurts my pride, Doctor," he said eventually. "It should have occurred to me that, as the owner of a third Redfern, she might be in as much danger as Molinet and Monckton. I'm a foolish old man. How long can it be before I must retire to that farm of my dreams?"

So accustomed was I to his invariable success that the very possibility of his failure had ceased to enter my head until that very moment. "But surely... there's still a chance... a chance to save anyone else who's become entangled in this sinister web. If any man can untangle it, that man is Sherlock Holmes."

Holmes gave a weak chuckle — he was always accessible upon the side of flattery. A moment later, he was the cold and practical thinker once again. "And faithful old Dr. Watson, of course," he added.

I knew at heart that he would not give up so easily. It was when he was at his wits' end that his energy and versatility were most admirable. "May I ask what our present objective might be?"

"Firstly, to ascertain whether anyone at the Tuttman Gallery might have a reason to wish harm to these three persons; secondly, to discover the names of anyone else who might have purchased a painting by Redfern; lastly, to locate the artist himself. It may be at odds with my method of observation and deduction, but I have an intuition that he might be at the center of this pattern of events."

And so it proved. Crabtree, the proprietor of the Tuttman Gallery, was a gentleman of amiable disposition, who was extremely distressed to hear of the deaths of three of his most frequent customers, and allowed us free reign to search his store, question his staff and examine his records. Given the outré nature of the deaths, I had no clear idea of what we might be looking for, but Holmes seemed satisfied that no-one at the Gallery was acting with malicious intent. It appeared from Crabtree's register that he had sold only one other Redfern, to a Mr. Phillimore. Holmes advised me that he had been consulted by Inspector Stanley Hopkins after Phillimore returned to his house one morning to fetch his umbrella and was never again seen in this world.

"I dislike ever having to hazard a guess," remarked Holmes, "but I think we have a fair idea of the reason for his disappearance, although I very much doubt whether even now we can count that case as one of my successes. Tell me, Mr. Crabtree, have you had any dealings with Mr. Redfern?"

"None personally, Mr. Holmes," the proprietor replied in a nasal whine. "All his paintings come to us through Mr. Milhause. You know him, I trust?"

"By reputation only. But it seems that we must make ourselves known to him. Mr. Crabtree, might we rely upon you to provide us with an introduction?"

"As if you needed one, Mr. Holmes," said a refined if somewhat effected voice behind us. We turned, and found ourselves facing a fellow I deduced to be Mr. Bartholemew Milhause himself. If I could have pictured a more suitable brother for the rotund Mycroft Holmes than my colleague, then it would surely have been Milhause. He was only slightly smaller than the obese civil servant I had encountered during the affair of the Greek Interpreter and the business of the stolen submarine plans, but in all other respects — the thinning hair, the deep-set grey eyes — he might have been his twin. However, where I commonly associated Mycroft with the faint odor of expensive cigars, Milhause had apparently drenched himself in a perfume better suited to a vulgar music hall artiste than an alleged patron of the arts.

He shook Holmes by the hand with an enthusiasm I considered unseemly. "An honor, sir, an honor!" he cried. "And you must be the other one," he observed caustically, eyeing me with distaste. I pretended to ignore the obvious slight.

"Mr. Milhause, you act for the artist Redfern, do you not?" Holmes enquired.

"A true talent, Mr. Holmes — a young fellow of genuine ability. An oasis in the desert of mediocrity that passes for culture in modern London. I make an exception for the items to be found in the Tuttman Gallery, of course." Crabtree, to whom this remark was directed, responded in similarly fawning terms. I glanced at Holmes, but he did not return my grimace.

"It just so happens, Mr. Milhause, that I am interested in sitting for a portrait."

"But surely Mr. Paget—"

"That was some years ago, and I am no longer the man I once was. I thought that if any artist in London might be capable of capturing my — well, my spirit..."

"That artist is Algernon Redfern!" Milhause declared, with a tiresome flourish. "Excellent, Mr. Holmes, excellent! Portrait work is not really in his line, you understand, but I doubt that he could pass up such a fascinating commission. Mr. Sherlock Holmes himself — how very unique!"

"It is simply 'unique', Mr. Milhause," I pointed out.

"But it is, my dear fellow — simply unique!"

Like every Londoner, I had, of course, heard of the artists' studios to be found off the long lean artery of the King's Road, but I had never seen them. Finding myself on that dark flagged alley, I must confess that I was not impressed by my surroundings. Indeed, the only hint of a bohemian air to the district was supplied by two disreputably-dressed young gentleman, no doubt on the way to their own studio. As they passed us, I heard the taller man say, "Honestly, Bunny, you really are the most frightful ass..." in a cultured fashion greatly at odds with his attire.

We halted at an unlatched door, and Holmes raised his hand to knock.

"It's open, Mr. Holmes, do come in!" called a male voice. My friend's expression betrayed none of the surprise I was sure he must have felt, and he pushed the door open.

I had imagined that the residence of a successful artist would be crammed to the rafters with sketches and paintings in various stages of preparation. But the lofty room in which we found ourselves betrayed little evidence of the tenant's occupation, save for an easel at the far side of the room and a small table in the center. The painting upon that easel faced away from us, but had, in any case, been covered by a stained towel. A completed work, rolled-up, rested against the easel.

As for Algernon Redfern himself, again my expectations were crushed. Given his flamboyant agent, and his apparent connection with a string of bizarre murders, I had begun to imagine him as a curious cross between Oscar Wilde and Edward Hyde; but such was not the case. Redfern was a man of approximately five-and-twenty, tall, loose-limbed, with black close-cropped hair and a pockmarked face.

"Forgive me for not shaking hands," he said, jovially, displaying his paint-smeared palms.

"How does it come about that you were expecting us?" I enquired.

He smiled, and I observed a row of uneven yellow teeth. "Perhaps as an artist, I have a keener instinct than most, Doctor. Or, a telegram might have reached me before your carriage. Then again, I might have that marvelously convenient invention, the telephone, installed somewhere on the premises. Pick any one you prefer. Cigarette?"

Under a copy of the *Pall Mall*, a plain cigarette box rested upon the small table. He brushed the newspaper to the floor and opened the box, revealing just one cigarette within.

"No thank-you, Mr. Redfern," Holmes replied.

"As you like," said the artist. In one swift movement, he placed the cigarette in his mouth and lit it. "This will probably be my last one, anyway. Plays hell with my chest. Is there any medical basis for swearing off them, Doctor?"

I must own that during my explanation — which took in findings made a century earlier regarding the connection between snuff-taking and certain nasal polyps, as well as my friend's frequent three-pipe sessions — I rambled more than a little, distracted as I was by Redfern's voice. That he was attempting to conceal his own nationality beneath a somewhat flawed English accent was clear.

"Well, Mr. Holmes," he said, jovially, "to what do I owe the honor of this visit?"

"What does your keen artist's instinct tell you?" Holmes asked, dryly.

Redfern chuckled. "Most assuredly, *not* that you are interested in having your portrait painted. From what I know of you from Dr. Watson's stories, I would not have said you were so vain."

"If you are an admirer of the Doctor's work, you have my condolences," said Holmes with, I felt, unnecessary relish. "But you are correct in stating that I have not come here today on my own account. I am more interested in your connection to James Phillimore, Anwar Molinet, Oliver Monckton and Mrs. Bernice Serracoult."

Redfern expelled a long, luxurious cloud of smoke before responding: "Sorry to say, I've never heard of any of them. Who are they?"

"They each bought one of your paintings," I explained.

The artist shrugged, before stubbing out his cigarette on the lid of the box and picking up a pad and pencil. "I only paint them," he said. "The charming Mr. Milhause handles the business side of things. You've met him, of course. Quite unbearable isn't he?"

"They are also, as Dr. Watson is too discreet to mention, all dead — Mrs. Serracoult as recently as this afternoon."

Algernon Redfern appeared unperturbed by this news. "I should call that a rather extreme reaction to my work." He began to scribble absent-mindedly on the pad.

"Are you English by birth, Mr. Redfern?" Holmes asked.

"How could you doubt it? I'm not native to London, however, but I've been here a while. And I'll remain until I've done what I came here to do."

"And that is?" I asked.

He looked up from his pad. "To sell my paintings, naturally. What else?"

I coughed to attract Holmes' attention.

"Your friend seems to have rather a nasty chest. Or is there something on your mind, Doctor?"

"You said... you said that Mr. Milhause dealt with the sale of your works. And I would not have imagined that a true artistic soul would be interested in such vulgar matters."

"I don't play any part in the sales — I couldn't even tell you where they're sold. But as a professional writer, you must know that any artist who says they're not interested in public acceptance is a liar. That's what it's all about. And money, of course. Only the air is free, gentlemen, and I have some doubts as to its quality."

"Dr. Watson likes to say that my pipe does little to add to the city's atmosphere."

"Another persuasive argument in favor of my giving up the cigarettes." Redfern dropped the pad at his feet, seeming not to notice. "I'm sorry I can't help you, Mr. Holmes, but as I told you, I've never met or even heard of those people you mentioned. And I'm certain that as a professional detective, you must have all sorts of ways of telling whether I'm telling the truth or not." Again, he flashed a sickly yellow grin, and I had the certain feeling that we were being manipulated, as a cat toys with a wounded mouse.

Holmes scratched his long nose. "Well, it was a long shot at best. Thank-you for your time, Mr. Redfern."

We made to leave, but the young man bounded across the length of the room, the rolled-up painting in his hand. "Wait!" he cried. "Mr. Holmes, as an... admirer of your work, I should very much like you to have this."

Holmes chuckled. "My services are charged at a fixed rate, Mr. Redfern. I doubt that I could afford one of your paintings."

"I'm not selling it — I'm giving it to you. It's mine to do with as I wish, and I wish you to have it. Take it, please."

I was already on my guard, and should never under any circumstances have accepted a gift from a man so patently false as Algernon Redfern, so I was astonished by my friend's reaction, unrolling the picture with an almost childish enthusiasm of which I would never have imagined him capable. Holmes' eyes glittered as he examined the picture.

"Why, this is really very fine!" he exclaimed.

"If I have captured the color of the mudstains, I take it you can identify the precise area of London depicted?"

"No need, Mr. Redfern, I am quite familiar with Coptic Street; I had lodgings not far from there some years ago, and it has featured in one of our recent investigations. Watson, you recall the case of the Coptic Patriarchs?"

I attempted to convey my concerns to Holmes in a surreptitious manner by means of a loud cough, but he seemed completely oblivious.

"Well, good-bye, Mr. Holmes," said the young man, his unhealthy grin now even wider. "It was nice to have known you, if only for a brief time. Good-bye, Dr. Watson — paregoric is the stuff."

"I suppose it has occurred to you, Holmes," I remarked, tartly, "that thus far in this case, everyone who has owned a painting by Algernon Redfern has died the most horrible death... and you are the latest owner of a Redfern?"

Holmes' mood during our cab journey back to Baker Street had been irrepressibly cheerful, and he refused to allow my grim observation to spoil his mood. "You know my methods, Watson — I am well-known to be indestructible. Besides, I trust that the two of us will be able to see danger coming in any direction."

"I wish us better luck than Anwar Molinet; we still have yet to determine the precise cause of his death, but I'd be prepared to wager a considerable sum that this fellow Redfern is behind it all somehow."

"Then perhaps it's wise that your checkbook is safely locked away in my drawer."

I ignored the sharpness of his retort. "I simply meant that I find it inexplicable that you choose to trust this fellow!"

"I did not say that I trusted him."

"But you said you were certain he was at the center of this pattern of events, and now you're accepting gifts from the fellow."

"Well, evidently, I was wrong about his precise connection to the case. I simply view him now as another stop on our journey, rather than our destination point."

This pronouncement baffled me; so far as I could see, we had no lines of enquiry left to pursue. Holmes evidently noted the confusion on my features, for he continued: "It's interesting that, as an artist, Mr. Redfern prefers to write rather than doodle. You noticed, of course, his furious scribblings as we conversed?"

"I noticed," I admitted, "but I placed no importance in it."

Holmes tutted. "Just when I think I have made something of you, Doctor. As we spoke, he wrote the words 'Do they know about Ferregamo?'"

"How could you possibly have seen that from where you were positioned?"

Holmes winced, and I found myself reaching for my service revolver, imagining that my friend was in some danger. But he simply smiled weakly.

"I really must speak to Mrs. Hudson about her cooking," he groaned. "I'm so sorry, old fellow, what were you saying?"

I repeated my question.

"No magic, Watson: one simply has to watch the end of the pencil in order to establish what is being written. It's a trick every detective should know. Now we have to establish who or what Ferregamo is—"

"That would be a Julius Ferregamo, of Bedford Square."

"Your average is rising, Watson. That's twice in a single day you've managed to render me speechless. I retract my earlier criticism. How do you come by this information?"

"No magic, Holmes. It just so happens that I met the fellow at a luncheon at the Langham Hotel. It was a good many years ago, but his reputation as London's premier art collector was unequalled even then. Many pretenders to the throne have come and gone in the interval, and Ferregamo retains his supremacy. Half-Italian, you know, but still quite a decent chap for all that."

"I'm sure he would appreciate your finding him so, Watson." Again, he winced, and clutched at his stomach.

"Holmes, you're unwell. We must get you back to Baker Street."

"If I am unwell, then I am extremely fortunate in having a physician at my side at all times." He rapped upon the roof of the carriage with his stick. "Driver, we've changed our minds! Take us to Bedford Square."

I shifted uneasily in my seat, as Redfern's painting brushed against my leg, and told myself that the chill I felt was entirely imaginary. I remembered Holmes' old maxim that the more bizarre a crime appears, the less mysterious it proves to be, and I wondered whether we might be witnessing the exception to that particular rule.

Julius Ferregamo was almost exactly as I recalled him from that luncheon so many years before. Where the years had taken their toll on my brow and waistline, he was as trim and dandified as ever, as he greeted us in the parlor of his lavish abode.

"Doctor, so good to see you again. Still producing your little yarns? How charming! And this must be Sherlock Holmes! You're very fortunate to catch me at home, you know. I've been in Amsterdam for some time, negotiating for a Hans Holbein. You're familiar with Holbein, I imagine?"

"Only with Anton Holbein, the Augsburg poisoner," Holmes answered. "The doctor will tell you that I have only the crudest notions about—" My poor friend's face had suddenly assumed the most dreadful expression. His eyes rolled upward, and his features writhed. For a fleeting moment, I feared he might be on the verge of collapse.

"Are you ill, Mr. Holmes?" Ferregamo enquired.

"Merely beginning to regret my dining habits, sir." He laughed weakly.

"I always dine at *Les Freres Heureux* when I'm of a mind, but as I passed it today, it seemed to be closed. I'm so sorry, Mr. Holmes, you were saying something about your crude notions?"

"Concerning art, Mr. Ferregamo. In fact, I came here today to ask your opinion on a piece I recently acquired. That is, if you would deign to cast your expert eye..?" He passed the painting to the Italian, who accepted it cautiously. As Holmes released his grip on it, a curious change seemed to come over his face, as though the cause of his discomfort had suddenly evaporated.

"For a friend of the doctor, how could I refuse?" He unrolled the painting with care. "I must warn you, if you are hoping to make a fortune from it, you are likely to be disappointed."

"Mr. Holmes is interested in art for its own sake," I explained. "But of late, I've learned a great deal about the importance of money in your world, Julius."

"Oh, indeed!" he beamed. "Why, that Hogarth etching behind you has probably appreciated in value about £100 since you entered my home. Why, this is very fine indeed."

Knowing that my own artistic impulses — though keener than Holmes' — were nowhere near as refined as Ferregamo's, I was cheered by the fact that our view of Algernon Redfern's abilities tallied.

"I should say that this would be the pride of your collection, Mr. Holmes," he went on. Given that Holmes' entire collection was made up of illustrations from the crime news, I was forced to agree.

"I am gladdened to hear that you like it, Mr. Ferregamo," Holmes said with uncharacteristic glee. "You must have it."

I was startled by this sudden act of generosity. What was Holmes thinking? Had he not accepted the same painting as a gift from Algernon Redfern an hour earlier?

"IIow much are you asking for it? As I said, it is not valuable, I merely appreciate it as a work of art."

"If you value it so highly, I am happy to present it to you as a gift. The doctor will tell you that I do not ordinarily act on impulse, but I feel very strongly that this painting should be yours."

A crease of doubt appeared on Ferregamo's high domed forehead. "Really? You know, I don't recognize the style, but there's something oddly... familiar. I pride myself that I can identify an artist's brushstrokes just as you Mr. Holmes, could spot the typeface of any newspaper."

"Not quite *any* newspaper. When I was very young, I once mistook the *Leeds Mercury* for the *Western Morning News*. But the artist in question is Algernon Redfern. Doubtless you're familiar with him?"

"As I say, I've been out of the country — I'm a little out of touch with recent developments. This Redfern... young fellow, is he?"

"In his early twenties, I should say," I answered. "Strange chap — claimed to be English, but he had an accent I couldn't place."

Without warning, Julius Ferregamo grabbed me by the lapels. "His teeth! His skin! Describe them!"

"Then you *do* know him!"

As quickly as he had accosted me, the frightened man released me, before staggering as though wounded. "My God!" he breathed. "Ruber! He's found me out! My God!" His face had reddened, and heavy beads of sweat ran down his brow. I feared his heart might be under some tremendous strain.

"Julius!" I cried. "Julius, what's happening to you?"

In describing what occurred next, I realize that I risk straining my readers' credulity. Even the famously eccentric Professor Challenger, the one man in London I imagined would be sympathetic to my tale, dismissed it as some form of narcotic delusion when I related this event to him. Nevertheless, I insist that I speak the absolute truth.

Ferregamo was acting like a madman, first scratching at the painting, then flailing about wildly. I attempted to restrain him, but without success. Holmes, meanwhile, was paralysed by the strange scene, his expression pale but exultant, his lips parted in amazement. At last, our host collapsed to the floor, heaving. But the worst was not over. It seemed from the unnatural movement in his gullet, that something was attempting to force its way out of his body... something alive.

When I viewed the remains of Anwar Molinet — was it really only that morning? — I thought I had witnessed the most hideous sight man could ever see. But now, crouching on all fours, Julius Ferregamo proceeded to disgorge a stream of bile... and live scorpions, more than could ever have been contained within a man's system, should he have chosen to swallow them whole in the first place. Freed from their unnatural prison, the creatures then proceeded to scuttle about the room, some of them heading towards Holmes and myself.

"Run!" Holmes cried, suddenly himself once more. Needing no further encouragement, I followed him out into the hallway, slamming the door firmly shut behind us.

"Holmes..." I gasped. "What just happened..." It was neither a question nor a statement, but Holmes nodded vigorously.

"It happened, Watson. But I'm at a complete loss as to explain why or how."

"When you start a chase, Mr. Holmes, you really do it!" With the passing of the day, Lestrade had become quite his old self. Holmes and I, however, were both exhausted and less than willing to accept the Scotland Yarder's customary twitting. "And you say this fellow's death is connected to the Molinet business?"

Holmes nodded, dumbly.

"And... you saw live scorpions coming out of his mouth? I don't mean to question your skill for observation, but really..."

"I am as dumbfounded as you, Inspector — not a sensation I much enjoy. But if you open that door, you will find that what we say is true. But please draw your pistol before doing so; you will have need of it."

With some hesitancy, Lestrade pushed lightly against the door to the parlor. Then, with a sly grin, he shoved it wide open.

"Having a laugh at the expense of the slow-witted policemen, eh? Well, no scorpions in here. Also no tarantula spiders and no venomous swamp adders."

Disbelieving, I pushed my way past Lestrade. Julius Ferregamo lay where we had left him, quite dead. But of the ghastly creatures, there was no trace.

"Impossible!" I breathed.

"Merely improbable, I should say." Sherlock Holmes brushed by and knelt to examine the body. "If there were no scorpions, then there remains the question of how Ferregamo was stung to death."

"Sounds as though I should have a word with the keepers at London Zoo," Lestrade suggested, unhelpfully.

I joined Holmes as he lifted Ferregamo's right hand gingerly. Under the fingernails were traces of paint. "He did begin scratching at the Redfern just before... the end," I observed.

"Perhaps he wanted to see this other painting underneath," said Lestrade. We both turned to see the police official examining the picture.

"Underneath?" I repeated. Looking closely, I could see that he was correct; there was a second picture, but it was impossible to tell what it might be.

"No doubt Mr. Holmes has some chemicals in his laboratory that could help reveal it."

"No need for that," Holmes responded, "I already know what it is. Lestrade, Watson and I have an appointment elsewhere. I can trust you to take care of the body before you begin waking up the zookeepers?"

Sherlock Holmes was transformed when he was hot upon a scent such as this. As the gleam of the street-lamps flashed upon his austere features, I saw that his brows were drawn in deep thought and his thin lips compressed. His face was bent downwards, his shoulder bowed, and the veins stood out like whipcord in his long, sinewy neck. His eyes shone out from beneath his brows with a steely glitter. Men who have only known the quiet thinker and logician of Baker Street would have failed to recognize him. But I recognized the battle-signs; the time of crisis had arrived.

It was close to midnight when we returned to Algernon Redfern's studio off the King's Road. Holmes did not wait, but simply pushed the door open and entered. I followed closely, my heart thumping so loudly in my chest, I was certain that I could be found in an instant by whoever or whatever awaited us.

I lack my friend's cultivated eyesight, but I doubted that even he could make out any details in the darkness. The lamps were unlit, the blinds drawn and were it not for the fact that I knew Redfern possessed virtually no furniture, I would have feared to take a step in any direction.

"You didn't knock, Mr. Holmes," said a familiar voice from the other end of the room. "I sensed at heart you were a poor sport. The artist in me... knows these things."

"Any pretence at sportsmanship vanished when you attempted to kill me, Mr. Ruber," Holmes replied, stridently.

I strained my eyes, but I could not make out the shape of Algernon Redfern. He chuckled. "Ferregamo told you my real name. Oh, please tell me he said it with his dying breath. It would mean so much to me. Or don't you propose to give me the satisfaction?" The last traces of his forced English accent were gone for good, I realized.

Holmes remained silent, a fixed point.

"Oh, very well," sighed the man I had known as Redfern. "If it helps — and I doubt it will — I'm sorry. Not about Ferregamo, of course, but about any discomfort you may have experienced."

I could remain silent no longer. "You seem to have forgotten, Redfern — I mean, Ruber, that four other people are dead, and I take it you are responsible."

"Haven't you told him, Mr. Holmes?"

"If I have kept the good doctor in the dark... so to speak... it is only because I find it difficult to credit that such a thing could occur in the world as I understand it. Very well, perhaps explanations are in order. All these terrible crimes were committed with just one target in mind: the late Mr. Julius Ferregamo. I realized that very late in the day — both figuratively and literally — when I passed on the painting that had been a gift from Ruber here, and all my digestive problems vanished."

"And were inherited by Ferregamo?" I asked, hardly daring to believe the implications.

"Had he not taken it, I daresay *I* should have suffered the same ghastly fate, a notion that should give fuel to my nightmares for some years to come."

From the tone of his voice, I knew that Ruber was mightily pleased with himself. "I was worried you might not have picked up on the little clue I left you — I never even saw you examine the paper I was writing on — but when word reached me about Ferregamo's death, well... I knew you'd done exactly what I'd wanted you to do."

"It was not as though I had any choice in the experience. Once you led me to him, I found I could do nothing but give him your painting. With the assistance of Watson here, I swore off the evils of cocaine because I disliked the sensation of not being in control of my thoughts and senses. All the works you created under the alias of Algernon Redfern — they were meant for Ferregamo, were they not?"

I had some vague notion of what Holmes was driving at, but it seemed simply too fantastic to credit. "What do you mean, Holmes?" I asked. "What are you saying?"

"I am saying that Ruber here..."

"*Felix* Ruber, in case you were wondering," the man in the darkness interrupted.

"Very well," Holmes continued, "*Felix* Ruber, you see, has... an ability. I cannot classify it scientifically, but it seems that his paintings are somehow able to affect their owner — adversely, I need hardly add. Hence, Mrs. Serracoult's fiery demise, the mysterious disappearance of James Phillimore, the invisible creature that clawed its way out of Molinet's stomach, and so on. You have a very vivid imagination, sir, if more than somewhat disturbed." Holmes touched my sleeve. Whether he could see my response or not, I nodded my understanding.

"Given that you have achieved your goal," he asked, "would you at least satisfy my curiosity and tell me your story?"

"If you're hoping that my story will contain an explanation of my gift, I'm afraid you're destined to be disappointed, Mr. Holmes. But why not?" As Ruber spoke, I began to take short, silent steps, tracking the voice to its source. "I was living on the streets of Vienna, when I first met Julius Ferregamo. I was little more than a child, trying to make money any way I could. You might think you've seen some terrible things today, gentlemen, but believe me, nothing can compare to the horrors I experienced growing up. Ferregamo was there to see what artwork he could snatch up for the so-called civilized world. The man was no better than a vulture. He'd heard some talk about my work... my abilities. You'd think that would have made me blessed. But once the word spread, life became impossible... I was the miracle-worker, the modern-day messiah. Believe it or not, I simply just wanted to paint. It is what I do, what I *am*. Ferregamo promised me a new life, away from that hell. I believed him. But he just wanted to use me like all the others. To be richer than he already was, to see his enemies crushed. It was my job to see that those things came to pass."

I remembered that Ferregamo had somehow retained his position as the premier art collector in London, perhaps even in Europe, but his competitors had all come and gone. Now I had some inkling of *how* they had gone. "So... you simply paint something and it happens?" I asked, and instantly regretted doing so. Had I given away my position?

"Not quite, Doctor. You have to possess the painting to feel its power. People must have thought Ferregamo was a very generous man — he was always giving them gifts."

"And those gifts were your paintings," Holmes responded. "Then you were his accomplice."

"I was his prisoner! Locked in a cell in his home, with a guard watching over me at all times. But finally, during my one mealtime a day, I was able to scratch a drawing into a metal plate with my fork — it was a drawing of a heart exploding. The guard took my plate and... I was free."

In his rage, he did not seem to have noticed my approach. I continued, step by careful step, as he expounded.

"I disappeared, studied, changed my style. Then returned to destroy Julius Ferregamo. But that wasn't easy if he had to possess my work. That was why, in addition to reinventing myself, I hid my revenge paintings under those rather more conventional landscapes. I found that using Brickfall and Amberley's lead-based paint seemed to block the effects for a time. Don't ask me to explain it; I don't really understand it myself. But, of course, I couldn't just send him one of my pictures, he would have known instantly. The only way was for him to buy one at auction. I had no idea he was out of the country until I saw it in the newspaper."

"And tell me, Mr. Ruber, does that make you any less of a murderer?" asked Holmes. In the gloom, I could see only the easel on which Ruber's last painting still rested. Where *was* the devil?

"I won't ask for your forgiveness. And I can't ask for it over... over all those other people you just mentioned who's names I'm ashamed to tell you I've already forgotten." I still could not see my quarry, but I was certain that I had traced the voice to its source, somewhere close to the easel.

"Of late, I've given a great deal of thought to questions of captivity and freedom... it strikes me that I have been a captive for my entire life — even these last few months, living in self-imposed imprisonment, unwilling to go out in public for fear that Ferregamo might recognize me. I have been my own jailer, Mr. Holmes; perhaps, in a way, that is true of us all. And I think that, for once, I should like to taste *real* freedom. The whole of Europe is open to me."

"I'm afraid that may not be possible. You must be called to account for the deaths you have caused."

Another chuckle. I knew that I was close. "I would not have categorized you as a wishful thinker, Holmes. It seems you still possess the ability to surprise me, after all. But you recall I said earlier today that I would stay in London until my work was completed? Well, Ferregamo has been dead some time now... and I departed the moment I knew."

I pounced. There was a crash — and then I experienced the sudden, overpowering numbness that comes seconds before the onset of great pain. My ribs burned, as I lay on the floor, and I could only hope that I had somehow succeeded in waylaying Felix Ruber as I fell. But I knew in my heart that I had not. Not only had he vanished without trace, but a search of the studio revealed no other entrance or exit. The windows had clearly not been opened in many a year, and we left some hours later, infinitely sadder but no wiser for our experience. Surely, I told myself, the voice could not have emanated from the self-portrait of Felix Ruber, which I had succeeded in knocking from the easel to the dusty floor?

Holmes and I did not discuss the incident upon our return to Baker Street, and we have talked little of the case since. If his own words are to be believed, Ruber is at large somewhere in Europe as I write, and though my friend could easily use his influence with the high officials of several international police forces to arrange a wide-scale search, he has not done so.

"Having given the matter further thought, it strikes me that it would be nearly impossible to bring the fellow to trial in a satisfactory manner," he explained, some months later. "The average British jury is not composed of massive intellects, and a prosecutor might just as well accuse hobgoblins and fairies of the crime. I fear that the finer scientific points would be lost on the great, unobservant British public."

For a man who has turned the docketing of fresh and accurate information into an art-form, it seems odd that he should be able to deny that these events occurred as they did, and as — so far as I am aware — the only other surviving witness, I fear that no-one will place any stock in this account. So I lay it aside for now, in the hope that perhaps my friend is at least partially correct, and by the time it is published, long after my death, we will at last have come to comprehend the nature of Felix Ruber's remarkable abilities.

I should add that I hear rumors, from time to time, of queer noises emanating from the vaults of Cox and Co, where the portrait of Felix Ruber is stored, but I have not felt a pressing need to investigate further.

Sherlock Holmes in the Lost World

by Martin Powell

Author's Note: John H. Watson, M.D. wishes to state that both the restriction for restraint and the libel action have been withdrawn unconditionally by Professor George Edward Challenger, who, being content that no criticism or observation in this narrative is meant in an offensive spirit, has guaranteed that he will place no obstruction to its publication.

The cave man's stomach felt as empty as his head.

Days and nights of starvation, by no means an uncommon happenstance upon the Plateau, had dimmed his distinctive wisdom and he'd reluctantly ventured down from the relative shelter of the vine-tangled trees in search of sustenance.

He crawled through the open grass on his hairy belly like a filth-encrusted beetle, short spear gripped in a black-bristled paw, with a razor-edge blade made of bone clenched in his broad square teeth. The deer was grazing only a few short yards away.

The cave man scarcely breathed, hungrily eyeing his quarry with mouth-watering expectation. He was down-wind of the slight breeze as planned — he'd not yet lost total reason — and rapid glances over each wide bushy shoulder did not yet reveal a rival predator stalking the same prey. From a kneeling position he raised his spear. Perhaps, this was his lucky day.

The deer's head sprang up in instant vigilance. The deadly double pair of antlers, and the Y-shaped horn upon its snout at once would have made the otherwise graceful creature utterly unearthly to the typical modern Londoner. Large liquid eyes darted for the coming danger. Before the batting of another long lash the fleet-footed deer sprang away in a series of lofty leaps that were almost miraculous in their prowess.

The cave man hadn't time for disappointment. At first he sensed the commotion rather than heard it, rather like the thudding of an inaudible drum-beat. Alarm flashed in his deep-set, sweat-reddened eyes as he suddenly felt the rumbling earth beneath him.

Stampede!

A bank of swirling grasses, twelve feet high, parted and exploded outward with an eruption of the thundering brontotherium and her galloping calf. The frenzied terror of the massive beasts prompted the cave man to race for the salvation of the high branches at least a hundred yards distant. Still, he had to try. The brontotheres feared few enemies.

A pack of creodonts swarmed after the massive grass-eaters in all their yellow-eyed, jagged jawed horror. The grisly devils virtually slithered rather than ran, their low, long, ductile feline forms fluidly racing and flowing in the heat of the hunt. Bone-crushing wolfish snouts dripped and snarled with the stuff of nightmares.

The clodding of the cave man's overly-wide, loutish feet betrayed him. A lone, lean creodont broke from the panting pack and instantaneously sized him up as easier game. No chance of out-running the racing red-tongued demon. The cave man whirled around, a bull-like bellow blasting from his thirsty lips as he hurled the stubby stone-tipped spear with all his shrinking, starving strength—transfixing the fiend from sternum to coccyx.

The dead beast's berserker brethren rampaged on through the grassy plain, unaware of the spoor of the cave man. After a bit, fearsome screams in the distant thicket gave evidence that the hunters would long be occupied with their ponderous feast.

He swatted away skulking black buzzards and little flying lizards, hastily slinging the weighty carcass over his apish shoulder. No time to waste. More formidable scavengers were certain to follow.

The cave man had lived past another noon.

⁙ ⁙ ⁙

As I alighted from the motorcar at the very doorstep of the Diogenes Club, I reflected upon the realization that, despite all the many years of our peculiar association, I didn't know Mycroft Holmes very well.

An urgent telegram demanding my presence in London upon that date at noon sharp vexed my good nature, but also piqued my curiosity. Such an august individual, who was once described by his own brother as the "British Government, Personified", could not easily be denied. Not even by an old retired army surgeon.

I was duly shown to the Strangers Room, the only place within the eccentric building that allowed normal conversation, and immediately recognized the imposing figure of Mycroft Holmes, much grayer and less corpulent than I remembered from our last encounter. Seated mournfully by a window was a small perfectly elegant lady, dark of hair and eye. She was very handsome, if worry-worn, her fine features denoting a more exotic heritage than usual in an attractive English woman. I would certainly have remembered if I'd met her before. Standing stalwartly beside Mycroft Holmes, much to no small amazement upon my part, was the solemn iron-mustached Prime Minister himself.

"Dr. Watson, good of you to come," Mycroft Holmes offered his great flipper of a hand. "You know the Prime Minister."

The Prime Minister hardly nodded, remaining nearly as motionless as his official portrait. Although the lady was not introduced, she favored me with a sad yet attractive smile.

Mycroft Holmes consulted his watch, snapping it shut again with a distinctive air of conviction.

"I perceive a multitude of queries forming behind your brows, Doctor. Pray remain silent one minute longer and all shall be revealed."

He spanned the space of the room in three prodigious strides, swinging open the door, revealing — to my great surprise — his celebrated brother, and my old friend, Mr. Sherlock Holmes, upon the threshold.

"Welcome, Sherlock. I apologize for the deception, but I surmised nothing less could lure you from those infernal bees," Mycroft Holmes tilted his massive head in my direction.

I hadn't seen Sherlock Holmes in nearly a year. He was leaner, and as a result seemed taller, than ever. At Holmes' first sight of me, the steely fierceness burning in his grey eyes immediately dimmed. I thought for a moment to detect something akin to sentiment settling on his hawkish features, but with a blink he was the aloof Holmes of old once more.

Without so much as a glance toward the Prime Minister, Holmes pressed my hand.

"My dear, Watson, it's quite gratifying to discover the full extent of my brother's rather imaginative exaggeration," he smiled faintly, presenting a crumpled telegram which I read with astonishment.

DR. WATSON DECEASED.
COME AT ONCE. MYCROFT.

I didn't know what to remark, so I remained quiet within the uncomfortable silence of the room.

"Well, Doctor," said Sherlock Holmes, "since I somewhat inexplicably find myself suddenly in London, I suggest that we take advantage of the new Greek and Etruscan vase exhibit at the British Museum. What do you say?"

My old friend hooked my elbow with his wiry forearm.

"Mr. Holmes, I protest your cavalier manner, sir," the Prime Minister came suddenly to livid life. "I ordered your brother to arrange your presence before us. He has done so, as was his duty. Your country has need of you, sir."

Holmes continued to spirit me hastily from the room.

"My country," replied Sherlock Holmes, "appears to suffer from a chronic form of reprehensible and unconscionable embellishment. Good day to you. Come along, Watson."

"The Prime Minister does not exaggerate, Mr. Holmes," the lady abruptly spoke out. "I am Mrs. George Edward Challenger. I understand you've met my husband."

Holmes halted, sighed slightly, and turned to face her.

"Once, more than a decade ago," a smile hinted at the notorious name. "I can certainly personally testify to the professor's scientific proficiency... as well as his rather brutal bare-knuckled straight left."

Mrs. Challenger beamed, brightening her dark beauty.

"However brief your meeting may have been, George always spoke of you with great respect, Mr. Holmes. A rare and difficult thing for a man like my husband, as I trust you can appreciate."

Holmes narrowed his eyes, regarding the lady for an instant, then stabbed rapid glances at his brother and, lastly, the Prime Minister. A shadow of apprehension veiled his pale gaunt features. Shoulders settling back he assumed his old unique comportment of authority.

"Allow me a moment to propose my suspicions as to my role in this dubious matter," he stated bluntly. "I take it that I have been engaged to locate and reveal the exact whereabouts of the infamous Professor George Edward Challenger, who — according to *The Times* — has been missing and is presumed dead these last twenty-seven months. I further infer that Mrs. Challenger believes that her husband is very much alive."

The Prime Minister's moustache visibly twitched in surprise.

"How in Hades did you guess that, sir?"

Holmes grimaced impatiently.

"I never guess," he snapped.

Mycroft Holmes stamped a boot heel.

"Now see here, Sherlock — these theatrical antics of yours are heinously out of place," the elder brother's neck bloomed a deep crimson. "I assure you that this is a desperately secret matter of the very deepest concern for all of England. Why, the very lives of hundreds of thousands are at stake —"

The Prime Minister touched Mycroft Holmes upon the sleeve.

"Your brother never spoke more truly, sir," his voice more grave by several degrees than mere moments before. "I demand to know exactly how you came by this information. If there has been some clandestine breach in our security I must know about it immediately."

Sherlock Holmes turned his back upon the bristling mustache and resigned himself to an armchair. His hooded eyes nearly disguised his growing interest in the matter, though his mouth remained fixed and determined. Automatically, he lighted a cigarette and blew the blue smoke toward the lofty ceiling.

"You may call off our watchdogs, Mr. Prime Minister, the secrets of the Crown are quite safe for now." Holmes exhaled with an exaggerated weariness. "You should be aware of my methods."

The Prime Minister puffed his annoyance.

"You mean to say, sir, that this is more of your deductive reasoning nonsense," his face was starting to purple.

Holmes allowed himself a slight smile.

"Is it nonsense to deduce, after being rather intimately aware of the workings of this government, that the presence of the presumed widow of a private scientific adventurer would suggest such an obvious inference? Why else would the lady be present within this selective company, were that not the case? As to Mrs. Challenger herself being convinced of her husband's survival, well, that is also simplicity itself. The lady would be wearing black, certainly not the stylish dove-grey dress we all perceive, if she were, in fact, in genuine mourning."

I noticed an immediate glint of affirmation in the lady's dark, lustrous eyes and a considerable weight of the earlier anxiety had perceptibly eased from her proud, yet delicate, shoulders.

The Prime Minister regained his stalwart composure. "I see," he nodded. "Now that you've explained yourself, it's really not so very clever at all. Well, sir, now that we understand each other—"

"There is one small detail I need to possess before we proceed," my friend interrupted. "Why is the Crown so interested in locating the Professor?"

The mustache fluttered angrily again.

"That is privileged information, sir," the Prime Minister glowered.

Holmes fully opened his eyes and tossed his half-spent cigarette into the fireplace. Abruptly, he rose to his feet and donned his top hat.

"Quite so. Good day, madam. Come, Watson, a gallery of Greek and Etruscan marvels await us."

The Prime Minister's violet complexion deepened.

"Very well," he spoke directly to Mycroft Holmes. "Show him the damned thing!"

The elder Holmes revealed a steel infantry helmet from a wooden case, handing it to my friend with the reverence of a Holy Relic. It was no different than any other soldier's helmet I'd seen, though I did notice immediately that it had been violently pierced by a rifle bullet.

"The Germans have advanced the effectiveness of their artillery, sir," the Prime Minister spat with no little amount of disgust.

Sherlock Holmes was upon the brink of an inquiry when his brother explained the meaning of the grisly artifact.

"Sherlock," he began, "Mrs. Challenger recently discovered a hidden notebook belonging to her husband wherein he had enthusiastically experimented with a formula, of his own invention, for a new lightweight steel alloy dozens of times stronger than what is currently possible."

I broke my long silence.

"I don't understand," I said, frankly. "It was my impression that Professor Challenger's expertise was, uh, rather is, zoology. How could a zoologist conceive of such a sophisticated formula?"

"My George has a restless mind, Dr. Watson. He rarely sleeps and constantly studies. I dare say, one day, he may well know just about everything," Mrs. Challenger smiled proudly, making her look younger and even more charming by some dozen years.

Sherlock Holmes rubbed his squared, prominent chin.

"The lady hardly exaggerates, my dear fellow," his long white finger morbidly traced around the helmet's bullet hole. "I've read Challenger's monographs on the practical applications of chemistry and physics with keen interest. Regardless of how he is ridiculed by his colleagues, they can't hold a candle to him. George Edward Challenger may well be the greatest scientific mind in all of Europe, if not the world."

The Prime Minister reinstated himself into the proceedings.

"A rather clumsy and discourteous scientific mind, I'll wager," he growled, peering at Mycroft Holmes.

"Yes, gentlemen," he explained to us, "it appears that Professor Challenger's actual formula resided purely within his own head."

"My George memorized everything," the lady sparkled. "He claimed it considerably reduced the clutter of his filing cabinets."

Sherlock Holmes moved to the window, putting a match to another cigarette.

"Allow me to refresh my own memory," his eyes took on a momentarily pensive aspect. "After Challenger returned from South America, he proposed to prove his claims of having discovered a hellish plateau, a lost world — if you will — still populated by the surviving denizens from the ancient Age of the Dinosaurs. As I recall, Challenger delivered such authentication by exhibiting, in person, a pterodactyl which he had captured and brought back alive to London."

Mrs. Challenger moved to my friend, her dark doe-like eyes suddenly tragic.

"That's exactly as it happened, Mr. Holmes," her fine porcelain features flushed with feminine ferocity. "But the creature escaped and the assembly of scientists almost immediately pronounced it a hoax. Two of my husband's most trusted colleagues, dear old Summerlee and young Mr. Malone of the *Daily Gazette* — both of them sworn eye-witnesses — were ridiculed into professional and public exile. My husband was furious. Even with such a temper like his, I don't think I ever saw him so close to cold-blooded murder as he was toward the entire academic community in those weeks that followed. In the end, George vowed that he'd go back to that primordial purgatory and, once and for all time, return with positive proof of its reality for the entire world to witness."

The heavy silence in the room was remindful of a wake. The dear lady fought back tears, more of outrage than of sorrow. Sherlock Holmes extinguished his cigarette and smiled at her kindly, if sadly.

"Madam, what you ask is impossible," he spoke to her as if they were alone together in the room. "Surely you must see that I am at my own limits, considering my age, and for me to even begin such a journey would be madness. It is my opinion that your brave, brilliant husband met an honorable end to his noble life somewhere upon that mysterious plateau. There are no existing maps or charts of this lost world. No way to even find it, let alone search for clues, now some two years old, of his possible where-abouts. I very much regret that services such as mine are useless to you in this endeavor."

Mrs. Challenger sank back against a chair as if all strength had left her. I felt powerfully sympathetic toward her plight, but Holmes, of course, was quite correct in his assertion. Without a map, without a guide, it would be like seeking a single lost speck of sand from among all the beaches of the world.

"Now see here, sir," the Prime Minister blocked the door. "We do not request, but rather, command this duty of you, Mr. Sherlock Holmes. It is by royal decree that you undertake this mission, regardless of your personal feelings in the matter. Whatever the chances, or the odds, England must have that formula or our boys fighting for our liberty in the trenches will be slaughtered like sitting fowl. Even if there's only the merest possibility of Challenger's miraculous survival, surely the World's Greatest Detective can discover this lone indispensable needle in a haystack for the sake of his nation?"

I didn't like the hot rapacious gleam in Holmes' eyes as he stalked so closely to the Prime Minister that his aquiline nose nearly brushed the suddenly fluttering mustache. A quiet knock at the door stayed his reply, for the moment.

Mycroft Holmes opened the door, receiving a calling card from the butler. His watery grey eyes were astonished as he read the name aloud.

"Apparently, Professor Challenger is... here."

The room was silent as a confessional until broken by the clack of a lady's boots.

Into the chamber stepped a tall, golden-haired young woman of twenty-eight or thirty. Her striking features were, somehow, familiar and yet the intense grey-green eyes almost buried her beauty behind a gaze of such piercing intelligence that I have never before witnessed in one so young and fair. She was, at once, Athena and Artemis, molded into the same divine being.

"Indeed, gentlemen," her voice was low though not unmusical, supremely confident in her rapid inflection. "Professor Jessica Cuvier Challenger — doctor of medicine, zoology, and anthropology."

Mrs. Challenger was clearly aghast.

"Jess... you promised—" she started and stammered, but the vivacious Amazon waved her aside.

"Not the first time I've broken such a ridiculous oath, Mother, dear," Professor Challenger held a telegram in her graceful hand. "As is my habit, I've managed to discover the very thing that all of you are so desperately searching for. I am, in truth, my father's daughter!"

She turned her cool scientist's eyes upon each of us and finally relinquished the telegram to Sherlock Holmes. After scanning it, Holmes handed it to me with a smile of satisfaction. It was sent from Central America. I'm reprinting the message below exactly as written:

DELIGHTED TO GUIDE MR. SHERLOCK
HOLMES TO LOST WORLD. WILL LAY ODDS
THAT OLD SON OF A BITCH CHALLENGER
IS STILL ALIVE.
— LORD JOHN ROXTON

⊹⊹ ⊹⊹ ⊹⊹

The cave man had slept for two full days. His belly again
gnawed at him to be filled, but it was the desiccation of
his painfully parched throat which provoked the descent
from his protective little grotto fortress in the limestone
cliff. He had chosen this refuge principally because of the
small stream of fresh water that poured continually near
its hidden entrance, but an aberrant ten-day drought had
caused the flow to vanish.

There was no avoiding it. Gathering up his club and
spear, slipping his treasured doeskin medicine bag around
his burly neck, a chill raised the hackles along the
caveman's spine. His aching, adventure-etched body was
already going through the motions before his clouded mind
caught up with it. He must return to that monstrous river
or die.

The long, snakishly winding, narrow river was an awful
place, indeed. It was there that many of the terrible, most
massive creatures of the Plateau came to sate their unfath-
omable thirst. Canopied in black-green shadows from
towering vine-webbed branches, even at high noon, the
river banks were a twilight world of creeping, crawling,
living delirium and unseen impending death.

The cave man waited impatiently behind a concealing
boulder, his swollen tongue raking across cracked lips. He
knew what he was doing, the strategy worked flawlessly
a thousand times past. The safest place among giants was
to form an alliance with them.

The massive jagged-spined stegosaur wouldn't do. The
hulking reptile was docile enough, except when roused,
but the two tons worth of meandering, slashing, spike-
tipped tail made the beast a companion of unpredictable
peril. The cave man warily kept his eye on the fin-backed

flesh-eating dimetrodons, but the entire pride was too immersed in glutting themselves with the muddy water to notice him.

He'd nearly resolved to select the company of two enormous exotically crested duck-billed hadrosaurs, but then a great baritone bellow trumpeted the arrival of a lone hundred-year-old deinotherium. Even better, the cave man recognized the elephantine goliath from long-healed foreleg scars caused from the claws of great saber-toothed cats, the splintered skulls of which were embedded forever in the pads of a ponderous front paw, resulting in a familiarly distinctive limp.

Gathering up a bouquet of succulent orchids, the cave man showed himself plainly to the colossal matriarch. Her melon-size left eye regarded the snack tentatively for just a moment, then the long muscular proboscis snatched the juicy blossoms high above to her pink hook-tusked mouth. The cave man had chosen his allies carefully, knowing from endless hours of observation that the deinotherium were predominantly gentle, intelligent and entirely fearless, even in the face of the Plateau's most fearsome flesh-eaters.

Confidently, the caveman followed alongside his lumbering guardian behemoth — safe in the shadow of her protective company — and drank his fill beside her from the edge of the beetle-infested, worm-writhing green-brown river. A swelling wave suddenly engorged the odious surface and for a scant second the cave man found his entire head submerged beneath the water. Coughing up the sulfur-flavored refreshment, he bitterly observed his leather medicine bag floating rapidly away from him. No chance of rescuing the precious little pouch, already it glided among sharp-beaked snapping turtles twice his own weight. The cave man's sole luxury, absolutely irreplaceable, was bade a tender farewell through his tear filled eyes.

Abruptly, the source of the rising river became alarmingly clear as a wading herd of leviathan long-necked sauropods emerged from the bend of the river, the thunder lizards enormously dwarfing every other colossus among them. These majestic treetop browsers, the cave man knew, were the real lords of the Plateau, especially when they gathered in such abundant numbers. The danger of a panicked stampede of the lesser giants around him was a very real possibility.

With a rapid, final, and regretful glance, the cave man scurried away to his lonely lair.

⊹ ⊹ ⊹

"There, lady and gentlemen, is our Plateau!" Lord John Roxton pointed with a weathered bronze forefinger.

Our ominous destination jutted up through the eerie morning mist like a dark green jungle-haunted obelisk. Already the dizzying height within the balloon's carriage had threatened to rob me of my meager breakfast as the humid tropical atmosphere rocked and swayed like an angry sea. It was, however, an excellent and even awe-inspiring view of our perilous objective. Lord Roxton remarked, jabbing an elbow playfully into my ribs, that he felt like a boy living out a Jules Verne adventure. Sherlock Holmes had said nothing at all since we'd cast off and he clung white-knuckled to the carriage handrails.

The last two months had been a flurry of planning, packing, and speeding away at a dizzying pace by motor, rail, sail, and steam. Twice Sherlock Holmes cautioned me that we were being followed, but would say no more about it afterward, even with me pressing him firmly.

Holmes had spent a goodly portion of our journey in silent study of Professor Challenger's recovered notebook. The missing scientist's distinctive barbed-wire scrawl contained enough chemical details on the mysterious super-steel formula to convince my friend of its possibility. Even so, he'd laboriously bemoaned leaving his little Sussex bee-farm and direly confided to me that all we were likely to find was Challenger's bones upon that Plateau, perhaps to eventually jumble with our own. A sobering prediction, indeed, especially as the terrible formation loomed up before us and was, at last, an incredible reality.

"Is that the region you and my father ascended?" the young professor indicated a treacherous slope seemingly somewhat more passable than the others in our sight.

Lord Roxton laughed cheerily.

"No, Miss, we can't see it from this angle. It's climb-
able, obviously, but more than a mite dangerous. I like this
balloon idea of yours much better — saves on lots of sweat,
blistered fingers, and potentially broken-necks!"

She glowered at him, lifting up her pretty chin.

"Refer to me as 'Professor', if you please, Roxton," her
tone was as cold as it was arrogant. "I'm not simply some
Kensington school mistress out on holiday."

Holmes took a sharp long breath and let it out slowly.

"Oh, beggin' your pardon, Mi— uh, Professor Challenger," Lord Roxton grinned, winking at me, then spoke
low into my ear. "Two of them in the world is rather over-
doing it — what?"

I must say, however frequently disagreeable she could
be, Professor Jessica Cuvier Challenger conducted the
piloting of our little airship with the valiant hand of a
seasoned expert. In truth, during the past several weeks
I'd come to the pleasurable realization that the young lady
was most remarkable in nearly every aspect.

Her knowledge of medicine was far in advance of my
own, having studied in both Vienna and America. She
flattered me personally, as well, with a profound familiarity of my written accounts of the cases of Sherlock
Holmes — correcting some of my careless chronological
blunders from her own prodigious memory — and finally
interrogated me most brazenly upon the exact anatomi-
cal location of my Afghan War wound.

Indeed, despite her arrogant, quick-tempered, and
almost artificial personality, the lady's keenly disciplined
brain, utter fearlessness, and her unrivaled physical beauty
had charmed me completely.

Suddenly I noticed and followed Holmes' gaze towards
a small flock of birds pursuing us at a distance.

"An impulsive beak or talon might well rend a hole in
this contraption," my friend mused matter-of-factly. "I take
it, Professor, that you've a perceived notion preventing such
a catastrophe?"

She lifted her excellent field-glasses, nodding calmly.

"The silk is chemically reinforced, Mr. Holmes. I doubt
that nothing less than a rifle bullet could pierce it. Also,

I noticed you warily detecting the electrical charge in the air. You needn't be concerned, there's no chance of fire as these pressure tanks contain helium, not hydrogen."

Holmes rolled his grey eyes at me. The altitude was making him a bit green.

"You seem to have thought of everything," he said curtly.

The Professor lowered the glasses, her breath slightly quickened.

"Everything, perhaps, but the simple fact that my father may have been absolutely correct in all his outrageous contentions. Roxton — have you a rifle handy? Those are most certainly not birds."

They were hideous creatures, such as the tortured nightmares of a madman might concoct. Indeed, the flying monstrosities were not birds nor like any other animal I've ever seen, rather they resembled flapping bat-like crocodilians with wingspans at least twice as great as that of an albatross. The enraged ear-splitting shrieks made it plain that our balloon was encroaching upon their aerial territory.

I'm delighted to confirm that Lord Roxton's marksmanship was every bit as legendary as reports of his worldwide adventures have claimed. Each time he shouldered his rifle; another winged demon squawked and spiraled away to vanish into the thick mists below. After the momentary danger died away, a different surge of excitement impressed us, even Holmes. Professor George Edward Challenger, and Lord John Roxton, had not exaggerated in the least. Such a "Lost World" as both men had long proclaimed, and established science had denounced, did, indeed, truly exist!

"Isn't it marvelous, Holmes!" I could hardly contain my exhilaration.

The passionless machine-like concentration had returned to his pale, gaunt face.

"I would suggest that those high limestone cliffs may be rather more imperative to the core of our quest, old fellow. I distinctly observed at least one cave located near the top that might have served as an excellent long-term refuge."

Professor Challenger focused her field-glasses once again, then lowered them with a quick nod and a beaming smile.

"Excellent, Mr. Holmes!" she agreed, looking quite lovely. "You are truly the first of detectives. Forgive me, in my excitement, I didn't notice those formations. Ptero-dactyls have been my favorites since I was a girl and seeing them alive is quite a thrill. Brace yourselves, gentlemen— we're going to land!"

Our landing was, if anything, even more dreadful than our daredevil launch. I've never had such a helpless sen-sation of vertigo. Densely dark jungle cloaked most of the Plateau's terrible denizens from our eyes, and perhaps that was for the best, but the hissing howls, blood-freezing screams, and thunderous footfalls could not be shut out.

At one point in our descent the balloon's carriage, which contained all our provisions, and us, slightly scraped the slime-skimmed surface of a prehistoric lake filled with such brethren of Hell as only Dante might have imagined. At first what I took to be gigantic swimming crocodiles were, in reality, undulating thirty-foot long marine monitor liz-ards. One of the beasts was lethally ensnared in the stran-gling tentacles of a massive snail-shelled octopus, the likes of which — according to the Professor — hadn't been seen upon this earth for over sixty-five million years. Swooping kite-tailed pterodactyls soared upwards again with fanged beaks full of lobe-finned silver-scaled fish, while magnifi-cent long-necked reptiles with the acrobatic streamlined bodies of sea lions gracefully rolled and sailed through the emerald, algae rich, waves.

We touched the earth, finally, near the base of Holmes' limestone cliff as there was no safe landing area upon its peak. Professor Challenger rapidly set about the task of deflating our balloon and sealing it, along with the cleverly designed collapsible carriage, inside a crate which she buried under a mammoth fern fully one hundred feet tall. At her orders, Lord Roxton, Holmes, and I stood guard with our rifles. She didn't need to tell us. We were taking no chances.

The Professor and Lord Roxton then commenced hurling grappling hooks, with stout lengths of rope attached, at the narrow cave entrance. I was amazed how swiftly and expertly that was accomplished. The cave above and beyond beckoned to be investigated.

"My father may be up there. Blood and brains before brawn, Roxton," Professor Challenger insisted after it was suggested there might be an element of danger within the cave itself.

She clambered up the cliff, in her high laced boots and riding britches, as effortlessly as a spider monkey. Before Lord Roxton could follow, Holmes surprised me by grasping the other rope.

"I'm afraid your old shoulder wound will be a nuisance here, Watson," he said ruefully. "However, I will trouble you for your service revolver. Take care of him, Lord Roxton. I'm lost without my Boswell."

With my pistol tucked into his belt, Holmes bounded up the line as fluidly deft as any man in his early sixties could ever hope to be. It was difficult to believe, at times like these, that he was only two years younger than me. When the scent of the chase was upon him, my friend could evoke an almost Herculean prowess as I'd witnessed, and chronicled, many times in our long association.

Lord Roxton let out a low whistle as he watched Holmes climb up and disappear into the cave. He grinned at me and revealed a silver hipflask.

"Is he a bloodhound or a squirrel — what? Care for a nip of whisky while we're waitin', Doctor?"

I confess to taking a few sips.

"After narrowly escaping from this Plateau seven years ago, I don't suppose that you'd ever imagined being back here again," I said to my famous companion, the steadying warmth of the whisky making me more social.

"Wouldn't miss it for the world," he sounded, between swallows from the flask, as if he meant it. "Besides this time there's more at stake than just the old bastard's bloomin' reputation, eh? What do you think of our young Miss?"

He offered me the flask again, but I thought better of it.

"A most capable lady, surely," I replied.

"She's that, and more," Lord Roxton's leathery face lapsed into a moment of solemnity. "Reminds me a bit of my son, Richard. Fearless. Head strong. Maybe even a little crazy. He's fighting against Germany even as we speak. Youngest major in the American infantry, so they tell me. Guess I'm here as much for his sake as anything. Say, Doctor, does Mr. Holmes really think we'll find old Challenger alive, and deliver him and his formula back to Mother England?"

World-famous adventurer and explorer, proud father, patriot — there was a depth and temperament to Lord Roxton that, even with just those few words, established not merely his profound decency but also elevated his character to the almost mythic level that one expected of him. I found myself very glad to have made his acquaintance.

"Well, I dare say we wouldn't be here now, if he believed such a thing was impossible," I answered, in all honestly.

A wiggle of the ropes caught our attention.

"Hope you're right, Doctor," his easy grin returned. "They're comin' back down — and I've never seen such a pair of long faces."

We scouted the base of the cliff for more caves, finally finding one more suited for our camp. Lord Roxton knew that night dropped swiftly, like a great black curtain over the Plateau, and we had a bright fire blazing at the cave entrance well before the first visible stars. Neither Holmes, nor Professor Challenger, had yet spoken of their morning adventure within the cave. Going along with her suggestion that we eat off the land, to lighten our packs, we were all dining on roasted Archaeopteryx, a bizarre toothed bird from the Jurassic Period, and some unknown, though very succulent fruits, when Holmes revealed his discoveries.

"This lady's father had, indeed, been a resident within the cave," my friend stated in his cool, unemotional manner. "There was evidence of scratches upon the cave floor, unmistakable nail-marks from the soles of worn-out British-made boots in his unusual size. Although we found no journals or scientific equipment, there were two rifles and a revolver in the cave, all without ammunition and badly rusted. Most telling, perhaps, were these..."

Holmes displayed a half dozen cigar stubs.

"The ends are cut, not bitten," the lady explained, "and Mr. Holmes has identified the tobacco which I easily confirmed as my father's special blend."

Lord Roxton kicked a stone into the fire and walked away, murmuring a quiet curse. I felt my own shoulders suddenly sag.

"So," I ventured hesitatingly. "Challenger was in the cave... but the condition of his weapons suggest that—"

"Without a good rifle, no one could survive twenty four hours in this infernal bloody jungle," Lord Roxton said, bitterly.

I wasn't ready to give up.

"Why, the Professor may have another rifle with him!"

Holmes shook his head.

"Challenger hasn't occupied that cave for better than a year, Watson," he said as he grimly filled his pipe. "The condition of the firearms, and especially the cigar stubs, make that plain. There also were signs that a more savage entity has since claimed the refuge. I must concur with Lord Roxton's opinion, tragic though it is. Professor George Edward Challenger, and his team of five companions, perished somewhere here upon the Plateau many months ago."

The lady herself remained even more aloof than my friend.

"Mr. Holmes and I are quite in agreement on this," she added, frankly. "There is no hope. We leave tomorrow. Tonight, I'll take the first watch — no arguments, Roxton. Get some rest, gentlemen."

Though exhausted, I little more than dozed for a few hours. The ache in my heart — and the incessant chattering drone of Plateau insects the size of alley cats — disrupted any chance for real slumber. While Holmes napped restlessly, I rose a bit after midnight, finding Lord Roxton dourly at watch. I observed that the Professor was not in her sleeping bag.

"Think she needed some privacy," he winked without the usual humor. "Headed off toward those reeds. Give her a few minutes."

I did as he suggested, but grew anxious as time wore on. Finally I found her sitting on a fallen log. Tears glistened on her exquisite cheeks in the blue moonlight. Silently, I sat down next to her and patted her soft cool hand.

"We never got on together, you know," she almost whispered. "He was never supportive of my education. Never believed women could be as clever as men. Father and I always argued, even when I was a little girl. From the pronouncements of Darwin, to my refusal to eat Mother's awful omelets, we fought about everything. He was always gone — distant — even when he was home. Brilliant as he was, he never really knew me. Now he never will."

She dabbed at her eyes with a dirty sleeve and somehow the effect was quite elegant. Gazing at her, torn and bruised from the adventures of yesterday, quietly weeping in utter heartbreak, I knew I was looking at the most beautiful woman I'd ever seen.

She regained her dignity with a purposeful shrug, her unpinned golden hair draping her shoulders.

"What would Father say if he saw me now, eh, Dr. Watson?" She managed a lovely, if sardonic, smile.

I smiled back, more gently.

"I've no doubt that he'd be very proud of that same little girl, who wouldn't eat her mother's omelets."

Jessica's lips dropped suddenly, but her sad eyes gleamed with tenderness as she leaned forward and kissed my rough old cheek.

Suddenly, it seemed the sky was falling.

From out of the dense jungle canopy, shaggy black hulks fell all around, surrounding us. An iron-gripped hairy paw snatched my revolver from my hand the very moment I stood, taking some of my skin away with it. The two of us were hopelessly, horribly outnumbered by a savage tribe of what I can only describe as subhuman ape-men.

Jessica managed one frantic shot with her rifle before the weapon was wrenched away, nearly tearing her arms from their sockets. Two of the devils leaped upon my back, crashing me to the fetid filth and decay of the jungle floor. I kicked and struck back like a madman, with no effect upon the beast-men at all.

Through the dim shadows I watched in horror as one of the larger brutes snared Jessica with a single long hooked arm, bounding back toward the trees. Fighting furiously, I was a mere child against monsters. I could do nothing, but die.

Abruptly, the ogre carrying Jessica shrieked then, limp as a puppet, flopped dead to the ground. The remaining horde paused, sniffing the air. Suddenly another one dropped dead. And another. There was no sound of a fire-arm, no indication at all of what was causing the mute, invisible slaughter happening inexplicably before my eyes.

The surviving ape-men fled back into the trees, screaming in terror as two more of their number were struck dead as they ran. The entire horrific incident had lasted probably less than a minute, yet we saw the lanterns of Holmes and Lord Roxton already rushing to our defense.

After rapidly establishing our safety, Lord Roxton scanned the branches with his rifle at the ready, while Holmes bent to examine one of the fallen fiends.

"Watson," he indicated the hideous creature in the lantern glow, "You've just witnessed the most mysterious assassination in history."

"I don't understand," I admitted.

"Observe for yourself," he smiled grimly as Jessica drew nearer, also fascinated. "We heard only one rifle report — presumably from one of you — and yet each of these creatures has been expertly shot through the skull, without noise or sufficient light in which to properly aim a weapon. Quite a puzzle. How do you explain it, my dear fellow?"

The magnitude of the weird circumstance suddenly dawned upon me in full. Immediately, one of Holmes' favorite axioms sprang to mind:

When you have eliminated the impossible, whatever remains — however improbable — must be the truth.

We were not the only human hunters upon the Plateau.

⊹⊹ ⊹⊹ ⊹⊹

The cave man spied on the predators from the high
jungle branches, watching them with a cold fascination.
Caught too far away from his cave while in pursuit of food,
he resigned himself to spending the terrible black night
in the comparative security of the trees. He'd been munch-
ing on tree lizards when he first heard the uproar of the
ape-men, rival hunter-scavengers, always dangerous in
numbers. The cave man furtively moved to investigate from
the gloom of the branches with the practiced ease of a
gibbon.

He'd arrived in time to witness their unearthly deaths,
almost the entire clan, slaughtered as if by a phantom killer.
The ape-men had simply dropped dead. Most of them
didn't even have time to scream. Their intended prey, a
burly old man and a tall, radiant-haired young woman,
seemed as perplexed as the cave man himself. Then, from
among the shielding high branches, he caught sight of the
executioners as they skulked away into the shadows among
the giant ferns.

Interestingly, the killers were only men.

Something more than instinct assured the cave man that
these three new invaders would murder him, too, if given
the chance. There was a feral, cruel press to their features.
Even in the darkness their evil nature was obvious. He
didn't take more than an instant to decide to alter the odds
of survival to his favor.

The cave man's spear and stone-headed club expertly
found their targets, and two of the villains fell dead almost
without a sound. Their older leader, more experienced and
mercurial, escaped wraithlike into the jungle.

A rare glint of humor brightened his deep-set hostile
eyes and the cave man allowed himself a rare chuckle of
amusement.

He was looking forward to tomorrow.

⊹⊹ ⊹ ⊹⊹

The hot, humid dawn couldn't come soon enough.
Hardly surprising that none of us slept.

Lord Roxton held his rifle ready in a steely vigil, while
Jessica and Holmes performed a grotesque firelight autopsy

on one of the dead subhumans. As for myself, I stood guard against whatever other horrors lurked in the maze of the jungle, puzzling fruitlessly over the inexplicable events of the night, and taking some small comfort in the weight of the high-powered rifle in my arms.

The first morning light had barely touched the damp mossy earth of the Plateau when I discovered Sherlock Holmes upon his hands and knees in the slime, intensely studying a boulder-heaped area about sixty yards from the massacre of the ape-men. He was there such a significant length of time, searching and researching, that Jessica and Lord Roxton anxiously sought us out.

"There were three of them, Watson," he refrained from glancing up, still scrutinizing the ground with his lens. "All Londoners, I'll wager, from the make of these square-toed boots. Two of them are young and very athletic, skilled mountaineers, no doubt. The other is quite a bit older and, although quite dependent on them, appears to be the leader. We really must remain at our most vigilant now."

Lord Roxton bent to one knee, nodding appreciatively.

"I'll be damned," he smiled, suddenly more himself again.

Jessica also inspected the tracks. She admirably hid her aching heart.

"I'd hoped for a moment... but, no. None of these footprints are nearly large enough to belong to my father. Even so, this is an extraordinary circumstance, Mr. Holmes!"

Sherlock Holmes sprang to his feet. The keen fire of the chase burned again in his eyes, much like in the old days. I could tell he was well satisfied with himself. For me, the mystery had merely grown murkier.

"Holmes," I was struggling to make sense of it, "do these mysterious saviours of ours have anything to do with your comment that we'd been followed since leaving London?"

We accompanied Holmes as he dashed back over the spongy terrain, to the ape-men killing ground. He minutely examined several of the great tree trunks surrounding us, selecting one; he then took his pocket-knife and dug meticulously into the scaly bark.

"I'd have thought that would be obvious, old fellow," he stated frankly. "And I'd hardly describe them as saviours. We're being kept alive for a practical purpose."

"You sound as if you already know these men," Lord Roxton couldn't quite hide the hint of skepticism in his voice.

Holmes withdrew the blade with a snap, letting a shapeless dull grey lump, about the size of a grape, drop into his hand.

"I suspect Watson does, too," he offered me the artifact.

I scraped its surface with my thumbnail, leaving a mark. It was made of lead.

"A soft-nosed rifle bullet," I mused aloud, when an incredible idea struck me. "My God — Holmes! But it can't be. He's dead."

"Are you so sure? I highly doubt it. This entire mystery is falling into place."

Without another word Holmes returned to the footprints, with the rest of us, again, breathlessly on his heels. He was utterly inexhaustible, racing and weaving through the thick undergrowth, on the scent of the almost invisible trail of our trio of stalkers. Less than five minutes later, we were investigating two more murders.

Holmes examined the corpses hastily, and with difficulty, as they were being devoured before our eyes by a fearlessly scampering flock of crow-sized winged reptiles.

"It's the young pair... dead about four hours," Holmes specifically pointed out their square-toed boots, which were barely intact. "However, they weren't killed by these little fiends. It appears that a stone-tipped spear and a heavy club were used against them, quite efficiently, too."

Lord Roxton eyed the upper tree boughs.

"Looks like we'd best find the other one quickly."

Sherlock Holmes indicted the single pair of continuing tracks, leading deeper into the swamp.

"Unless I am entirely mistaken," he motioned for us to follow. "I highly suspect that it is he who will find us."

The swamp was crawling with an unimaginable multitude of vermin and parasites. Anemic-hued needle-toothed lampreys plagued us, biting through our clothing.

Dragonflies as huge as hawks swooped over our heads, the droning of their wings almost deafening. Extremely bizarre coin-sized arthropods — Jessica identified them as trilobites — attached themselves to us like armored leeches, oozing even into our boots.

The sticky mist surrounded us, swirling in dense steaming ribbons. Every step we took was a calculated risk. None of us, not even Sherlock Holmes, could see more than twenty feet away in any direction. Abruptly, and with no small alarm, we discovered our path blocked by two huge saurians, each easily heavy as elephants, and at least thirty feet long. Their ponderous faces, vaguely horse-like despite the thick scaly hide, seemed unimpressed by our diminutive stature.

"It's only a couple Iguanodons," Jessica's educated tone was in contrast to her expression of wonder. "They're harmlessly herbivorous, unless we get stepped on."

Almost as if on cue, the hulking dinosaurs became visibly agitated and galloped away, narrowly missing us. A series of tremors, each growing stronger, vibrated through the soles of our boots. A tremendous splashing followed, as if a barrage of boulders were being plummeted deep into the swamp. The creature that began to emerge from the mist was so immense, so utterly colossal, that it seemed to eclipse the sun.

The long serpentine neck arched slightly downward, its lizard-like head bowing toward us suspiciously. Even standing there in its regal presence, it was difficult to comprehend how something so enormous could actually be alive.

"A Diplodocus!" Jessica breathed. "I saw some egg casings along the edge of the swamp. She thinks we're invading her nesting ground. We've got to get away from here quickly — without panicking her."

Without warning, the hundred foot long behemoth began a rhinoceros-like charge at us, a living avalanche of muscle, scale, and bone. There was nowhere for us to run.

Then, quite rapidly, before our astonished eyes, the monster began to explode into pieces. Yet, perhaps, that is the wrong word, for we heard no sounds of explosion at all — though the effect was as if the beast was caught in a bombardment of canon-fire. The ground rumbled as the ravaged remains of the mangled giant crashed wetly to the earth.

We gazed at each other, silent in the moment of our reprieve. Each of us, so I believe, knew the real storm was about to strike.

"Drop all your weapons to the ground," an English voice growled from behind us. "You're not going anywhere."

I could barely see his outline, simply a tall stoop-shouldered figure standing in the curtain of mist. An extraordinary-looking firearm was pointed in our direction. We complied, relinquishing our rifles.

Even unarmed, Sherlock Holmes moved assertively toward the intruder.

"On the contrary, Colonel Moran," Holmes said coldly, "it would appear that it is you who aren't going anywhere. Not without us, that is. And you damn well know it."

Colonel Sebastian Moran glared at Holmes with pure hot murder in his eyes.

"Aware of the fate of my companions, are you, Holmes?" he snarled beneath a heavy iron-grey mustache.

"I know much more than that," Holmes stepped closer to the barrel of Moran's amazing weapon. "How tragic for your scheme, that Challenger's secret formula has died with him. No doubt, had you tortured the data from him, you would have possessed a King's ransom. More than enough to rebuild the late and unlamented Professor Moriarty's decayed criminal empire."

Colonel Moran grimaced, showing his stained tusk-like teeth.

"That's quite close enough, Holmes," he raised the remarkable rifle against his ursine shoulder. "You're correct, of course. The existence of such a formula made this damnable gamble a risk well worth taking. Not that there haven't been other rewards for a man such as myself. Never in all the world, since the beginning of time, has there been such a hunt for big game — the biggest game — as I have relished in this Primordial Hell. I've proven myself as the chief predator, almost a god. Ironic, isn't it, Holmes, that I was protecting all of you from harm, just so the World's Greatest Detective could guide me to Challenger and all his secrets!"

The grizzled old murderer was nearly raving. There was a mad yellowish cast to his eyes that bespoke, perhaps, of malaria, syphilis, or both. Moran was no longer the roguishly distinguished tiger-hunter Holmes and I once battled, but he was every bit as dangerous as he was more than twenty years before.

"Your cleverness has faded, Moran," Holmes smiled thinly. "You need us to help you escape from this Plateau. You cannot possibly leave the way you came, aided by your mountaineering henchmen. Even as demented as you are, it should come as no great surprise that we utterly refuse to grant you passage."

Moran pressed a lever with his thumb and the fantastic rifle softly hummed like an electrical dynamo.

"You're wrong, Holmes," Moran sneered as he pointed the weapon directly at me. "Quite an improvement upon my old silent air-gun model, eh? You observed what it did to that forty-ton monstrosity. There won't be enough left of Dr. Watson to fill a jelly jar — unless you do as I demand."

Both Lord Roxton and Jessica made angry motions toward Moran.

"Pull that trigger and this Plateau will be your damned grave," Lord Roxton swore to the madman.

Jessica gazed at me with tear-rimmed eyes. The pain apparent on her bruised, scratched face intensified her beauty.

"I'd say this is as good a time as any, if you please," Holmes said, with a studied ease, directing his voice toward the branches above us.

No sooner had the first furrows of confusion appeared on Moran's murderous face than he was pinned to the earth, impaled with a Stone Age spear.

We stood aghast as the troglodyte dropped down into our midst from the trees. He was covered with filth, crusted blood, and animal skins only slightly shaggier than his own brutish nearly naked hide, and a rich blue-black beard flowed nearly to his waist. Although his height was scarcely a few inches over five feet, the bull-like shoulders and broad apish chest gave the impression of a powerful hammered-down Hercules. In nearly every respect, except one, he was the very image of a Neanderthal Man museum exhibit brought to life. The only major disparity was the unusually high-domed intelligent forehead.

The cave man paid us no heed, leaping toward Moran and snatched up the weird rifle.

"Under normal circumstances, I'd sooner deface the Mona Lisa than destroy such an ingenious instrument," he, astonishingly, said to Holmes and then smashed the weapon against a boulder.

Moran uttered a wet rattling groan, coughing up blood. I immediately went to his side, but there was nothing I could do. The spear had pierced his left lung, narrowly missing the heart by less than an inch. He would be dead in a matter of minutes.

Holmes and our shaggy champion studied each other for a moment in silence. Jessica was pale as a ghost, and even Lord Roxton's bronze complexion had become ashen. Then, the savage's piercing blue-grey eyes fell briefly upon each of us.

"Sherlock Holmes... but why...?" he mused aloud to himself, then slapped an enormous hand against his naked thigh. "Of course! This is about my steel, isn't it? I doubt they sent you here out of concern for my health. The war-mongering bastards."

He nodded at Lord Roxton.

"Obviously you still know your way around, Roxton. Full marks, you damned old campaigner. Delighted to see you."

Next, his eyes narrowed at Jessica, who'd started to tremble slightly.

"No keeping you away, was there?" he said almost reproachfully, then smiled. "You get it naturally, I suppose. Remind me to describe the peculiar sub-species of living pseudosuchian that I discovered, as yet unknown even in the fossil record. I think you'll be very interested."

Finally, he bowed to me, formally as any English gentleman might.

"Ah, yes," his smile brightened. "Dr. Watson, I presume?"

Only Holmes was left unfazed and still capable of speech.

"Forgive me, dear fellow, I'd forgotten that the two of you never met," he said as if in the normalcy of a London street. "Allow me to present Professor George Edward Challenger."

He stood before my eyes, yet I could hardly believe it. Challenger, the man we'd come to find had not only survived — but had even thrived in this terrible place.

Challenger's surprisingly amiable smile abruptly vanished. I was startled and disturbed to see him literally sniff the humid breeze.

"Starved as I am for human conversation," he spoke with some haste, "I'm not the only hungry biological entity upon this Plateau. The blood-scent of the slain sauropod, and this wicked son of a bitch, is luring—"

Before he could say another word, a horrendous creature, more terrible than the most nightmarish dragon of myth, leapt suddenly from the green-black jungle, pouncing upon the saurian carcass with a meteoric impact. I would dream, in a cold sweat, of this forty-foot long scaly demon in the years that have followed this adventure. It was an Allosaurus, the Challengers later explained, although both scientists conceded the animal was considerably larger than its fossilized kin. Perhaps best described as a composite of bipedal crocodile and a wingless bird of prey, the fiend's grinding, snapping jaws towered twenty feet, or more, above the ground. In hideous rips and gulps it swallowed whole masses of meat and bone half as large as a London cab.

As can well be appreciated and understood, all of us ran for our lives — not daring even the quickest backwards glance. We couldn't help but hear Moran, still barely alive, wailing one last shrill and piteous scream of terror.

A hellish death, even for such an evil man.

As for we who survived, our only thoughts were of our balloon and the safety of the skies above. I'm certain that even Holmes relished the notion of leaving this wretched place.

⊹ ⊹ ⊹

Two months later, the secret formula for Professor George Edward Challenger's super-steel had reached the battle-fields and the tide of the Great War turned to Britain's advantage. It was amusing to Challenger and to Sherlock Holmes that they both had the distinction of refusing knighthoods as a result.

Holmes and I had received a special invitation to Challenger's long-planned, and highly anticipated, lecture at the prestigious Zoological Institute — the very place that a few years before had decreed his experiences within the Lost World a fraud. Unfortunately, the weight limitations of the balloon, and our frenzied speed of departure from the Plateau did not allow for the collection of specimens to submit as evidence. However, Challenger and his daughter had written prodigiously since their return to civilization and were prepared to publish their proclamations following the lecture.

Both seemed unaffected by the probability that, once again, the scientific community would ridicule their discoveries.

We found them waiting for us just outside the Hall. Challenger struck quite a different figure in his immaculate white tie and tails, with his great black beard re-sculpted to spade-shaped perfection. Jessica Cuvier Challenger was radiant, reveling in the company of her father, and bravely ready to face the stormy trial of mockery that, doubtlessly, awaited them.

"Listen," Challenger scoffed, beard bristling. "You can already hear the bloody vultures deviously calculating how best to pick us apart. No matter to them that all of my courageous exploration team — and their own hand-picked associates — perished by beast and disease in the very place whose existence they all continue to deny."

His daughter affectionately touched his muscle-thick shoulder.

"No matter, sir," she laughed. "Last time even a live pterodactyl didn't convince them. After it escaped though the window, flying out to sea, all were convinced they'd witnessed nothing more than an elaborate conjurer's trick. We know what we saw, and studied. No one can ever take that away. And, believe us or burn us, they will damn well hear us out."

Challenger laughed uproariously, embracing Jessica and lifting her high above his head, as if she was still a toddler.

"Ah, one thing before you start," Holmes remarked, "Dr. Watson and I have a small presentation. For the both of you."

This was news to me. I was as curious as the Challengers when Holmes drew a cigar box from his inner coat pocket.

"Ah—!" Challenger's eyes gleamed and, again, he laughed uproariously. "My only weakness! I've become even more addicted to the damned things since returning to London. I'd saved a single cigar while on the Plateau, wearing it in a pouch around my neck, resisting the temptation to put a match to it for over a year. It was a very sad day when I lost it in the river."

Jessica laughed heartily, as well.

"A presentation for both of us? You're suggesting, perhaps, that I take up the odious habit, Mr. Holmes?" she genuinely sparkled, ever so lovely in the glow of the street lamps.

Holmes nodded to her with hooded eyes.

"Open and see," he calmly directed.

She laughed again and opened the box, then became solemnly silent. Challenger also looked at the contents. He glanced up at Holmes, back to his daughter, then down again into the box. He was, finally, at a loss for words.

"Lord Roxton delivered it to me. It had managed to conceal itself in his boot," Sherlock Holmes explained. "Fascinating little creature — and extremely tenacious, I might add. As you'll observe, somewhat miraculously, it has remained very much alive."

Jessica reached inside and extended her palm as the trilobite energetically scuttled across the fabric of her glove.

The Grantchester Grimoire

by Chico Kidd & Rick Kennett

Between the years of 1894 and 1901 Sherlock Holmes was an extremely busy man; although by 1902, however, the number of cases that stirred his interest had diminished, and he began to speak of retiring. In that same year my interests also lay largely elsewhere, as I had met the charming lady who would eventually fill the great void left by the death, some years previously, of my wife Mary. Naturally I was spending as much time as I could on the serious business of wooing and during that time, Holmes, I fear, found me a less than congenial comrade when I was thrown into his company instead. Nonetheless I still found myself unable to ignore his occasional appeals for assistance.

Some weeks after my return from the Continent in search of Lady Frances Carfax, we were breakfasting together and listening to the sound of a late-summer downpour battering against the windows of our old Baker Street rooms. Earlier that month I had reached my half-century, and the rain was making my old war wound ache, to say nothing of the new scar on my leg, a souvenir of our recent adventure with the American 'Killer' Evans. Opposite me at the breakfast table, Holmes was reading a letter which had arrived in that morning's first post. Whatever was in it made him cock an eyebrow. I looked at him inquisitively, and he handed me the single sheet of notepaper, on which I read the following:

> *Grantchester, 26th August*
> Dear Mr. Sherlock Holmes,
> I hope that you will be able to help me
> on a matter that, to you, may initially
> appear trivial. My husband, Professor
> Henry Westen, who has spent many years
> cataloguing the chained library here at
> Grantchester Abbey, was working in the
> library last night and did not come home
> for his supper. I went to look for him and
> found him lying unconscious upon the
> floor. I could not wake him. He has still
> not woken and our physician says he can
> find no reason for it, but that my husband
> appears to be more like a man sleeping
> through nightmares than one in a coma.
> The police have washed their hands of the
> matter since they could find no sign of an
> intruder, yet I believe a book to be
> missing — one that had been hidden in a
> secret compartment in the library. I do
> not know what the book might be, but I
> believe that someone has stolen it all the
> same, and rendered my husband uncon-
> scious to do so. I am at my wits' end and
> can only hope that you will consent to
> look into this matter.
> Yours sincerely,
> Eleanor Westen.

While I was reading this missive, Holmes took to his feet and pulled the huge index volume that was his reference bible down from the shelf. Having cleared a space on the breakfast table by the simple expedient of pushing everything to one side with an almighty clatter, he set the book down on the table and began leafing through it.

"Let us see what C has to contribute. Carbuncle, ha! Of the blue ilk, eh? Carfax, Lady Frances — quite a trip you made, Watson. Carnacki, Thomas. Curious name. Perhaps derived from Karnak in Egypt. I wonder why

I made a note of *him*. 'Ex-mariner, gifted amateur photographer'... Bah! 'Occult Detective'. What manner of creature can that be, other than *genus* Charlatan?" He turned pages noisily. "'Chained Libraries in General: Usual practice to provide security for reference libraries from the Middle Ages to approximately the 18th century. Existing Chained Libraries by Location: Mappa Mundi at Hereford Cathedral. Wimborne Minster, Oriel College, Oxford. Guildford.' Finally! 'Grantchester Abbey: These books are chiefly of an occult and alchemical nature, some of them extremely rare.' Not a great deal of help, though it might tempt a book collector." He indicated the letter which had set off this flurry of activity. "So, Watson, what do you make of it?"

I handed him back the letter. "It is all rather thin stuff, Holmes."

"Life itself is made of thin stuff; it is the weaving together that makes for interest." My friend took up the letter again. "I *believe* a book to be missing," he read. "A hidden book, Watson, a secret book stolen from a chained library. Does that not strike you as significant?"

"Belief is not the same as fact," said I. "You taught me that."

"Belief is a strange thing," replied Holmes quietly. "My three years wandering the world after my encounter with Professor Moriarty at the Reichenbach Falls taught me not to be as dogmatic on certain subjects as I once was."

"It still seems hardly worth your consideration. There may not have even been a crime committed."

Holmes shot me an amused look. "Well, Watson, since you are so sure this is not worthy of serious attention it might be as well that I go to Grantchester alone. I would not wish you to waste your time and I don't doubt that Professor Westen's nightmare state is quite beyond your medical experience."

This stung me, as of course it was meant to. I said, "Where you go, Holmes, so go I. Even if it be a fool's errand."

"Splendid!" And he gave one of his rare laughs. "Hand me the Bradshaw, if you will."

Although the rain had mercifully eased, it was certainly chilly enough for us to don our ulsters for our trip to St. Pancras station. With a telegram dispatched via the boot-boy, we had ample time to hail a hansom; but the traffic in the Euston Road was, as usual, a disgrace — not helped by a brewer's dray which had shed its load, adding the pungent odor of spilled beer to the usual city stinks. I wrinkled my nose.

"Sometimes I completely sympathize with your desire to retire, Holmes," I said.

But his mind was elsewhere. "What do you suppose this curious sleep of Professor Westen's might be?" he asked. "'Like a man in a nightmare' — and we may surmise it has lasted some two days or more. Even normal sleep goes through stages, Watson, does it not?"

"Mesmerism?"

"Hypnotism, I believe it is now more commonly termed. And yet he was alone within a locked room. Watson, there is more to this than a simple theft. I feel it! But here we are at St. Pancras."

I confess that the thrill of the chase had thus far passed me by, but Holmes was evidently in his element, so I devoted some thought to Professor Westen's plight. Without examining the gentleman I could only make educated guesses, and as Holmes had often said, it was a capital mistake to theorize without data. Nonetheless, when we were seated in our carriage and fairly on our way I hazarded a guess.

"Opium? Or some derivative thereof?"

Holmes shook his head. "Not if the subject is still unconscious. And his physician would have detected it."

"Then some other poison, one a provincial doctor might not have encountered?"

"Poison seems likely, I agree. Yet my mind keeps circling back to the idea of hypnotism. Yes, Watson, I do believe we have an interesting case before us."

His sudden eagerness caught my own fancy and swept aside my original misgivings. "The game's afoot, Holmes!" I said, with a genuine smile.

"Indeed it is, Watson," replied my friend. "Indeed it is."

Grantchester, in pleasant contrast to London, was bathed in brilliant sunshine. The station was deserted, although we were not the only passengers to alight. A young man in, I judged, his early thirties also disembarked, and strode purposefully towards the exit, giving us a polite nod as he passed. I touched my hat in response.

"That gentleman was a merchant seaman until a few years ago," remarked my companion in a conversational tone.

"Indeed? What makes you draw that conclusion? He is a long way from any port of significance."

"His gait, mainly. The sailor never quite loses that nautical roll."

"He might've been a Navy man."

"No. That nod of the head was entirely too casual."

We emerged from the station into a pretty English country lane, just behind the ex-seaman. A pony and trap stood outside, and he was endeavouring to persuade the driver to accommodate him.

I indicated the conveyance. "I fancy that he was sent to meet us."

"Hush," Holmes whispered and placed a finger to his lips. "Let us hear what our sailor has to say."

"No, sir," the driver was telling him. "I were sent to fetch those two gentleman to t'Abbey."

"But we are all going to the same place — oh, never mind." He turned to face us. "I beg your pardon, gentlemen. As I too am going to Grantchester Abbey, would you be so kind as to let me accompany you?"

"Do you know Professor Westen?" Holmes enquired.

"I am... a friend of the family."

"Mr. Thomas Carnacki, if I am not mistaken," said Holmes.

"At your service, sir," replied the other, his face taking on a bemused expression.

I shot an astonished glance at Holmes.

"Yes, a singular coincidence, Watson. Our 'Occult Detective' has an interest in this as well." Then, ignoring the ex-mariner's extended hand, he said stiffly, "I am Sherlock Holmes, and this is my associate Dr. Watson."

Carnacki's face broke into a grin. "I don't know which surprises me more — meeting the famous Mr. Holmes here of all places, or having a demonstration of your equally famous deductive powers. What gave me away, may I ask?"

"Your history as a sailor and photographer are readily available to anyone who knows where to look," Holmes replied. "You have had a tattoo of an anchor removed from the back of your hand, but a trace remains. Also you have a discoloration on your hand that is peculiar to the chemicals used in the photographer's dark room. Finally, there is a certain esoteric value in this case which I am sure would attract a person in your dubious 'profession.'"

"Holmes!" I expostulated.

"It's quite all right, Dr. Watson," said Carnacki. "When I took up this line of work I quickly learnt to tolerate sneers and suspicion." He nodded to Holmes. "Might I be so forward as to ask why you are here?"

"Probably for the very same reason that you are, to investigate the probable theft of an ancient manuscript."

"My God!" Carnacki exclaimed, then muttered something that sounded like, "Is that what he was trying to tell me?"

"Mr. Carnacki," said I, "just what does an 'Occult Detective' do?"

Carnacki smiled, a little self-deprecatingly, seeming to recover himself. "Mostly I investigate hauntings — both hoaxes and those which might not be hoaxes. Recently I have been exposing fraudulent mediums. Was it Mrs. Westen who called you both in?"

"It was. And yourself — are you here as a family friend or in your 'official' capacity?"

"Probably a bit of both. It was during the course of investigating a séance that I learned of trouble at the Abbey. Professor Westen came to me in astral form. He was holding a particular scroll and appeared very distressed, so I knew I had to come."

"Interesting," said Holmes silkily, though I had noticed his lips purse at Carnacki's mention of astral travelling.

"But we should not linger here talking while there is work to be done. We can all sit fairly comfortably in the trap, although I fear Watson here has grown a little stout of late."

I was a little hurt by this remark, but Holmes is often careless of people's feelings and I did not take it to heart. I was more concerned for Carnacki and felt a pang of sympathy for him. Holmes could be intimidating, and he had obviously taken against the young man.

We boarded accordingly; the driver flicked his whip, and off we lurched in the direction of Grantchester Abbey.

A short while later we passed a picturesque ruined pile showing little evidence of the substantial edifice it must have been, save for the remains of a Gothic arch. Behind it, hedged by yews, stood a sturdy grey church with a solid-looking tower from which the sound of bells was pealing. Carnacki, who had been silent for the course of our journey, indicated the ruin with a wave of his hand.

"Grantchester Abbey," he said, somewhat superfluously. "And *that*," he continued, pointing to the end house of a row of cottages, "is where Professor Westen lives."

"What on earth is going on?" I exclaimed, for an extraordinary commotion was centered upon this house. A middle-aged woman in housekeeper's dress was apparently having a bout of hysterics in the middle of the front lawn, while a younger lady, presumably Mrs. Westen herself, was endeavouring to calm her down; around them a small terrier was tearing, barking furiously and pursued, with little success, by a red-faced maidservant.

There was an element of farce about the scene; but I could not fault Carnacki's reaction. He sprang to the ground, vaulting over the side of the trap, and sprinted towards the ladies, stooping to gather up the dog en route. I seized my medical bag and followed more sedately, having at least smelling-salts to offer.

Carnacki was now hesitating, the squirming terrier in his hands. I turned to the maid, who was nearest. "You seem a sensible girl — what's your name?"

"Susan, sir."

"Take the dog, Susan," I said. "That will help the most. And then I will see to Mrs.—?"

"Mrs. Allison, sir," she replied, holding out her hands for the terrier and tucking it under her arm with an air of long practice. Carnacki nodded distractedly in thanks.

Mrs. Allison responded to the *sal volatile* and subsided into weeping, and I was eventually able to make out what she was saying.

"It was like Frank— but... but..." She put her hands to either side of her eyes and howled anew.

"Frank was her husband," said Mrs. Westen who was looking almost as agitated as the housekeeper. I looked up and saw her properly for the first time: she had a heart-shaped face with a determined set to her jaw, and dancing dark eyes that would be very attractive when not red from her own grief. "It... it stood at the window. It stood at the window and stared in at us with big empty eyes," she said in an oddly strained voice. Then, seeming to collect herself, she went on more calmly, "You must be Dr. Watson."

I straightened and held out my hand to her. Susan, having stowed the dog somewhere, helped Mrs. Allison to her feet. "At your service, Mrs. Westen." I turned as my friend hurried up to our little group. "And here is Sherlock Holmes," I said.

"*Was* her husband?" Holmes asked.

"Yes," replied Mrs. Westen. "He died two years ago. Good Lord, Mr. Holmes, he died two years ago and yet something that looked very much like him stood at the kitchen window not a minute before."

By the expression on my friend's face I could see he was already dismissing all this as female hysteria. But Carnacki was wide-eyed with interest and looked first to the two women, then at the window and back again.

"Has this ever happened before?" he asked Mrs. Weston.

"No!" she said and shook her head vigorously. "No, never!"

"Sudden ghosts," he muttered.

The housekeeper showed no sign of becoming more coherent, and was in such evident distress that I judged it best to administer a sedative before yielding Mrs. Allison's care to Susan.

"Pray tell us what happened, Mrs. Westen?" Holmes asked with ill-concealed impatience.

"Yes, of course," the lady replied. "I was discussing menus with Mrs. Allison in the kitchen when someone rapped on the window. We looked up and both of us saw... something that was the image of Frank Allison but with great, deep, dark hollows where his eyes should have been. When I went outside there wasn't a soul to be seen."

"I meant with *your* husband, Mrs. Westen," said Holmes.

I saw Carnacki hide a smile. "Mrs. Westen," he said, "with your permission, I think my time would be put to better use if I could now see the library."

She nodded, and ran a hand over her hair. "Yes, of course. Ask Susan if you need anything. She is still rather new here, but a bright girl."

Our Occult Detective took his leave.

"What is Mr. Carnacki's interest in this matter?" asked Holmes.

"Oh, he helped my husband with the library a few years ago. I'm not entirely sure what he did, but I'm convinced it had something to do with the missing book."

"Ah yes, the putative missing book." Holmes smiled. "I am still not entirely clear as to why you think a volume is missing."

She shot him a sharp look. "I *deduced* it, Mr. Holmes. Henry was lying unconscious in a locked room. A secret compartment whose existence I previously knew nothing of stood open and empty. Something must have been in it, and the room is a library after all. What else was I to think?"

Holmes is often not at his best when confronted by the more intelligent members of the fair sex — and for just a moment his expression resembled that of a man who had unexpectedly bitten into a hot pickle, though he quickly recovered himself.

"I think we should see Professor Westen now," said Holmes. "Come, Watson, your expertise will be needed."

Mrs. Westen bustled ahead of us, ushering us into the cottage and up a flight of stairs. We reached a landing and passed through an open door. There, in a bed, Professor Henry Westen lay still beneath a coverlet. He had a full head of hair, dark like his drooping and untrimmed moustache, without any trace of grey, which gave the impression of a man young for his academic distinction. His face was thin, pale and immobile, but as I stooped for a closer look he began to move his head in an erratic, agitated way upon the pillow and made incoherent grunts and growls deep in his throat. Here indeed was "a man sleeping through nightmares" as Mrs. Westen had described him in her letter.

"Has he been able to drink anything?" I asked, opening my bag for thermometer and stethoscope.

Mrs. Westen nodded. "When he is calm and quiet I can press him to take a little water or tea. He will swallow, but he simply will not wake." This last she spoke in a distinct tone of frustration.

"A good indication, Watson, that our hypnosis supposition may be close to the mark," said Holmes, examining the professor's hands, particularly some slight skinning of the right knuckles, before turning his attention to the clothes draped over a bedside chair.

"Indeed," said I. "His temperature is normal, his pulse is slow and even and his breathing is that which I would expect of a man in deep sleep. The question now is, who was the hypnotist?"

"Why not ask him? If this is a case of hypnotism it naturally follows that the professor is in a highly suggestive state."

I bent closer and said, "Professor Weston, who has put you into this trance?"

The man in the bed began to toss and turn again, and I became aware that his harsh grunts and growls concealed words, or rather *a* word, though it made little sense: it sounded like "Sigsand," repeated over and over.

Holmes, with a pair of the professor's shoes in his hand, turned to Mrs. Westen with a frown. "Who or what is Sigsand?" he asked.

"It is an ancient book — or rather manuscript in the form of a scroll — of forbidden lore," replied Mrs. Westen, "on which Henry and Mr. Carnacki worked some time ago. They were very secretive about it, but I believe they were engaged in translating it."

"Could it be the missing book?"

Mrs. Westen went deathly pale and gasped, "Heaven help us! Might someone think they could use it for wicked purposes, Mr. Holmes?"

The man in the bed gave a horrible moan, exclaimed, "I will not!" in a terrible voice and dropped back into growled incoherencies.

"Professor?" said I. "Can you hear me?"

His eyes snapped open. I jumped.

Mrs. Westen gasped. "Henry?" and someone else said, "John."

It was a woman's voice, but so muffled and distant that I could not tell from whence it came, nor for the moment recognize it, though I should have.

A tap at the bedroom window turned my attention there — and my heart flew to my throat. There at the glass, staring in at me with black hollows where her eyes should have been, was the face of my late wife.

"Mary!"

My brain felt like a lump of ice within my skull and the room rocked about me in a giddying dance as the spectre of my dead wife and I gazed at each other across an unknowable abyss. And all the while I was vaguely aware of Westen repeating, "Sigsand... Sigsand," in a voice that spoke of effort and pain.

As if from a great distance, I heard Holmes gasp, followed by the double thump of the shoes he had been examining hitting the floor. The sounds seemed to break the spell for we rushed across the room together, and as Holmes flung open the window the ghastly visage of she whom I had once loved seemed to sweep away from the glass and fall beneath the level of the sill. We craned our heads out, but there was nothing to see — no face, no ladder, no strings or wires, nothing but a curious mist thickening about the lower portion of the cottage many feet below.

"Did you see her, Holmes?" I gasped.

"*The* woman," he said with a queer, intense expression.

"*The* woman?" I repeated dully, puzzling at his words until I recalled that this was how he habitually referred to Irene Adler, the American adventuress who had bested him in the Bohemian scandal affair. "Holmes," I said as levelly as my shaky voice allowed, "It was the image of my wife Mary."

"No," he said. "It was..." We looked at each other in silence for a moment, then Holmes said very quietly, "Mrs. Westen, was there anything at this window just now?"

"Nothing, Mr. Holmes," she answered, as much mystified by our actions and exclamations as by the question. "We are twenty feet from the ground. What could possibly be at the window?"

"What indeed?" said Holmes. "I think, Watson, we should repair to the library."

"I'll ring for Susan to show you the way," said Mrs. Westen, but my friend demurred and said we would find our own way to the church and its chained library.

Once out of the door, however, I began to wonder if that might be easier said than done, for we were shrouded within the thickest fog I had ever encountered. It was like being encased by masses of grey wool, and almost as palpable. Not at all like the wet yellow London particulars. Yet, for all that, it was still a fog. We could barely see a yard in front of us, and the moment we left the door of the cottage we were groping like blind men along the wall. Presently we rounded a corner and found ourselves in that open space of coarse grass upon which stood the abbey ruins.

"Quite an *outré* case this missing book affair has turned into, eh, Watson?" I heard Holmes say somewhere immediately ahead of me as we picked our way along. I voiced some vague agreement, and he continued, "Which may yet prove to be less than it seems."

"What I saw was utterly convincing... as I believe it was for you, at least momentarily."

"Remember, Watson, there is hypnotism at work in this case. For the present I shall give human trickery equal consideration with spectral manifestation. You observed how friend Carnacki absented himself immediately upon arrival?"

"The library was of immediate interest to him," said I, defending the Occult Detective. "Do you suspect him?"

"I make no accusations. I merely note the fact. In any event, Watson, you will agree with me that I have not led you on a fool's errand... that was the phrase you used, I believe?"

I gave a non-committal grunt as we shuffled on through the fog. Its dullness deepened, it grew thicker and closer, claustrophobic and suffocating, our footsteps as queerly distorted as were now our voices.

"I think there's something distinctly unnatural about this fog," said I, as much to break the deadening silence as to state the disturbingly apparent.

"Yes," said my friend, but refrained from further comment. I knew he detested any suggestion of the supernatural, and yet I was certain he would welcome a ghost over stagnation any time. Indeed, I was beginning to think that the supernatural was what we had run up against. It was not a wholesome thought there with the close greyness about us, creeping among the ruins of an ancient abbey, edging past broken arches and columns. It became a simple matter to imagine ghostly monks with nothing but darkness beneath their cowls walking silently close behind or looming up before me out of the fog.

Then, as if my wandering imagination had overtaken reality, there was a loud crash, followed by a piercing cry, such that I had never heard issue from either man or beast. I stared uselessly into the fog, unable to tell from whence the sounds came. Then a hand clutched at my arm and I almost yelled with fright.

"Watson!" said Holmes, invisible at my elbow. "Listen. Something approaches."

Something was indeed approaching. I did not hear it, I could not see it, but I *knew* something was coming all the same, as I'm certain did Holmes at that instant. And I knew that its motion through the fog was swift and unerring, exuding a sense of its utter wrongness as it rushed silently and invisibly upon us. Within seconds this grew in me to an unreasoning fear, to horror, to animal terror, to a sure knowledge of this thing's hatred of my very humanity. The sensation overwhelmed me like an ocean wave of pure malignity. I cried out as it all but crushed me down into the rank grass. Then as swiftly as it had come, it was gone, passed unseen and the horror of the moment faded like the dwindling memory of a fevered dream.

"Did you... did you feel that, Holmes?" I gasped.

"Yes... an experience I should not wish to repeat," he replied in a voice that struggled to regain its composure, part amazement, part disgust, as his figure grew more distinct before me. The fog was rapidly lifting.

"Thank God," said I, never meaning it more literally.

We were, I saw now, within a few steps of the church. Its great oaken door was wide open, flung back upon its hinges.

"Carnacki!" Holmes shouted, but his cry went unanswered and rang hollowly about the church. All manner of dire thoughts passed through my mind as the silence lengthened. Cautiously we made our way through the church to the chapter house, which contained the famed chained library of Grantchester. Carnacki was sitting on the floor in the shadow of a great octagonal table upon which lay ancient books bound by links of chain. He was surrounded by what looked like a hastily chalked five-pointed star, and as we approached he began an extraordinary and complicated gesticulation with both hands.

"Good Lord!" said I.

Holmes chuckled. "The First Sign of the Saaamaaa Ritual, Watson. A supposed defence against occult forces."

Carnacki visibly relaxed. "Jove! You're real. I had to make sure you were who you seemed," he said, standing up. "So, Holmes, you understand?"

"I understand, which is not the same as belief, which in turn is not the same as fact, as Watson was remarking earlier."

"Is Professor Westen all right?"

"As well as can be expected for a man in a deep and protracted trance," said I.

"Trance? Ah... yes. A psychic attack would explain both the astral projection that brought me here and what has happened just now. I was making a search of the library in the hope Professor Westen may have shoved *The Sigsand Manuscript*—" here Carnacki indicted the secret niche, now open and empty, within the octagonal table, "—into a cupboard or shelf... when something came unbidden into the room."

"Some*thing*?" said Holmes.

Carnacki frowned, as though he were trying to recall a dream. "The bell-ringers had just left — I heard the door close — and there was a time of silence while I looked about the shelves and cupboards. Then a dog barked briefly somewhere outside and it was after this that I heard the church door open again, but very stealthily it seemed. I remember thinking how queer this was, and then I remember turning around and seeing... a small figure, I think, at the library door." Carnacki spread out his hands at his inability to describe it further. "It approached me slowly. I don't know what it was, nor exactly what shape it took, but I know that something else crawled or slithered along the floor beside it. And as it crept nearer I seemed to be trying to fight off a terrible need for sleep as someone was whispering 'Sigsand... Sigsand' over and over. I recollect snatching a piece of chalk from my pocket... and then had no more sense of time passing until you entered."

"Extraordinary," said Holmes in a neutral voice while his gaze roved around the library: now on the octagonal table with its burden of chained books, now on the surrounding shelves and cupboards, now on the radiators, with their grey heating pipes, spaced at intervals along the wall. Finally he looked again at the drawn five-pointed star within which Carnacki remained, as if still unsure of our corporeality. "I wish I had thought to invest in a piece of chalk. It might have saved me untold trouble throughout the years."

"Make mock if you wish, Mr. Holmes," said Carnacki, though without rancor. "Even a rough pentacle is a fair defence against most Aeiirii developments, though I might not have survived even a minor Saiitii manifestation. It is the wisdom that is behind such as this pentacle that is the soul of the book we seek. Deduction and knowledge of all things worldly is your school. Mine is the lore of magic as written by Sigsand and others — that and arcane wisdom combined with modern science. We both seek the truth, but our adversaries are of different stuff: the criminal and the Abnatural."

Carnacki's words, though in places incomprehensible, impressed me with their heartfelt sincerity, and I could see that Holmes too had also taken them in with a measure of acceptance he might not have displayed earlier. He was about to speak when, from the tail of my eye, I noticed a small figure appear in the library doorway. I swung around with a shout, expecting to see heaven knew what, startling Holmes and Carnacki in the process.

It proved to be Susan, the maid.

She regarded our reaction with an odd, bemused expression. "If you please, gentlemen, Mrs. Westen said I should make certain you found your way."

"You may tell your mistress," said Holmes, "that we are all quite safe and that we will be back to the house presently. I'm afraid it appears the *Sigsand Manuscript* has in fact been stolen and is quite beyond recovery. There is nothing further either Mr. Carnacki or I can do here."

"What—" began Carnacki, but stopped as Holmes waved his hand behind him in a quick, shushing gesture.

"Very good, sir," said Susan. After bobbing a curtsy she left to convey the news to Mrs. Westen. I could not imagine her receiving it with any equanimity.

"What is this, Holmes?" I asked indignantly. "Surely you're not frightened that there really are ghosts at the bottom of this business?"

"Not at all, doctor," said Holmes. "Mr. Carnacki, have you by chance a sounding hammer?"

In reply Carnacki produced a small hammer from his bag. "It's invaluable in finding hollows in walls and false panels. More than one ghost has been laid with its use."

Climbing onto one of the radiators, which lined the library walls, Holmes methodically tapped along the length of its brass feed pipe, rapping out several high notes before hitting a dull *thunk*. A moment more and he had unscrewed the pipe joint, dislodged the pipe itself and was carefully knocking the end of it against the palm of his hand where fell, like a conjurer's trick, an antique parchment scroll.

"Jove!" said Carnacki. "*The Sigsand Manuscript!*"

"But who put it there?" I asked.

"Is it not obvious?" said Holmes. "Professor Westen. There were scuff marks on his trousers and shoes which indicated to me that he had been doing a bit of climbing. The injury to his right knuckles suggested his hand had likely slipped while undoing the pipe joint."

"And he did this," said Carnacki, "to hide it from whomever held him in trance to steal it?"

"Precisely. And our mysterious hypnotist is someone who knows about the books, covets the knowledge this scroll contains, but has no easy access to the library."

"But how are we to catch him?" said I.

Holmes smiled. "I have already set the trap, Watson, when I gave the girl Susan that message to take to Mrs. Westen. To win our little victory, we must first admit defeat."

Our interview with Mrs. Westen in her downstairs sitting room was as embarrassing as it was awkward. Holmes had rarely tasted of defeat, and as he explained to Mrs. Westen his inability to help he made it plain that he was finding it a sour dish indeed. Carnacki also was clearly feeling humiliated in being "utterly stumped" as he put it, so early in his unique and peculiar career, which could only reinforce the impression of the '*genus* Charlatan.' As for myself, I had to claim that as a general practitioner, I knew little about exotic trance states.

Against this there were, from Mrs. Westen, recriminations of the bitterest kind, all of which we thoroughly deserved. To her accusations that we had not even attempted to find a solution we had no answer. She implored us to stay at least one night to see whether her husband's condition improved, but we denied her even that. Our behavior toward the lady was wretched and beastly. It pained me, as I know it pained Holmes, but what else could we do?

And so we took our leave, trooping along the road to the station with our long shadows trailing after us. We must have looked a quite dejected trio, which of course was the impression we hoped to give.

Over a light repast at a nearby public house we laid out our plans for the coming night. We were back again at the church with twilight deepening perceptibly around us. The vicar had been told by Mrs. Westen of our arrival and business, but had yet to be informed of our failure and departure, so he was quite amenable to loaning us the church keys and a dark-lantern.

By the time we entered the building it was all but night, and this made Carnacki distinctly uneasy. *"Forces and entities rejoice and gather pow'r in darkness,* according to Sigsand," he said, as we made our way down the aisle with Holmes leading, lantern held aloft. Its light chased shadows out before us like dark conspirators surprised, and though I did not quite believe the essence of Carnacki's quotation, his uneasiness at the approach of night communicated itself to me. I glanced over my shoulder, I peered into corners, I fancied following footsteps and looming attackers.

We reached the library and all was as we had left it.

By the light of our lantern and with Holmes looking on bemused from beside the octagonal table, Carnacki first swept a part of the floor with a broom of hyssop (as he called it), then took careful measurements before drawing a pentacle around both himself and me with a stick of blue chalk.

"I've recently learnt that some colors are just as effective as particular substances and shapes in providing a defense," Carnacki explained. "Doctor Watson, before I complete the pentacle please empty your pockets of all smoking paraphernalia. Light can act as a path for certain of the forces we may encounter, and I don't want you forgetting yourself."

I tossed my matchbox and cigarette case over to Holmes whose part was to stay outside this magical protection, no matter what occurred.

"It appears you're traveling in a non-smoking carriage tonight," said my friend cheerfully.

"And your role, Holmes," said I a little testily as I eased myself down to sit upon the cold floor, "might be better suited if you were tethered by a rope and making the noise of a goat."

"Bravo, Watson!" He began to laugh, then sniffed and asked, "Is that garlic?"

"It is, and it's a smell I hate," Carnacki said, wrinkling his nose and producing from his bag several cloves of garlic strung on a sturdy cord, followed by a gold chain from which depended a glittering pentacle. He stepped through the gap in the yet unfinished chalked star. "Humor my eccentricities, please, Mr. Holmes, and put these on." He draped the strange necklaces around Holmes' neck. "Garlic is a wonderful protection against the more usual Aeiirii forms of semi-materialization that I am supposing this to be."

"And what if it proves to be a Saiitii manifestation, as you call it?" Holmes asked. There was, I noticed, a lack of banter in his tone now, and I wondered if his prejudices were beginning to weaken a little, as were my own.

"I consider it unlikely," said Carnacki, returning to the pentacle to smudge a clove of garlic in lines parallel to the blue chalk. "The hollow-eyed ghost Mrs. Westen and the housekeeper witnessed, and the similar images you told me Doctor Watson and yourself saw in the window, lead me to suspect there is a human will behind this, but uncertain and amateur. Those ghosts were mistakes, I believe. Tentative experiments. Anyone so inexperienced meddling with Saiitii matters would be dead by now... or worse than dead."

"Experiments in what?" said I.

"Avatars."

"Avatars?"

"Hindu mythology, Watson," said Holmes. "Manifestations of their gods on Earth, or in this case a projected persona."

"You put the idea very neatly," said Carnacki. "Doctor, do you have your gun?"

In answer I produced my service revolver from my coat pocket.

"Good. There's no telling what level of materialization may take place. It may prove useful." Carnacki finished both the garlic and chalk stars, enclosing us both.

Holmes sat down upon the floor, back against the wall and closed the shutter over the lantern, plunging us into darkness. So we began our night watch.

How shall I ever forget that dreadful vigil? I could not hear a sound, not even the drawing of a breath, and yet my companions sat open-eyed and close by, Holmes within a few feet and Carnacki beside me with our shoulders touching. From outside came the occasional cry of an owl and once I fancied hearing something scratch at one of the high windows. There in the dark and the quiet, without connection to the world, save for the now fading smell of bruised garlic, I felt adrift in the night. My old wound began to remind me of its presence with a dull but persistent ache. It did not like this long and enforced inactivity where the minutes dragged like hours, and neither did I.

Suddenly I felt Carnacki stir beside me.

"Something is about to happen," he whispered.

Wondering how he could know this, I was overcome with an odd feeling of nervousness. Then Holmes shifted uneasily where he sat, the first sound he had made since closing the dark-lantern. He was, I supposed, experiencing the same weird sensation.

Outside, somewhere in the dark, a dog barked, giving two or three brief yaps and nothing more. It brought to mind the little dog presumably owned by the maid Susan that had caused such a commotion at our arrival. For some unaccountable reason, however, identifying the sound did not make me feel any better.

Then came another sound that did nothing for my nerves — the slow and stealthy opening of the church door, just as Carnacki had described before the attack on him that afternoon. Footsteps echoed faintly through the church, and presently there came a fumbling at the library door.

From nearby came the sound of squeaking metal and I knew Holmes had picked up the lantern by its handle in readiness to fling open its shutter. I drew my revolver from out my coat and aimed into that part of the darkness where I knew the door to be. I heard it too open in a slow and stealthy manner. Something was entering the library.

It came on in the dark, bearing no light, but with a quick, uncanny step amidst the furniture. I was certain it could see us plainly, and I dreaded a sudden attack out of the blackness. The footsteps stopped quite near to me and I heard something scuff against the radiator in what was surely an attempt to surmount it. It had evidently not seen us at all, and it occurred to me in a queer fashion that if there was anything to this magic of chalked stars and garlic it might not only protect but also obscure.

Just above me and to the left someone gave a grunt of exertion, a sound patently human. Light flashed across the room as Holmes unshipped the cover to his lantern, disclosing Professor Westen, still in his bed-clothes, holding onto the radiator's piping as he attempted to unscrew a large connecting joint.

"Is this what you seek, Professor?" said Holmes, and swung the light away from Westen, playing it instead on the ancient scroll of *The Sigsand Manuscript* that he retrieved from his coat pocket.

The light veered again onto the Professor, shining into his unblinking eyes as he stiffly climbed down from the pipe and lumbered towards my friend with arms outstretched like a soulless automaton. Westen was all but upon him when the Professor flinched back, and I saw the pentacle around Holmes' neck flash in the lantern light. Taking advantage of the confusion, Holmes threw the scroll deftly over the Professor's head to where Carnacki, already rising, caught it between both hands. But in catching the precious grimoire he had reached too far forward and began to over-balance. The scroll fell from his hands, hit the floor and began to roll out of the pentacle. Dropping my revolver I grabbed the scroll with one hand while with the other clutched at Carnacki's coat-sleeve as he began to pitch forward over the barriers — gripping him with all the fright and desperation I might feel rescuing a man teetering on the brink of a mighty chasm.

We seemed to swing in a moment of vertigo along the lines of garlic and blue chalk as though they were the very edge of the world. Then I pulled back with all the weight that Holmes had been so unkind about earlier, and we tumbled backwards together. I heard Carnacki gasp with relief, and it was only then I had a queer realization as to the danger we had been in.

But there was no time for reflection. "He's coming your way!" I heard Holmes shout somewhere behind the glare of the lantern which now silhouetted something like a drunken string puppet stumbling blindly on toward us.

Carnacki and I were on our feet now. Professor Westen reeled closer, and attempted to cross the protective lines. As his foot hit the outer garlic barrier we made to grab him and haul him into the pentacle, but he staggered back as if struck and our fingers slid from him.

Westen stood quite still a few feet away, looking in at us with an odd, bewildered expression, his eyes unfocused in a way that made me think he could not really see us, despite the light. Then he tilted his head as if listening to something, a sound, or a voice that only he could hear.

"Yes," he said. A moment later he began to choke, his face turning purple, spittle flecking his lips, his tongue beginning to protrude.

"He's choking!" I cried and tried to move forward to help, but Carnacki thrust out a muscular arm, barring my way.

"No, Doctor! You mustn't cross the lines!"

Before I could even begin to struggle or protest, Holmes was upon Westen and with a mighty shove propelled him across the pentacle. We had him in our grasp in an instant, but it was as though we were pulling the man out of the Grimpen Mire. The resistance was simply incredible. After some seconds struggle, utilizing my weight and Carnacki's strength, we wrenched Westen forward and the power holding him outside gave way so suddenly that we stumbled back. Much to my relief the Professor immediately lapsed into a bout of coughing, which cleared after a few seconds, and I knew he was breathing normally again.

"Hallo, it's Thomas Carnacki," the Professor said, smiling bemusedly at his old acquaintance. "What are you doing here?" He glanced about. "What has happened? What is *The Sigsand Manuscript* doing on the floor? Why am I in my night-shirt?" He then swung around to find me standing at his elbow and with a look of frank astonishment said, "And who the deuce are you, sir?"

"He is my colleague Dr. Watson and I am Sherlock Holmes," said my friend, stepping forward with the lantern.

"The detective? What crime has been committed?"

"Only the strangest case of attempted theft I have ever come across. What do you last remember, Professor?"

"It is important we know," Carnacki said, soothing Westen's obvious indignation at this questioning.

"Well... I was working here in the library," he said. "That was a few minutes ago."

"It was in fact some days ago," said I.

He glanced at me doubtfully, then continued. "I turned and saw someone at the library door, which I thought odd as I'd not heard any of the church doors open, and I was locked in at any rate, and then... and then you three were suddenly here."

"You were induced by hypnosis to steal *The Sigsand Manuscript*," said Holmes. "But you resisted to a degree, so that you were able to hide it, although the trance still held you fast as you struggled to resist so that you lay in your room in a kind of mental limbo for some days. I was sure another attempt to steal the book would be made when we feigned defeat."

"And we were not a moment too soon," said Carnacki. "It seems you finally succumbed to the will commanding you, and having failed you would have destroyed yourself in obedience to the controlling mind. Indeed it may still be active. You should stay within the pentacle until morning. You will still be in peril until then." Carnacki paused, glanced to the side and added, "And so are we all."

"From what, pray?" said Holmes.

"From that." He pointed to the library doorway where stood a small shifting, rippling column of translucent white mist, vaguely human-shaped and watching us with two dark pits where the eyes should have been. It shimmered as if seen through a heat haze, though I felt the room go distinctly chill. As I looked, part of it sloughed off to drop silently to the floor as a horizontal bar of mist, which, as I continued staring, began to shape itself into some indistinct crouching beast.

It growled, a sound part tiger, part wolf, and most horribly... part human.

"Get ready, Watson," said Holmes. The unaccustomed quiver in his voice made me glance around, and I saw he had his revolver at the ready. I knelt and picked up my own weapon. At my first movement the crouching thing sprang, coming at us in a curious lope while still congealing its substance from the mist it had been, a nightmare beast of fangs, fur and shining scales. It hissed, it screamed, it roared and flung out clawed arms as it came.

"Now!" cried Holmes, and together we fired shot after shot into the unholy thing, the reports echoing and re-echoing from the ancient stone walls. The beast was visibly hindered by our efforts, shuddering back momentarily before plunging forward again. Impeded but far from stopped.

It rushed past Holmes, ignoring him as he emptied his last chamber into it. My final shot was at point-blank range, fired just as it flung itself across the barriers of the pentacle, straight for Professor Westen. The three of us fell back. The thing hung in mid-air, checked an instant in its leap, and fell back, giving a single scream far more human than its cries hitherto. It clawed the air with its terrible arms. Carnacki, Westen and I rushed forward, grappling with those flailing limbs, thin and incredibly strong, touching something rough and hot and strangely soft while Holmes on the other side hammered at it with his revolver.

The thing surged forward a little more, scything wicked claws this way and that. I heard Carnacki yell and felt warm blood splatter across my hands.

It edged closer, its claws slashing, its fangs and slavering jaws alive with hunger.

It was crossing into the pentacle!

An arc of glittering gold caught my eye and I saw Holmes, having wrenched off his gold pentacle, swing it like a medieval knight's mace and land it smartly down upon the creature's head. Though it had resisted his hammering and was overcoming our three-fold fight against it, the gold pentacle smote with a sharp *crack* and in an instant it lost all vitality, slid to the floor and melted away to nothing.

It took me a moment to realize we had won, but a glimpse of the blood upon my clothes and hands reminded me victory had not been won without cost. I turned to Carnacki standing beside me, his face a mask of dazed horror, his right coat sleeve in ribbons and soaked in blood.

As I thought of suture and needles, disinfectant and morphine, the rents in his clothing sealed up and the blood faded, as did his expression of pain. He rolled up his sleeve and found no marks at all.

"If it had cut at your throat," said Sherlock Holmes, shining the light full on Carnacki's unbroken skin, "I fancy your mind would have killed you instantly."

"Yes," said Carnacki, nodding grimly.

"The ghost!" Westen suddenly exclaimed.

We looked to the library doorway but the watching apparition had gone.

We found the body of Susan the maid among the ruins of Grantchester Abbey early the next morning. In her right hand were hawthorn and rowan berries and what later proved to be cuttings of St. John's Wort. In her left was a rag doll shaped into the form of some uncertain species of beast.

"I am shocked," said Sherlock Holmes quietly as we looked upon the girl lying dead in the grass. "Shocked, but not surprised that such simple beauty should hide such diabolical evil."

Later that day we apologized to Mrs. Westen for the fiction we had told her with such straight faces; apologies which were readily and gracefully accepted. The nightmare had been ended, and her husband returned to her, alive and healthy.

In the maid's room, under the roof, we found further evidence that she had been meddling in the Mysteries, amongst her possessions were found two grimoires — The Book of the Cypress Tree and The Book of the Forty Words. Their contents, Carnacki assured us, were not for the uncertain and the amateur. As he leafed through her secret notebooks he shook his head sadly, declaring her a poor student.

"Who knows what disasters she might have wrought had she tried to put Sigsand's text into practice," he said, and shuddered a little. "We all strive to better ourselves, but she clearly had little idea of where her particular path would ultimately lead."

Strangely enough there was no sign she had ever kept a dog. In fact the dog that had been seen with her many times since she had taken service in the Professor's household was never seen again.

Two days after our adventure, as we rattled down to Grantchester station in the dog-cart, Holmes leaned across and said to me in confidential tones, "You know,

Watson, my faith in all that is rational and real is as unshaken as always. You see that?"

"Of course, Holmes," said I, although I was still inclined to speculate. He *did* think to strike with the gold pentacle even after our revolvers had failed to stop it.

"But for all that, I do believe that our Mr. Thomas Carnacki has a fascinating career before him."

The Steamship Friesland
by Peter Calamai

For reasons that will presently become obvious I have instructed my solicitors to withhold this tale from publication until 75 years after my death. It could be argued that I should have specified that span after the death of my companion and friend of many years, Mr. Sherlock Holmes, since he is the central character of the tale. Holmes, who so often came close to death during our adventures, bids fair to outlive me by many years, removed as he is from the unhealthy miasma of London to the pure air of the Sussex Downs and rejuvenated by the Royal Jelly, of whose regular use he believes me ignorant.

As I write, the nightmares of the Great War have eclipsed much of the previous public fascination with spectral happenings. Only a few years ago it was not thought frivolous to believe in an afterlife and in shadowy beings who could inhabit both the world of the living and that of the dead. Perhaps when this tale appears there will be still some who can remember the world of 1894 when ghosts moved among us.

My tale begins in the early summer of that year, just a few months after Holmes had effected the capture of Colonel Sebastian Moran, an event which I recorded in 'The Adventure of the Empty House'. Although that is now more than two decades ago, I am able to draw upon the customary accurate and complete notes that I kept of many of my friend's unusual and important cases.

My wife had once again abandoned me for some ailing relations, so I was spending time in our old rooms at 221B Baker Street. I had retired early, but the deep ache from the Jezail bullet that had long ago pierced my flesh kept me from sleep. I was reading one of Kipling's fine stories about Mowgli when my attention was diverted by unusual sounds from the sitting room. Long association with Holmes had inured me to the acoustical disturbances of violin playing, explosive chemical experiments and even indoor revolver practice. That night, however, it was the great detective himself who was the source of the troubling sounds.

Through the heavy oak door it first seemed as if Holmes was carrying on an agitated discussion with a late-night visitor who had somehow contrived to mount the 17 steps to our rooms without alerting Mrs. Hudson, our long-suffering landlady. When I inched open the door, however, I could clearly see that my colleague and friend was alone in the sitting room, apparently talking to himself.

"Are you quite sure it is the same three men behind this trouble?" he asked. Then he waited for some moments in quiet repose, his gaze fixed to a spot in front of and above his head and his hands grasping tightly his favorite cherrywood pipe.

"Would they not have taken great care to avoid drawing undue attention to themselves?" Another pause, much shorter than the first. "Their emotions concerning the matter are that strong, then?" Pause. "But is there any reason to suppose their accusations of miscegenation to be well founded?" Pause. "And Brouwer paid for that with his life!"

To my ears this one-sided exchange was devoid of any meaning. Nonetheless, hearing it served to heighten a fear that had been mounting for some days. Since his dramatic return from the supposed dead that Spring, Holmes had been pushing himself beyond the limits of normal human physical and mental endurance. His days consisted of repeated bursts of frenetic activity, and he appeared not to sleep at night. He ate little and even then at most irregular hours. His features were contorted in a permanent expression of anxiety, and his eyes stared wildly from their sockets. Several times in the past week I had observed him injecting himself from a hypodermic needle. Even his iron constitution could take only so much of such mistreatment, and I had begun to fear that, once again, he might be on the cusp of a breakdown. Now my worst fears seemed to be borne out. But the next morning when I taxed Holmes with the fruits of my nocturnal observations and my deep concern for his health and sanity, his response baffled me even further.

"Watson, I believe you are well acquainted with a fellow medical man of some repute here in London who is an eye specialist, of Irish heritage but trained in Edinburgh and familiar with ophthalmic practices on the Continent. I now desire to consult him on a professional matter. Would you be so kind as to request such a meeting for me?"

"Of course, Holmes, but I should tell you that he put aside medical practice a few years ago to devote himself to writing historical novels. Perhaps I should arrange a meeting with another ophthalmological surgeon instead, one active in the field?"

"I would prefer the original, Watson. We had a brief chat at a social function once, and I was impressed with his clear-headedness and brisk intelligence on matters other than his specialty."

"Can you give me some indication of the subject matter. He is bound to ask."

My friend said he had been reading about the study of the blood vessels and light receptors at the back of the eye, work that had begun more than a half century ago, and made rapid strides recently with advances in the capabilities of dark-field microscopes and in photography. He believed this scientific technique could yield a means of identifying people by their eye patterns, a potentially invaluable tool in the investigation of crime, and he was considering a monograph on this subject.

I dispatched a telegram to South Norwood, home to my medical colleague turned author. He replied instantly that he was pleased to give time to the world's greatest con-sulting detective, and the meeting was arranged for the following day.

When Holmes returned to our rooms, he was a changed man. If anything he appeared even more drawn and fatigued but now his features were in repose and his eyes stared no longer. He sank into the basket chair and, after charging his pipe, spoke: "Watson, I fear that I have not been entirely open with you, but I beg you for the sake of our long friendship to hear my defence of this deceit. I also urge you to keep an open mind concerning what I am about to tell you. I ask you to remember that you have professed to regard me, despite some minor personal foibles, as a man of sound moral character and the highest degree of rationality."

After this astonishing preamble and without waiting for my response, Holmes proceeded to unfold a tale, the telling of which here will, I believe, explain my decision to delay publication for so long. He began by revealing that he had not gone to the former ophthalmologist to pursue the identification of criminals by retinal scans, but instead to discuss communication with the dead.

"Holmes, even broaching such a subject is unbecoming in a man of your intellect and reputation for strict ratiocination ," I protested.

"As you know, my dear Doctor, I have often compared my reasoning in these recondite matters that come my way to the approach of a serious historian like Macaulay. Using indications culled from various documents, he recreates a picture of a time, a place and the great actors who shaped events. In my own way, using observations of everything from a woman's spatulate fingers to traces of clay on a shoe, I construct an imaginary picture of how a crime was committed and by whom.

"So I have no patience with accounts of table-rapping, messages spelled out using Ouija boards, emissions of ectoplasm, or other instances of spirits being able to communicate only through mediums and then only imprecisely. I am also convinced that the spirits of the departed would have neither the desire nor the ability to project some sort of physical presence. Surely projecting an intellectual presence would suffice, especially when communicating with a powerful and attuned mind."

That was precisely the possibility Holmes had explored in his visit to the author and former ophthalmologist, who turned out to be well studied in spiritualism. But what had prompted this interest, I asked, as my bewilderment and anxiety increased. In silent answer he extracted a newspaper clipping from his pocketbook and handed it to me.

> A shocking discovery was made late last night by members of the River Police from the new Blackwall Station. A police launch, on patrol in the Thames, came upon the body of a man floating in the water at the entrance to Blackwall Basin. Although the body was already partly decomposed, papers in an oil skin pouch identified the unfortunate soul as Jan Brouwer, the First Officer of the steamship *Friesland* out of Rotterdam which tied up at the West India Docks here only days ago.
>
> Because there were no signs of violence upon the body, the authorities are treating the death as the type of misadventure that is sadly all too common along a waterfront populated by establishments where sea-going men are encouraged to consume excessive amounts of alcohol.

"That is very regrettable, to be sure. But I fail to see anything that would lead anyone to a belief that the spirits of the departed could communicate with us, either corporeally or by intellect alone," I said with some asperity.

"Of course you are correct, Watson, that the newspaper account by itself contains no obvious indication that spiritualism plays any part in this unfortunate incident. Yet when I read about Brouwer's death I experienced a reaction that has happened to me only twice before. Somehow I knew there was more to this tragedy than met the eye."

Spurred by what he frankly admitted to be nothing more than a non-rational 'intuition,' Holmes had hurried to the police and was fortunate to find the case in the charge of an old acquaintance, McFarlane. He observed at once that the police examination had overlooked the absence of discoloration around the mouth common in drowning. With McFarlane's approval he was able to open Brouwer's chest cavity.

"The incompetence of the police is quite astounding, Watson. There was no water in Brouwer's lungs. The man was dead before his body went into the river. With that knowledge I examined the body closely and discovered that he had suffered a blow to the head, not enough to break the skin but almost certainly sufficient to render him senseless. As well, his eyes betrayed tell-tale sign of asphyxiation, and inside his nostrils I detected several small fibres of wool. From this evidence I concluded that the poor man had been smothered after being knocked unconscious, quite possibly with a cap held fast over his mouth and nose.

"I left the morgue convinced that Brouwer's death was the result of an assault, almost certainly premeditated, and therefore murder. But I had no client, no particular reason to place the investigation of this commonplace crime above the others on which I am engaged, and so I resolved to simply forget about it.

"But here's the rub, Watson. I couldn't banish Brouwer's tragedy from my thoughts. No matter how much I willed it otherwise, my mind returned constantly to that subject throughout the day. I began wondering whether I was suffering from a malignant brain fever brought on by overwork. Then that night, sitting in this chair, I heard a voice."

"Sherlock Holmes hearing voices!" I ejaculated. "My good friend, why did you not confide in me immediately?"

"If I myself had begun to doubt my own mental stability, my dear doctor, I could well imagine how you would have responded. Until now I had always insisted there were no such things as spirits and ridiculed anyone who believed in them. Yet you see me before you today apparently rational and sane, so I implore you to listen to the rest of my tale."

Of all the stories I had heard in that sitting room over many years, the one that Holmes told that evening was the most astonishing, and it was but the first act of the even more astonishing drama that was to follow shortly and which nearly cost us our lives.

The first phrase that my friend heard urgently repeated by that spectral voice was chilling. "Brouwer was murdered by the same men who murdered me," Holmes quoted.

"I tried to ask questions, but I had no more success at first than Hamlet and his colleagues when they were addressing the ghost on the battlements of Elsinore," Holmes said. "Then abruptly the voice varied its refrain.

"'Brouwer was murdered by the same men who murdered me, John Openshaw.'"

Holmes said that he almost bit through the stem of his pipe in astonishment. As contemporary readers of my writings would have known then (and possibly readers of this account will still recall) Openshaw was a young man who sought Holmes' help when threatened by former members of the Ku Klux Klan. They believed he had custody of family papers implicating them and some now-prominent Southerners in criminal activities in the years after the American Civil War. My friend had outlined a course of action that might have placated the KKK, but Openshaw was fatally assaulted and dumped into the Thames that very evening. As I recounted at the time, this had a profound effect on Holmes, who vowed to make retribution for Openshaw's murder a personal crusade, saying:

"If God sends me health, I shall set my hand upon this gang. That he should come to me for help, and that I should send him away to his death—!"

Within the day, by making full use of his remarkable deductive and reasoning powers, Holmes had identified Openshaw's killers. They were the captain and two other crew members of the barque *Lone Star* out of Savannah in the state of Georgia. That very morning the ship had sailed for America, but Holmes instantly put into motion a plan that would guarantee the three murderers were brought back to London to stand trial. Alas, that never happened. A shattered sternpost carved with the initials "L. S." was spotted far out in the Atlantic, and the barque and all aboard her were presumed to have perished in a fierce equinoctial gale.

"But in fact the barque did not founder in the storm. Openshaw explained that to me, once we began talking freely. That and very much more," declared Holmes.

I regarded my friend closely. It was obvious that he was in deadly earnest and not deceiving me with some cunning stratagem, as when he led me a few years previously to believe he was dying from a nameless 'coolie disease from Sumatra'. I decided to remain silent, although harboring grave misgivings about where the conversation was leading. Holmes may have sensed my unease, for he begun speaking more and more rapidly, rushing through the next part of his story.

To his astonishment and relief, Holmes had found this supposed spirit of John Openshaw bore him no malice and was not seeking revenge for having been so casually sent to his death. Against the three KKK members, however, he was set on deadly retribution. For that reason his spectral form had joined the *Lone Star* before it quit the Albert Dock.

"Openshaw told me that what did founder in those dreadful gales was the mail-boat carrying my letter to the American authorities laying out the case for a charge of murder against the three men. The faster mail-boat had overtaken the barque before the storm struck, and the bag containing that note was among the wreckage recovered by the *Lone Star*. Hoping for negotiables or even currency, the KKK murderers opened all the envelopes and thus discovered that their crime was to be exposed.

"As I remarked at the time, they are cunning devils. Openshaw told me how they dumped overboard the sternpost and some other fittings to make it appear that their own ship had sunk with all hands. Then they put into a port in the Caribbean, paid off the Finns and Germans who made up the rest of the crew, changed the name of the ship and sold it."

Seldom pausing even to draw breath, Holmes continued with this remarkable tale of what he had learned from a bodiless spirit. The three men signed on to a Dutch steamer called the *Friesland*, where the ringleader, James Calhoun, was quickly appointed Second Officer on the basis of having his captain's papers. The *Friesland* had called at London several times in the intervening years, but Openshaw had not been able to contact Holmes anywhere in London using mental projection.

"Of course, he had no way of knowing that I, too, was then deceased," Holmes said with what sounded suspiciously like a chuckle.

Finally, there arrived the necessary confluence, with the *Friesland*, the three murderers, the spirit of Openshaw and a very much alive Sherlock Holmes all present in the great metropolis at the same time. Before Openshaw could attempt to penetrate the consciousness of the master detective, however, fate once again intervened. The First Officer had resigned when the *Friesland* docked. Calhoun confidently expected to be promoted, but was pipped at the post by one Jan Brouwer, whose father was a significant investor in the shipping line and a prominent planter in the Dutch Antilles. While some resentment on Calhoun's part was perhaps understandable, his animosity toward Brouwer escalated into pathological hatred after hearing a rumor of Negro blood in the Dutchman's family several generations back. Aided by his two KKK companions on the *Friesland*, he staged a repetition of the murderous attack on John Openshaw seven years previously. All this was witnessed by Openshaw's spirit.

As my companion finally paused for breath, I testily interjected. "Holmes, do you honestly believe in the existence of spirits and credit what one of them supposedly tells you as a true account of events?"

"Pray keep your mind open just a short time longer, my dear doctor. Initially, as you might imagine, I was distrustful and convinced that I was suffering from what Shakespeare called 'paper bullets of the brain.' I was also concerned that Openshaw, if indeed this spirit was a true manifestation of the man, must bear me some ill will for the cavalier treatment he suffered at my hands. That second fear evaporated as we talked at length over the course of several nights. I feel more attuned to him now than to any other person, save yourself of course."

At this juncture Holmes shot me a bemused glance. "Indeed, you may have gathered that much from your covert overhearing of our most recent nocturnal consultation."

"The concern about my mental state I addressed by my visit to your medical colleague in South Norwood. You may not be aware that he is a member of the Society for Psychical Research and also, most importantly, a man of science utterly devoted to the supremacy of rationality. He assured me that communication with the departed has been scientifically documented in a number of cases. As well, it is widely believed among psychical researchers that communication from spirits is the basis for what we sometimes term intuition. That would certainly help explain my actions the day I learned of Brouwer's death."

Here Holmes came to a stop and arched his eyebrows at me in obvious inquisition. Reluctantly I responded.

"I remain far from convinced of the existence of either an afterlife or of spirits of the dead who communicate with the living. All you have told me so far could be explained as the workings of your own mind pulling together items, as you said earlier, to construct an imaginary picture of how a crime was committed and by whom."

"A hit, a palpable hit, Watson. And it is because of the risk of real hits that I entreat you, on the basis of our long friendship, to set aside these doubts for the moment and join me in the investigations I must undertake to keep faith with John Openshaw. I have reason to believe these may involve serious physical danger, and I would be far more comfortable with you beside me, armed with your service revolver."

I immediately assured Holmes that he could rely on me, for indeed I could not possibly have declined such an appeal. He explained the need for quick action, since the *Friesland* would undoubtedly leave port once new cargo was loaded. A quick journey in a hansom cab had us climbing that ship's gangway within the hour. The captain, a stolid Karl Neustaedter, was most co-operative. He took pains to emphasize that Brouwer had been appointed First

Officer on the basis of merit, not family connections. They had sailed together previously on another ship where Brouwer had been a conscientious and more than competent Second Officer. He had upgraded his qualifications since, and the captain had been pleased to find him available in London on such short notice.

"Have you signed on another First Officer then?" I asked.

"Mr. Calhoun has been named to that position on a probationary basis. It was obvious from the start that he expected to get the post, but I had misgivings about his close friendship with the two other Americans aboard. Any suspicion of favoritism would have quickly created tensions and resentment among the rest of the crew, who mostly hail from Asia. I am trusting that Mr. Calhoun will keep a check on his deplorable tendency to disparage anyone not of the white race. But here he comes now."

The man who approached had skin that shone like burnished mahogany, made the more striking by a white goatee and the blazing white of a dress uniform.

"Request permission to go ashore, Captain. I need to complete arrangements for Brouwer's service and burial tomorrow."

"Of course, Mr. Calhoun. But first these two gentlemen were wanting a word with you about Mr. Brouwer's mishap. Let me introduce the famous detective Sherlock Holmes and his colleague Dr. Watson."

Betraying no surprise, the First Officer spoke even before we had finished shaking hands. "I'm right pleased to make your acquaintance, gentlemen, and am willing to give you whatever time is needed for your inquiries. But the undertaker is even now expecting my arrival. Would it be possible for you to return this evening, say at two bells of the first watch, when we could talk at our leisure?"

So it was that in the last rays of daylight Holmes and I again made our way along the narrow and unsavory passages which led to the vast West India Docks. We had just started down Preston Road when an unexplained premonition of deep foreboding caused me to spin round, and

I realized that I had unconsciously drawn my service revolver from my overcoat. I shouted a warning to Holmes before I became fully aware of the gang of swarthy ruffians bearing down upon us. The nearest drove his knife toward my left forearm just as I managed to shoot him in the leg. Arms around one another, we fell to the greasy stone surface and grappled for some moments until I was able to subdue my attacker.

Meanwhile Holmes was engaged in routing the others. Although they were armed with knives, cudgels and weighted coshes, they were no match for a man skilled in baritsu and the art of singlestick combat. As they fled down the alley, Holmes prised my assailant off me and slammed him roughly against the wall of a brick warehouse.

"If Watson is seriously hurt you will not live another minute," he growled.

"There is no need for such desperate action, Holmes," I said. "My heavy coat deflected his blade and I have suffered little more than a scratch. But I had better bind up the gunshot wound in that fellow's thigh before he bleeds any more."

The ruffian was understandably relieved to receive such immediate medical attention and readily answered all of our questions. He and his comrades had been hired by a 'Yank' from the public bar of The Gun, a pub on a nearby thoroughfare called Coldharbour. They'd been given our description, probable route and likely time of arrival. After the assault they were to dump our bodies into the water.

"He didn't say nuffink about you being armed, Guv'nor, or about your mate being able to use a cane like that."

His description of the 'Yank' left no doubt that it was Calhoun. Holmes and I gave our attacker into police custody and continued on our way to the *Friesland's* berth. Captain Neustaedter was waiting at the top of the gangway. With him were two Lascars holding tight the arms of a struggling man in his mid-twenties.

"They've flown, Mr. Holmes. Mr. Calhoun and his older American friend lit out of here just about a half-hour ago. They commandeered a tug that was at the dock here and already had steam up. But we laid hands on their younger confederate as he was climbing over the side."

"Have the River Police been notified?" asked Holmes.

"Yes, and they are in pursuit."

"Then we will have to possess our souls in patience and use the time to get some account of the affair out of Billy here." Somehow it was no great surprise that Holmes knew the scoundrel's name without being told.

Obtaining the information proved to be easier than I would have imagined. Holmes explained to Billy that he would undoubtedly swing for the murders of Openshaw and Brouwer unless he could provide convincing testimony that the other two men were chiefly to blame. With such inducement the frightened young man was quick to tell all he knew.

In most particulars his account tallied with what Holmes said he had learned already from the spirit of Openshaw. For example, Holmes had wondered at the time how Openshaw was lured to the edge of the Embankment, well away from his most direct route from Baker Street to the railway at Waterloo Station. Billy explained that he had been the decoy. As a mere youth then, he had found it simple to imitate a woman's voice and had cried out for help as Openshaw came down Wellington Street toward Waterloo Bridge.

"But it was Jim and Darrell that did the poor man in, not me, Mr. Holmes," Billy pleaded. "They coshed him and then Jim pressed his cap down on the fellow's face till he stopped breathing. He was already dead afore he went into the water."

Even more striking was his confirmation of what had happened on the high seas, an explanation that I felt came too close to fantasy when Holmes had first relayed the spirit-transmitted version. Yet, unprompted, Billy described exactly the same sequence of improbable events: the survival of the *Lone Star* in the storm-tossed ocean, the providential discovery of wreckage from the mail-ship and the interception of Holmes' accusatory letter. Then the staged disappearance of the *Lone Star* at sea, followed by its real disappearance in a Caribbean port.

"Jim said the ship's owners were little better than car-pet-baggers anyway, so we were merely getting a little bit of our own back, as real Southerners."

Billy's eagerness to talk began to abate, however, as we approached the death of Jan Brouwer. He confirmed that Brouwer's preferment had festered with Calhoun. "It wasn't just that he got the job because his Daddy owned part of the shipping line. And it wasn't only that he was obviously a Nigra-lover, what we could see right away by the way he treated the rest of the crew the same as us. But Jim said that Brouwer had a touch of the tar brush, and there was no way we should be taking orders from a man whose blood was impure."

"So you followed the same method as with Openshaw: the cosh to the head, suffocation and then into the water. Is that correct?" Holmes asked. Billy nodded silently, and it seemed likely that his hand had wielded the cosh or at least helped tip Brouwer's body overboard.

At that point a grim-faced Captain Neustaedter in-terrupted our interrogation. "Blackwall Station has sent over a message, Mr. Holmes. They have had a cable from Tilbury. The River Police lost sight of the tug in the fog just past there and the scoundrels have made their es-cape."

We were a dispirited duo as we made our way back to Baker Street. "To have failed John Openshaw once was a blow to my pride, Watson, but for it to happen twice is almost too much to bear. I cannot believe that he will have enough magnanimity to forgive me twice. The next visit of his spirit to our rooms will be painful for all con-cerned, but most of all for me."

Not for the last time, Holmes was to be proven spec-tacularly wrong. Two days later, the afternoon newspa-pers reported the finding of two bodies washed up on the north Kentish shore near the mouth of the Medway. They were identified as the men sought by police in con-nection with the suspicious death of the First Officer of the Dutch steamship *Friesland*. There was, however, no sign of the stolen tug.

As we sat quietly that night, each lost in his own thoughts, Holmes suddenly started. "He's here, Watson. Can you sense his presence?"

"I sense nothing beyond this fug of tobacco smoke, Holmes."

But his attention was already elsewhere, eyes focused on a patch of empty air and ears cocked like a whippet on the hunt. A one-sided colloquy ensued.

"Yes, I wondered if you played a part in that. How exactly was it managed?" A long pause and then a high-pitched laugh. "Oh what a fitting end!" Holmes glanced my way. "Dr. Watson does not hear you speak. Why is that?" He listened for some moments and then looked at me again, and smiled.

"This will be our last night-time chat, I surmise?" Pause. "It is my business to know what other people don't know, and I now realize that can also include spirits. Thank you for lifting this burden from both our souls. Perhaps we shall meet again nonetheless."

For some minutes Holmes continued to gaze into that empty space and to strain his ears. Finally he sighed.

"You must promise me, my dear Watson, never to chronicle this adventure. It would be hypocrisy in the extreme for me to claim any credit for the solution of these crimes, and I fear the table-rappers would seize upon what happened as support for their nonsense."

"Of course, I will honor your wishes, Holmes. But I feel that I am owed an account of what you learned from the visitation that apparently just took place."

"Good old Watson, you truly are the epitome of the firmly rooted Englishman. Your colleague may be hearing voices and talking to himself, but you will nevertheless take pains to insist upon fair play."

He continued: "I learned that the drowning of Calhoun and Darrell were no accident but the final retribution from the spirit world. Openshaw was, of course, aboard the fleeing tug in spirit form. When it had passed safely beyond the mouth of the Thames and it became apparent the two murderers were once again likely to vanish into the shadowy maritime world, he took action."

"But you said these spirits cannot assume corporeal form, so Openshaw could have no way of checking their flight physically."

"That is correct, Doctor. Nor was there aboard that tug an independent agent such as myself with an intellect capable of communicating with the spirit world and a desire to interfere. Instead, Openshaw said he 'clouded their minds', causing the scoundrels to run the tug into a navigation buoy with such force that it took on water and then quickly sank. Neither man could swim, as is common among sailors, and they drowned."

"How did Openshaw 'cloud their minds?'" I asked.

"He did not provide details about that. It is my belief that the spirits can modulate the force of their mental emanations to suit different circumstances. In this case I suspect Openshaw projected into the minds of those two murderers an image that obscured the true risk of striking the navigation buoy with some even more imminent hazard, perhaps a phantom ship steaming upriver through the fog. Taking evasive action to avoid the imaginary danger, Calhoun and his henchman rammed the real one.

"You also asked why I couldn't hear the spirit's voice. What did he answer to that?"

For a long time Holmes said nothing, and I began to think that he was deliberately ignoring my question. In a low voice, he finally spoke:

"I once feared death, Watson. Not the disintegration of this body, which will all too soon begin to betray me, but the snuffing out of this intellect which I have spent so much effort to fashion into an unequalled thinking machine. My experience with Openshaw has vanquished such fears. When we die, our spirits can continue as the purest form of intellect, ratiocination elevated to this highest conceivable level. I will not rush to embrace death, nor actively seek it out, but I will not despair when it finally comes.

"Moreover, I now appreciate the reason that Openshaw could project his thoughts into my mind only when we were in the same room and why he had to be present on the tug to be able to fatally confuse the thinking of those murderers. As you noted in your published account, he was but two and twenty when he met his death. His mind was nowhere close to reaching its full potential, so the power of his emanations was limited. I, on the other hand, have honed my mind over the years to such a degree that I will no doubt be able to project my thoughts over great distances and continue my work on behalf of the living.

"You wonder what all this has to do with the question I posed to Openshaw's spirit about you. Well, let me ask you a further question in turn. What caused you to draw your revolver on Preston Road and spin about, thereby no doubt saving both of us from serious injury and possibly even death?"

"I had a sudden premonition of danger. I don't know why."

"I do. Openshaw says he shouted a warning at you. You perceived it instantly in the most primitive portion of your brain, the part that prompts us to flee or fight. And being Watson, you fought."

I did not intimate to Holmes that I accepted this explanation nor did we discuss it again. But in the years following I observed Holmes talking to the thin air on numerous occasions. As for myself I subsequently held many fascinating discussions with a certain doctor who had become quite famous as a writer.

The Entwined

by J. R. Campbell

She strode across the neatly trimmed grass, immune to the charms of the day around her. Spring was in full bloom, the wind rustling the leaves in the trees and carrying the season's fresh scents to the fortunate and unfortunate alike. Her feet were bare as she walked across the lawn; tracing out a path perceived by none but her. She walked with her head bowed. Whether to watch the rise and fall of her hesitant steps or to shelter her frighteningly pale skin from the sun's warmth I could not say but her posture and slack expression telegraphed an utter disinterest in everything and everyone around her. The pleasant English countryside unfurled its full lush glory but, for all the pleasure she took from it, a bleak, arctic wasteland would have served her as well. Slender and pale, her wispy hair tousled by the breeze, she seemed almost insubstantial until she turned her remarkable brown eyes to you. Confronted with the depths of those ravishing eyes a man realized this young woman was meant to be beautiful. In those dark eyes was a promise unfulfilled, a potential thwarted by the insidious affliction from which she suffered.

Dark circles gave her face a hollow-eyed aspect. Next to her pallid skin, even the grey clothes of the asylum appeared bright. Her footsteps, her translucent skin, her painfully thin form all but lost in the asylum clothes, all combined to make the young woman insubstantial. Seeing her I found myself in agreement with the opinions I had read in her case file. The poor creature suffered from nothing which food and rest could not cure, nothing save a flaw in her mental process preventing her from accepting that which her body craved. We followed her unnoticed, despite my friend Sherlock Holmes' attempts to gain her attention.

"Miss Drayson!" Holmes, impatient and frustrated, called once more. He moved to stand directly before her. She lifted her head slowly, careful not to lift her feet from her unseen path as she dealt with this interruption.

"You must be Sherlock Holmes," Catherine Drayson said, offering the detective a shy smile. "I trust you received my letter?"

"Yes," Holmes said impatiently. "However I do not understand what it is you require of me."

Her smile, so small a thing, slipped from her features as she examined my friend. "I thought I had explained myself adequately, Mr. Holmes," she said, a charming childlike lilt in her voice. "I require you to determine whether or not I murdered the men I listed. Obviously this matter is of the utmost importance to me. Until my guilt or innocence is proven I am trapped here. Abandoned. Uncertain which world I am to be a part of..."

Having spoken, she lowered her head and resumed marching along her invisible path. She appeared startled when she encountered Holmes who, unmoving, remained directly before her. Looking up, her expression of concern was replaced by a shy smile. "Mr. Holmes," she greeted him as if meeting him again after a lengthy absence.

"Miss Drayson." Holmes returned the courtesy. "I can assure you: These murders are not of your doing."

"That is wonderful news," she said, bringing her hands together in delight. Her shy smile expanded into something more substantial. "You must tell me how you were able to determine this. Was the investigation difficult?"

Holmes cast a concerned look at me before returning his attention to the young woman. "It was not difficult at all."

"You mustn't be so modest Mr. Holmes," Catherine Drayson said.

Holmes, a man seldom accused of modesty, was momentarily nonplussed by this assurance. Nevertheless he pressed on. "It is quite impossible for you to have committed any murders. You have been confined here in this asylum, under constant observation, for the last twenty-three months. I have reviewed your medical file, Miss Drayson. I have spoken to the doctors and staff charged with your treatment. They assure me you have not left the asylum grounds for almost two years."

Catherine Drayson listened patiently to Holmes as he explained his findings. When he finished she laid her small hand on his forearm in a friendly, familiar gesture obviously intended to lessen the sting of her reply. In her musical, untroubled voice, she chided the detective. "Now really Mr. Holmes, I have no wish to be difficult but I did expect better from you. Reading a medical file to solve such ghastly crimes? And everyone says you are so very clever. If you do not wish to accept my case that is one thing, but to stint on an investigation is quite another. I am relying on you Mr. Holmes, is that not clear to you? I must know one way or another before I can decide which world I should direct my efforts towards."

It was a rare instance indeed when Holmes cast a look of desperation my way, I will confess to being somewhat flattered as he did so now. I cleared my throat, drawing Miss Drayson's attention to me. "Excuse me Miss Drayson, but that's the second time you've mentioned different worlds. May I ask which worlds you are referring to?"

"There is this world," Catherine Drayson said, waving her hand in a dismissive gesture towards the blue skies, the looming asylum and the lush, green woods. "Here I am a daughter to a kind man. A child whom everyone likes and pities at the same time. I fear I am a disappointment to those who know me here although they cling to a fading hope. This world is, I confess, a difficult one for me. Often it is a remarkably lonely and frustrating place. Yet it is not without its attractions."

"I see," I said. "And the other world?"

"In many ways the other world is much like this one," she answered earnestly. "Yet in that world I am different. In that world I have neither friends nor family yet, somehow, I am never alone. It is as if there is another me, a part of myself which is missing in this world. When I am there

I know myself to be a fearsome thing, capable of the most vicious violence, yet in that world I am untroubled by my nature. Under the red sun of that world, the only frustration I know comes from my inability to unseat my rider."

"Rider?" I interrupted. "Like a horse?"

"Much more dangerous than a horse." Her words bore a strange flash of bravado, very much at odds with her feminine voice. "The person I am in that world has tasted the flesh of men and gloried in the spilling of their life-blood. My rider believes I can become great. A beast so fearsome I will carry him beyond the red sun to where all his ambitions might be realized. Although I know such a path will be bloody indeed yet, when I am in that world, I find myself eager for the bloodshed."

"When I look up to the red sun the memories of my life here disgust me. Everything seems so weak and lonely, devoid of purpose or companionship. But when I am here the memories of the other world horrify me, such cruelty and wickedness. You see how I am trapped, don't you? There is a choice to be made. I cannot exist between such extremes. I must be one thing or another. I am not large enough to encompass both. So when my rider commanded me to murder those men, I did so eagerly. I knew it would solve my unendurable riddle."

"Solve it how?" I asked.

"I should think it obvious." Catherine Drayson explained pleasantly, her brown eyes captivating as she spoke to me of murder. "If I have indeed killed men from this world then it proves the other world is more than a delusion. It follows then, having spilled the blood of living men, I no longer belong here. Knowing this I am free to commit myself to the world beneath the red sun. Oh, I admit I shall miss the compassion and independence of my life here but one cannot deny one's nature. Besides, if I am truly a murderer, I cannot harbor any expectations of continued kindness on my behalf. Then again, if Mr. Holmes can prove my innocence, I shall abandon the other world. While I will miss my rider and — how shall I put it? — my savage half, it will be a relief to know such frightening deeds are nothing but a delusion."

"I see," I spoke with a confidence I did not entirely feel.

Holmes' frown deepened as he listened to Miss Drayson's explanation. "These men you claimed to have murdered, how did you learn their names?"

The question seemed to puzzle her. For a moment she was silent as she considered her answer. "Yes," she said. "I can see where that might trouble you. In truth I know their names only because I tasted their lives. You see, in the other world, when creatures such as I feed on our prey we gain a sense of our victims. Perhaps it would be more correct to say we gain a sense of who our victims were, for it is only in the last swallow of blood the knowledge appears. I knew their names because I tasted their names. Can you understand that Mr. Holmes? No, I see you do not but I have no better explanation to offer. However I came to know their names, you must admit I did know them. These men did exist and each of them was recently murdered."

"That has not yet been proven," Holmes said.

"It hasn't?" Catherine Drayson's childlike voice betrayed an adult note of hopefulness. Yet even as it built I could see it fade. "Oh, of course, Mr. Pursey was aboard a ship, wasn't he? I should have recognized that I suppose. The small room with the ocean all about. Have you been able to contact him?"

"Not as of yet," Holmes admitted with ill grace.

"And the other names I gave you?" Miss Drayson asked.

"Mr. Mulchinock has been reported missing," Holmes said. "His fate has not been determined. I should remind you that India is a savage land, full of perils for unwary travellers."

"Those are but two names from my list of five," Catherine Drayson reminded him. "Nor have you disproved my contention they have been murdered. What of the remaining gentlemen on my list?"

Holmes scowled, his expression answering her question more eloquently than words could have. The remaining gentlemen had been murdered and Holmes did not wish to admit it to her. Instead of answering her question, Holmes countered with an argument.

"You could not have murdered any of these men," Holmes insisted. "You were confined here, in the asylum."

"In the other world, Mr. Holmes," Catherine Drayson said earnestly, "I have wings."

"Like an angel, Miss Drayson?" I asked.

She smiled an ironic, humorless smile. "No, Dr. Watson, not in the least like an angel. You see Mr. Holmes? I doubt the guards who watch over us are prepared for inmates who sprout wings and disappear into other worlds."

Almost against my will I nodded as she said this, feeling she had spoken the simple truth. It was unlikely, after all, asylum guards would be instructed to watch the unimposing Miss Drayson in the event she unfurled hidden wings and flew off to sea with the intent of determining a sailor's name by drinking the last drop of his blood. Still my unthinking nod was noticed by Miss Drayson who graced me with a grateful, pretty smile. Holmes also noticed my reaction, and glowered furiously at me.

"You see Mr. Holmes," Miss Drayson continued. "Your investigation has only just begun. You'll wish to be paid of course, my father will see to the details. You understand they do not allow us currency in the asylum else I would settle our account now. Oh, and Mr. Holmes, there is one more thing I feel I should mention. I did not include it in my note as I was uncertain how to properly explain such a thing to you but now that you're here, now that you've heard my explanations, perhaps you will understand. The last victim, Mr. Wolfe, as he perished I tasted a fear in his blood, a concern that his friend — Mr. Willingham — was in grave danger. I understood this to mean Mr. Willingham was likely to be my next victim. You understand I know nothing of Mr. Willingham beyond the fact Mr. Wolfe feared for him. I do hope you will be able to prevent his murder. When I am in this world I find thoughts of death and murder most distressing."

"Of course," Holmes agreed, his expression humorless. "Miss Drayson, who told you of these murders?"

Smiling in a friendly manner at Holmes, she answered sweetly. "If you have looked in my file, Mr. Holmes, and spoken to the doctors and staff here, you know I receive no visitors aside from my father. No doubt you will have noticed how newspapers and the like are not permitted within the institution? The staff feels news from the outside world is not helpful to those suffering nervous disorders. If that is all Mr. Holmes?"

Holmes looked as if he wished to say more but was unable to articulate his questions. Instead he merely tipped his head to the slight girl. "I trust you will have a pleasant day Miss Drayson," he said in farewell.

"And you Mr. Holmes," Miss Drayson returned the courtesy with a smile. "A pleasant and productive day."

Holmes stepped aside and, as if a switch had been thrown, Miss Drayson bowed her head and her expression slackened as she resumed her joyless walk along her invisible path. For a moment Holmes and I watched the young woman walk away from us. The detective's hands twitched as he watched her. It seemed to me he was reaching for the pipe and tobacco which he'd unthinkingly left behind in Baker Street. Then Holmes turned and indicated with a tilt of his head that we should be leaving.

"Holmes," I asked when we were in the cab leaving the asylum behind us. "What on Earth was all that about?"

In answer Holmes reached into the pocket of his jacket, pulled out a small, carefully folded note and handed it to me. The stationary was plain, the woman's writing somewhat ornate but easily read.

> *Dear Mr. Sherlock Holmes,*
> *I am writing to you in hopes of securing your services. Much to my dismay, I have been witness to a series of ghastly murders. I wish for you to investigate the following deaths:*
> *Russell B. Wolfe: Killed in a room overlooking London's Hammersmith Bridge.*
> *David J. Johnson: Killed in a flat with a large brass clock.*
> *Ronald A. Pursey: Killed in a small room with the ocean all around.*

Robert W. Elliott: Killed out of doors,
on a city street.
Jonathan E. Mulchinock: killed in a
library not his own.
It may make no difference however I feel
compelled to add that each of these
gentlemen's murders occurred quite late at
night.
As to the matter of your fee, I have
enclosed my father's address and a note to
him explaining how very important this
matter is to me. You must understand that
there are decisions I am compelled to make
but, until I know the truth of these crimes,
I lack the information necessary to make
such choices. Obviously if I am guilty of
five murders such knowledge will affect the
future I must select for myself.
Appreciatively yours,
Catherine Drayson

I handed the note back to Holmes. "The Elliott murder was a sensation, of course. Anything so ghastly in such a public place attracts the curious. No doubt she read of it in the papers."

"As Miss Drayson correctly pointed out, news of the outside world is not permitted within the confines of the asylum," Holmes reminded me. "Still, what are an institution's rules against the power of gossip? I've no difficulty believing Miss Drayson learned of the unfortunate Mr. Elliot's murder through the careless whispering of the asylum staff."

"And the other names on the list?" I asked.

"Aye, there's the rub," Holmes said. "Mr. Wolfe was found murdered last week in his home and, before you ask Watson, he was killed in a room overlooking Hammersmith bridge. Like the sensational Elliott murder his death was both bloody and violent. Mr. Wolfe was beaten and repeatedly stabbed. Scotland Yard believes someone attacked him with an unusually large sword, possibly a weapon from the Far East. Unfortunately they did not think to allow me the opportunity to examine the body."

"Pity," I remarked.

"Indeed," Holmes agreed. "David Johnson was murdered in the Charing Cross Hotel. His body was found beneath a large brass clock. Like Mr. Wolfe and Mr. Elliot, Mr. Johnson was cut several times with some manner of large weapon. As neither Mr. Johnson nor Mr. Wolfe's deaths were as public as Mr. Elliot's, the newspapers have shown little interest in their cases."

"Then Miss Drayson's observations have been correct," I said. Seeing Holmes' frown, I quickly amended my statement. "At least, she has been correct three out of five times."

"I fear her average is better than that Watson," Holmes admitted. "Mr. Mulchinock has not returned from a trip to the sub-continent. I placed a telegram to the hotel where he was meant to be staying. Although they disavow any knowledge of murder, they assure me the blood in the library has been thoroughly cleaned."

"Leaving just one, what was the name? Pursey?"

"Departed on a lengthy sea voyage six weeks ago," Holmes said. "I've received no word of his murder, nor have I been able to confirm his well-being. If, as Miss Drayson suggests, the gentleman was killed while at sea we will be obliged to wait before receiving word of it. If we disregard Mr. Pursey, whose status can neither be confirmed nor denied, it appears Miss Drayson is correct in all of her descriptions. Each of the known victims was, in fact, killed during the night. Furthermore, with the possible exception of Mr. Pursey, she has arranged the names in chronological order of their deaths. Mr. Wolfe being the most recent murder and Mr. Mulchinock being the first. Strange, is it not?"

"Very strange," I agreed.

"Apparently Miss Drayson is being informed of these murders somehow," Holmes said. "It is possible these deaths are connected. At least three of the deaths were achieved by similar means. Given these circumstances, if we could discover the source by which Miss Drayson learns of the crimes it may well lead us to the perpetrators. Ah, here we are!"

The cab rattled to a stop and Holmes eagerly clambered out. "Where are we Holmes?" I asked as we emerged into the brightness of the day.

"In her time at the asylum Miss Drayson has only received one visitor," Holmes reminded me. "Likewise there is only one person with whom she has exchanged correspondence."

"Her father," I said.

"And we have been invited to discuss the matter of my fee with him," Holmes said, his face alight with a hunter's grin. "Many criminals feel an inexplicable compulsion to confess their crimes. Perhaps this father feels his confessions safely hidden in his daughter's insanity. Let us discover what manner of man this Drayson is."

Confident the answer to his mystery was close to hand Holmes marched purposefully into the Drayson residence. Sharing Holmes' enthusiasm I followed but nothing in the man's home bespoke a murderous nature. Neat and ordered, it seemed a bachelor's residence although here and there photographs and other mementos gave evidence of a happier past. Photographs of a child and her mother were scattered about, the resemblance to Catherine Drayson obvious in the mother's attractive features. Other portraits showed young Catherine at various stages of her childhood, telltales of a doting father.

"Mr. Holmes, is it?" Drayson greeted the detective uncertainly. Despite his immaculate apparel, Mr. Drayson appeared a tired, worn man. His was a thin face with a drooping, grey moustache arranged in a permanent frown. The father's form betrayed the same slenderness as the daughter's, and soulful brown eyes peered at us from behind round, wire-rimmed glasses.

Holmes quickly explained our business, handing over the note Drayson's daughter had prepared. Catherine Drayson's father read the missive carefully and then pulled a checkbook from the drawer of his desk.

"I do not think you fully understand the implications of your daughter's message sir," Holmes said as Drayson readied his pen. "You have not inquired if there is any factual basis to the murders your daughter describes. For all intents and purposes she has confessed to a series of monstrous crimes yet you have not requested any further information from us. You seem remarkably trusting sir, perhaps you've heard my name before?"

"I have not," Drayson said, his pen filling in the cheque as he spoke. "To be honest Mr. Holmes, it makes no difference to me if you are what you say you are or a charlatan. As a father I cannot afford to overlook any action that might result in a betterment of my daughter's condition. In her note she claims you may be able to help her. Your fee Mr. Holmes? Please."

Holmes stated a figure.

Drayson's eyebrows rose and the father looked over the top of his spectacles at the detective. "Is that all Mr. Holmes? May I include an incentive, to insure this matter receives your full attention?"

"Unnecessary," Holmes assured the man. "My professional charges are upon a fixed scale. In any instance, a trail of five murdered men cannot help but attract the attention of one such as I."

"There have been murders then?" Drayson inquired as he completed the cheque. "As she describes them?"

"Yes," Holmes answered. "Though how your daughter knows of them is something of a puzzle. Her confinement is such that she should have no knowledge of such brutality. Unless you know some way by which such news might reach her ears?"

"I do not," Drayson assured Holmes as he handed the detective his payment. "Had Catherine been outside the asylum she would have told me of it and I know of no one there who would speak of such things to her."

"Yet she possesses more than a passing knowledge of these deaths," Holmes observed. "I believe someone connected with these murders has spoken to her about them."

"I don't understand," Drayson said without suspicion. "You suspect a member of the staff?"

"No sir," Holmes said bluntly. "I do not."

"Oh," Drayson said, blinking in surprise as the implication of Holmes' statement became apparent. "As far as I know, I am the only visitor my daughter receives."

"That is true," Holmes said with a pointed stubbornness.

"You think I committed these crimes?" Drayson removed his spectacles and cleaned them thoughtfully. "I see the suggestion does not surprise you. Very well, I keep a diary of my appointments and activities. It reaches back several months and the older ones should still be here someplace. My diary should supply a reasonably complete record of my comings and goings. Would that be helpful to you Mr. Holmes? Is there anything else I can provide you with that may prove my innocence?"

Holmes spent the better part of the next two hours interrogating the unfortunate Mr. Drayson about his whereabouts, his daily practices and the sad history of his family. I listened but had nothing to add to the proceedings. To my ear it sounded as if Drayson was exactly as he seemed to be: A man whose life, through no fault of his own, had been marked by tragedy. A father surviving as best he could in the somewhat desperate hope that his daughter's health might be restored. As we left the Drayson residence I saw Holmes' scowl had returned.

"Baker Street." Holmes informed the cabbie curtly. His eyes were distant as he considered the problem before him. As we were dropped before the familiar door of the 221B lodgings Holmes impatiently pushed past me, hurried up the seventeen steps to where his pipes and rough-cut tobacco waited. By the time I had ascended the stairs pungent smoke was already thickening the atmosphere.

For the remainder of the day Holmes smoked his pipes, the great engine of his brain grinding away at the puzzle. As night approached he removed his ash filled pipe, grimaced and exclaimed, "It won't do Watson, it simply will not do!"

"Perhaps we should return to the asylum," I suggested. "Interview more of the staff."

"In case I overlooked something significant!" In another man's mouth such a statement might sound reasonable. Holmes spat it like a curse. My friend was not accustomed to doubting his own formidable abilities. Holmes shook his head. "No need for that Watson, we still have fresh earth to turn. You recall Miss Drayson mentioned a Mr. Willingham."

I nodded. "She suggested he would be the next victim but not how we would find him."

"But she also suggested he might be a close friend of the last victim," Holmes reminded me. "Mr. Wolfe had a business partner, a Theodore Willingham. An interesting coincidence, isn't it? I have the address here. We best leave if we are to arrive before nightfall. And Watson—"

"My service revolver," I finished the thought, already in motion to retrieve the deadly weapon. Holmes allowed himself a small smile as he left to hail a cab.

My old wound ached as we climbed the stairs to Mr. Willingham's fourth floor lodgings. As I navigated my way upwards it occurred to me that living in the upper reaches of a London residence offered a strange protection. Perhaps Holmes had a formula to calculate the frequency of crimes in proportion to the number of steps between the criminal and his desired felony. At last we stood before the thick oaken door of Mr. Theodore Willingham. I might have hesitated, uncertain as to what welcome we should expect given the improbable tale we carried with us, but Holmes had no such compunction. His determined knock echoed in the cramped confines of the hallway like a series of artillery shots.

The stout door opened fractionally, barely enough to reveal the concerned eye of the occupant. Holmes paused long enough to determine there would be no further introduction unless he initiated it. "My companion and I were hoping to speak to you regarding the unfortunate Mr. Wolfe."

Curiously, Mr. Willingham's response to this was to thrust his hand out into the hallway so that Holmes might shake it. The heavy door opened no further. The distrust gleaming in the watching eye did not lessen. Nor did Mr. Willingham offer a single word in way of greeting.

"Of course," Holmes said, as if the out-thrust hand explained everything. Holmes took the offered hand and shook it briskly and deliberately.

"Thank God," Willingham welcomed us with a desperate sincerity as he withdrew his hand. Holmes cast a self-satisfied look my way. Bringing a finger to his lips, he warned me to silence. While I did not understand the need for my quiet, I knew Holmes well enough to trust he would explain his odd request when the opportunity presented itself. I nodded as Willingham pulled open the heavy door and hurried us inside.

Our host, Willingham, was a tall man of imposing stature. Haunted eyes in a weather-beaten face looked worriedly up and down the hallway. His wide, dashing moustache and the tuft of beard on his chin put me in mind of an adventurer, like a knight from the tales of chivalry beloved by schoolboys across the Empire. Closer inspection revealed a nervousness, an unshakable fright, such as I had witnessed during my military service. Willingham seemed to me a once dashing figure who was now haunted by his intimacy with the battlefield.

As we stepped into the small apartment I was surprised to see a long sword leaning against the wall beside the doorframe. Should our meeting evolve into something less than cordial the weapon was within easy reach.

Our host held out his trembling hand to me but as I reached for it Holmes interrupted. "The Doctor is with me," Holmes said. I did not understand what he meant by the comment but Willingham nodded. Pulling back his hand, he crossed the room to an open liquor cabinet.

"Can I offer you gentlemen something to drink?" Willingham said as he reached for a bottle. An empty tumbler waited on a table. Pouring himself a measure of amber liquid, Willingham looked over the table and out a large window.

"Thank you but no," Holmes said.

Drink in hand, Willingham turned to face us. "I cannot tell you how relieved I am to see you. When Wolfe was murdered I thought myself quite alone. All the members of my detachment are either dead or out of the country."

Holmes shifted in his seat. Looking regretfully to Willingham, he spoke. "We have heard reports suggesting Pursey and Mulchinock have been killed as well."

The color drained from Willingham's lined face. The tumbler in his hand fell to the floor, forgotten. Fearing the poor man might faint I hurried to his side and guided him into a nearby seat.

"We have not been able to confirm these reports," Holmes hastened to add. "Obviously, we hope the information is false and both men are well."

"Of course," Willingham said. He raised his hand but discovered his drink gone. Holmes rose and poured the poor devil another. The taste of it seemed to restore the forsaken figure somewhat. "It appears I am the last of the detachment. It will come for me next."

"Most likely," Holmes agreed reluctantly.

"So the Brotherhood sent you to check on me." Willingham made no effort to conceal his bitterness. "To see if I'd break before the end? I've no assurances to offer gentlemen. You may inform them that I know what duty requires of me. My hope is that I will go down fighting, in keeping with the Brotherhood's glorious history, but I'll not pretend to be grateful for the opportunity."

Glancing at the sword leaning by the door, Holmes spoke speculatively. "Perhaps the Doctor and I might—"

"Would you?" An expression of gratitude softened Willingham's face, making him seem younger. As quickly as it appeared, the expression was gone. Willingham's voice was firm.

"No. God bless you for offering but that's exactly what they want. I've no idea how they've breached the gate but obviously they're seeking out as many of the Brotherhood as they can. They can't beat us there, our fortifications are too strong, but here — at home — we're all vulnerable. No, my detachment may be lost but I've no wish to bring down another. Much as I appreciate your offer I cannot accept. You gentlemen will have to leave."

Holmes frowned. "Is there anything you wish us to report to the Brotherhood?"

Willingham emptied his drink, rolling the spirits over his tongue.

"A deathbed statement? Very well. Tell the Brotherhood my detachment served with an honor which exceeded our situation. I know how desperately the Elders seek the forbidden knowledge of the *Melvaris*. Tell the brotherhood such partnerships are not meant for men. My situation is hopeless. I cannot defeat the abomination which comes for me. Even so, I would rather die a man than know victory as such a monster. Tell the Brotherhood to remember us as we were: Men who stood together beneath the red sun. We earned our conquest, fighting as comrades. Do not let the Elders corrupt that victory. Remember the courage of men. Do not let them turn brave men into a blasphemy of foreign sorcery. Alone I cannot match a creature of the *Melvaris*, but if we stand together, as men, none can defeat us." Willingham looked out the large window at the lights of London. "How strange to have travelled so far only to learn we had no need of the magic we sought."

Visibly composing himself, Willingham tore his gaze away from the window. Looking at Holmes and I, the man set down his glass. "You should leave now."

Holmes opened his mouth to protest but Willingham strode to the door and took the long sword into his hand. Despite the alcohol he'd consumed the man still appeared quite formidable. "Thank you for coming but you must go if you are to carry my message to the Brotherhood. Farewell."

There was simply no way we could remain. In short order Holmes and I found ourselves in the hallway, the sturdy door closed behind us.

I started for the stairs. Holmes' hand fell on my shoulder, stopping me. With a nod of his head, Holmes indicated we should proceed in the opposite direction. I followed as Holmes walked to the flat next to Willingham's. He tapped lightly on the door and, receiving no answer, pulled a familiar, but illegal, set of tools from his pocket.

"Holmes!" I protested as my friend made short work of the door's lock.

"The apartment is vacant," Holmes explained as he stepped into the dark room beyond. "You did not notice the 'Room to Let' sign downstairs? Come, it serves our purpose to remain close to Mr. Willingham. If he is attacked, as he obviously expects to be, it would be best if we remain near enough to render assistance."

As Holmes predicted, the flat was empty of occupants and furniture. Striding across the empty room Holmes walked up to the tall window, opened it and leaned out. Satisfied with what he saw he pulled himself back in. "Nothing unusual on the street or dangling from Mr. Willingham's window. This flat is empty, leaving the hallway as the only avenue of attack. Unless this killer flits about on angel's wings."

Miss Drayson, I recalled, had insisted her wings were nothing like those of an angel. Refusing to be baited, I asked, "What was all that business in Willingham's? Who did he think we were?"

"Oh yes," Holmes replied, amused. Opening the door to the hallway fractionally the detective placed a small mirror against the doorframe so he could watch the comings and goings in the hallway unobserved. Seating himself on the floor, settling himself for a long wait, Holmes explained. "You noticed how Willingham refused to speak until I had shaken hands with him?"

"Yes." I recalled the incident.

"Apparently Mr. Willingham belongs to some manner of secret society," Holmes explained. "A club fond of secret handshakes and the like. Having made a study of such things I decided to risk passing myself off as a member, thinking he would be more willing to discuss his situation with a fellow."

"It worked," I said.

"Too well I'm afraid," Holmes confessed. "Having bluffed my way in, I couldn't very well admit to having no idea what the man was talking about. *Melvaris?* The term is not one I am familiar with, although I suppose it may be the name of some rival society."

"He spoke of their secrets," I remembered.

"Yes," Holmes replied dismissively. "What use is a secret society without secrets? No doubt they have a closet full of all manner of mystical refuse. It makes no difference. Whatever nonsense Willingham said our interview has confirmed two important points. Firstly, there is a definite, if secret, connection between the murdered men. Secondly, Willingham himself believes he will be attacked tonight. All we need do is wait for his attackers. Once we have taken them into custody I am confident they shall lead us to the answers we seek."

"If we can take them into custody," I amended Holmes' statement. Holmes, ever confident, merely shrugged.

We settled in for a long night's watch. Holmes sat by the door, his eyes never wavering from the mirror and its reflection of the hallway. I sat with my back against the wall shared with Willingham's flat, occasionally pressing my ear against the barrier and listening. Willingham seemed to be spending his time pacing back and forth. The hours stretched on and we endured them silently.

Checking my watch, I noticed it was just after three o'clock. Pressing my ear against the wall again, I checked on Willingham once more. My hope was the man had ceased his pacing and retired for the night. Certainly by that point I was wishing the same for myself. Rather than the even tread of a man's stride however, I heard the unmistakable sound of a deflected sword thrust. Hurried footsteps jostled for position. The battle had begun.

"Holmes!" I leapt to my feet, weariness forgotten.

"There's been no one," Holmes insisted, pressing his ear against the wall. Hearing the sounds of combat from the other side Holmes uttered a curse and hurried to the window.

I looked to the door and Holmes, seeing my confusion, called for me. "Willingham's door is too thick to breach," Holmes said. "Expecting an attack, he'll have locked it securely. No, the window is our only way. Check your revolver Watson."

Holmes disappeared out the window. I checked my service revolver, it was loaded and ready, and placed it back in my jacket pocket. Reluctantly I followed Holmes out the window. A small, wrought iron balustrade surrounded the small balcony. Climbing over it, Holmes leapt from our window to the next. The space between was not great but the distance to the street below was daunting. Climbing into the brisk, night air I caught a glimpse of Holmes frowning as he kicked in the glass of Willingham's unbroken window.

Summoning my courage, I leapt into the air in pursuit of my friend. Climbing over the metal railing, I was startled by the sound of a loud collision. Heart in my throat I saw Holmes thrown against the windowsill. His head connected loudly against the ledge. Pulling my pistol, I hurried through the broken window.

Holmes lay crumpled on the floor, unconscious. Blood flowed from a wound to his head. Across the room stood Willingham, his clothing dishevelled, bleeding from several wounds. All of this I noticed in a glance for my attention was drawn to the unearthly creature hovering above the overturned furniture in the room's centre.

She'd spoken truly. Her wings bore no resemblance to those of an angel. They were great, curved muscles. Bones sharp as blades over taut, grey skin. Her legs merged together like a serpent's tail. Along her flanks rows of articulated bones emerged like knives. Despite these and other changes, I knew the face which turned to me. I had looked into the depths of those brown eyes before.

Her new form must, I know, seem hideous as I describe it. Indeed, it was hideous. And yet — there was a grace, a beauty, to the creature. The potential for loveliness I had glimpsed earlier was fulfilled in ways both unexpected and chilling. The Catherine Drayson I'd seen was present but her youthful anatomy had been melded with that of a monstrosity. The flesh of her savage half, for that was how she'd termed it, shared an appalling intimacy with the woman I had met earlier. Her faintly green skin seemed, in places, to roughen into blue-edged scales. Dagger-like teeth crowded her newly grown snout, making it impossible for her to smile. Still the curve of her back, the swell of her breasts, those dark brown eyes, all remained deliriously female. For a moment I simply stared, terrified and captivated, at the apparition before me.

She raised her hands and reached towards me. I saw her fingers had become daggers. Seeing that, I understood Scotland Yard's confusion over the murdered men's cuts.

First her hands would pierce my flesh then she would spread her fingers. The resulting wound would seem like a puncture left by an unusually wide sword. Yet, even knowing this, I made no move to defend myself. Catherine Drayson and her savage half stepped towards me. Eagerness shone in her eyes. I waited.

Behind her Willingham swung his sword. The blade was deftly turned aside by the bony edge of one slender wing. Her expression angered. In a quick, powerful twist she turned to face Willingham. She thrust a closed hand at the dishevelled man. He parried the lunge and stumbled backwards. Looking down I saw the revolver still in my hand. Raising the gun, I took aim at the back of the creature's head and squeezed off a round.

Somehow sensing the attack, a wing twitched and deflected the bullet. Disbelieving, I fired two more rounds but each time the edge of the creature's wing deflected the bullet before it could reach its target. Behind me Holmes lay on the floor, bleeding. Unwilling to leave him undefended yet powerless against the strange hybrid I looked about frantically for something, anything, that might serve as a weapon.

Returning the revolver to my jacket pocket, I took hold of the empty bottle Willingham had been drinking from earlier. Breaking the glass against the table allowed me to fashion a crude knife. I watched in sick fascination as the creature battled the swordsman. Despite Willingham's obvious skill, it seemed to me the creature was toying with him. Blocking his escape. Allowing him to strike only where the creature could easily deflect the thrust. Willingham knew it too. Looking over the creature's shoulder he cast me a desperate look.

Unfurling its wings, the creature blocked my view of Willingham. Between the outstretched wings I saw a long, black ridge. Vividly I recalled Miss Drayson describing her savage half. I also remembered her speaking of her rider. Seeing that long, black, snake-like ridge between her shoulders, I was struck with the notion this was the rider she'd spoken of. I did not hesitate. Lunging forward, I plunged the broken glass bottle into the black ridge.

Battered by the surprisingly strong wings I wasn't certain I had found my mark. With a hideous scream, the creature lunged forward and thrust its hands into Willingham. Blood splattered on the floor as those terrible fingers spread within the man. Willingham, his face twisted in agony, threw himself forward. The unexpected action slowed the creature. Rather than pull its hands free, the hybrid lifted Willingham off the ground and drank deeply of the man's flowing blood.

Finding myself on the floor, I reached into my jacket pocket and pulled out my revolver. Black ichor oozed from the wound on the creature's back but the ridge, revealed now as a dangling snake, still held fast to the creature. I fired at it. The wings moved but not quickly enough. The bullets found their mark. The hybrid creature shuddered and screamed. With a savage gesture it pulled its hands free of Willingham, tearing the man in half as it did so. Turning to me, it staggered. The snake fell from its perch. The hybrid creature's wings flapped in a vain, uncoordinated effort to keep itself aloft. It fell to the floor.

I stood. Finding my revolver's ammunition spent, I reloaded. Standing over the twisting, struggling snake I emptied my revolver into it. At last it stopped moving. Was this the *Melvaris* Willingham had spoken of? I turned to the fallen winged creature Catherine Drayson had become and wondered: Was this the secret magic the Brotherhood sought? The ability to entwine the flesh of two distinct beings to form something new? Willingham had been correct. The creature was an abomination, its reptilian creator a blasphemer.

The winged creature turned on its side. It looked up at me with those brown eyes. Fallen, it was still captivating and horrible. Reluctantly, seeing no alternative course of action, I started to reload my revolver again but there was no need. Whatever magic held the creature together was coming undone.

I watched as the two halves pulled free of one another. The sundering was horrible to witness. Each wailed in sorrow as their unnatural intimacy ended. Somehow the creature they had been was greater than the sum of their individual parts. Each of them knew it. They mourned the loss as they were torn from each other. My eyes remained on Miss Drayson. Uncertain if either of them would survive, I could only give witness to the horrible process of separation.

When it was done they were both gone. There had been a green light, bright enough to make me avert my eyes. When I looked back both had disappeared. Holmes lay where he had fallen. I hurried to his side.

So it was that Scotland Yard found us — in the centre of a bloody room that stank of gore and spent ammunition. It was indeed fortunate that we were known to the officers of the Yard. Had Holmes and I not been so familiar I do not doubt we would have found ourselves locked in a cell to await charges of murder.

I told the police Willingham had been attacked by a large, foreign-looking man with an uncommonly wide sword. Willingham, I explained, was dead when we entered the room. Upon our arrival the attacker knocked Holmes to the ground, giving me time to draw my revolver and fire six shots into the brute. The assassin screamed and left by way of the window. Rather than give chase, I remained behind to tend to Holmes.

"Watson." Holmes shook his bandaged head as he listened to my tale. "Your aim is slipping."

"So it would appear," I agreed. Holmes listened to the account I gave to Scotland Yard without comment or question. Nor did he make any inquiries as we journeyed back to Baker Street. Very quickly the matter became just another case. Other crimes took Holmes' fancy. A letter of gratitude arrived from the much-improved Catherine Drayson. Another grateful missive from her father informed us of her release from the asylum. Such tokens were nothing new to Holmes and, as was his custom, he ignored them. Holmes quickly put the case behind him. However, as you might suppose, I have thought of the matter often.

It is not my custom to hide the truth from my friends. Sherlock Holmes is dauntless in the face of horrors which chill my blood. Murder and violence, the screams of the innocent and the doings of evil men, all part of Holmes' environment and as natural to him as water to a fish. Yet, as courageous as he undoubtedly is, Holmes is not without his personal demons. He lives a life built upon small but unshakable truths, upon what is and is not possible. Catherine Drayson and her savage partner disappeared from Willingham's apartment. In Sherlock Holmes' world such things cannot be.

Sometimes I assure myself I acted to protect my friend. When confronted with a horror not of this world, I feared his skills, as a detective, would be rendered useless. Robbed of the very foundations of his courage, how would Holmes react? Such an event could well push him back into the drug usage we had struggled so hard to put behind him. The reality of other worlds, of beings such as the *Melvaris* and their unexplainable magic, seemed a truth which might unravel Holmes. A revelation capable of tainting the detective's skills with doubt, poisoning his future work. At such times I am convinced my response was entirely appropriate and that my actions were those of a loyal friend.

Yet there are other times. Late at night, when sleep is inexplicably elusive, my thoughts stray into the shadowy realms of doubt and I wonder. Were my actions those of a friend or was it simple cowardice? If Holmes had witnessed the truth, had seen the creature sent to kill Willingham, where would he be now? In his own way Holmes has always been a hunter of terrible monsters. A man who exposed secrets. Given the choice would he remain here, solving crimes in London, or would he venture forth to explore that world under the red sun? I find myself reaching for the answer but it eludes me still, eclipsed by another, more troubling question. If Holmes were to leave this world, would I follow?

Merridew of
Abominable Memory

by Chris Roberson

The old man reclined on a chaise-longue, warmed by the rays of the rising sun which slanted through the windows on the eastern wall. In the garden below, he could see the other patients and convalescents already at work tending the greenery with varying degrees of attention. The gardens of the Holloway Sanatorium were the responsibility of the patients, at least those tasks which didn't involve sharp implements, and the nurses and wardens saw to it that the grounds were immaculate. Not that the patients ever complained, of course. Tending a hedge or planting a row of flowers was serene and contemplative compared to the stresses which had lead most of the patients to take refuge here, dirty fingernails and suntanned necks notwithstanding.

No one had asked John Watson to help tend the garden, but then, he could hardly blame them. Entering the middle years of his eighth decade of life, his days of useful manual labor were far behind him, even if he wasn't plagued by ancient injuries in leg and shoulder. But it was not infirmities of the body that had led John here to Virginia Water in Surrey; rather, it was a certain infirmity of the mind.

John's problem was memory, or memories to be precise. The dogged persistence of some, the fleeting loss of others. Increasingly in recent months, he had found it difficult to recall the present moment, having trouble remembering where he was, and what was going on around him. At the same time, though, recollections of events long past were so strong, so vivid, that they seemed to overwhelm him. Even at the best of times, when he felt in complete control of his faculties, he still found that the memories of a day forty years past were more vivid than his recollections of the week previous.

John had been content to look upon these bouts of forgetfulness as little more than occasional lapses, and no cause for concern. When visiting London that spring, though, he had managed to get so befuddled in a fugue that he'd wandered round to Baker Street, fully expecting his old friend to be in at the rooms they once shared. The present tenant, a detective himself as it happened, was charitable enough about the episode, but it was clear that Blake had little desire to be bothered again by a confused old graybearded pensioner.

After the episode in London, John had begun to suspect that there was no other explanation for it than that he was suffering from the onset of dementia, and that the lapses he suffered would become increasingly less occasional in the days to come. In the hopes of finding treatment, keeping the condition from worsening if improvement were out of the question, he checked himself into Holloway for evaluation.

Warmed by the morning sun, John found himself recalling the weeks spent in Peshawar after the Battle of Maiwand, near mindless in a haze of enteric fever, something about the commingling of warmth and mental confusion bringing those days to mind.

His reverie was interrupted by the arrival of an orderly, sent to fetch John for his morning appointment with the staff physician, the young Doctor Rhys.

As the orderly led him through the halls of Holloway, they passed other convalescents not equal to the task of tending the emerald gardens outside. There were some few hundred patients in the facility, all of them being treated for mental distress of one sort or another, whether brought on by domestic or business troubles, by worry or overwork. Not a few of them had addled their own senses with spirits, which brought to John's mind his elder brother Henry, Jr., who had died of drink three decades past.

There were others, though, who had seen their senses addled through no fault of their own. Some of the patients were young men, not yet out of their third decade, who seemed never to have recovered from the things they did and saw in the trenches of the Great War. Their eyes had a haunted look, as they stared unseeing into the middle distance.

John well remembered being that young. If he closed his eyes, he could recall the sounds and smells of the Battle of Maiwand as though it had occurred yesterday. As he walked along beside the orderly, he reached up and tenderly probed his left shoulder, the sensation of the jezail bullet striking suddenly prominent in his thoughts.

Finally, they reached Doctor Rhys's study, and found the young man waiting there for them. Once John was safely ensconced in a well-upholstered chair, the orderly retreated, closing the door behind him.

"And now, Mr. Watson, how does the day find you, hmm?"

"Doctor," John said, his voice sounding strained and ancient in his own ears. He cleared his throat, setting off a coughing jag.

"Yes?" Rhys replied, eyebrow raised.

"*Doctor* Watson."

Rhys nodded vigorously, wearing an apologetic expression. "Quite right, my apologies. How are you today, then, *Dr*. Watson?"

John essayed a shrug. "No better than yesterday, one supposes, and little worse."

Rhys had a little notebook open on his knee, and jotted down a note. "The staff informs me that you have not availed yourself of many of our facilities, in the course of your stay."

It was a statement, though John knew it for a question. "No," he answered, shaking his head.

In the sanatorium, there was more than enough to occupy one's day. Those seeking exercise could use the cricket pitch, badminton court, and swimming pool, while those of a less strenuous bent could retire to the snooker room and social club. In his days at Holloway, though, John had been content to do little but sit in an eastern facing room in the mornings, in a western facing room in the afternoons, sitting always in the sunlight. It was as though he were a flower seeking out as many of the sun's rays as possible in the brief time remaining to him. The less charitably minded might even accuse him of seeking out the light through some fear of shadows, since by night the electric lights in his room were never extinguished, and when he slept it was in a red-lidded darkness, never black.

"Tell me, Dr. Watson," Rhys continued, glancing up from his notes, "have you given any further thought to our discussion yesterday?"

John sighed. Rhys was an earnest young man, who had studied with Freud in Vienna, and who was fervent in his belief that science and medicine could cure all ills. When John first arrived in Holloway weeks before, he had taken this passion as encouraging, but as the days wore on and his condition failed to improve, his own aging enthusiasms had begun to wane.

Had Watson ever been so young, so convinced of the unassailable power of knowledge? He remembered working in the surgery at St. Bartholomew's, scarcely past his twentieth birthday, his degree from the University of London still years in his future. The smell of the surgery filled his nostrils, and he squinted against the glare of gaslights reflecting off polished tiles, the sound of bone saws rasping in his ears.

"Dr. Watson?"

John blinked, to find Rhys' hand on his knee, a concerned look on his face.

"I'm sorry," John managed. "My mind... drifted."

Rhys nodded sympathetically. "Memory is a pernicious thing, Dr. Watson. But it is still a wonder and a blessing. After our meeting yesterday I consulted my library, and found some interesting notes on the subject. Are you familiar with Pliny's *Naturalis Historia?*"

John dipped his head in an abbreviated nod. "Though my Latin was hardly equal to the task in my days at Wellington."

Rhys flipped back a few pages in his moleskin-bound notebook. "Pliny cites several historical cases of prodigious memory. He mentions the Persian king Cyrus, who could recall the name of each soldier in his army, and Mithridates Eupator, who administered his empire's laws in twenty-two languages, and Metrodorus, who could faithfully repeat anything he had heard only once."

John managed a wan smile. "It is a fascinating list, doctor, but I'm afraid that my problem involves the *loss* of memory, not its retention."

Rhys raised a finger. "Ah, but I suspect that the two are simply different facets of the same facility. I would argue, Dr. Watson, that nothing is ever actually forgotten, in the conventional sense. It is either hidden away, or never remembered at all."

"Now I am afraid you have lost me."

"Freud teaches that repression is the act of expelling painful thoughts and memories from our conscious awareness by hiding them in the subconscious. If you were having difficulty recalling your distant past, I might consider repression a culprit. But your problem is of a different nature, in that your past memories are pristine and acute, but your present recollections are transient and thin."

John chuckled, somewhat humorlessly. "I remember well enough that I described my own condition to you in virtually the same terms upon my arrival."

Rhys raised his hands in a gesture of apology. "Forgive me, I tend to forget your own medical credentials, and have a bad habit of extemporizing. But tell me, doctor, what do you know of Freud's theories concerning the reasons dreams are often forgotten on waking?"

John shook his head. "More than the man on the Clapham omnibus, I suppose, but considerably less than you, I hazard to guess."

"Freud contends that we are wont soon to forget a large number of sensations and perceptions from dreams because they are too feeble, without any substantial emotional weight. The weak images of dreams are driven from our thoughts by the stronger images of our waking lives."

"I remember my dreams no better or worse than the next man."

"But it seems to me, based on our conversations here, that the images of your past *are* stronger and more vivid than those of your present circumstances. The celebrated cases in which you took part, the adventures you shared. How could the drab, gray days of your present existence compare?"

John rubbed at his lower lip with a dry, wrinkled fingertip, his expression thoughtful. "So you think it is *not* dementia which addles my thoughts, but that I forget my present because my past is so vivid in my mind?"

Rhys made a dismissive gesture. "Dementia is merely a name applied to maladies poorly understood. The categories of mental distress understood in the last century— mania, hysteria, melancholia, *dementia*—are merely overly convenient categories into which large numbers of unrelated conditions might be dumped. More a symptom than a cause." He closed his notebook and leaned forward, regarding John closely. "I think, Dr. Watson, that you forget because you are too good at remembering."

Rhys fell silent, waiting for a response.

John was thoughtful. He closed his eyes, his thoughts following a chain of association, memory leading to memory, from this drab and gray present to his more vivid, more adventure-filled past.

"Dr. Watson?" Rhys touched his knee. "Are you drifting again?"

John smiled somewhat sadly, and shook his head, eyes still closed. Opening them, he met Rhys' gaze. "No, doctor.

Merely remembering. Recalling one of those 'celebrated cases' you mention, though perhaps not as celebrated as many others. It involved a man who could not forget, and who once experienced a memory so vivid that no other things could be recalled ever after."

⁎⊹ ⊹ ⊹⁎

We have spoken about my old friend Sherlock Holmes, *John Watson began*. It has been some years since I last saw him, and at this late date I have trouble remembering just when. I saw little of Holmes after he retired to Sussex, only the occasional weekend visit. But as hazy as those last visits are in my mind, if I close my eyes I can see as vividly as this morning's sunlight those days when Victoria still sat upon the throne, and when Holmes and I still shared rooms at No. 221B Baker Street.

The case I'm speaking of came to us in the spring of 1889, some weeks before I met the woman who was to become the second Mrs. Watson, God rest her, when Holmes and I were once again living together in Baker Street. The papers each day were filled with stories regarding the Dockside Dismemberer. He is scarcely remembered today, overshadowed by other killers who live larger in the popular imagination, but at the time the Dismemberer was the name on everyone's lips.

At first, it had been thought that the Ripper might again be prowling the streets. Holmes and I, of course, knew full well what had become of *him*. But like the Ripper before him, the Dismemberer seemed to become more vicious, more brutal, with each new killing. By the time Inspector Lestrade reluctantly engaged Holmes' services in the pursuit of the Dismemberer, there had been three victims found, each more brutally savaged than the last. On the morning in which the man of prodigious memory came into our lives, the papers carried news of yet another, the Dismemberer's fourth victim.

By that time, we had been on the case for nearly a fortnight, but were no nearer a resolution than we'd been at the beginning. The news of still another victim put Holmes in a foul mood, and I had cause to worry after his health. Holmes was never melancholic except when he had no industry to occupy his thoughts, but to pursue such a gruesome killer for so many days without any measurable success had worn on my friend's good spirits.

"Blast it!" Holmes was folded in his favorite chair, his knees tucked up to his chest, his arms wrapped tightly around his legs. "And I assume this latest is no more identifiable than the last?"

I consulted the news article again, and shook my head. "There is to be an inquest this morning, but as yet there is no indication that the authorities have any inkling who the victim might be. Only that he was male, like the others."

Holmes glowered. "And doubtless savaged, as well, features ruined." He shook his head, angrily. "The first bodies attributed to this so-called 'Dismemberer' had been killed and mutilated, with the apparent intention of hiding their identities. These more recent victims, though, appear to have been killed by someone who took a positive delight in the act itself."

I nodded. We'd had opportunity to examine the previous three victims, or rather to examine what remained of them, and Holmes' assessment was my own. Even the Ripper had only approached such degradations in his final, and most gruesome killing.

I turned the pages of the paper, searching out some bit of news which might raise my friend's spirits, or distract him for the moment, if nothing else. It was on the sixth page that I found what I was seeking.

"Ah, here is an interesting morsel, Holmes," I said as casually as I was able. "It is an obituary notice of an Argentinean who, if the story is to be believed, was rather remarkable. Ireneo Funes, dead at the age of twenty-one, is said to have had a memory of such singular character that he could recall anything to which it was exposed. Witnesses are quoted as saying that Funes could recall each day of his life in such detail that the recollection itself took an entire day simply to process."

Holmes still glowered, but there was a lightening to his eyes that suggested my gambit had met with some small success. "Have I ever told you about Merridew, Watson?" I allowed that he hadn't. "He was a stage performer I once saw, while traveling in America as a younger man. A mentalist performing under the name 'Merridew the Memorialist,' he appeared to have total recall. I myself saw him read two pages at a time, one with each eye, and then a quarter of an hour later recite with perfect accuracy texts he had glimpsed for only a moment."

Had I but known of Pliny's list of prodigious memories, Doctor Rhys, I might have suggested this Merridew for inclusion in the rolls. As it was, Holmes and I mused about the vagaries of memory for a brief moment before our discussion was interrupted by the arrival of a guest.

Our housekeeper Mrs. Hudson ushered the man into our sitting room. Holmes recognized him at a glance, but it wasn't until our visitor introduced himself as one Mr. Dupry that I knew him. A scion of a vast family fortune, Dupry was one of the wealthiest men in London, and in fact in the whole of the British Empire.

"Mr. Holmes," Dupry said, dispensing with any pleasantries. "I want to engage your services to investigate a theft."

Holmes leaned forward in his chair, his interest piqued. "What is it that's been stolen, Mr. Dupry."

"Nothing," Dupry answered. "Not yet, at any rate. I'm looking to you to make sure that remains the case."

Holmes uncrossed his legs, his hands on the armrests of his chair. "I'll admit that you have me intrigued. Please continue."

Dupry went on to relate how a number of his peers and business associates — Tomlinson, Elton, Coville, Parsons, and Underhill — had in recent months been the victims of bank fraud. Someone had gained access to privileged financial information and used it against their interests. The amounts stolen from Tomlinson and Elton had been so relatively small as to remain unnoticed for

some time, while the funds taken from Coville and Parsons were more substantial, but poor Underhill had been
rendered all but destitute. After seeing so many of his
contemporaries fall victim to the machinations of parties
unknown, Dupry felt certain it was only a matter of time
before he himself became a target, and thus his interest in
securing the services of Sherlock Holmes.

Suffice it to say, Holmes took the case.

I explained to Dupry that we were still engaged in the
matter of the Dockside Dismemberer, and so would have
to continue to address matters relating to that investigation
while beginning to look into his own concerns. We had the
inquest of the fourth victim to attend that morning, after
which we would meet Dupry at his home to survey the
grounds and make a preliminary assessment.

At the inquest we were met by Inspector Lestrade, who
seemed even more foul-tempered than Holmes at the lack
of progress so far accomplished. Of substantive findings
relating to this fourth victim, there were scarcely any. The
body had been recovered from the Thames near Temple
Stairs, in a state of early decomposition. Aside from a tattoo
on the victim's upper arm, depicting an anchor ringed by
a rope of intertwining vines, there were no distinguish-
ing marks. It was the opinion of Scotland Yard that the killer
was not the so-called "Torso Murderer," who had been
depositing body parts around the greater London area for
the better part of two years, given the markedly different
nature of the wounds and the condition of the remains,
and the suggestion in the popular press that it was Jack
the Ripper walking abroad once more was not even merited
with a response.

Following the inquest, Holmes and I accompanied
Lestrade to the chamber in New Scotland Yard in which
the remains had been laid. In all my years, both as a medical
man and as a seeker after criminals, I have seldom seen
so gruesome a sight. The condition of the wounds suggested that the victim had been alive for some time before
expiring from them. The oldest of the wounds had begun

partially to heal over, while the newest were ragged and unhealed. The police surgeon and I agreed that the killer may well have taken a period of days inflicting cuts, severing digits, and slicing off appendages, one by one, before finally delivering a killing blow.

Insult was added to injury by the innumerable tiny incisions all over the body, which could be nothing but the bites of fish that had attempted to make a meal of the corpse as it drifted in the Thames.

I had seldom seen so gruesome a sight. Little did I realize then that it would pale in comparison to what came after.

With our business at Scotland Yard completed, Holmes having made a careful study of the victim's tattoo for future reference, the two of us traveled across town to Kensington, to the home of Dupry.

"Have you come about the position?" asked the servant who answered the door.

"What can you tell us about it?" Holmes said, carefully phrasing his response neither to confirm or deny.

The poor man seemed haggard. He explained that the under-butler had run off in the night, and that the house steward was now in the process of interviewing candidates. The servant at the door was normally occupied in the livery, and so was unaccustomed to dealing with visitors, a task which normally fell to the under-butler. When we revealed that we were not, in fact, applicants for the position, the servant apologized profusely, and ushered us into Dupry's study.

"A damn nuisance," Dupry blustered, when Holmes mentioned the missing under-butler. "He seemed a stout enough fellow, and here he's disappeared without warning. If I can't hire a trustworthy man for twenty pounds a year, where *am* I to find good help, I ask you?"

"I'm afraid I have no idea, Mr. Dupry," Holmes answered as solicitously as he was able. "Now, with your permission, may we examine your home? In particular, can you show me where you keep materials of a, shall we say, sensitive nature?"

For the next three quarters of an hour, Dupry showed us around his home, paying particular attention to his study, and to the wall safe there. When it was opened, though, revealed to contain neatly bound stacks of pound notes, bullion, and other valuables, Dupry held up a single piece of paper as the most valuable item in his possession.

"This, gentleman," he said, careful to keep the document's face away from our view, "is the key to my fortune. You see, the vast majority of my liquid holdings are held in an account in Geneva."

I was confused, but Holmes nodded in understanding. "You see, Watson," he explained, "Swiss bankers are obliged by law to keep a numerical register of their clientele and their transactions, but are prohibited from divulging this information to anyone but the client concerned. You and I might need our balance books to access our account at Child & Co., but one would only need the appropriate register numbers to access a Swiss account, as even the bank clerk's themselves are unaware of the identities of the clients they serve."

"Quite right," Dupry said, appearing impressed. He returned the document to the wall safe, careful to keep the printed side from our line of sight, and then closed the door, spinning the combination to lock it. Even with his precaution, though, I managed to glimpse the paper's front for the briefest second, though I couldn't begin to call to mind the words and numbers I'd seen in that instant. "And if that information were to fall into the wrong hands, I would be ruined. I suspect that my colleagues who have seen their fortunes plundered allowed information regarding their own Swiss accounts to be learned, and that the thief took advantage of the anonymity of the Swiss system." He turned and fixed Holmes with a stare. "I keep my information safely under lock and key, Mr. Holmes. I am hiring *you* to ensure that it remains there."

After we had completed an initial investigation of Dupry's home and its locks, bars, and other security features, Holmes suggested that we visit some of the men whom Dupry indicated had fallen victim to the thief before.

First on our agenda was Underhill. The younger son of a well established family, Underhill lived in a large Cubitt-designed home in Pimlico. If the state of the residence when Holmes and I arrived was any indication, though, it was clear that Underhill would not be in residence for much longer. The man answered the door himself, dressed only in shirt sleeves, harried almost to the point of tears. After we explained who we were, and our connection to his associate Dupry, Underhill admitted us, and explained that he was now all but destitute. He had been forced to let the majority of his household staff go, having lost the funds with which to pay them. It had been difficult to keep them even before, though, having lost two men from the staff in as many months before his fortune was even lost.

From there, we visited the homes of Coville, Elton, and Parsons who, if they were not as badly off as Underhill, seemed hardly much better. All three, too, mentioned having lost members of their domestic staffs in recent months.

When we called at the home of Tomlinson, we found him not in, having left the city to visit the continent. We were instead welcomed by his house steward, a man named Phipps.

"What is it I can do for you, gentlemen?" Phipps asked, with more urgency than seemed necessary. Standing in close proximity, I detected a strangely familiar but confusing scent wafting from him, which it took me a moment to recognize as an exceptionally strong cleaning agent, such as those used to clean tiles in large houses. Given the size of the staff apparently on hand in the Tomlinson home, it seemed odd that the house steward, the head of the staff, would lower himself to cleaning kitchen tiles.

Holmes explained that we had been engaged by Dupry, and that in connection with that engagement were investigating the rash of bank fraud whose victims had included Phipps's employer, Mr. Tomlinson.

For the briefest instant, I fancied that panic flitted across the steward's face, but as quickly as it had come it had passed, and he treated us to a friendly, open smile. "I'm happy to help in any way I can, of course." Still, I couldn't help but notice the sunken quality of his cheeks, the sallow coloration of his skin. He was clean scrubbed, for all that he smelled like bleach and lye, but I could not escape the impression that he was less than entirely healthy.

"Tell me, Phipps, have any members of your staff gone unaccountably missing in the recent past?"

The house steward continued smiling, but shook his head. "No, sir," he said, his voice even and level, "not a one." He paused, and then chuckled. "I took a brief vacation myself, this past winter, to visit family abroad, but returned to my post just as expected, so can hardly be considered 'missing.'"

As the day ended, we returned to Baker Street, to find Inspector Lestrade waiting for us.

"We've identified the tattoo," Lestrade said, without preamble, "and the man."

Holmes nodded. "So you have found a man who sailed the Atlantic Ocean as a deckhand onboard a ship of Her Majesty's Navy, I take it?"

Lestrade's eyes widened, and as I smiled he began to glare at Holmes. "Blast it, Holmes, how did you know that?"

"Simple observation, my dear fellow," Holmes answered. "Now, who was our late seaman, and who was it identified him?"

Lestrade grumbled, but answered. "His name was Denham. Until a few weeks ago, he was employed as a footman in the Parsons household."

Holmes and I exchanged a glance. "Parsons?"

Lestrade nodded. "I spoke to the house steward myself. Seems Denham just stopped showing up to work some weeks back. Stranger still, his replacement, an American chap, went missing a short time after."

"Was this before or after Parsons discovered a portion of his fortune had been stolen?"

Lestrade raised an eyebrow. "Now how did you know about *that*?"

Holmes explained in cursory detail our other ongoing investigation, and in particular the fact that we had earlier questioned Parsons himself.

"Well, the steward *did* mention the theft, at that, and said that for a brief time he'd suspected the two missing men of playing a part. But Parsons had felt sure that there was no way that a retired sailor or an addled American could possibly have been responsible, and had instead blamed the whole mess on a conspiracy of the Swiss."

That certainly was in line with what Parsons had told us earlier that day.

"Why addled?" Holmes asked. "Why did Parsons regard the American as addled?"

Lestrade lifted his shoulders in a shrug. "Something about him becoming easily distracted. The American had come highly recommended, but seemed a poor hand at his duties, always staring at a patch of sunlight on the wall, or counting the number of trefoils on a rug, or some such, and his conversation rambled all over the place." Lestrade chuckled. "Of course, it seems to me the steward had little room to talk, given how long he banged on about the whole matter. Seemed hungry for conversation, I suppose."

I failed to see the significance of any of this, save that several of the men on Dupry's list had lost members of their domestic staffs before their fortunes were ransacked, and that one of the missing servants had apparently fallen victim to the Dockside Dismemberer. But Holmes appeared to divine a much more subtle truth in it all.

"Come along, Watson," Holmes said, slipping back into his great coat and making for the door. "You'd better come, too, inspector. Unless I'm mistaken, we have only a short time left to prevent another fortune being stolen, and perhaps even another murder from being committed."

It was late afternoon, the sun still lingering in the western sky, when we reached Dupry's house. The unfortunate stable-hand had evidently been sent back to his duties, as Dupry's butler answered the door.

"Can I help you gentlemen?"

"Where is Mr. Dupry?" Holmes asked, abandoning all courtesies.

"Interviewing a prospective applicant for the under-butler position, sir." The butler sniffed, haughtily. "I am confident that by this interview's conclusion the position will be filled."

"Why does everyone take me for a domestic?" Holmes fairly snarled. "Tell me quickly, man! This applicant? He comes to you well recommended, seemingly perfectly suited for the task and able to start immediately?"

The butler was a little taken aback. "W-why, yes," he stammered. "We had the most glowing report of his services from the house steward at the Tomlinson estate..."

"Take me to Dupry right away," Holmes interrupted, shouldering his way through the door. The butler, a portrait of confusion, merely bowed in response and hurried to do as he'd been bid. Lestrade and I followed close behind, neither of us any more aware of what Holmes was about than the other.

We came upon Dupry in his office, interviewing a man of middle years. The interviewee was speaking as we entered unceremoniously, and I detected a distinct accent to his speech, Canadian or possibly American.

"What's the meaning of this?" Dupry blustered.

Before the butler could answer, the interviewee in the chair turned, and when his eyes lit on Holmes it was with visible recognition.

After only a moment's pause, Holmes' own face lit up, and he snapped his fingers in sudden realization. "Merridew!" he said.

I recalled the name of the mentalist Holmes had reported seeing in America, years before.

"The Hippodrome Theatre, Baltimore, January 5th, 1880," the man said in a strangely sing-song voice. Then, the syllables running together like one elongated word, he recited, "What art thou that usurp'st this time of night, Together with that fair and warlike form, In which the majesty of buried Denmark, Did sometimes march? By heaven I charge thee speak!"

"It is some years since I trod the boards," Holmes said, not unkindly. "You have gotten yourself mixed up in some messy business, I fear, Merridew."

The American lowered his eyes, looking somewhat shamed. "Horatio, thou art e'en as just a man, As e'er my conversation cop'd withal."

"What is this, Holmes?" Lestrade demanded, pushing forward. "What the devil is he talking about?"

"Memories, inspector," Holmes explained. "This is a man who trucks in memories."

"See here," Dupry said, slamming his hand down upon his desk, "I demand an explanation."

Holmes clasped his hands behind his back. "A moment, Mr. Dupry, and a full accounting will be presented." He turned to the American in the chair. "You didn't hatch this one yourself, Merridew. You haven't the stomach for the darker work this scheme requires. So who was it?"

Merridew, surprisingly, did not even attempt to dissemble. He calmly and patiently explained that he had come to England some months before with an eye towards performing his mentalist act on the English stage, but that he had fallen in with another passenger on the ship, a man who gave his name only as Stuart. When Merridew had demonstrated his ability for total recall, Stuart had hit upon a scheme. It appeared that he had recently come into a considerable amount of money, having gotten hold of confidential financial information belonging to his employer. The sum Stuart had embezzled was scarcely large enough to be noticed by his wealthy employer, but was a small fortune to him. And now he was hungry for more. Stuart could not take much more from his employer without tipping his hand, though, and so he would need to gain similarly sensitive information from other wealthy men.

Stuart identified their targets by looking over his employer's business transactions to locate those with the largest fortunes invested in the appropriate ways. Once the target was chosen, Stuart would select a member of their household staff, and eliminate them. With a position vacant, Stuart would equip Merridew with a flawless resume and sterling recommendations, put in perfect position to be hired as the missing man's replacement. Then Merridew would simply wait for the chance to get even the barest glimpse of the target's financial documents. Only an instant was needed, and then he would be able to recall all of the information in perfect detail.

"And this man Stuart," Holmes said, "which doubtless was merely an alias? Where did you meet with him?"

Merridew gave an address in the East End, and said that he'd been instructed by Stuart to meet him there at the conclusion of each assignment.

Holmes turned to us with a smile. "Gentlemen? Anyone fancy a trip to the East End?"

We hired a growler in the street outside Dupry's home, and the four of us rode east, Holmes and Merridew on one side of the carriage, Lestrade and I on the other. There was a strange, almost childlike quality to Merridew. He seemed lost in a world of his own, and would answer truthfully any question put directly to him, unless he had some prepared answer already provided. It appeared that was how this "Stuart" had been able to work Merridew's skills to his advantage, training him to act and speak just enough like a household domestic that he could pass a few days in the wealthy households, just long enough to catch a fleeting glimpse of a piece of paper such as the one Dupry had shown us. And with eyes that could read an entire page of text in a single glance, it was a task of complete ease to recall only a string of digits and a few words. And with that information, this Stuart would have complete access to the target's Swiss account.

As we rode west, away from the setting sun, Holmes plied the alienist, asking Merridew questions about the man in pursuit of whom we rode. It was hard for me not to feel sorry for this idiot savant, who seemed little more than a dupe in this business. But as Merridew described the man with whom he worked; I was reminded that four men lay mutilated and dead at this Stuart's hands, and that in a just world some of the blame for that carnage had to be laid at Merridew's feet as well. His hands may not have been red with their blood, and he claimed never to have seen the men whom he was positioned to replace, alive or dead, but he was still implicated in their deaths.

Urged by Holmes' questioning, Merridew explained that Stuart appeared to have grown unsettled in recent weeks. Stuart had arranged a set of signals by which he and Merridew could communicate, without ever coming face to face unless necessary. There was a north-facing window on the top floor of the building in which they met, visible from the street, at which hung two drapes, one red and one black. If the window was curtained in black, Merridew was to mount the stairs and enter, where he would find Stuart waiting for him. If the red curtain was instead drawn, Merridew was to stay away, and not to approach under any circumstances.

"Red curtain," Merridew said as we stepped down from the growler to the street. "Stay away."

"Come along, Merridew," Holmes said, taking the American by the elbow and steering him towards the door. "The signal suggests that your Mr. Stuart is in, and he is a man that my friends and I would very much like to meet."

When we reached to the top of the stairs, in the deeply shadowed gloom of the ill-lit interior, I caught a strong smell of bleach and lye, overlying something stronger, ranker, more unsettling. Through the flimsy wooden door at the landing, I could hear faint moaning, somewhere between the cry of a child and the mewling of a drowning cat.

"Red curtain, stay away," Merridew repeated, looking visibly shaken.

"You've been here before," I said, feeling the irresistible urge to cheer him, if possible. "What is there to be afraid of?"

Merridew shook his head, and fixed me with a pathetic gaze. "When I came before, it had always been cleaned. Now, I think, it is still dirty."

"Enough of this nonsense." Lestrade pushed ahead of us, and pounded on the door. "Open up in the name of her Majesty!" He pounded again, louder. "It'll only go harder on you if you resist."

The moaning on the door's far side took on a different quality, and I could hear the sound of scuttling, feet pounding against wooden boards, as if someone were trying to flee. But the room occupied the entire floor of the narrow building, and the only out would be through the window.

"He's trying to scarper," Lestrade said.

"Not today, I think," Holmes said. Stepping back, he carefully studied the door in the dim light. "There, I think." He pointed to a spot midway up, near the jamb. Then, after taking a deep breath, he lashed out with his foot, kicking the door at the point he evidently felt the weakest. He'd been right, as it happened, for the thin door flew inwards, shattering into three pieces.

The stairway and landing had been darkened, a gloaming scarcely lighter than a moonless night, but in the room beyond candles burned in their dozens, in their hundreds. Their flickering light cast shadows that vied across the walls and floor, shifting archipelagoes of light and darkness. The room itself might once have been suitable for a human dwelling, but had been transformed into an abattoir. Bits of viscera hung like garlands from the rafters; blood and offal painted the walls and floor. A pair of severed limbs had been transformed into grotesque marionettes, strung up on bits of intestine tied with ligaments, a kind of macabre Punch and Judy awaiting some inhuman audience.

It took an instant for me to recognize the figure that lay stretched on the floor as being that of a human being at all, so little was left of him, the rest having been spun out and excised to decorate the room. And a further instant to recognize as human the figure crouched by the now-open window, his arms and face covered with blood as red as the curtain he'd torn out of his way. In one hand, the man held a knife, in the other what appeared to be some severed piece of human anatomy. The blood-covered man regarded us with crazed eyes, lips curled in a snarl baring red-stained teeth, his cheeks sunken.

"Don't do it, Phipps," Holmes shouted, taking a single step forward, and only then did I recognize the steward of the Tomlinson household.

There must have been some confusion when Merridew and the man first met, and the American's strange recall had fixed on a term he'd misunderstood. Phipps had simply never corrected him when Merridew assumed his *name* was Stuart, not his *profession* that of steward.

Phipps snarled like an animal. "Money is power, blood is power, both are mine." He threw one leg over the window's sash. "You cannot stop me, nothing can."

I don't know whether Phipps truly believed in that moment that he could not be hurt, or even that he might be able to fly. When he struck the cobblestones below a heartbeat later, though, he quickly learned that neither notion was true.

While Lestrade rushed to the window, already too late to do anything about Phipps, Holmes and I turned our attention to the man on the floor. He was alive, but only barely, and would doubtless perish before any help could arrive, or before he could be transported anywhere else.

"Dupry's under-butler," Holmes said, his hand over his nose and mouth to block the worst of the smell.

"Poor fellow." I held a handkerchief over my own nose, but still the fetid stench of the place threatened to overwhelm me.

Lestrade stepped over from the window, his expression screwed up in distaste. "The man 'removed' so that Merridew could take his place, I take it."

"The most recent of five," Holmes corrected. "Most recent and final victim of the so-called Dismemberer."

It was only then that I thought to see where Merridew had got to. I turned, and saw him standing there in the doorway, just as he had been when Holmes had kicked the door down. The American idiot savant had not moved, but had stood stock still with his eyes wide open and fixed on the scene before him, his mouth hanging slightly open, slack-jawed.

"Merridew?" I said, stepping towards him.

But it was clear that Merridew would not be answering, not then, not ever. He could not look away from the horrible carnage that his erstwhile partner in crime had wrought, and for which he in some sense at least had been responsible. Eyes that could recall entire books in a single glance, that could find untold levels of detail in the patterns of shadows' falling or the curve of a cloud, took in every detail of the grisly scene. And having seen it, Merridew would never see anything, ever again. He would live, but his mind would be so occupied by that macabre sight in all its untold detail that his mind would refuse to allow any other sensations or impressions to enter. He would live forever in that moment, in the horrible realization of the horrors he had, however inadvertently, helped to accomplish.

I remember that day as if it were yesterday, and yet I know that I can not recall even a scintilla of the detail that Merridew retained. But even that tiniest amount, even that small iota of recollection, is enough to haunt me to the end of my days.

⊹⊹ ⊹⊹ ⊹⊹

Doctor Rhys regarded John Watson, his eyes wide with sympathetic horror.

"I can't help but think of all those young men," John continued, waving towards the door and indicating the whole of Holloway Sanatorium beyond, "those tending the garden, or around the snooker table, or else just lounging in the corridors. So young, with so much life ahead of them, and yet their minds are fixed on the horrors of the trenches, their attentions forever fixed on the Great War."

John leaned forward, meeting the doctor's gaze.

"If it were up to me, doctor," John went on, "you would spend less time studying how it is that we remember, and marveling over the prodigious memories of the past, and instead devote your attentions to discovering how it is that we *forget*."

John closed his eyes, and eased back in his chair.

"Memory is no wonder, Dr. Rhys, nor is it a blessing."

John pressed his lips together tightly, trying to forget that awful day, and the smells that lingered beneath the scent of bleach and lye.

"Memory is a *curse*."

Red Sunset
by Bob Madison

The sky was red when a hot wind blew in from the south. Sunset in Los Angeles can be a funny thing. It can make a man feel beaten and maybe a little lonely. Whichever, it didn't make me feel good.

I had never met the old man before. They moved him over the big drink for safe keeping when Hitler started bombing London. They said that morale would crumble if the Nazis took him out, so he was smuggled into New York by submarine and wheeled over like a pasha to the coast. Then, we pretty much forgot about him, warehousing him with the other fossils once we got into the war ourselves. I heard that the old guy was screwy, but I thought screwy was just what I needed about now.

They set him up in an old folk's home near Santa Monica Boulevard. It was a gray old dump, crumbling and shaky, just like the people who lived there. The nurse at the front desk made a big show getting me 'approved' to see the old man, even though I flashed my badge and explained that it was business. When she thought I had waited long enough, she led me down a dimly lit hall and knocked on the door.

A reedy voice said, "Yes?"

"Visitor for you," she said.

"Send him away."

She smiled at the door. A cruel smile, I thought. "He always says that. Just go in."

I watched her walk away before I took hold of the door-knob and entered.

It was rank in the old man's room. It smelled of stale clothes and medicine and something vaguely sick in the air. There were two windows facing south and the room was flooded with the red sunset. Books, some opened, some not, were scattered about, and the floor was littered with copies of *The Times*. The drapes were a little ragged and the carpet frayed. On the desk was an old photograph of a good looking man with a thick moustache.

The old man sat huddled in a wheelchair, small and brittle in his clothes. He wore an over-sized dressing gown and the collar of his shirt needed ironing. He had a beaky face that was a battlefield of wrinkles, and his gray hair was pulled far back from his temples. His lips were thin and blue with age, his teeth brown with nicotine. I heard he was over one hundred, and it was a miracle that the old man was still alive.

His brows came together and he squinted at me. "You smoke cigarettes, I perceive."

I nodded.

"Give me one."

I fished a pack of Luckies from my jacket pocket and handed it to him. His clawed fingertips touched mine and they were cold. "They think that smoking is bad for me and have taken away my pipe," he wheezed. "Colossal stupidity."

The old man wheeled over to his desk and took down a large box of wooden matches. He lit a Lucky and inhaled gratefully. Then he coughed, his bones rattling. When he started breathing again, he looked at me.

"Oh," he croaked. "Thank you. That will be all." He put the cigarettes in his dressing gown pocket.

"Wait a minute. I need to talk to you."

He sighed heavily and blew smoke at the ceiling. "You want me to do the trick? Young man, I was quite elderly before you were born. I am not a performing flea and will not entertain you in return for a cigarette."

"You kept the whole pack," I said.

He took another drag and gave me a dirty look. It was a thin smile that could curdle milk. He clawed at his chest for a satin ribbon and pulled an old fashioned *pince-nez*

from the folds of his robe. He held these up to his eyes,
which magnified like big, gray headlights.

"Very well. You," he said, "are a dick."

"I beg your pardon?"

"That is, I believe, the American vernacular for a consulting detective. You're an operative for one of the larger
firms, Chandler or Continental, perhaps. You have smoked
cigarettes for some thirty years. You are from the American
mid-West, Nebraska or some other wild territory. You are
unmarried and not engaged or in any other permanent
arrangement with a woman. You never eat at home and
your diet is appalling. It is quite some time since you've
bought a new suit of clothes. You write your reports with
a typewriter on which the 'A' key is loose. You own a motor
car, a rather gaudy one, I should think. You carry a revolver
and have recently been in an altercation that has occasioned
the use of fisticuffs."

I looked at him.

"You've been in a fight."

"Yeah."

That curdled smile again, then another drag. "Haunt-
ingly concise. Thank you and good-bye." He wheeled
around, his back to me.

"I've come here for help."

"I'm not interested. I'm retired. I'm too old. I don't care.
Go away."

"I shot a man yesterday."

"I understand from the cinema that your type often
does."

"I shot him three times."

"Once I could shoot my Sovereign's initials in my parlor
wall. Do better."

"I shot him twice in the chest and once in the head. Then
he got up and walked away."

Silence. Then he slowly wheeled around again to face
me. His eyes had caught the red light outside. He pursed
his lips, thinking of what to say next. "You have another
package of cigarettes in your left breast pocket, I perceive.
Give them to me."

I handed them over and he squirreled that pack away with the other. "Pray take a seat."

I pulled up the only other chair in the room — a wooden straight-back that was once part of a kitchen set. I took the violin off of it and placed it gently on the desk before sitting. "Do you have a smoke?" I asked.

He smiled thinly, giving one of my cigarettes back to me. He kept the pack. I struck a light on my shoe and puffed. "About five days ago a dame comes into my office. She's just what you want, you know? Long and slinky, blonde, but probably not natural, her eyes were puffy and she had that haunted look, but not enough that it would put her on the shelf. I sit her in the chair across from my desk and offer her a drink. The light played on her rings when she moved her hands, and—"

He cut me off. "Do you talk like this all the time? Could you please dispense with the poetry? I'm over one hundred years old and I don't have much time."

I made it short. "She says that her husband's vanished. He's an importer. His business was mostly through Europe, but with the war business has dried up. They were doing OK — better than most, I'd say. But times have been tough for the past few years."

"Does this *dame* have a name? Or her husband, for that matter?"

"Landau. Monica Landau. Husband is Miles Landau. He started the business, Landau Consignments, in the early '30s. Business did well and he made enough for a big spread in Marina Del Rey. He and his wife moved there in '38. Aside from the problems with business because of the war, she thought they were happy."

"What were the circumstances of his disappearance?"

"There were no circumstances. He just never came home."

"You searched his office, naturally."

"Yeah. Landau Consignments is down by the Vivica Docks. It's the swankiest building there — he didn't do things on the cheap. He's got only one full-time employee, an old dame named Theresa Vincenzo. Everyone else he uses is freelance or part of the importation crew. Vincenzo has to be a hundred. No offense, of course." I stubbed my cigarette into the clean ashtray on the desk. "Went through his phone book. No dames. No tell-tale signs of hanky panky, either."

"I beg your pardon?"

"He was the age, you know? Don't get me wrong, Monica Landau is a doll, but Miles was pushing fifty, and that's when a man is looking for a little excitement."

"I believe I understand. Pray continue."

"Well, when a guy pushing fifty disappears, it's usually one of three things. Either he's got a broad on the side or he's gambling or drinking — something that gets him into trouble. Or, sometimes, he's had some kind of accident and no one knows it yet."

"Astonishing," he said, blandly, lighting another of my cigarettes. "I could, with a modicum of imagination, create hundreds of reasons for a man to disappear, but no matter. I assume you followed your usual lines of investigation."

"Yeah. Nothing large missing from the bank account. No booze hidden in the office. Vincenzo says no unexplained phone calls. I even went to the cat house four blocks down, you know, on Lindstrom?"

He blew smoke. "I can't say I do, but I shall take your word for it."

"Never heard of him. So, I get a picture from the Landau dame and go to each and every hospital and morgue in town. Nothing. Check with the police on the car. Nothing."

"Come back to the motor car, please. What do you mean, *nothing*?"

"It could still be on the road, but it hasn't turned up wrecked or abandoned. A black sedan."

"I see. So Landau drove to work in a motor car?"

"Yeah. Why?" He just brushed the question aside, so I went on. "So, then I'm thinking that maybe it's the dame, you know? Maybe she's getting me in on it, so, after her husband's body turns up, no one would know she killed him. You know?"

The old man crushed his butt in the ash tray. "It is a considerable deductive leap to suddenly believe this young lady would commit murder simply because you cannot find her husband."

"Yeah, but you know dames." He gave me that smile again, really venomous this time. "What's wrong?"

"Nothing. When I'm around you it's just a pleasure to be alive. Now tell me. I assume that Monica Landau had also gone to the police and reported her husband missing. I also assume that you found nothing to incriminate her in his disappearance. And, I conclude that you returned to the case with that indefatigable energy that you have thus far demonstrated. Would that be an accurate summation?"   '

"Yeah. So, then I figured, hell, maybe it was something to do with his business."

"Ah ha, a colleague after all. Pray continue."

"As I said, business for Landau had not been so good since the war. I went over his import/export records for the last few years. He shipped all around the world, but there was nothing consistent that got me suspicious. He worked the Orient, but not enough for him to be big into dope, you know? And he did enough with Germany, but that all dried up in the late 30s, so I didn't think he was a Fifth Columnist, either. And he did just as much with the French and Brits as he did with the Germans.

"For the past few years, though, he's been concentrating mostly on Canada and Mexico... a little to Alaska, too. Nothing there, though, just business as usual as far as I could make out. And then, going through the records from four months ago, I come across something that got me thinking. He had a client who needed fifty boxes shipped out of Romania. Bam. Out of nowhere, he's dealing with Europe again.

"So, I looked into it. It was right around the time that the King Michael coup over there deposed Antonescu and got Romania out of the Axis and back with the Allies. It was legit enough, but, like I said, it came from out of nowhere. Fifty boxes, six and a half feet long, three feet wide and three feet deep."

The old man leaned back in his wheelchair. He looked like I spat on him. "What's the matter?"

He stared into the distance. "Nothing. Just renewing an acquaintance. Pray continue."

"Well, I checked the manifests and records. The boxes arrived on Tuesday, April 30."

"Walpurgis night," the old man said. He motioned me to go on.

"That's the last day Monica Landau saw him alive."

"Where are these boxes now?"

"That's where it gets screwy. I was in his office all day yesterday. Vincenzo is still putting in full days; I think she manages the cash flow and she's paying herself, hoping that Landau comes back and that there's still a job for her. I was getting close to the end of his business records, so I stayed on until late into the night, paging through them. Landau Consignments is right across from the Beroil Club, you know. I had my feet on the desk and I was smoking a cigarette. The air was unusually hot and my tie was open. The Beroil has a neon sign and—"

The old man smacked a desiccated fist on the arm of his wheelchair. "Yes, yes, yes. *And the neon light beat a steady tattoo on the wall and somewhere I heard a melancholy saxophone play.* I know. Get on with the story man!"

He got on my last good nerve so I gave it to him hard and plain. "I suddenly felt that someone else was in the room. I looked up and there was Landau, standing in the doorway. I had been carrying his picture with me for the past few days, and he's impossible to miss. Tall guy. Was blond once, but now a little gray at the temples. Jowly, but not fat. He was wearing a dark suit, probably the one he was wearing the day he vanished because it has dirt stains on the knees and elbows.

"I got up and made my way around the desk. I was about to ask him where he'd been and let him know his wife was worried when he snarled at me like an animal and grabbed me by the wrist. He pulled me forward and I slammed into the wall hard enough to crack it. I shook my head to work the brain when he came at me again. His eyes were glowing red... I swear to God, his eyes were glowing red. And his breath. Jesus, he smelled like rotten meat and stale farts. He reached for my collar and I ducked and weaved around him.

"I'm not brave. I knew something was wrong with him, and I wasn't about to try and make friends with the guy. I slammed my fist into the nape of his neck. It's a punch that would've floored an elephant, but he stayed standing.

"Without missing a beat, he takes a backhanded swipe at me. I had ducked back a bit, but he caught me on the shoulder and I staggered back and over the desk. I came down on his office chair, and it slid between me and the wall. Good thing. I was able to haul myself up out of it and pulled my gun. I drew a bead on him and told him to raise his hands and get nice and quiet.

"But he didn't. He just... growled. It was low and guttural, like he went blood simple. His teeth were, well, huge. And his eyes... red light shone out of them... like hot coals burning inside of his head. I don't scare easy, but I felt my insides melt and turn to mush. I didn't know what I was doing. I just aimed and fired."

The old man was silent for a minute, staring into space. I let him think before I talked again.

"The first shot hit him square in the chest, maybe eight inches under his chin. A black hole burned through his tie and white shirt, but no blood. He stopped at the impact and looked down at the bullet hole. A little wisp of smoke was coming out of it when he looked up at me. I panicked and fired again, making another hole right next to the first one, but closer to the heart. It ripped through his suit jacket, but still no blood. I didn't wait for him to react to that one. I took my gun in both hands and aimed at his head. I heard the bullet smack into his skull.

"The force of the shot knocked him against the wall and he buried his face in his hands. Then, slowly, he looked up at me again. His forehead had torn open, and ragged strips of flesh hung down around his eyebrows. Gray, moldy pulp that I knew to be his brains dribbled down his nose, but still no blood. He wiped the mess away from his face with his sleeve and snarled. And that was it, I knew I was dead.

"But as he took his first step, we heard the sirens blare. There had to be a squad car parked right near the Beroil, or maybe a security guard in the building called. Either way, the cavalry was coming. Landau comes on me slowly and stops so close I can smell him. It was a stink like something long dead. He smiles at me with those teeth and then wags his finger at me like I was a naughty kid. Then he turns and walks out.

"Well, I'm not going to stand around and explain this to the bulls, so I pocket my gun and get out of there. I was thinking about it all day, and the only person I figured I could come to was you."

He was still silent, looking over at the old picture of the moustached man. "I only called him John, you know," he said. "Never his surname. I don't know why he said otherwise in those lurid accounts of his, but I knew him only as John."

"Excuse me?"

He turned to me. "Nothing. The curse of old age is long memory. You have something to show me, I perceive."

I reached into my jacket pocket. "Yeah. I pulled the last few pages from the ledger when I left. It had the address on Edgecombe of where the boxes were shipped. I was at the city office today... it's an old house that was recently bought. Landau acted as agent for the sale. It's not far from his office."

"Your motor car is outside, I presume? Then fetch my hat and coat. We haven't a moment to lose."

Getting him out of there was not that easy. I asked him if he could walk and he said yes, but slowly. I helped him out of his dressing gown; it had gone unwashed so long that parts of it had petrified. Though it was now May and summer heat had already hit California, he insisted on a tweed suit with vest and a greatcoat that had seen better days. Into this he stuffed a large flask of whiskey. He grabbed a heavy, black walking stick with a weighted knob as the handle and a battered gray homburg, which surprised me. "Blame the illustrator," was all he said when he caught my look.

For convenience, I pushed him out in his wheelchair. The nurse's station was empty, which was lucky, and I got him down to my car, a '34 green La Salle that a Chinaman gave in payment for a case years ago. The old man gave it one look and murmured, "right again." I virtually picked him up and put him in the front seat before folding the wheelchair into the back.

"Is that a wireless?" he asked as I got in, pointing at the dashboard. I said yes. He pulled a heavy turnip watch from the folds of his vest. "Time for *The Shadow*," he said, reaching for the knob. "I'm slavishly devoted to it."

He listened to the show as I drove, paying no attention to me whatsoever. During the station break he lowered the volume and spoke. "Outlandish fiction, of course, but it pales beside reality. What can you tell me of our destination?"

I shrugged. "Large brownstone. Private home forty years ago, but pretty much abandoned when the neighborhood changed. Has a large foundation, which makes me think it's got a big basement."

"Yes, he would need that."

"Who?"

"Nothing. Is that a petrol station I see up ahead? Capital. Let's stop there."

I looked at the gage. "We don't need gas."

"Ah, it's starting again," he said, turning up the volume. "Be a good fellow and get a small canister of gasoline. I'll just wait for you in the motor car. Invisibility is quite ridiculous, isn't it?"

I figured that if he knew what he was doing, it would be best if I just followed orders. And if he didn't, well, what did I have to lose? There's a dead man walking around Los Angeles with three of my bullets in him, and I was ready to do or believe anything. I got the gas can out of the trunk and had the attendant fill it. Then I put it in the trunk and started the car.

"It would've been best if we started out in the morning," the old man said, "but some things can't be helped. By the way, have you reloaded your revolver since last night? Well done. It won't be of any practical use against our antagonists, but it may help create a diversion. Isn't it curious how life is like a wheel?"

"If you say so."

"It is," he wheezed, taking out another of my cigarettes. "Like a wheel it goes round and round and the same spoke comes up. I had thought all of this was finished in '97, but, of course, I couldn't go to the Continent for the end of it, so the job wasn't finished properly in my absence. It creates an unhealthy optimism in the criminal classes once I'm outside of London." He took a long drag on his cigarette. "So it all ends in the New World, I suppose."

I let him rant.

"John never believed a word of it, of course. But, you know, it's fascinating that he was completely taken in by that whole fairy business a few years later, which is the most extraordinary thing. Of course those photographs were faked! A child could see it."

"Sure," I humored him.

"I'm of the opinion that images will provide our greatest deceptions in years to come. Imagine, a society that looks instead of thinks. Have you seen those ridiculous moving pictures supposedly based on my life? And I accused John of being lurid. And that actor is ridiculous. Imagine people thinking my nose is *that big*."

"Edgecombe is about three blocks away."

"Wonderful. Please stop the car here. We should walk the remaining few blocks."

I circled around once and found a spot. When I helped the old man out, he wheezed deeply, leaning on his cane for support. His bones popped like a car backfiring.

We slowly made our way down to Edgecombe. The night was hot and damp, the mean streets slick and dangerous in the light mist. The old man would sometimes bump against my arm, and it was then that I could feel the lump of my .45 in its holster. It made me feel good.

I saw the house we wanted up ahead. "Stop. Landau is here."

The old man was all attention. "How do you know?"

"That's his car." I pulled out a matchbook on which I had made a note of his plate number. The numbers on the black sedan matched. "Yeah, that's his."

"Capital," the old man said. He let go of me and hobbled over to the car, moving faster than I expected. "Now, I understand you can lift the bonnet and disable it?"

It took five minutes to pull out the sparkplugs. "Capital. All of that stuff about bats is nonsense, you know. But, still, we should cut off all opportunities for escape."

"What about bats?"

"Never mind. Let's see if there is anything else here to be learned. Must you break the window to get inside of this thing, or can you pick the lock? My specialty is safes, and I'm afraid I'm a little rusty."

I started working on the lock while the old man talked, something he liked doing a lot. "Of course, I have had a somewhat limited experience with motor cars, but I do believe that they can be invaluable to the logician. Don't you agree? Fewer things offer more opportunities for deduction, except, of course, boot laces and belt buckles. Wrist watches will never be as instructive as pocket watches, I daresay, but they too have points of interest. Can I help you with that, young man?"

Fortunately the door opened and he shut up. The old man gingerly lowered himself into the driver's seat and ran his hands along the wheel, reached into the ashtray, poked and prodded the door pockets. He pulled his *pince-nez* from under his vest and peered at the neighboring seat and then, to my surprise, sniffed it.

"Interesting," he said, "and good news, as well."

"What?"

"No blood. The contagion could not have gone very far. Possibly no farther than Landau. My friend is biding his time."

"What contagion? And what friend? You said something before about renewing an acquaintance."

He only smirked in reply and I called him an infuriating old bastard. He pretended not to hear. I helped him out of the car and traveled up to the brownstone. I reached for my lock pick, but the old man simply turned the door handle and let us in.

"He has nothing to be frightened of," he said, stepping inside. "Of course, I doubt he knew that I was in America.

Fascinating how these Continental types underestimate their foes. Rather like Herr Hitler, right? A ludicrous figure, of course, but never, never underestimate the incalculable damage one unstable personality can do."

The hallway was dark. The old man took a pocket flashlight out of his coat and aimed it toward the living room. Like a lot of old houses, it had a high ceiling and lots of carved details over the doors. The furniture was covered with white sheets, and at the far end of the house, a gauzy white curtain fluttered in the faint breeze. "Our denouement will take place in the cellar, most likely. They do have a predilection for underground spaces. Only natural, I suppose. Or perhaps I should say unnatural. Just what to say is so confusing in situations like this, don't you think?"

"Yeah."

He flipped the light switch and the living room chandelier came alive. "Appalling taste," he said, looking around. "But I do like the chandelier. The Professor tried to kill me with one just like it in '05."

Something crashed overhead. I reached for my .45; the old man blandly looked up.

There, at the top of the stairs, was Landau. He had changed his clothes since last night, so the two bullet holes in his chest were now hidden. There was a long, jagged line of stitching where he tried to sew up the hole my bullet left in his head. The torn bits of flesh had been pulled away, leaving pale white pockmarks. His teeth, white and bestial, gleamed. His eyes were red and they squinted when they took in the old man.

"Mr. Landau," he said, leaning on his cane as he stepped closer. "This is a rather lamentable state of affairs, and I assure you that I understand it all came about through no fault of your own. You were only doing your job and fell victim to a most despicable nobleman. He has a history of exploiting and then victimizing such as you. Perhaps the Fabians had a point after all. At any rate, I'm afraid that we must swim through bitter waters before we reach the sweet, and what must be done must be done. A heavy heart and all that, but it can't be helped." The old man turned to me. "Shoot him dead, there's a good fellow."

I didn't think this was the time to point out that I had already shot him three times, but I didn't argue. I brought my gun up and aimed for his head once again. I fired three shots, knocking him against the stairwell wall. The first shot took off the top of his head, splattering the wall with what looked like gray, moldy bread. The second tunneled into the stitching he used to fix the first head wound, and my third shattered his cheekbone, pulling out the check and forever exposing half of his teeth. Then Landau slowly slid down the wall and crumpled on the stairs.

The room was filled with smoke. I lowered my gun as the room cleared; I could hear the old man's raspy breathing. "Did we do it?" I asked, but the old man shushed me with a hand.

I looked up at Landau. His right hand twitched, then his left. Slowly, he grabbed the banister and pulled himself upright. His head was nothing more than a ruin — hair pulled away from the first shot, most of his forehead missing now and half his face cleared away to the skull. The half of his mouth still there smiled wickedly. And then... he *hissed*. Deep and guttural, it was a sound like nothing I ever heard before.

The old man turned to me. "Here it comes."

Before I could say anything, Landau leapt from the top of the stairs, sailing across the length of the living room with hands outstretched, and careened directly into me. He knocked me over, my .45 flying across the room. In seconds he was kneeling on my chest, his horrible breath like the blast of a slaughterhouse choking me. I couldn't focus my vision, bits of brain dribbled from his head and splashed into my face. I screamed and grabbed his lapels to pull him off, but it was like he was made of stone.

I writhed underneath Landau as he tore at my collar with one hand, and pushed up on my chin with the other. He drooled a bit as he got closer to my throat.

And then, a sound like rain, or a pipe leaking. I shook some of the goo out of my eyes and squinted up. It was the old man, standing over us like the referee at Friday night's fight. He was slowly emptying his whiskey flask over Landau's back. With a nonchalant gesture, he tossed the flask over his shoulder and took one of my cigarettes from his jacket pocket. He lit that with a wooden match, and then dropped the match on Landau.

One moment, a very solid dead man is holding me down and making a beeline for my throat; the next, the back of him is up in flames. His eyes popped wide open and his head shot up. He howled and jumped to his feet, spinning around in circles. He clawed at the flames, but his jacket and shirt went up fast — the fire burning away what hair was left on his head. He looked at the old man for help. The old buzzard only took another drag on his cigarette and watched him burn.

Landau continued to spin, screaming as the room filled with black smoke. I fought the urge to puke as his flesh burned. Then, the old man toppled him with the tip of his cane and the flaming husk that was Landau fell, writhed and went still. "Use one of those sheets to put him out, there's a good fellow."

I whipped a sheet from one of the armchairs and beat what was left of Landau with it. His corpse smoldered and stayed down.

"Thank you for creating a diversion," the old man said. "Come along. I suspect we'll finish all this in the lower regions."

I hunted around for my gun and put it back in my shoulder holster. Then I took the flashlight from the old man and led the way through the dining room and into the kitchen. The basement stairs were there, beside an old servant's door. I reached into the darkness and hit the switch. Dim light came from below.

"There may not be more of those things," the old man said. "Things like that poor devil Landau. But, of course, I could be wrong." He gestured towards the stairs. "After you."

The first step creaked loudly. I was down two or three stairs before the old man had even made it down the first. Something scurried in the dark corners and I caught sight of rats running for cover. "More of his friends," the old man said. "He has a marked taste for vermin. He's down here, I'm sure of it. Do be careful. He can control rats, you know."

"Control rats?"

"Though I wouldn't worry. He's hardly had time to gather too many of them. Still, you never know. Maybe we'll need your revolver after all."

The stairs curved round and, halfway down, I saw the main portion of the basement for the first time. It was filled with boxes... fifty coffin-sized boxes of simple, unvarnished wood. Romanian words were stenciled in black paint on most of them. I hurried down and into the room, now a deep ocean of pine.

One box leaned upright in a corner, separate from the others. This, too, was stenciled with Romanian words, but it also had some weird oval marking on the lid, like a family crest. The crest featured a castle and four bats. I thought of what the old man said outside and wondered again what the hell was going on.

The old man caught up behind me. "That would be his. Odd question of etiquette, isn't it? I wonder if one just knocks, like a Sunday visitor? Of course, he may not be home." He hobbled over to the box and smartly rapped on the lid with his cane. "Come along, come along. The game is afoot and it's getting late."

The box... moved. Something was inside and shifted its weight. Then... things happened too quickly for me to fully grasp it.

First, the box lid exploded outward, shooting across the room. Then a wave of fetid air washed over us and I moved back a step. I could hear roaring in my ears, and, suddenly, rats squealed all around me. I looked around my feet and then in the corners of the basement, but didn't see anything. And when I focused my attention back on the box, *he* was stepping out.

He was tall, very tall. I top about six feet, and he towered over me. He was dressed all in black from head to foot, and the high gloss of his boots caught the gleam of the light. His face was long, fierce and cadaverous. He had thick white hair brushed back over a high forehead. His face was aquiline, with a large nose. His bushy eyebrows met over the bridge of his nose, and his top lip was invisible under a large, gray moustache. Sharp, animalistic teeth protruded onto his bottom lip. Then I caught his eyes.

They were red, and burned like coals. Like Landau, he looked more animal than man.

He flexed his hands and I heard his knuckles crack. His fingers were tipped with long, pointed nails, and his palms were hairy. He raised his right hand, gesturing first to me, then he turned to the old man. His eyes locked on him, and the fires there burned brighter.

The old man bowed slightly, steadying himself on his cane. "Count," he said. "Journeys end in lovers meeting, as they say in the old play. I am happy to see that your flair for the dramatic has not deserted you."

"You!" he hissed. He had a heavy Romanian accent, like the bad guy in a spy picture. His voice was deep and seemed to echo, like he was speaking from a tunnel. "You're still alive!"

"Surely longevity is nothing to surprise you. It is indeed disagreeable to find you here, in the United States. The California climate has nothing to recommend it. What do you want here?"

The red eyes turned to me. "Who is he?"

"Fresh blood, if you'll pardon the expression," the old man answered. "Now, I believe I asked a question of you."

The man in black turned away from me. "I've come to help."

The old man blinked, surprised. "I beg your pardon?"

The man in black took a step closer. "I escaped from Europe as soon as I could. I could not stand idly by while that maniac destroyed the country I had lived and died for. But the forces of darkness are sometimes too much, even for the Prince of Darkness Himself. So, I have come to offer my services to the Allies."

"And what would those services be?" the old man asked.

"An army. An army of my kind, led by me, their king! We would be invincible. With sword and mace we would sweep over the Continent and take back what was once ours. We could form an alliance, your kind and mine, the warm and the cold. It would be sweet, yes? The blood

would run in the gutters and the world would be safe
again, yes, safe for the strong and for those willing to
sacrifice. The time has come... *to fight back with claw and
fang!*"

The old man was silent as he thought. "How many like
you are there in the United States?"

"I am not a butcher," the man in black said, "despite
what the Dutch doctor and the others claimed. I took
Landau because I had to. You... put him at permanent
rest?"

"Yes." Then the old man turned to me. "Mad as a hatter,
you know. Is it your experience, too, that once you get
them talking, it's obvious that they are insane? Oh, forgive
me, Count. You'd expect greater respect for a royal personage from one raised under Victoria, I'm sure, but the
world is changing rapidly. Too rapidly, I think, for the
likes of you to find any place in it. I'm afraid that your
little American adventure must end here."

I didn't wait for instructions. I rammed my shoulder
into the man in black and he staggered into his upright
box, both of them thundering to the floor. Then I pivoted,
grabbed a corner of a whole stack of coffin-shaped boxes
and pitched them onto him.

"What the devil are you doing?" the old man asked,
his voice high.

"Trying to stay alive." Landau had taken six of my
bullets, whatever he was. And the man in black had
turned Landau into that thing, so I was dangerously out-
classed. I'd have to keep him off balance if I was going
to find a way to take him out.

But he didn't stay down long. The was a cracking
sound, and I saw the man in black chopping his way out
of the boxes with the edge of his hand. The hard wood
cracked apart like toothpicks.

"Perhaps it's time you shot him, too?" the old man said.

The man in black had just made it to his feet when I
pulled my gun and emptied it into him. Unlike Landau,
he wasn't knocked back at impact. Instead, he just stood
there, glaring at me.

"Now hit him with something else," the old man suggested.

Some of the boxes that landed on him were now badly splintered. I grabbed a loose board and held it like a baseball bat. The man in black inched closer and I smacked him hard on the side of the head. He didn't even wince. I reared back and brought the wood down again, but he stopped it in midair with one hand and held it tight. Then he pulled it closer to him and I dragged along with it. We were torso to torso, and I could see his red lips grin wolfishly when I was close. There was a loud squeak, and the wooden club pulped as he crushed it in his fingers.

The other hand wrapped around my tie. He pulled down and I fell to my knees before him. He pushed my head to the side, exposing my neck. I heard him growl like a punk in a stag film. I thought of what Landau had become and struggled with everything I had, but I couldn't pull away. I pulled at his arm, screaming.

Then, a horrible, swishing noise, and I was drenched with a vile smelling filth. The man in black fell to his knees opposite me... but his head was missing. The top of his old fashioned black suit was drenched in blood, and great gouts of it spurted from the horrible, gaping hole that topped his shoulders. Then the body fell back, still gushing red muck.

I put my hands on the floor to keep steady, and that's when I saw his head lying about three feet away from his body. The red eyes were open with a look of surprise. Then I looked up. The old man was wiping blood from a sword with a long, lavender handkerchief. He then tossed the handkerchief aside and lowered the sword back into the heavy black walking stick that concealed it. "Useful thing," he said. "Very handy in Whitechapel back in '88. Now *there* was a madman. I say, are you well enough to fetch that can of petrol from the car? This all must be burned, you know, both the bodies and the boxes. Then we'll call the fire brigade before it gets too out of hand. I don't want to repeat all the trouble I had in San Francisco in '06. Don't see why I was blamed for all that, but there you are. Need a hand up?"

The Red Planet League
by Kim Newman

(Being a reprint from the Reminiscences of Col. Sebastian Moran, Late of the 1st Bengalore Pioneers)

As my many devoted readers — hullo *mater*, gout still playing up, eh what? — know, Professor Moriarty excelled in *two* fields of human endeavour.

Mathematics, for one. Never was there such a fellah as the Prof for chalking up sums, or the rigmarole with more squiggles than numbers. Equations. Did 'em in his head, for fun... damn his eyes.

Neverthehowsoever, your humble narrator — Colonel Sebastian 'Basher' Moran, to whit: me — would wager several pawn tickets held on the family silver that you lot have little or no interest in fractional calculus or imperfect logarithms. You'd all be best pleased if I yarned up the *other* field in which James Moriarty was top of the class.

Crime. Just the word gets you tingly, don't it?

Well, tough titty... as the house-captain who tried to roger me when I was a whelp at Eton used to say, because this story is *all about* mathematics. I got my pen-knife to the house-capt's goolies, by the way. Preserved my maidenly virtue, as it were. Blighter is Bishop of Brichester these days. Wouldn't care to be a boy soprano in *his* choir. That's beside the point: maths is the thing!

Get your thinking caps on, because I might put in some sums. Make you show your workings in the margin and write off for the answers. It will cost an extra 3d and a stamp just to find out if you're as clever as you think you are. Probably, you ain't. Most fellahs (including — I'm not ashamed to admit it — me) aren't as clever as they think they are. Moriarty, though, was *exactly* that clever, a *rara avis* indeed. More dodos are around than blokes like that. According to Mr. Darwin, that's good joss for the rest of us. Elsewise, we'd have long since been hunted to extinction by the inflated cranium people.

Drifting back to the subject in hand, Professor Moriarty was Number One Heap Big Chief in both his vocations. Which meant there was something he was even better at than complicated number problems or turning a dishonest profit — making enemies.

Over the years and around the world, I've run into some prize-winningly antagonistic coves. I recall several of that species of blood-soaked heathen who bridle under the yoke of Empire and declare war on 'the entire White Christian Race'. Good luck to 'em. Pack off a regiment of curates and missionaries led by Bishop Bum-Banger to meet their savage hordes on the field of carnage, and see if I care. In India, some sergeants wear armor beneath the tunic because no soldier serving under them can be trusted with a clear shot at their backs. I've also run into confidential police informants, which is to say: grasses. Peaching on one's fellow crims to escape gaol is guaranteed to get you despised on both sides of the law. Fact is: no bastard born earned as many, as various, and as determined enemies as Moriarty.

First off, other crooks *hated* him. Get your regular magsman or ponce on the subject of Professor Jimmy Bleedin' Moriarty, and you'll expand the old vocabulary by obscenities in several argots. Just being a bigger thief than the rest of them was enough to get their goats. What made it worse was villains were often forced to throw in with him on capers, taking all the risk while he snaffled the lion's share of the loot. If they complained, he had them killed. That was my job, by the bye — so show some bloody respect or there's a rope, a sack and a stretch of the Thames I could introduce you to. To hear them tell it, every cracksman in the land was *just about* to work out a foolproof plan to lift the jewels from Princess Alexandra's knickers or rifle the strong-boxes in the sub-basement of the Bank of England when Professor Moriarty happened by some fluke *to think of it first*. A few more tumblers of gin and their brilliant schemes would have been perfected — and they wouldn't have to hand on most of the swag to some evil-eyed toff just for sitting at home and drawing diagrams. You might choose to believe these loquacious, larcenous fellahs. Me, I'll come straight out and say they're talking through a portion of their anatomy best employed passing wind or, in certain circumstances, concealing a robin's egg diamond with a minimum of observable discomfort.

Then there were coppers. Moriarty made sure most of them had no earthly notion who he might be, so they didn't hate him quite as *personally* as anyone who ever met him — but they sure as spitting hated the *idea* of him. By now, you've heard the twaddle... vast spider squatting in the centre of an enormous web of vice and villainy... Napoleon of Crime... Nero of Naughtiness... Thucydides of Theft, *et cetera, et cetera*. Detectives of all stripe loathed the unseen King of Krooks, and blubbed to their mummies whenever they had to flounder around after one of his coups. *Scotland Yard baffled again*, as if that were news. Hah!

One man above all hated Professor Moriarty, and was hated by him.

Throughout his dual career — imagine serpents representing maths and crookery, twining together like a wicked caduceus — the Prof was locked in deadly struggle for supremacy — nay, for *survival* — with a human creature he saw as his arch-enemy, his eternal opposite, his *nemesis*.

Sir Nevil Airey Stent.

I don't know how it started. Stent and Moriarty were at each other's throats well before I became Number Two Heap Big-ish Chief in the Consortium of Crime. Whenever the Stent issue was raised, Moriarty turned purple and hissed — and was in no condition to elucidate further. I do know they first met as master and pupil: Moriarty supervised young Nevil when the lad was cramming for

an exam. Maybe the Prof scorned the promising mathematician's first quadratic equation in front of the class.
Maybe Stent gave him an apple with a worm in it. Upshot
is: daggers drawn, eyes a-blaze, lifelong enmity.

Since this record might be of some academic interest,
here are a few facts and dates I've looked up in back
numbers of the *Times*.

1863 — boyish Nevil Stent, former pupil of James
Moriarty, rocks the world of astronomy with his paper
*Diffractive Properties of an Object-Glass with Circular
Aperture*. Not a good title, to my mind — which runs
more to the likes of *Heavy Game of the Western
Himalayas* or *My Nine Nights in a Harem* (both, as it
happens, written by me — good luck finding the
latter: most of the run was burned by order of the
crown court and the few extant volumes tend to be
found in the collection of the judge who made the
ruling).

1869 — Stent appointed to the Lucasian Chair of
Mathematics at Cambridge University, succeeding
brain-boxes like Isaac Newton, Thomas Turton and
Charles Babbage. Look 'em up — all gems, so I'm
told. If said Chair were a literal piece of furniture,
it would be hand-carved by Chippendale and covered
in a three-inch layer of gold flake. The Lucasian
Professorship comes complete with loads of wonga,
a free house, all the bowing and scraping students
you can eat and high tea with the dean's sister every
Thursday. Stent barely warms the Lucasian with his
bottom before skipping on to occupy an even more
exalted seat, the Plumian Chair of Astronomy and
Experimental Philosophy. It's only officially a Chair
— everyone in Cambridge calls it the Plumian *Throne*.

1872 — the book-length expansion of *Diffractive
Properties* lands Stent the Copley Medal of the Royal
Society. This is like the V. C. of science. Wear that little
ribbon and lesser astronomers swallow their chalk
with envy when you walk by.

1873 — Stent publishes again! *On an Inequality of Long Period in the Motions of the Earth and Venus* so radically revises the Solar Tables set out a generation earlier by Jean Baptiste Delambre that the Delambre Formulae are tossed into the bin and replaced by the Stent Formulae. J-B is dead, or Moriarty would have to queue up behind him for the job of Nev's arch-enemy, methinks.

1878 — Stent knighted by Her Majesty, Queen Victoria — who couldn't even count her own children, let alone calculate an indice of diffraction — and is therefore universally hailed the greatest astronomical mathematician of the age. Rivals choke on their abacus beads. Naturally, Sir Nevil is also appointed Astronomer Royal and allowed to play with all the toys and telescopes in the land. Gets first pick of which bits of the sky to look at. Can name any cosmic bodies he discovers after his cats. The AR position comes with Flamsteed House, an imposing official residence — Greenwich Observatory is tacked onto it, rather like a big garden shed. Lesser mortals have to throw themselves on the ground before Sir Nevil Airey Stent if they want to take so much as a shufti at the man in the moon.

Cast your glims over that little lot, and consider the picture of Sir Nevil in the rotogravure. Tall, fair-haired, eyes like a romantic poet, strong arms from working an alt-azimuth mount, winning little boy smile. Mrs. Sir Nevil is the former Caroline Broughton-Fitzhume, second daughter of the Earl of Stoke Poges, reckoned among the beauties of the age. Tell me you don't hate the swot right off the bat.

Now... imagine how you'd feel about Stent if you were a skull-faced, reptile-necked, balding astronomical-mathematical genius ten years older than the Golden Youth of Greenwich Observatory. Though recognized as a serious brain, your career has scarcely stretched beyond being ousted from an indifferent, non-Plumian chair — no more than a stool, they say — at a provincial university few proper dons would toss a mortar-board at. If you aren't grinding your teeth with loathing, you probably lost them years ago.

Stent. It's even a horrible name, isn't it?

All the *Dictionary of National Biography* business I found out later. When Professor Moriarty, tense as a coiled cobra and twice as venomous, slithered into the reception room of the digs we shared in Conduit Street brandishing a copy of *The Observatory* — trade journal for astronomers, don't you know — I'd have been proud to say I had never heard of the flash nob who was giving that evening's lecture to the Royal Astronomical Society in Burlington House.

My understanding was that my flat-mate and I were due to attend an exclusive sporting event in Wapping. Contestants billed as 'Miss Lilian Russell' and 'Miss Ellen Terri' in the hope punters might take them for their near look-alikes Lillian Russell and Ellen Terry, were to face off, stripped to drawers and corsets, and Indian-wrestle in an arena knee-deep in custard. My ten bob was on Ellen to shove Lilian's face into the yellow three falls out of four. I was scarcely best-pleased to be informed that our seats at this cultural event would go unclaimed. We would be skulking — in disguise, yet — at the back of the room while Sir Nevil Stent delivered his latest crowd-pleasing lecture.

His title: *The Dynamics of an Asteroid: A Comprehensive Refutation*.

"Has it not been said that *The Dynamics of an Asteroid* 'ascends to such rarefied heights of pure mathematics there is no man in the scientific press capable of criticizing it'?"

Sir Nevil Stent smiled and held up a thick volume.

I was familiar with the blasted book. At least a dozen presentation copies were stuffed into the shelves in our study. It was the Professor's *magnum opus*, the sum total of his knowledge of and contribution to the Whole Art of Mathematical Astronomy. In rare moments of feeling, Moriarty was wont to claim he was prouder of these six hundred and fifty-two pages (with no illustrations, diagrams or tables) than of the Macao-Golukhin Forgery, the Bradford Beneficent Fund Swindle or the Featherstone Tiara Theft.

"Of course," continued Stent, "we sometimes have our doubts about 'the scientific press'. More sense can be found in *Ally Sloper's Half Holiday.*"

A tide of tittering ran through the audience. Stent raised his eyebrows, and shook the book in humorous fashion, as if hoping something would fall out. Chuckles ensued. Stent tried to read the book upside-down. Something which might be diagnosed as a guffaw erupted from an elderly party near us. Moriarty turned to aim a bone-freezing glare at the old gent — but was thwarted by his disguise. He wore opaque black spectacles and held a white cane in order to pass himself off as a blind scholar from Trinity College, Dublin.

Stent slammed the book down on the lectern.

"No, my friends, it will not do," he said. "Being beyond understanding is of no use to anyone. Astronomy will never progress from simple star-gazing if we allow it to be dominated by such... and I don't hesitate to use the term... *piffling tripe* as Professor Moriarty's pound and a half of waste paper. This copy of the book was taken by me this afternoon from the library of the Greenwich Observatory. As you know, this is the greatest collection of publications and papers in the field. It is open to the finest scholars and minds on the planet. Let us examine this *Dynamics of an Asteroid*, and see what secrets it has to tell..."

Stent picked up the book again and began to leaf through it. He showed the title page. "A *first*, and indeed *only*, edition!" Then, he turned to the opening chapter, and drew his finger down the two-columned text, turned the page, and did the same, then turned the page and...

"Aha," he exclaimed. "After only three pages of actual text, we find that the next leaf is uncut. As are all remaining leaves. What can we deduce from that? This book has been in the library for six years. I have a list of academics, students and astronomers who have taken it out. Seventy-two names. Many I see before me this evening. It seems no one has managed to read beyond the first *three pages* of this masterwork. Because I am not averse to suffering for my field, I *have* read the book, cover to cover. Six hundred and fifty two pages. I venture to say I am the only man in the room who can claim such a Herculean achievement. Is there any comrade here, to whom I can extend my condolences, with whom I can share my sufferings? In short, has anyone else managed to finish *The Dynamics of an Asteroid*? Hands up, don't be shy. There are worse things to admit to."

The handle of the Professor's cane snapped. He'd been gripping it with both knotted fists. The sound was like a gun-shot.

"So you *have* joined us, James," said Stent. "I rather thought you might."

A sibilance escaped Moriarty's colorless lips.

"We shall have need of you later," said Stent, producing a long thin knife — which he proceeded to slip into the book, cutting at last its virgin leaves.

"You can take off those ridiculous smoked glasses," said Stent. "Though, if you have suffered some onset of blindness which has not been reported in the press, it would explain a great deal. Gentlemen of the Royal Society of Astronomers, it is my contention that no man who has ever looked through a telescope with sighted eyes would ever be able to make the following statement, which I quote from the third paragraph of page one of *The Dynamics of an Asteroid...*"

Stent proceeded to dissect the book, wielding words like a scalpel, and flicking blood in Professor Moriarty's face. It was a merciless, good-humored assassination. Entertaining asides raised healthy laughter throughout the evening.

The sums were well above my head, but I snickered once or twice at the amusing way Stent couched his refutations. I should have kept a stonier face: the next day, Moriarty had Mrs. Halifax, who kept brothel under our rooms, despatch Fifi, my favorite French dollymop, to Alaska as a mail-order bride.

At every point, Stent invited a response from Moriarty. None came. The Professor sat in silence as his theorems were shredded, his calculations unpicked, his conclusions burst like balloons.

It occurred to me that Sir Nevil Airey Stent had no idea that the Professor's interests extended beyond equations.

Blithely, the Astronomer Royal continued his lecture. Though I knew only too well what the clot was getting into, I could scarcely blame him for digging his own grave in public.

No one would have believed, in the next-to-last years of the 19th Century, that his lecture was being watched keenly and closely by an intelligence greater than his own; that as he blathered on and on he was scrutinised and studied, perhaps almost as narrowly as a berk with a microscope might scrutinise the tiny wriggly bugs that swarm and multiply in a drop of water. With infinite complacency, Stent read from his little sheaf of notes, serene in the assurance that he was royalty among astronomers.

Yet, across the gulf of the lecture hall, a mind that was to Stent's as his was to those of the beasts that perish, an intellect vast and cool and unsympathetic, regarded the podium with envious eyes, and slowly and surely drew his plans against him.

"In brief, sirs," said Stent, wrapping things up, "this asteroid is off its course. Heavenly bodies being what they are, this cannot be allowed. Stars are inexorable. The laws of attraction, gravity, propulsion and decay are immutable. An asteroid does not behave in the manner our friend Moriarty alleges that it does. This august body will fall prey to... to *men from Mars*, with three legs, eyes the size of saucers and paper party hats... before the asteroid will deviate one whit from the course I have charted. I would wager five pounds that Professor Moriarty can say no different. James?"

The pause stretched on. Moriarty said nothing. It was summer, but I felt a chill. So did the rest of the audience.

The silence was broken by Markham, the adenoidal twit who had introduced Sir Nevil. He stood up and called for a round of thunderous applause, then announced that the gist of the speech was now available as a pamphlet at the cost of 6d. There was a rush for the stall outside the lecture room, where a brisk trade was done.

Moriarty remained in his seat as the room emptied.

"James," Stent said cheerfully from the podium as he gathered his notes, "it's pleasant to see you in such evident

health. There's actually some color in your cheeks. I bid
you a respectful good night."

The Professor nodded to his nemesis. Stent left by a rear
door.

Moriarty didn't move from his chair. I wondered if he
even could.

Stent had set out to murder Moriarty the Mathematician. He didn't suspect his victim had another self. An
unmurdered, unmerciful enemy.

"Moran," he said, at last, "tomorrow, you will call on
The Lord of Strange Deaths in Limehouse. The Lord is out
of the country, but Singapore Charlie will act for him. You
remember the Si-Fan were able to import the swamp adder
we supplied for Dr. Grimseby Roylott. I wish to place an
order for a dozen *vampyroteuthis infernalis*. That is not yet
an officially recognized *genus* of *coleoidea*, but specimens
come on the exotica market from time to time."

"Vampyro-whatsit?"

"*Vampyroteuthis infernalis*. Hellish vampire squid. Often
mistaken for an octopus. Don't let Singapore Charlie palm
you off with anything else. They are difficult to keep alive
above their spawning depth. Pressurized brass contain-
ers will be necessary. Von Herder can manufacture them,
reversing the principle of the Maracot Bell. Use the funds
from the Hanway Street jeweller's, then dip into the re-
serve. Expense is immaterial. I must have my *vampyroteuthis
infernalis*."

I pictured what a hellish vampire squid might be. And
foresaw unpleasant experiences for Sir Nevil.

"Now," said the Professor, consulting his watch, "there
is just time to catch the last falls. Would you be interested
in making haste for Wapping?"

"Rath-er!"

The next few weeks were busy.

Moriarty dropped several criminal projects, and devoted
himself entirely to Stent. He summoned minions — familiar
fellahs from previous exploits, like Italian Joe from the Old
Compton Street café poisonings, and new faces nervous

at being plucked from obscurity by the greatest criminal mind of the age. 'P. C. Purbright', a rozzer kicked off the force for not sharing his bribe-takings, was one such small fish. A misleadingly strapping, ferocious-looking bloke and something of a fairy mary, P. C. P. specialized in dressing up in his old uniform and standing look-out for first-floor men. He had a sideline as a human punching bag, accepting a fee from frustrated criminals (and even respectable folk) who relished the prospect of giving a policeman a taste of his own truncheon. If you paid extra, he'd turn up while you were out with your darby girl and pretend to make an arrest — you could beat him off easily and impress the little lady with your fightin' spirit. Guaranteed a tumble, I'm told. He came out of the Professor's study with wide eyes, roped into whatever bad business we were about.

I was sent out to make contact with reliable tradesmen, all more impressed by the color of Moriarty's gelt than the peculiarity of his requests. Paul A. Robert, a pioneer of praxinoscopists, was paid to prepare materials in his studio in Brighton. According to his ledgers, he was to provide 'speculative scientific educational illustrations' in the form of 'rapidly-serialized photograph cells from nature and contrivance'. Von Herder, the blind German engineer, bought himself a week-end cottage in the Bavarian Alps with his earnings from the pressurized squid-tanks and something called a burnished copper parabolic mirror. Singapore Charlie, acting for a mad chink who had cornered the market in importing venomous flora and fauna, was delighted to lay his hands — not literally, of course — on as many squid as we could use.

The pets were delivered promptly by Chinese laundry-men straining to lift heavy wicker hampers. Under the linens were Herder Bells, which looked like big brass barrels with stout glass view-panels and pressure gauges. A mark on the gauge showed what the correct reading should be, and a foot-pump was supplied to maintain the cozy deep-sea foot-poundage the average h. v. s. needs for comfort. If this process was neglected, they blew up like balloons. Snacks could be slipped to the cephalopods through a funnel affair with graduated locks. The Professor favored live mice, though they presumably weren't usually on the *vampyroteuthis* menu.

Mrs. Halifax supplied a trembling housemaid — rather, a practiced harlot who *dressed up* as a trembling housemaid — to see to the feeding and pumping. Pouting Poll said she'd service the entire crew of a Lascar freighter down to the cabin boy's monkey rather than look at the ungodly vermin, so hatches were battened over the spheres' windows at feeding time. Not wanting to follow *ma belle Fifi* to Frozen Knackers, Alaska, Polly did her duty without excessive whining. The Prof spotted the doxy, and promised her a promotion to 'undercover operative' — which the poor tart hadn't the wit to be further terrified by.

The squid were quite repulsive enough for me, but Moriarty decided their pale purplish cream hides weren't to his liking and introduced drops of scarlet dye into their water. This turned them into flaming red horrors. The Professor, cock-a-hoop with the fiends, spent hours peering into their windows, watching them turn inside-out or waggle their tentacles like angry floor-mops.

Remember I said other crooks hated Moriarty? This was one of the reasons. When he was on a thinking jag, he couldn't be bothered with anything else. Business as usual went out the window. While the Professor was tending his squid, John Clay, the noted gold-lifter (another old Etonian, as it happens), popped round to Conduit Street to lay out a tasty earner involving the City and Suburban Bank. He wanted to rope in the Professor's services as consulting criminal and have him take a look-see at his proposed scam, spot any trapfalls which might lead him into police custody and suggest any improvements that would circumvent said unhappy outcome.

For this, no more than five minutes' work, the firm of Moriarty, Moran & Company, could expect a healthy tithe in gold bullion. The Professor said he was too busy. I had some thoughts about that, but kept my mouth shut. I'd no desire to wake up with a palpitating hellish vampire squid on the next pillow. Clay went off in a huff, shouting that he'd pull the blag on his lonesome and we'd not see a farthing. "Even without your dashed Professor, I shall get away clean, with thirty thousand napoleons! I shall laugh at the law, and crow over Moriarty!"

You know how the City and Suburban crack worked out. Clay is now sewing mailbags, demonstrating the finest needle-work in all Her Majesty's prisons. A flash, smug thief, he'd been an asset on several occasions. We'd never have got the Rajah's Rubies without him. If Moriarty kept this up, we wouldn't have an organization left.

One caller the Professor did deign to receive was a shifty-eyed walloper named George Ogilvy. I took him straight off for a back-alley chiv-man, but he turned out to be another bally telescope tosser. First thing he did was whip out a well-worn copy of *The Dynamics of an Asteroid* (with all its leaves cut) and beg Moriarty for a personal inscription. I think the thing the Professor did with his mouth at that was his stab at a smile. Trust me, you'd rather a *vampyroteuthis infernalis* clacked its beak — buccal orifice, properly — at you than see those thin lips part a crack to give a glimpse of teeth.

Moriarty got Ogilvy on the subject of Stent, and the astronomer poured forth a tirade. Seems the Prof wasn't the only member of the We Hate N. A. Stent Society. I drifted off during the seventh paragraph of bile, but — near as I can recollect — Ogilvy felt passages of *On an Inequality of Long Period* owed a jot to his own observations, and that credit for same had been perfidiously withheld. It was becoming apparent that mathematician-astronomers, as a breed, were more treacherous, determined and murder-minded than the wounded tigers, Thuggee stranglers, card-sharps and frisky husband-poisoners who formed my usual circle of acquaintance.

Ogilvy happily signed up as the first recruit for the Red Planet League and left, happily clutching his now-sacred *Dynamics*.

I ventured a question. "I say, Moriarty, what *is* the Red Planet League?"

His head oscillated, a familiar mannerism when he was pondering something dreadful. He looked out of our window, up into the pinkish-brown evening sky over London.

"The League is a manufacturer of paper hats," he said. "Suitable apparel for our friends from beyond the vast chasm of interplanetary space."

Then Moriarty laughed.

Pigeons fell dead three streets away. Hitherto-enthusiastic customers in Mrs. Halifax's rooms suddenly lost ardor at the worst possible moment. Vampire squid waved their tentacles. I quelled an urge to bring up my mutton lunch.

Frederick Nietzsche witters on about 'how terrible is the laughter of the *übermensch*' — yes, I have read a book without pics of naked bints or big game! — and establishes there is blood and ice in the slightest chuckle of these superior beings. If Fathead Fred ever heard the laugh of Professor Moriarty, he would have shat blood, ice and sauerkraut into his German drawers.

"Yes-s-s," he hissed. "Paper hats-s-s."

From the Diary of Sir Nevil Airey Stent.

September 2: Notices are in!

My lecture — an unparalleled triumph! *The Dynamics of an Asteroid* — in the dust-bin! Moriarty's hash — settled for good! I may draw a thick black line through the most prominent name on the List.

Now — on to other things.

Remodelling of Flamsteed House continues. All say it's not grand enough for my position. Workmen have been in all week, installing electric lamps in every room. In my position, we must have all the modern, scientific devices. Lady Caroline fears electricity will leak from the wiring and strike dead the servants with indoor lightning. I have explained to her why this is impossible, but my dear featherhead continues to worry and has ordered the staff to wear rubber-soled shoes. They squeak about the place like angry mice.

Similarly, the Observatory must expand, keep apace, draw ahead.

At 94 inches, our newly-commissioned optical reflecting telescope shall be the biggest in the world! The 'scopes at Birr Castle and the Lick Observatory will seem like tadpoles! I almost feel sorry for them. Almost. That's two more off the List!

Kedgeree for breakfast, light lunch of squab and quail eggs, Dover sole and chipped potatoes for supper. Congress with Lady C. — twice! Must eat more fish.

Reviewing my life and achievements on this, my forty-fifth birthday, I concede myself well-satisfied.

All must admire me.

Looking to the planets and stars, I feel I am surveying my domain. My Queen has her Empire, but she has gifted me the skies for conquest.

Mars is winking at me, redly.

September 6: A curious happening.

Business took me to the lens-grinders' in Seven Dials. Old Parsons' work has been indifferent lately, and I made a personal visit to administer a metaphorical boot to the seat of his britches.

After the booting was done, I left Parsons' shop and happened to notice the premises next door. Above a dingy window was a sign — 'C. Cave, Naturalist and Dealer in Antiquities'. The goods on offer ran to dead birds, elephant tusks, shark-maws, fossils and the like. I'd thought this site occupied by a bakery, but must be misremembering. Cave's premises had plainly stood for years, gradually decaying and accumulating layers of dust and dirt.

My attention was drawn to the window by a red flash, which I perceived out of the corner of my eye. A stray shaft of light had reflected off an odd object — a mass of crystal worked into the shape of an egg and brilliantly polished. It might do for a paperweight if I were in need of such a thing, which I was not.

Then, I heard voices raised inside the emporium.
One was known to me — that upstart Moriartian
Ogilvy. Alone among the fraternity of astronomers,
he has written in defence of *The Dynamics of an
Asteroid*. His name was on the List.

I stepped back into the doorway of Parsons', but
kept my ears open. Og. was haggling with an old
man — presumably, C. Cave himself — over the
crystal lump, for which the proprietor was asking
a sum beyond his purse. An opportunity.

Casually, I wandered into the shop.

Cave, a bent little fellow with egg in his stringy
beard and a tea-cozy on his head, had the odd mannerism of wobbling his head from side to side like
certain snakes. I thought for a moment that I knew
him from somewhere, but must have been mistaken.
He smelled worse than many of his antiquities. I
say, that's rather good — must save the line for my
next refutation.

Og. was going through his pockets, scraping together coins to up his offer.

Upon seeing me, Og. said "Stent, how fortunate
that it's you," with undue familiarity as if we were
the closest of friends. "Could you extend me a small
loan?"

"Five pounds," insisted Cave. "Not a penny
less."

Og. sweated like an opium-addict without funds
for his next pipe. Most extraordinary thing. I hadn't
thought he had the imagination to be so desperate.

"Of course, my dear fellow," I said. His face
lifted, and his palm came out. "But first I must
conclude my own business. My good man, I should
like to purchase that *curious crystal* in your window."

Og. looked as if he had been punched in the gut.

"Five pounds," said Cave.

"Stent, I say, you can't... well, that is... I mean,
dash it..."

"Yes, Ogilvy, was there something?"

I drew out my wallet and handed over five pounds. Cave entered the sale in an ancient register, then fussed about extracting the object from the window.

I looked at Og. He tried unsuccessfully to cover fury and disappointment.

"Now about that loan," I said, wallet still open.

"Doesn't matter now," he said — and left the shop, setting the bell above the door a-jangle.

Another name off the List!

Cave came back with the object, cradled in black velvet. It struck me that I need only say I'd changed my mind to reclaim my outlay. But Og. might creep back and get the blessed thing after all. Couldn't have that.

Cave held up the crystal and said something about 'the inner light'. Strange phrase. He meant the refraction, of course, but a lecture on optics would have been out of place in this circumstance. No fee would be forthcoming, and it doesn't do to cheapen the currency of scholarship by dishing out lectures *gratis*.

I took the thing away with me. Perhaps I can use it as a paper-weight after all.

Roast boar with apricots at the Lord Mayor's. Congress with Lady Caroline in the carriage on the way home. Whoosh!

September 7: An odd day.

Luncheon at Simpson's in the Strand with Jedwood, my publisher. Cream of turbot, hock of ham, peppered pear. An acceptable muscadet, porter, sherry. The *Refutation* pamphlet is shifting briskly, and J. is eager for more. Pity Moriarty hasn't fired other literary clay pigeons I could blast to bits. J. proposes a collection of *Refutations* and suggests I consider expanding the arena of combat, to launch my intellectual ballista against other so-called great minds of the age. J. is a dolt — he doesn't understand the List, or that it is as important to choose the proper enemies as the proper friends. Nevertheless, I'm tempted. Tom Huxley, Darwin's old bulldog, could do with having *his* ears boxed for a change. And I didn't care for the way George Stokes hovered over Lady Caroline at the last Royal Society formal. Those Navier-Stokes equations have their tiny little cracks.

Most extraordinary thing. As J. and I were leaving the restaurant, a wild-haired, sun-burned fellow accosted us in the street, gabbling "The Martians are coming, the Martians are coming!" Ever since Schiaparelli put about that nonsense about canals, there has been debate about how one should address the notional inhabitants of the planet Mars. I am firmly of the belief that 'Marsian' is the only acceptable term. I took the trouble to correct the moonatic on this point, but he was in no condition to listen. He grabbed my lapels with greasy fingers and breathed gin in my face. He called me by name, which was discomforting. "Sir Nevil," he said, "keep watching the skies! Look to the Red Planet! Look into the Crystal Egg!"

J. summoned a hefty constable, who laid a hand on the madman's shoulder. The fellow writhed in the grasp of the law, and a look of heightened terror passed over his face. It is no wonder men of his stripe should fear the police, but the extent of his pantomime of fright struck me as excessive even for his situation. Curiously, the constable seemed humpbacked, tailored uniform emphasizing rather than concealing a pronounced lump on one shoulder. I assumed the Metropolitan Police imposed strict physical requirements on their recruits. Perhaps this fellow's condition has worsened in recent years? Something was not quite right about his hump, which I could swear wobbled like a jelly on a plate. His eyes were glassy and his face pale — indeed, our lawful officer was evidently in as poor a shape as our degenerate semi-assailant.

"Don't let them take me," begged the madman, "they wraps round you... and they bites... and they sucks your brains... and you ain't you no more. I've seen it!"

"Let's... be... 'avin... you... my... lad," said the policeman, voice like a prolonged death rattle, monotonous and expressionless. "You... don't... want... to... be... a... botherin'... these... gentlemen..."

The madman's face contorted in a silent scream.

There was something peculiarly hideous about the constable's voice, as if he were a music hall dummy manipulated by a wicked ventriloquist.

"Mind... 'ow... you... go... sirs!"

The policeman lifted the madman — not a small individual, by the way — one-handed. He marched off stiff-legged, bearing his whimpering prisoner down the Strand. As he walked, his hump seemed to *shift* under blue serge, as if it were a separate entity. I had a sense of evil eyes cast at me.

J. asked me if I had any idea who the maniac was.

He had something of a military mien, I thought — though come down in the world, perhaps having frazzled his brains out in some sunstruck corner of Empire. It came to me that I *had* seen him before — perhaps in the audience at one of my many popular lectures, perhaps skulking on the street waiting for the chance to accost me. J. pointed out that he had known who I was, but — of course — everyone in England knows the Astronomer Royal.

"It should definitely be 'Marsian'," I insisted. "The precedents are many and I can recall them in order..."

J. remembered he had forgotten another appointment — with a lesser author — and left, before I could fully convince him. Must send him my monograph on planetary possessives. Some still rail against 'Mercurial' and 'Jupiteric', though a consensus is nearly reached on 'Moonian' and 'Venutian'. By the end of this century, we shall have definitively colonized the sunnar system for proper naming!

September 7, *later.*
I had thought to dispel completely the unpleasant
memory of this afternoon's strange encounter... but
the words of the madman resounded.

By some happenstance, this was literally true.

The long-necked cabbie who conveyed me back
to Greenwich bade me a jovial farewell with "keep
watching the skies, sir." An unusual turn of phrase
to hear twice in one day, perhaps — but a sentiment
naturally addressed to a famous astronomer in the
vicinity of the biggest telescope in the land.

Galvani, the Italian foreman of the gang who have
completed — at last! — the electrification of
Flamsteed House, handed me a sheaf of wiring diagrams marked 'for the attention of the householder'
and clearly said "*look to the Red Plan, et...* es essential for to understan' the current en the house". There
was, indeed, a red plan in the sheaf, but it seemed
to me he had stressed the first part of his sentence,
which echoed the words of the madman, and thrown
away the second, which conveyed his particular
meaning.

Then, before supper, I was passing the kitchens
and happened to overhear Mrs. Huddersfield, the
new house-keeper, tell the butler to "look into the
crystal", referring to our fresh stock of Waterford
glassware, a scant instant before Polly, the new undermaid, exclaimed "egg!" in answer to a question about
the secret ingredient of the face-paste which keeps
her complexion clear. To my ears, these separate
voices melded to produce a single sentence, the
madman's "*look into the Crystal Egg*".

Lady Caroline is at her sister's, and I dined alone,
unable to concentrate on supper. Every detail of the
business on the Strand resurfaced in my mind.

I was shocked out of my reverie only by the sweet-
ness of dessert — and looked down into a crystal
bowl to see a quivering scarlet blancmange, with a
curiously eye-like glacé cherry at its summit. In its

color, the dish reminded me of the planet Mars, and, in its movement, the somehow-unnatural hump of the strangely-spoken police constable.

Only then did I remember the paperweight snatched out from the grasp of the odious Ogilvy yesterday.

A mass of crystal, in the shape of an egg!

A Crystal Egg! Could the madman of the Strand have been referring to this item of bric-a-brac?

Unable to finish my dessert for thinking.

September 7 — *still later*: a great discovery!

After supper, I repaired to my study, where I keep my collection of antique and exotic optical and astronomical equipment: telescopes, sextants, orreries and the like. Signor Galvani's men have disturbed them greatly while seeing to the electrification of the room.

A new reflecting telescope arrived this morning, a bulky cabinet affair on trestles, with an aperture where a separate lens must presumably be attached. It is an unfamiliar design — a presentation, in honor of my achievements in mapping the night skies, from an august body who call themselves the Red Planet League. I have had had my secretary respond with an autographed photograph and a note of thanks. Entering the study, I saw at once that the workmen had mistaken this gift for a species of lamp, and wired it up to the mains. I would be inclined to chide Galvani most severely, had this error not nudged me on the path to discovery.

I unwrapped the supposed paperweight and made close examination of it under the steady illumination of the electric lamps. Cave, the vendor, had mentioned an 'inner light' — a phenomenon I soon discovered for myself. It is a trick of the optics, of course — if held up to the light, the interior of the crystal egg coruscates, seeming to hold multiple refractions and reflections.

By accident, when Polly reached into the room and turned off the lights at the wall-switch, I discovered the crystal had the unusual property of retaining luminosity even when the light-source was gone. I did not measure the time of glow-decay, because the undermaid was fussing and apologizing for not seeing I was still in my study when she plunged me into darkness. She whimpered that these new-fangled inventions were not like proper gas. I fear Lady Caroline's 'indoor lightning' theory has infected the servants with irrational terror.

"What's that egg?" exclaimed the maid, meaning my crystal. "And why's it lit up?"

I ventured to explain something of the laws of refraction, but saw my learning was wasted on this simple soul. Nevertheless, it is to Polly that I owe my next, most extraordinary discovery. She picked up the crystal egg, rather boldly for a person in her position I might say.

"Doesn't it go here, sir?" she said, slipping the egg into an aperture of the Red Planet League's reflecting telescope. It was a perfect fit. Before I could chide her, Polly had fiddled with a switch which triggered an incandescent lamp inside the cabinet — projecting a beam through the crystal, which diffracted out into the room. Suddenly, the opposite wall was covered by a swirling, swarming red cloud. Polly yelped, and fled — but I hadn't the heart to pursue and chastise her.

I was transfixed by the pictures on the wall.

Yes, pictures! Pictures that move! With a faint flicker, accompanied by a definite whirring from inside the reflecting telescope. I had never before seen the like.

At once it came to me that my crystal egg was in fact a crystal *lens*. When light passed through it *just so*, the crystal egg — by some means as yet undetermined by science — transmitted images from its interior.

The *process* was astounding, but I was more overwhelmed by the *picture*. It was as if I were looking
out of a window which floated high over a ruddy
desert far from Greenwich. Faintly visible above the
horizon were familiar stars, skewed in the sky — as
observed not from our home-world, but from a body
which must be considered (on a cosmic scale) our
near neighbor. I perceived the tiny blue-green circle
of Earth, and knew with utter certainty that this
window looked out onto the plains of Mars.

The Red Planet.

All the tiny incidents of the last two days impelled
me, inch by inch, towards this discovery.

I knew the subject of my next lecture, my next
book. Indeed, the remainder of my career could be
devoted to this. I am Master of Mars. No other can
come close. Og. must have had some inkling, but this
is to be Stent's triumph — not Ogilvy's. From hence-
forth, this acreage of red dust will be Stent's Plain.
In the distance, I saw slumped, worn hills, more
ancient than the sharper peaked mountains of Earth
— the Caroline Range! A deep channel grooves across
the landscape, flowing with a thick, red, boiling mud
— Polly's Canal, to commemorate the child whose
unknowing hand urged me to this discovery! Nearby,
a gaping pit was scraped raw like a bloody gouge
in the Marsian soil. I named this Victoria Regina
Chasm in honor of the gracious lady who has be-
stowed so many honors on my name.

Inside V. R. Chasm, something stirred. My heart
stopped, I am sure — for long, long seconds. Pads
like large leaves, a richer scarlet than the crimson of
the desert dirt, flopped over the rim and anchored
in the soil. These were the tips of sinewy tentacles,
which held fast and contracted as *a Marsian being*
hauled itself out of its hole.

What manner of men might inhabit the Red
Planet? Not men at all, it seems — but creatures
beyond classification.

I saw its bulging, filmed-over eyes. Its beak-like mouth. Its mess of limbs. Its swelling carapace.

The thinner atmosphere of Mars and a colder, drier climate have shaped that planet's ruling species differently from us. I had no doubt that I was looking at a Man of Mars, not a brute animal. All around were signs of an intelligent species, a civilization perhaps older than our own.

There were structures — a Marsian factory, perhaps, or a school. The Marsian hauled itself across metal frames, fighting the pull of its planet, and came closer to the window.

I confess to a moment of stark, irrational fear. As I could see the Marsian, could it see me? Did the crystal egg have a twin on Mars?

With no earthly object for comparison, it was difficult to get a sense of scale. The Marsian could be the size of a puppy or an elephant.

It wriggled closer to the 'window'. Its features grew gigantic on the study wall. I could see the wallpaper, the bookshelves and pictures through its phantasmal image. Then, suddenly, it shut off. There was a flapping sound, and a brief burst of bright, blank light — that died too, along with the incandescent bulb inside the Red Planet League's reflecting telescope.

How ironic that a body named after Mars should provide the device which led me to gain such an unprecedented view of our planetary neighbor!

I turned the switch on and off, and I fiddled with the crystal in its aperture, trying to re-open the line of communication, but the window closed as mysteriously as it had opened.

Still, I am too excited to be frustrated. I am certain that the phenomena shall be repeated.

Otherwise, I fear I have a head-cold coming on. It may be the turn in the weather. I took a solution of salts, in lemon and barley-water. Though especially prepared by Mrs. H. from her own curative recipe, this concoction served only to exacerbate my condition. I passed an indifferent night, with frequent recourse to the c. p. and my handkerchief.

September 8: Invasions!

That confounded cold has set in, in my head and chest. The servants have plainly been lax in tending draught-excluders. Or else Signor Galvani's foreign crew have imported alien bacteria into the household — for which they will be reprimanded. I am known for my good health, and these minor ailments do not normally afflict me.

Breakfast — porridge, honey-glazed gammon, courgettes, preserved pears. More of Mrs. H.'s vile (and inefficacious) home remedy. It'll get worse before it gets better, I am assured — which is scarce comfort. I have instructed the housekeeper to dispense with her brews, and procure proper medicine from the chemist's.

My digestion was incomplete when Flamsteed was impertinently invaded. In my study, making a start on notes for my Marsian Announcement, I became aware of a great ringing on the bell and knocking at the door. My first thought was that barbarians were at the gates. This proved to be the case — though, a singular barbarian, the opprobrious Ogilvy, rather than a horde.

I ventured out into the hallway and found Mrs. Huddersfield in the process of calling the stable-boy to throw Og. off our front step. Much as it would have pleased me to see the inky git tossed into the gravel and given a good kicking, it occurred to me that he should be consulted. Plainly, he had some dim perception of the importance of the crystal egg. It would be best to find out what he knew.

I instructed Mrs. H. to let Og. into the house. She stood aside and I had momentary pause about my decision. Having run across a superfluity of madmen in recent days, I saw at once that Og. was one

of their number. His collar was exploded and his
cravat tied carelessly. The skirts of his frock-coat bore
singe-marks as if he had jumped through a bonfire.
There was a peculiar burned smell about him. He had
no eyebrows left and a serious case of the sun. It had
been overcast lately and I doubted Og. was freshly-
returned from some tropical adventure.

"Brandy," he insisted. "Brandy, for God's sake,
Stent."

Mrs. H. frowned, but I told her to send Polly to
fetch a decanter of the third-best brandy. No sense
in wasting the good stuff on an hysteric. I'll need it
to fight off this cold.

In my study, Og. saw the egg, still fit into the aperture of the new telescope.

"So you know what it is?" he exclaimed.

"Indeed."

"A window — a portal — to the Red Planet. Have
you seen the Martians?"

"Marsians," I corrected.

"Their tripod machines? Their firing pit? Their
heat-devices? Have you determined their purpose,
Stent? Their hideous purpose?"

The fellow was ranting, but I expected as much.

"I have made notes of my findings," I told him.
"I will reveal my conclusions when I am ready to
publish."

"Publish!? Who will there be to type-set, print and
bind your conclusions, Stent? Who to read them? Do
you hope to amuse our new masters with your book?
They don't seem the types to be great readers, but
I suppose you never know..."

Og. was laughing, now — bitterly, insanely, irri-
tatingly. Polly arrived, and Og. snatched the decanter
from her tray. He drew a mighty quaff, then wiped
his mouth with the back of his hand. Never the most
savory of characters, he had apparently decided to
become a wild Indian.

"There were four eggs," he said. "As far as we can
tell."

"We? Of whom are you speaking?"

"The Red Planet League," he said. "What there is left of it. When you took the final egg, we had this telescope delivered to you. I am loathe to admit it, but you are the greatest astronomical mind of the age..."

"True, true..."

"...and if anyone has a chance of cracking the egg's secrets, it is you."

"No doubt."

I fancied I caught a slight smirk from Polly, and told her she could be about her business. She left.

"It must have been fate that brought you to Cave's emporium. Cave is dead, by the way. The police report says "spontaneous combustion", if you can credit it. There has been a rash of such phenomena. Almost an epidemic. Colonel Moran and I had a brush with the heat weapons, two nights back. We were separated afterwards. His nerve snapped. Terrible thing when a brave man's nerve goes. He's faced tigers and native rebels and charging elephants, but that flash from the copper tube boiled away all his heart. You saw Moran yesterday, I believe — before *they* caught up to him."

"I saw no one yesterday."

"In the Strand, outside Simpson's. Moran would have seemed, ah, irrational. Lord knows, we all act like cuckoos. With what we have in our heads. It's only to be expected. A big man, Moran. Red-complected, after our experience..."

I remembered. The madman who was taken away by the hump-backed policeman.

"Moran brought me into the League. He's a big-game hunter and adventurer. He found the first of the eggs, in a temple in India. It was the eye of an idol worshipped by an obscene cult. When the light fell into the temple on certain days of the year, the portal opened and the cultists saw their "Gods". You know what they really saw, Stent. The men of Mars. Those tentacles, those eyes, those mouth-parts!

Another crystal was looted from the collection of the Emperor of China, carved into a goblet. I would not drink from that goblet for all the tea in its rightful owner's dominions, would you? A third was found fresh, among the hot fragments of a new-fallen meteorite in the Arizona desert. All these came to the League, and all have been *taken* — taken *back*, one might say."

Og. kept glancing at the crystal. I worried that he would snatch it from the telescope and flee the house.

"This one was sent here, to England. I don't know how Cave came by it. Dishonestly, I suppose."

"It is mine," I reminded him. "Paid for and bought."

He wasn't listening to me. "Stent, have *they* seen *you*? The portal opens both ways. That we can see them is incidental, an accident, a flaw in the great plan. From the other side, from *Mars*, they spy us. Spy *on* us. It's what the eggs are for. They are taking our measure, making a study. Drawing plans. At first, the meteorites just brought the eggs. It's only recently that *they* have come. Just a few, but enough — for their purpose. Across millions of miles of empty space! What explorers they must be, what conquerors. They ready their armada, Stent, their fleet..."

I concede that Og. was alarming me. A great deal of what he said struck me as fanciful drivel. Conquerors, indeed — what nonsense, as if creatures without hands or clothing could hope to stand up to the military might of Great Britain! But I worried there were eggs in other hands. Dangerous hands — other scientists eager to 'scoop' the Great Stent. If half of what Og. said is true, someone else might publish first.

I can not let that happen.

The doorbell rang. Mrs. H. came into the study, and presented a *carte de visite*.

Colonel Sebastian Moran, Conduit Street.

"Your comrade in the League has extricated himself from the police," I told Og.

The fellow looked further stricken, which was not what I expected. I got little sense from him. I feared this would also be true of Moran — yesterday, he had been singing from the same hymnbook.

"Don't let him in," said Og., grabbing my lapel. "In the name of all that's..."

"There's a policeman with the caller, sir," said Mrs. H. "Constable Purbright."

I could not have been more relieved. With all the ranting, raving and lapel-grabbing, a policeman might be just what the doctor ordered. Clap these madmen up in irons, and leave me to conclude my Marsian studies.

"Show them in," I said.

"Very good, Sir Nevil. Don't you be straining yourself. Remember you're not a well man."

Og. threw himself into an armchair, in a pose of stark terror. Under his sunburn, he even went pale.

"Hullo... Sir... Nevil... Hullo... Ogilvy..."

It was the madman from the Strand, but much changed. His demeanor was more sober, respectable. His voice was uninflected, somehow metallic. And, since yesterday, he had grown a humpback. A long, red scarf wound around his neck, ends trailing down his back.

"Good... morning... gentlemen," said the police constable beside Moran.

They could have been brothers, with the same shifting deformity, the same strange manner of speech.

"Keep them away from me," shrieked Og. "They're... *them!*"

"Don't... make... a... fuss... old... chap."

Moran and Purbright spoke in unison, like a music hall turn. Their voices scraped the nerves. I was overcome by a powerful wish that all my visitors should leave. I could do with a medicinal tot, and some peace.

The constable walked, stiff-legged, across the room, to the telescope. He laid a hand on the crystal egg.

"That's delicate scientific equipment," I warned Purbright.

"Evidence... sir," he said, twisting the egg free.

"I must protest..."

"Obey... the... law—" said Colonel Moran.

Moran was in my way. Beyond him, I saw the constable slipping the crystal egg into his tunic.

"I paid five pounds for that!"

"Stolen... goods," said Moran.

I tried to strong-arm him out of the way, but he was immovable. My hand fell on his hump, and his long scarf unwound, showing where his jacket seam was split by the swelling. An angry, inhuman eye looked out from the hole! Sinewy, venous scarlet ropes wound around Moran's exposed neck. A beak-like barb was fixed to his throat, under the ear, blood dribbling from the conjunction.

A cowardly knee met my groin, and I doubled over.

When I righted myself, Moran had rearranged his scarf. I knew what I had seen.

Og. leaped up from the chair and flew at Moran.

From a pocket, Moran pulled a curious object — a tube with a burnished copper disc at one end. A beam of light seemed to project from this — and fell on Og., whose jacket started smoking. With a scream, Og. fled from the room, down the hall, and out of the house. His clothes were on fire.

Moran turned to me. Purbright had also produced one of the heat-casting devices. Both were aimed in my direction.

I sensed I was in danger. But if the egg left the house, I would have no proof, no basis for my findings!

Og.s' screams still echoed.

"We... must... be... going..." said Moran.

"Not with my crystal egg."

The copper discs were glinting at me but I was resolute. No somnambulists, puppeteered by angry-eyed inhuman humps, would stand between me and recognition for my achievements.

"I am Sir Nevil Airey Stent, the Astronomer Royal," I reminded them. "I will thank you to return my property. On this world, sirs, I am not to be sneezed at."

"Sneezed... at?" they both said.

At that inopportune moment, my cold struck again — and I had a sneezing fit.

This had the most peculiar effect on my threatening guests. They turned tail, in something like panic, and ran. Purbright dropped the egg which — mercifully — did not shatter. As they ran, they slumped over, arms dangling uselessly, heads lolling — as if they were piloted by their tentacular humps, who could no longer concentrate on even the semblance of normal conduct.

My sheer physical presence, and the dignity of my office, had overwhelmed these creatures.

But I did not doubt they would be back.

I took some brandy, for my chest and sinuses, and reflected over my triumph in this skirmish of the spheres.

Mrs. H. called me to the garden. On the gravel driveway lay a human-shaped pile of ashes, already drifting in the wind. It seems I don't have to worry about Ogilvy horning in on my findings any more...

Feeling much better, despite sniffles, I returned to my study.

In Lady Caroline's continued absence, attempted congress with Polly — but, for some reason, was thwarted. Have much on my mind.

D— this cold!

September 8 — *later:* I Capture a Marsian!

Mrs. H. has obtained a supply of a patent medicine, Dr. Tirmoary's Infusion for Coughs, Colds and

Wheezes. According to the label, it is mostly *diacetyl-morphine hydrochloride*. The stuff burns in a basin, and is inhaled under a damp towel. I spent ten minutes breathing acrid fumes before supper — dressed Cornish crab, lamprey *surpris*, calamari, conger mousse, langoustines — and, finally, gained some measure of relief from congestion, sniffles and associated symptoms. Not only am I sneezing less, I am thinking more clearly.

After a fresh, post-prandial infusion of Dr. Tirmoary's, I retired to my study, determined to tinker with the crystal egg until it yielded its secrets. But, light-headed and with a sense of fullness in my stomach and other parts, I fell into a doze in an arm-chair...

I was awakened by a whirring, which I recognized as the sound of the telescope when the egg-portal was open. The room was bathed in a red, flickering light. The window to Mars!

Again, I saw Stent's Plain, the Victoria Chasm, the Caroline Range. Now, there was great activity. Structures had changed, been erected or expanded. Many Marsian creatures could be seen, crawling about their purpose — which seemed to me to be the construction, within the Chasm, of a great cannonlike device. This could be aimed, I saw at once, at the tiny bluish speck on the Marsian horizon.

I recalled Og.'s ravings about a Marsian armada readying for a trip across the gulf of space.

Poppycock and nonsense!

My study door opened, and Polly came in. The possibility of a renewed attempt at congress arose, and I bound from my chair, into the beam of egg-light. For a moment, I was distracted by my own silhouette, cast on the wall as images from Mars played across my body.

Something was amiss. Polly, hunched over, wore a heavy shawl — not suitable for indoors. She carried a wicker basket, which I had not asked to be brought to me. Emboldened, I tore away her shawl. A red, wct creature pulsed on her shoulder, tentacles wound around her neck, face buried in her throat.

My maid was host to a Marsian!

I tripped over the carpet and fell back into the armchair. My nerve was resolute, but my limbs betrayed me — some side-effect of Dr. Tirmoary's, I'll be bound, for which the manufacturer will receive a stern letter from my solicitor. I could not stand. The room became a swirling red blur, as much Mars as Greenwich. I fancied that the beings I saw working on their cannon could see me across the void, and might crawl through the portal.

Polly set down the wicker basket.

She attempted a clumsy curtsey, and craned her cheek against her Marsian master, stroking its slimy hide as if she were indulging a kitten. The creature, bereft of its native atmosphere, was in evident difficulty. I'll wager they can't last long among us. Susceptible to all manner of Earthly ailments, drowning in our alien air, boiling in what was to us a cool evening.

The lid lifted from the basket, and a curious contraption rose from within — like a brass diving bell, on three mechanical legs. Some sort of clockwork enabled it to 'stand', and 'walk'. A thick window showed the tentacle-fringed, scarlet face of a Marsian. Within the sphere, it was comfortable — sustained by some sort of liquid atmosphere, doubtless rich with the nutrients of Mars.

This must be the chief of the Marsians on Earth, leader of the expedition, the planet's most able diplomat. I looked it — him! — in the eyes, and began to introduce myself.

"We... know... who... you... are... Mr.... Stent..."

The words came from a hooded figure who had slipped into the room. I realized at once that the superior creature in the bell could exert mental control over a human without the need for physical contact. This facility must be developed among the higher castes of the planet. The hooded figure was a meaningless person. His head bobbed from side to side like an imbecile's as the Marsian Master spoke through him.

"It strikes me that you have not conducted yourselves in the proper manner," I told him. "You should have come to me first, not wasted your time with this rag-tag Red Planet League."

Meaningless syllables stuttered from the hooded puppet. The laughter of Mars!

"Well you may laugh, sir! A serious misunderstanding could have come about between our two great planets, as a result of your congress with the likes of George Ogilvy. He holds no great office. Now you have come to the proper person, the Astronomer Royal. You are in communication with someone best-placed to reveal your presence to the worthies of Great Britain. Treaties can be brokered, as trade agreements are being made in our world's Orient. If travel between planets is possible, we may send you missionaries, medical staff, advisers. We must form a limited company. Anglo-Marsian Trading. I perceive you get scant use from your famous canals, but a few Scots engineers will have a railway system up and running across your red sands in no time. You have a surfeit of coolies, I see."

The syllables continued. Not laughter, I think — but song! A native hosanna at the prospect of deliverance from a state of ignorance and depravity.

I looked into the Marsian's huge, lidless eyes.

The hooded man spoke. "I... speak... for... you... would... call... him... Roi... Marty... King... of... Mars."

I was impressed that such an exalted personage should be my guest.

"And what service may I do the King of Mars?"

Polly and the hooded figure raised now-familiar copper tubes, which caught the red light from the telescope. I sensed Marsian treachery!

"You... can... *burn...*"

Then, things happened swiftly.

A sturdy broom scythed down on Polly's shoulder, squelching her alien master — which detached from her with a hideous shriek and flew across the room to explode against the mantelpiece, swollen organs bursting through its skin. The redoubtable Mrs. Huddersfield was in my study, swinging her broom like a yeoman's quarterstaff. The hooded figure turned, and fire broke out on the wall where fell the beam from his copper tube. Mrs. H. tripped him, and he tumbled in a heap.

"Take that, you fiend from another world, you," shouted Mrs. H., with some relish. "I'll not have you botherin' the *Astronomer Royal!*"

Polly, bereft of a controlling mind, stood staring, still as a statue, angry weals on her neck and bosom. Mrs. H. took to battering and sweeping the King of Mars's puppet, driving him from the room, and — indeed — out of the house.

The King's Bell began to move, edging away on its three legs. With all the skill of my days as a varsity three-quarter, I fell on the contraption, pinning it down, preventing its escape.

Robbed of its puppet, the King had no way to converse. Its eyes bulged in mute, frustrated fury.

"Your highness, you are captured!" I told it. "You will surrender yourself to my authority."

The spell of the crystal egg was broken. A last unsteady image held for a few moments, then bright red light replaced the vista of Mars. The whirring sped up after the picture was lost. Something flapped loosely inside the telescope before it shut off entirely.

Mrs. H. returned, broom over her shoulder, and the puppet's hood in her grip. She reported that she had seen the puppet — a demented tramp, she believed — high-tailing it down the drive. He was unimportant, I knew. No more than a set of vocal chords.

Polly was recovered from her upright faint, but still in a dazed state. She did not relish the memory of communion with the creature which lay dead in a jumble in the fireplace. All she could say was that its touch was slimy and sharp. I suggested a dose of Dr. Tirmoary's, but she turned it down — she has promised her mother not to have truck with such potions, apparently. Mrs. H. similarly passed up the opportunity to taste her own medicine, but I felt another dose would be restorative and invigorating. I am becoming quite partial to its effects. A certain gaiety is upon me after each infusion. Of course, I am in a heightened state of excitement just now, in the midst of these great events.

War is over before it is begun! I have captured the Marsian King!

Also, I have one of the copper tubes. A gun of Mars. I must find out how the hot-beam works. The burned patch on my study wall has a chemical smell, as if some reactive compound were smeared on the paper and left to ignite — but I sense the truth of the process is to do with transforming light into heat. I shall experiment with this device in safer, less expensively-decorated premises.

The King squirms and writhes in his metal shell. The three legs are wired together, so it may not 'walk' free.

I have communicated by telegram with the Royal Society, setting a date three days hence for my Marsian lecture. I shall use the crystal egg and display the terrain and inhabitants of the Red Planet to those who would call themselves my scientific peers. I shall demonstrate the use of the copper tube — maybe singe the trousers of some of my more disbelieving colleagues, to make a point. Then, as the crowning moment, I shall present the King of Mars!

Surely, ennoblement must follow. I shall be Lord Flamsteed of Mars!

Considered congress with Mrs. H. and/or Polly, but was persuaded instead to cap off the evening with another infusion of Good Old Dr. Tirmoary's.

I am Conqueror of Mars!

Being a reprint from the Reminiscences
of Col. Sebastian Moran, Late of the
1st Bengalore Pioneers — continued

Pah! Ever read such rot, eh? Believe me, those were the
interesting pages. The rest of Stent's journal is fit only to
start fires. His entries are stuffed with menus and 'con-
gresses' and remarks about how brilliant, acclaimed, well-
loved and admirable he is. By my count, the Astronomer
Royal penned seventeen thousand heated words about a
controversial boot-scraper installed, removed, installed
again, relocated by six inches and finally removed from
outside the servants' door at Flamsteed House.

How did I get hold of the journal? Stole it, of course.
Not that Stent was in any state to complain.

By pasting in these pages, I've saved myself a deal of
pen-work, which is all to the good. More time down the
pub, rather than filling up an exercise book with this
scribble.

Of course, you knew me at once when I turned up in
Stent's narrative — doing my old 'madman' act, which has
proved persuasive in many a tight spot. When I start froth-
ing and raving, you wouldn't want to be around. Avoided
being fed to crocodiles once by throwing a similar wob-
bly. The queer... halting... voice... took more effort, and
Moriarty had to coach us — me, P. C. P., Polly — in the
proper hollow tones. We used Punch and Judy swizzles,
as well. *That's the way to do it!*

As for the rest of it, the Professor only let us into as much
of his grand scheme as he deemed necessary. Like his
imaginary Squid King, Moriarty puppeteered his subjects,
speaking words through us, chivvying Stent along until
the fathead fancied himself Conqueror of Mars. Of course,
Ogilvy didn't know how flammable the gunk poured on
his jacket really was. The cretin hopped around outside
Flamsteed House, on fire from head to foot, until a bucket
of merciful water was sloshed over him. By then, he was
almost in as poor shape as the ash and cinder outline laid
out on the gravel to represent his incinerated remains.

Threw a sulk about that, he did. Still, can't make an omelette
and all that. In Ogilvy's case, it's true. He lost the use of
his arms and hands, and so literally can't make an omelette,
or perform many other everyday tasks. That's what you
get for volunteering.

I've rarely had cause to remark upon Professor
Moriarty's genius for disguise and impersonation. There's
good reason for that. Anyone less wholly shoved up his
own bum than Sir Nevil Stent would have seen through
Moriarty's beards and hoods and skullcaps and spectacles
in a trice. That snake-oscillation mannerism *always* gave
him away. He didn't list card-sharping among his favored
crimes, or he'd have known about 'tells' and taken steps
to suppress his. On one occasion, I tried to raise the matter
in as tactful a fashion as possible, venturing to suggest that
the Professor moderate his 'cobra-neck tell' when incognito.

"What are you talking about, Moran? Have you been
at the *diacetylmorphine hydrochloride* again?"

There was no sense in pressing the matter further.
Genius or no, Moriarty truly didn't know about the thing
he did with his neck. I wondered if he was unconsciously
trying to make it difficult for the hangman in anticipation
of an eventual date with the gallows. Probably not. It was
just a habit. Other men scratch their balls, fiddle with their
watch-chains or chew their moustaches. That's when it's
a good time to double up, throw the mortgage into the pot
and slide an ace out of your cuff.

Nevertheless, Moriarty acquitted himself adequately
in the multiple roles of 'C. Cave', filthy shop-keeper, 'long-
necked cabbie', dispenser of jovially ominous sentiments,
and 'Hooded Man of Mystery', mouth-piece of Martian
Royalty. (Stent never did persuade anyone else to say
'Marsian'.) As you can tell from the diary, the worthy Mrs.
Halifax, pouting Polly, Italian Joe (Signor Galvani), P. C. P.
and some nobly self-sacrificing specimens of *vampyroteuthis
infernalis* also strutted and fret their weary hours on the
stage.

It's a shame there wasn't any money in it. The whole
palaver cost the firm a great deal, exhausting the proceeds
of five good-sized blags, and sinking Moriarty into debts

we had to work hard to pay off. I know we have a reputation as rotters and crooks and all, but it doesn't do to
default on payments owed someone who *likes* to be called
the Lord of Strange Deaths. Hellish vampire squid wouldn't
have been the half of it.

For the Prof, the pay-off came at Stent's lecture.

This time, the Royal Astronomical Society wasn't a grand
enough platform for Sir Nevil, but we were back in
Burlington House. The edifice is also H. Q. of *the* Royal
Society, a body so sniffily superior it feels it doesn't even
need to give you the full name — which, as it happens,
is The Royal Society for the Improvement of Natural
Knowledge — when you are expected to prostrate yourself
before the hallowed altars of high science and furthermore
purchase an illustrated souvenir program booklet to
memorialize the hours you spent snoozing through a lecture. Chairman at the time of these occurrences was Thomas
Henry Huxley, and you know what the Astronomer Royal
thought of *him*. I don't doubt Huxley thought the same right
back at Stent, who — for reasons which by now must be
glaring — was not as popular with the general community of test-tube sniffers and puppy-vivisectors as he was
with his home crowd of star-gazing toadies.

Again, we took our seats. Sans disguises, on the assump-
tion Stent wouldn't notice us in the crowd — at least, not
until the crucial moment. The hall was packed, as if word
had leaked out that Lola Montez would be tightrope-
walking nude over the audience while Jenny Lind sang
all eighty-six verses of 'The Ballad of Eskimo Nell'. Every
branch of science was represented, for Stent had announced
his lecture would radically affect all of them equally. A lot
of text-books would need revising (or burning) after this
one, the rumor-mill insisted. To me, the mob looked like
an unkempt crowd of smelly schoolmasters on a spree, but
the Prof clucked and tutted to himself, listing the great
names who had shown up. Besides our home-grown brain-
boxes, there were Yanks, Frogs, Krauts, Eye-ties, dressed-
up darkies of assorted hues and an authentic Belgian —
all trailing more degrees, honors, doctorates and profes-
sorships than you could shake a stick at. It would have

been humbling if they weren't mostly aged and chalk-covered. We had salted the room with a few of our own fellahs, who carried hat-boxes or picnic hampers and were a bit fidgety in clean, respectable clothes. A squeaky-voiced draper's clerk tried to squeeze in on a platform ticket, but was properly ejected for being a lower-class bounder.

This time, Stent went for dramatic effect.

The house-lights dimmed, and a spot came up on the lectern. The Conqueror of Mars posed dramatically, in a vestment-like long white coat.

"Gentlemen," he began, "we are not alone..."

He whipped a dust-cloth from the 'reflecting telescope' which incorporated the 'crystal egg'. In the end, Polly had been forced to draw him a picture to show how she had 'accidentally' made it work. Between shows, someone had to reset or replace the strip of exposures inside the box and put in a new incandescent bulb — which meant getting Stent away from his toy. Fortunately, he'd quite a nose for Dr. Tirmoary's Infusions and was often in a daze.

"I give you... the Planet Mars!"

Stent toggled a lever and electric current made a motor grind. Red images were cast on a white board erected on the platform. Squid crawled across a sandbox, gagging for water. There were gasps of awe, though a few coughs of scepticism too. A few sequences wound backwards, which gave an eerie, unnatural effect — as if pictures that moved weren't unnatural enough.

I'd seen some of these views 'taken' by Mr. Paul A. Robert of Brighton. Urchin assistants had to hand-color the scenes, picture by picture. Robert has a glass-roofed studio under construction on the downs. I had to be blind-folded and driven up and around country lanes before visiting it because he fears some Yankee swine is out to poach the process and present it as his own invention. Good luck to him, I say. Apart from making a fool of the Astrono-mer Royal, all Robert's whateveroscope is good for is giving anyone who stares too long at the stuttering pictures a blinding headache. I daresay few in the audience had seen the like. There was still that damned whirring and flap-ping as exposures passed in front of the incandescent. The bloody racket is why Robert's Box Pictures in Motion will never 'catch on', if you ask me. They'll never replace the stereopticon.

After the images from the crystal egg passed, Stent was assailed by questions. Some were about the creatures, but most were about Robert's Box — which several in the audience had heard of before. One or two had even seen the thing demonstrated while the inventor was soliciting funds for development of his annoying wonder of the age. When Stent repeated his assertion that the Box was a 'reflecting telescope', someone called him an 'blithering idiot'. He looked displeased. Several helpful souls shouted out the principles on which the Box worked. A couple of young fellahs got into a heated argument about 'persistence of vision' and 'Muybridge strips'. No one cared much about *what* they had seen (it could have been a chuffing train or a couple snogging, for all they cared) but many were intrigued by the *process* whereby moving images were cast on a board. Stent had caused a sensation, but not the way he expected.

Moriarty smiled to himself.

Seeing things not going his way, Sir Nevil hastened on to what would have been his grand finale.

"Sirs, men from Mars are among us! They have been here quite some time!"

Hoots, whistles, laughs.

Stent lifted another drop-cloth from an exhibit.

"This is the King of Mars," he announced.

There was sudden hush. The window in the bell had a magnifying effect, and the hideous red face of the creature trapped inside loomed. The buccal orifice clacked angrily.

For a moment, everyone was struck quiet and frozen. Swollen alien eyes, set in angry red facial frills, seemed to range over the assembled scientific multitudes, as if ready to direct a 'hot-beam' across their ranks and wipe out the great minds of Earth before calling down a sky-fleet of tentacled horrors. Red tentacles writhed, ready to crush human resistance before hauling up the Martian standard on the blackened ruins of Burlington House.

The Robert's Box was forgotten, and this new horror held the attention.

Stent, sensing that he was on the point of winning a few converts, radiated a certain smugness, as his thick hide recovered from the earlier pinpricks. His shirt-front puffed out a bit, like a squid rising above its spawning-depth, and he allowed himself to look on the audience with his old superior attitude. If this King of Mars could cow the Royal Society, then Stent might transfer his allegiance from the lesser, terrestrial monarch he had hitherto served. If his mighty brain went unappreciated on this poor planet, then perhaps he should look elsewhere for patronage...

Then, just as Stent was on the point of recapturing his audience, the Professor stood up and shouted "where's his party hat?"

Stent was horror-struck at the sight of an enemy he'd thought bested. His mood turned. For a moment, I assumed he'd seen through the whole business and understood how he'd been gulled, but it was a passing doubt. The Astronomer Royal remained firm in his convictions. He believed what Moriarty had made him believe.

"I insist," he said, holding up a copper tube, "this is a visitor from another world."

Seconds ago, he had been taken at his word. Now, the sceptics and rationalists — for is this not an age of doubt? — were inclined to get close to the old gift horse and pay close attention to his choppers.

An elderly Frenchman from the front row got up and took a closer look at the bell, squinting through pince-nez.

"This is a 'hot-beam' device," said Stent, voice cracking. "A weapon of Mars!"

He aimed it at the now-bewildered crowds, as if willing it to burst them into flame. Of course, we weren't smeared with the slow-acting chemical concoction which provided the fire when the pretend-guns were used in Flamsteed House.

"This is a squid," announced the Frenchman. "Someone has cruelly dyed it red. An uncommon specimen, but not unknown."

Some laughter was forthcoming. A paper dart, folded from a program, zoomed from the back of the room and sliced past Stent's head.

"This is the Marsian King," Stent told the onion-eater. "Roi Marty. You, sir, are an unqualified dolt. You know nothing of alien worlds."

"*Eh bien*, perhaps," the Frenchman admitted. "But I, *monsieur*, am Professor Pierre Arronax, greatest living authority on denizens of the deep. In debate about the courses of the stars, I would allow you are far more expert than I. However, in matters of marine biology, you are a child of five and I am an encyclopedia on legs. This, I repeat, is a squid. An unhealthy squid."

"I say, Stent, is that the sick squid you owe me?" brayed one wit.

"Here here," shouted a vocal clique of Arronax supporters. "A squid, a squid!"

Stent's world was collapsing. He knew not what to say. His mouth opened and closed, but no words issued forth. I saw he was desperate for an infusion of Dr. Tirmoary's — damn fine stuff, let me tell you, though even I would caution against excessive use. The Astronomer Royal pressed his fists to his temples as if to shut out the catcalls and retreat into his own 'sunnar system'. There, many-limbed things crawled across the sands of Mars, intent on climbing into three-legged suits of armor, hurling themselves at the Earth to subjugate humanity for food and amusement.

Moriarty's facial tendons were tight as leather drumskin dried in the sun, making his face a skull-mask rictus of glee. His eyes lit up like Chinese lanterns. I'd wager every muscle in the old ascetic's stringy body was tight with sordid pleasure. He got like that when he had his way. Other fellahs might pop a bottle of fizz or nip down to Mrs. H's for a turn with a trollop, but the Professor just went into these brain-spasms of evil ecstasy.

Huxley left the hall in disgust, followed by a dignified procession. Some of his colleagues, perhaps pettier, stayed to jeer. The draper's clerk poked his head in, and asked if he'd missed anything.

"Wait, don't leave," said Stent, vainly. He viciously pressed a stud on his copper-tube. No one caught fire. "There's danger in disbelief. The Martians are coming! You fools, you must listen. If you don't support me, you're next! They're here! The Martians are among us!"

At that moment, Moriarty gave a signal.

Our people stood up in their seats — one or two were stationed 'backstage' — and lobbed struggling missiles at Stent. Out of water, the squid didn't last long — but they fought hard, as Polly and I can bear witness, getting tentacles around something convenient and squeezing madly while internal pressure blew them up like balloons. It was a sight to see, but most of the paying customers were gone.

A volley of squid fell upon Stent. He yelled and slipped, knocking over the lectern. Tentacles wound around his legs, his waist, one hand. A squid fixed to his lower face like a mask, beak thrust into his mouth in a ghastly kiss, shutting off his screams. Plastered with *vampyroteuthis*, he threw a full-on fit, back arching, limbs twitching. Eventually, attendants came and pried burst, dead creatures off him.

Arronax tried to lodge a protest at this mistreatment of rare specimens, but slipped into French to do it and was properly ignored. There are idiot Englishwomen (of both sexes) who would be generally happier to see children whipped, starved, laughed at, shot and mounted in the Moran den than brook any abuse of their 'furry or feathered friends' — but it was a rare crank, like Pop-eyed Pierre, who gave two hoots for anything with tentacles and a beak.

With all our wriggling shots fired, the Professor gave the nod — and our picked men melted into the crowds, well-paid and frankly little the wiser for tonight's business. When Moriarty handed over coin and told you to bowl a squid at an astronomer, your wisest course was to ask 'over-arm or round-arm?' and get on with play.

As his arms were slipped into a strait-waistcoat, Stent begged for an infusion of Dr. T's. He had the shakes, the sweats and the abdabs at the same time. All his strings were cut.

It so happened that the director of Purfleet Asylum — a far less pleasing official residence than Flamsteed — was in the audience, and well-positioned to take the babbling madman off Lady Caroline's hands. I think she had papers already drawn up, assuming control of all Sir Nevil's estates and monies. Being the second daughter of an Earl doesn't come with much ready cash, but getting hold of the Stent fortune would do her for a while. I made a note to look her up.

The Astronomer Royal was carried from Burlington House, strapped to a stretcher.

We lingered in the imposing hallway, lined with portraits of past presidents. The attendants paused for a moment. Moriarty leaned over his now-broken nemesis.

Stent's eyes rolled upwards. His cheeks were striped red and dotted with horribly familiar sucker marks. He tried to focus on the face looming over him, the thin-lipped leering countenance of the author of *The Dynamics of an Asteroid*.

"I have, I think, made my point," said Professor Moriarty. "And you, Stent, have finally learned your lesson."

Editors

J. R. Campbell is an occasional presence tolerated by the eminent Sherlockians of Calgary's Singular Society of the Baker Street Dozen, where he is considered something of a dilettante. Despite this he has managed to co-edit two previous anthologies of Sherlock Holmes mysteries, *Curious Incidents* and *Curious Incidents 2* as well as providing the great detective a chance to fill his pipe on Imagination Theater's radio series *The Further Adventures of Sherlock Holmes*. He lives in Calgary with his wife and three children, none of whom are impressed by his acquaintance with Sherlock Holmes. Quite correctly, they point out writing about someone clever and observant does not make the writer clever nor observant.

Charles V. Prepolec is co-editor of two previous Sherlock Holmes anthologies *Curious Incidents Vols. 1 & 2* and has contributed articles and reviews to *All Hallows, Sherlock Magazine, Scarlet Street, Canadian Holmes*, and his website www.bakerstreetdozen.com. An active Sherlockian for more than 20 years with Calgary's The Singular Society of the Baker Street Dozen, he was designated a Master Bootmaker in 2006 by the Bootmaker's of Toronto — Canada's national Sherlock Holmes Society. He lives in Calgary, AB, Canada with his wife Kristen and their cat Karma.

Artists

Timothy Lantz is a full-time illustrator and graphic artist with degrees in art education and communications. During his career, Lantz's work has included such far-flung projects as weather maps, television commercials, book covers and tarot cards. He is the author and artist of *The Archeon Tarot*, available from U. S. Games Systems Inc. You can find more of his work on his website, www.stygiandarkness.com

Phil Cornell was born in Sydney, Australia in 1954. He first came into contact with Sherlock Holmes at the age of ten when given an anthology containing 'The Speckled Band.' The infection was instant and incurable. He lives in Sydney with his twelve year old son, two cats and more Sherlockian books and videos than can comfortably fit in a fairly small home. He holds the position of "Expedition Artist" in The Sydney Passengers Sherlock Holmes Society. He is also a member of The Unscrupulous Rascals of South Australia and The Sherlock Holmes Society of London. He works as a commercial artist.

Authors

Peter Calamai, a journalist for more than four decades as a reporter, foreign correspondent and editor (winner of four National Newspaper Awards), is an enthusiastic Sherlockian. The author of numerous pastiches and scholarly Sherlockian and Doylean articles, he is a Master Bootmaker and invested in The Baker Street Irregulars as "The Leeds Mercury," befitting his special interest in Late Victorian newspapers. He lives in Ottawa.

J. R. Campbell's fiction has appeared in a wide variety fo publications including *Spinetingler Magazine, Wax Romantic* and *Challenging Destiny*. He has also contributed to various anthologies including *Bone Ballet* and *Fantastical Visions IV*. His work can also be heard on radio's Imagination Theater (jimfrenchproductions.com)

David Stuart Davies is a playwright and the author of five Sherlock Holmes pastiches. His survey of the detective's screen career *Starring Sherlock Holmes* was published by Titan in 2007. He is the former editor of *Sherlock* magazine and currently edits *Red Herrings* for the Crime Writer's Association and serves as general editor of the Wordsworth Mystery and Supernatural series. His latest Johnny One-Eye mystery *Without Conscience* was published in March of 2008. www.davidstuartdavies.com

M. J. Elliott's writing credits include episodes of many US radio series. Among the collections he has edited for Wordsworth Publications are several volumes of stories by H. P. Lovecraft and Robert E. Howard. On the lighter side, Matthew has lent his voice and writing talents to the *Rifftrax* website, masterminded by the makers of *Mystery Science Theater 3000*.

Since publishing her first fantasy novel, *The Time of the Dark*, **Barbara Hambly** has published more than 40 novels. Although she's written across many genres, her work displays a special fondness for both fantasy and historical mysteries. A Guest of Honor at the 2008 World Fantasy Convention, Barbara's recent projects include *Renfield: Slave of Dracula* and the historical *Patriot Hearts*.

Since 1979, **Chico Kidd**'s stories have been published in the UK, the USA, Canada, Australia and Europe. Her first novel, *The Printer's Devil*, came out in 1996. First hardback anthology: *Summoning Knells* (2000). Chico's and Rick Kennett's collection *No 472 Cheyne Walk* was published in 2002. Since 2000 she has been busy with the Da Silva sequence of novels and stories. *The Mammoth Book of Best New Horror 13* and *Dark Terrors 6* featured three between them. Others have appeared in *Supernatural Tales, Acquainted with the Night* and elsewhere.

Rick Kennett is a resident of Melbourne, Australia, and works in the transport industry. His ghost stories have appeared in many magazines and anthologies. He's co-author with Chico Kidd of *472 Cheyne Walk: Carnacki, the Untold Stories* (Ash Tree Press 2002). His hobbies include naval history and wandering cemeteries (necrotourism).

Bob Madison is the editor of *Dracula: The First Hundred Years*, published in 1997, and the author of the kid-oriented *American Horror Writers* (2000). He has also written for *Wonder Magazine, Cult Movies* and *The Dinosaur Times*. He has appeared on WABC-TV's *Good Morning America*, WOR's *Joey Reynolds Show* and WABC's *Morning News*, among others, and DVD documentaries for the classic movie versions of *Frankenstein, The Bride of Frankenstein, Dracula* and *Abbott and Costello Meet Frankenstein*.

Kim Newman is a novelist, critic and broadcaster. His fiction includes *Anno Dracula, Life's Lottery* and *The Man From the Diogenes Club*. His non-fiction includes *Nightmare Movies, Horror: 100 Best Books* and *BFI Classics* studies *of Cat People* and *Doctor Who*. He is a contributing editor to *Sight & Sound* and *Empire*. His website is at johnnyalucard.com.

Martin Powell is the author of the Eisner nominated Sherlock Holmes/Dracula adventure, *Scarlet in Gaslight*. Although he has returned to the character many other times, Powell considers *Sherlock Holmes in the Lost World*, contained in this volume, as his personal favorite among his own stories featuring the Great Detective.

Chris Roberson's novels include *Here, There & Everywhere, The Voyage of Night Shining White, Paragaea: A Planetary Romance, X-Men: The Return, Set the Seas on Fire, The Dragon's Nine Sons, Iron Jaw* and *Hummingbird, End of the Century*, and *Three Unbroken*. Along with his business partner and spouse Allison Baker, he is the publisher of MonkeyBrain Books, an independent publishing house specializing in genre fiction and nonfiction genre studies. Visit him online at www.chrisroberson.net.

Barbara Roden is one-half of the World Fantasy Award-winning Ash-Tree Press, and co-edits *All Hallows*, the journal of the Ghost Story Society. She is a longstanding member of the Bootmakers of Toronto, and in 2005 was investitured in the Baker Street Irregulars as "Beryl Stapleton".

Christopher Sequeira has written for *The Passengers Log — the journal of The Sydney Passengers — Sherlock Holmes Society of Australia*. He's also worked on scripts for international comic-book publishers including DC Comics and Marvel Entertainment and had horror and mystery stories appear in a range of publications.

**Our titles are available at major book stores
and local independent resellers who support
Science Fiction and Fantasy readers like you.**

EDGE Science Fiction
and Fantasy Publishing

Tesseract Books

Dragon Moon Press

www.edgewebsite.com
www.dragonmoonpress.com

Our titles are available at major book stores
and local independent resellers who support
Science Fiction and Fantasy readers like you.

Alien Deception by Tony Ruggiero -(tp) - ISBN: 978-1-896944-34-0
Alien Revelation by Tony Ruggiero (tp) - ISBN: 978-1-896944-34-8
Alphanauts by J. Brian Clarke (tp) - ISBN: 978-1-894063-14-2
Apparition Trail, The by Lisa Smedman (tp) - ISBN: 978-1-894063-22-7
As Fate Decrees by Denysé Bridger (tp) - ISBN: 978-1-894063-41-8

Black Chalice, The by Marie Jakober (hb) - ISBN: 978-1-894063-00-7
Blue Apes by Phyllis Gotlieb (pb) - ISBN: 978-1-895836-13-4
Blue Apes by Phyllis Gotlieb (hb) - ISBN: 978-1-895836-14-1

Case of the Pitcher's Pendant, The: A Billybub Baddings Mystery
   by Tee Morris (tp) - ISBN: 978-1-896944-77-7
Case of the Singing Sword, The: A Billybub Baddings Mystery
   by Tee Morris (tp) - ISBN: 978-1-896944-18-0
Chalice of Life, The by Anne Webb (tp) - ISBN: 978-1-896944-33-3
Chasing The Bard by Philippa Ballantine (tp) - ISBN: 978-1-896944-08-1
Children of Atwar, The by Heather Spears (pb) - ISBN: 978-0-88878-335-6
Clan of the Dung-Sniffers by Lee Danielle Hubbard (pb) - ISBN: 978-1-894063-05-0
Claus Effect, The by David Nickle & Karl Schroeder (pb) - ISBN: 978-1-895836-34-9
Claus Effect, The by David Nickle & Karl Schroeder (hb) - ISBN: 978-1-895836-35-6
Complete Guide to Writing Fantasy, The - Volume 1: Alchemy with Words
   - edited by Darin Park and Tom Dullemond (tp)
   - ISBN: 978-1-896944-09-8
Complete Guide to Writing Fantasy, The - Volume 2: Opus Magus
   - edited by Tee Morris and Valerie Griswold-Ford (tp)
   - ISBN: 978-1-896944-15-9
Complete Guide to Writing Fantasy, The - Volume 3: The Author's Grimoire
   - edited by Valerie Griswold-Ford & Lai Zhao (tp)
   - ISBN: 978-1-896944-38-8
Complete Guide to Writing Science Fiction, The - Volume 1: First Contact
   - edited by Dave A. Law & Darin Park (tp)
   - ISBN: 978-1-896944-39-5
Courtesan Prince, The by Lynda Williams (tp) - ISBN: 978-1-894063-28-9

Dark Earth Dreams by Candas Dorsey & Roger Deegan (comes with a CD)
   - ISBN: 978-1-895836-05-9
Darkling Band, The by Jason Henderson (tp) - ISBN: 978-1-896944-36-4
Darkness of the God by Amber Hayward (tp) - ISBN: 978-1-894063-44-9
Darwin's Paradox by Nina Munteanu (tp) - ISBN: 978-1-896944-68-5
Daughter of Dragons by Kathleen Nelson - (tp) - ISBN: 978-1-896944-00-5
Digital Magic by Philippa Ballantine (tp) - ISBN: 978-1-896944-88-3
Distant Signals by Andrew Weiner (tp) - ISBN: 978-0-88878-284-7
Dominion by J. Y. T. Kennedy (tp) - ISBN: 978-1-896944-28-9
Dragon Reborn, The by Kathleen H. Nelson - (tp) - ISBN: 978-1-896944-05-0
Dragon's Fire, Wizard's Flame by Michael R. Mennenga (tp)
   - ISBN: 978-1-896944-13-5
Dreams of an Unseen Planet by Teresa Plowright (tp) - ISBN: 978-0-88878-282-3

Dreams of the Sea by Élisabeth Vonarburg (tp) - ISBN: 978-1-895836-96-7
Dreams of the Sea by Élisabeth Vonarburg (hb) - ISBN: 978-1-895836-98-1

Eclipse by K. A. Bedford (tp) - ISBN: 978-1-894063-30-2
Elements of Fantasy: Magic edited by Dave A. Law
    & Valerie Griswold-Ford (tp) - ISBN: 978-1-8964063-96-8
Even The Stones by Marie Jakober (tp) - ISBN: 978-1-894063-18-0

Fires of the Kindred by Robin Skelton (tp) - ISBN: 978-0-88878-271-7
Firestorm of Dragons edited by Michele Acker & Kirk Dougal (tp)
    - ISBN: 978-1-896944-80-7
Forbidden Cargo by Rebecca Rowe (tp) - ISBN: 978-1-894063-16-6

Game of Perfection, A by Élisabeth Vonarburg (tp)
    - ISBN: 978-1-894063-32-6
Gaslight Grimoire: Fantastic Tales of Sherlock Holmes
    edited by J. R. Campbell & Charles Prepolec (pb)
    - ISBN: 978-1-8964063-17-3
Green Music by Ursula Pflug (tp) - ISBN: 978-1-895836-75-2
Green Music by Ursula Pflug (hb) - ISBN: 978-1-895836-77-6
Gryphon Highlord, The by Connie Ward (tp) - ISBN: 978-1-896944-38-8

Healer, The by Amber Hayward (tp) - ISBN: 978-1-895836-89-9
Healer, The by Amber Hayward (hb) - ISBN: 978-1-895836-91-2
Hounds of Ash and other tales of Fool Wolf, The by Greg Keyes (pb)
    - ISBN: 978-1-894063-09-8
Human Thing, The by Kathleen H. Nelson - (hb) - ISBN: 978-1-896944-03-6
Hydrogen Steel by K. A. Bedford (tp) - ISBN: 978-1-894063-20-3

i-ROBOT Poetry by Jason Christie (tp) - ISBN: 978-1-894063-24-1

Jackal Bird by Michael Barley (pb) - ISBN: 978-1-895836-07-3
Jackal Bird by Michael Barley (hb) - ISBN: 978-1-895836-11-0
JEMMA7729 by Phoebe Wray (tp) - ISBN: 978-1-894063-40-1

Keaen by Till Noever (tp) - ISBN: 978-1-894063-08-1
Keeper's Child by Leslie Davis (tp) - ISBN: 978-1-894063-01-2

Lachlei by M. H. Bonham (tp) - ISBN: 978-1-896944-69-2
Land/Space edited by Candas Jane Dorsey and Judy McCrosky (tp)
    - ISBN: 978-1-895836-90-5
Land/Space edited by Candas Jane Dorsey and Judy McCrosky (hb)
    - ISBN: 978-1-895836-92-9
Legacy of Morevi by Tee Morris (tp) - ISBN: 978-1-896944-29-6
Legends of the Serai by J.C. Hall - (tp) - ISBN: 978-1-896944-04-3
Longevity Thesis by Jennifer Rahn (tp) - ISBN: 978-1-896944-37-1
Lyskarion: The Song of the Wind by J.A. Cullum (tp)
    - ISBN: 978-1-894063-02-9

Machine Sex and other stories by Candas Jane Dorsey (tp)
    - ISBN: 978-0-88878-278-6
Maërlande Chronicles, The by Élisabeth Vonarburg (pb)
    - ISBN: 978-0-88878-294-6

Tesseracts 1 edited by Judith Merril (pb) - ISBN: 978-0-88878-279-3
Tesseracts 2 edited by Phyllis Gotlieb & Douglas Barbour (pb)
- ISBN: 978-0-88878-270-0
Tesseracts 3 edited by Candas Jane Dorsey & Gerry Truscott (pb)
- ISBN: 978-0-88878-290-8
Tesseracts 4 edited by Lorna Toolis & Michael Skeet (pb)
- ISBN: 978-0-88878-322-6
Tesseracts 5 edited by Robert Runté & Yves Maynard (pb)
- ISBN: 978-1-895836-25-7
Tesseracts 5 edited by Robert Runté & Yves Maynard (hb)
- ISBN: 978-1-895836-26-4
Tesseracts 6 edited by Robert J. Sawyer & Carolyn Clink (pb)
- ISBN: 978-1-895836-32-5
Tesseracts 6 edited by Robert J. Sawyer & Carolyn Clink (hb)
- ISBN: 978-1-895836-33-2
Tesseracts 7 edited by Paula Johanson & Jean-Louis Trudel (tp)
- ISBN: 978-1-895836-58-5
Tesseracts 7 edited by Paula Johanson & Jean-Louis Trudel (hb)
- ISBN: 978-1-895836-59-2
Tesseracts 8 edited by John Clute & Candas Jane Dorsey (tp)
- ISBN: 978-1-895836-61-5
Tesseracts 8 edited by John Clute & Candas Jane Dorsey (hb)
- ISBN: 978-1-895836-62-2
Tesseracts Nine edited by Nalo Hopkinson and Geoff Ryman (tp)
- ISBN: 978-1-894063-26-5
Tesseracts Ten edited by Robert Charles Wilson and Edo van Belkom (tp)
- ISBN: 978-1-894063-36-4
Tesseracts Eleven edited by Cory Doctorow and Holly Phillips (tp)
- ISBN: 978-1-894063-03-6
Tesseracts Twelve edited by Claude Lalumière (pb) - ISBN: 978-1-894063-15-9
Tesseracts Q edited by Élisabeth Vonarburg & Jane Brierley (pb)
- ISBN: 978-1-895836-21-9
Tesseracts Q edited by Élisabeth Vonarburg & Jane Brierley (hb)
- ISBN: 978-1-895836-22-6
Throne Price by Lynda Williams and Alison Sinclair (tp)
- ISBN: 978-1-894063-06-7
Time Machines Repaired Whie-U-Wait by K. A. Bedford (tp)
- ISBN: 978-1-894063-42-5
Too Many Princes by Deby Fredricks (tp) - ISBN: 978-1-896944-36-4
Twilight of the Fifth Sun by David Sakmyster (tp)
- ISBN: 978-1-896944-01-02

Virtual Evil by Jana Oliver (tp) - ISBN: 978-1-896944-76-0

Writers For Relief: An Anthology to Benefit the Bay Area Food Bank
edited by Davey Beauchamp (pb) - ISBN: 978-1-896944-92-0

1/09